CURTAIN
CALL

Other books by Denise Grover Swank:

Magnolia Steele Mystery
Center Stage
Act Two
Call Back
Curtain Call

Rose Gardner Investigations
Family Jewels
Trailer Trash
For the Birds

Rose Gardner Mystery
Twenty-Eight and a Half Wishes
Twenty-Nine and a Half Reasons
Thirty and a Half Excuses
Falling to Pieces (novella)
Thirty-One and a Half Regrets
Thirty-Two and a Half Complications
Picking up the Pieces (novella)
Thirty-Three and a Half Shenanigans
Rose and Helena Save Christmas (novella)
Ripple of Secrets (novella)
Thirty-Four and a Half Predicaments
Thirty-Four and a Half Predicaments Bonus Chapters
Thirty-Five and a Half Conspiracies
Thirty-Six and a Half Motives
Sins of the Father (novella)

The Wedding Pact
The Substitute
The Player
The Gambler
The Valentine (short story)

Bachelor Brotherhood
Only You
Until You

denisegroverswank.com

CURTAIN CALL

A Magnolia Steele Mystery
Book Four

Denise Grover Swank

Copyright 2017 by Denise Grover Swank

Developmental Editor: Angela Polidoro
Copy editor: Shannon Page
Proofreader: Carolina Valedez Miller
Cover design by James T. Egan, www.bookflydesign.com

chapter one

"Ms. Steele? I'm Detective Maria Martinez with the Franklin Police. I'm here to talk to you about what happened Saturday night at the Middle Tennessee Children's Charity Masquerade Ball."

I stared at the woman on my mother's doorstep, wondering why it had taken two days for the police to show up asking questions. I'd recognized Martinez before the reintroduction, of course. She'd interrogated me at the Franklin, Tennessee, police station a month ago, after I'd stumbled upon Max Goodwin's body. It wasn't exactly the kind of thing you could forget. Insults had been flung by both of us, and the small smile on her face told me she was eager for the chance to get another crack at me.

"I'd be more than happy to talk to you, Detective," I said, "but can we reschedule this for a later date? I'm currently hosting my mother's *wake*."

She made an apologetic face but held firm. "It's only a few questions. It won't take long." Then she gave me a smile that made her look constipated.

She thought I was involved in the murders.

She wasn't wrong—not totally—but I couldn't tell her the truth . . . and I didn't know if I had the fortitude to hold myself together and convincingly lie. I'd buried my mother only hours ago, and a wave of people had descended upon her house and hadn't left. My patience and emotional strength had been tested again and again by everything I'd endured over the past few days, let alone the last month, and from the look in Detective Martinez's eyes, that was what she was counting on.

I stepped out onto the porch, closing the front door and quieting the chatter of the mourners behind me. The air was cooling as the sun set, and the wind had picked up. I wrapped my arms across my chest to stay warm, and it occurred to me that I could use the chilly air and the people in my mother's house as an excuse to get away, should the need arise.

And knowing Detective Martinez's tenacity and her fast and loose relationship with the truth when it didn't fit her theories, I suspected the need would arise.

I lifted my eyebrows and gave her a look that said, *Go on.*

That little smile grew into a satisfied smirk, the kind that mean girls got when they thought they'd bested you.

I tried to look bored. "Do you have any questions, Detective Martinez? Or do you just plan to stare at me? If you're admiring my dress, it was a gift from a designer in New York," I lied. "It's one of a kind." . . . the only one in the New York City vintage thrift store where I'd bought it two years ago.

Anger filled her eyes. "Did you attend the ball this past Saturday night?"

I couldn't hide my surprise. "Don't you talk to your partner? Brady saw me there. This question seems like a waste of my time *and* yours." It was stupid to goad her. I knew it. But I still held a grudge for the way she'd treated me in connection with the Goodwin case. How she'd attacked my character. While some part of me knew she had been doing her job, there was no denying she'd been overzealous with her interrogation and her insults.

Her eyes went flat. "Detective Bennett has been reassigned, so *I'm* asking you, Magnolia Steele. Did you or did you not attend the masquerade ball at Savannah House last Saturday night?"

Brady had been reassigned? What did that mean? Last I'd heard, he was working the murder of my attorney, Emily Johnson. He'd linked it to a serial killer— the same one who'd carved his mark onto my leg ten years ago. Only, no one else had made the connection, and Brady had asked me to keep it quiet. Not hard to do since only four people knew about my connection to the serial killer—Brady, my mother (who was now dead), my sister-in-law Belinda, and Colt Austin. And Colt had bigger secrets to keep.

The look in Detective Martinez's eyes told me she blamed me for her partner's reassignment.

There was no denying that I'd stayed with Brady for several days last week. After all, he'd told me that half the force knew, which was how he'd always seemed to know where I was and what I was doing. Apparently members of the Franklin PD had been giving him regular reports.

I'd never intended to stay with Brady, but a week and a half ago, my apartment had become a crime scene after I'd been attacked and nearly killed by Geraldo Lopez, a Nashville dentist. He'd faked his own kidnapping and then shown up at my apartment looking for one million dollars' worth of gold bullion. My father had stolen the gold and hidden it in a ceramic dog I'd given him when I was a kid, something I'd found by chance in my mother's garage.

After the attack, Brady had suggested that I stay with him for a while, and I'd folded like a paper towel. While he had made it clear he was interested in a romantic relationship, I'd held him off . . . at first. Being with him had felt wrong, though, like I was a problem for him to solve or a damsel for him to save, and I was far from sure that I could trust him. Not to mention that the serial killer, who'd been sending me threatening texts all month, had amped up his threats because of all the time I'd spent in the company of a member of Franklin law enforcement.

Brady had never known the truth about the gold, only that Geraldo Lopez thought I had something of my father's. The only person who knew about it was the aforementioned Colt Austin, part-time employee at my mother's catering business and aspiring country singer.

And now my sort-of boyfriend. (It was complicated . . . but I felt like myself when I was with him, and that was something.)

Except two bad people had also figured out that I had the gold . . . but they were the two who had been killed in front of me on Saturday night. Rowena Rogers and her lackey.

And that was why Detective Martinez was standing on my mother's front porch right now.

"Detective," I said in a tone that suggested we should try to reach a truce. Pissing her off wasn't the smartest thing to do. "As you undoubtedly know, I *was* there, but only for a very short time before I was called to the hospital. That was the night my mother died."

She gave me an expectant look. "She died from . . . ?"

I gasped. "Are you seriously asking about my mother's *cause of death*?"

"You have to admit that a significant number of people around you have died since you came back to Franklin a month ago."

While what she said was true, I couldn't handle that she was treating my mother's death so impersonally, not when we'd just buried her. "You're talking about my mother, Detective Martinez. Please show a little more respect."

The woman had the good grace to look slightly embarrassed.

"My mother had cancer. Something to do with her blood. She'd kept it a secret for several years."

"Is that why you came back to Franklin?" she asked, the snide tone back.

"You know perfectly well why I came back to Franklin." I was starting to get pissed. "The detective in charge of Max Goodwin's murder case made it very clear the whole department knew why I'd returned to Franklin. He'd watched the videos. But then," I said with cool disdain, "I suspect you've watched them too."

Her smirk was back. "There's much better porn out there." She leaned forward and said in a stage whisper, "I'd suggest a boob job if you decide to continue down *that* career path."

I gasped again, beyond outraged. The YouTube videos of my stage oops in my first (and only) performance as the lead in Broadway's hottest new musical, *Fireflies at Dawn*, *hardly* qualified as porn.

I was just about to tell her off when the front door opened and my sister-in-law, Belinda, poked her face out. "Magnolia, I wondered where you'd got off to."

"Belinda," I said, my anger simmering. "This is Detective Martinez, and she's inquiring about Momma's cause of death."

Belinda flicked on the porch light, then stepped outside and shut the door behind her. She glanced at both of us with a confused expression. "What does that mean?" Then her eyes widened and she turned a furious glare on the detective. "Are you insinuating her death was foul play? Did *Roy* put you up to this?"

10

I nearly groaned. I was sure the detective's question had only been intended to shake me up so I'd be more likely to tell her everything I knew about the murders at the ball. But she was bound to latch on to Momma's death now. Maybe that was a good thing. When it came to this, I didn't have anything to hide.

"Roy?" the detective asked, cocking her head to the side. She did a poor job of hiding her excitement, and it was equally obvious that she didn't need us to ID him for her.

Belinda looked even more confused. "My husband. Magnolia's brother."

"Belinda." I drew out her name. "Detective Martinez came here to ask if I was at the masquerade ball on Saturday night. Then she decided to ignore that we're *grieving* and callously suggested Momma died due to nefarious circumstances."

"Why in the world would she do that?" Belinda asked.

"Because she thinks it's curious that a few people around me have died."

"A few?" Martinez released a snort and started ticking off with her fingers. "Max Goodwin, Neil Fulton—"

"I didn't personally know Neil Fulton," I interjected, but I *had* known Max Goodwin. The sleazy talent agent had propositioned me a couple of years before, which was how I'd become a suspect in his death after finding his body.

Her eyebrows rose. "But your father sure did." She lifted another finger. "Amy Danvers. Walter Frey, Steve Morrissey—"

I started to protest that one. Amy had been Belinda's friend, and I was the person who'd discovered Walter Frey's body, but the only encounter I'd had with Steve Morrissey was at the fundraiser the night of his death. It hadn't gone well, sure, but I had an alibi for the rest of that evening.

The detective lifted her other hand. "Geraldo Lopez, Emily Johnson, and now your mother." She held up both hands. "That's eight people. All with ties to you. All dead within a month."

Little did she know there were more.

Belinda lifted her chin and gave Detective Martinez her best glare, a difficult feat given how sweet my sister-in-law was. "Magnolia had nothing to do with her mother's death. The chemo weakened Lila's immune system, and she died from an infection."

"Then why would you think Roy sent me?" the detective asked.

"Because Lila refused antibiotics at first and Roy wanted to hire an attorney to try to get the hospital to disregard Lila's DNR directives. He was looking for someone to blame, and since he has . . . *issues* with his sister, she's an easy target."

"Your brother," Detective Martinez said with a frown. "The one who hurt you?"

I wasn't sure if it was good or bad that she remembered that. My brother had pinched me hard enough to leave bruises, which Detective Martinez had been all too eager to link to her theory that I'd killed Neil Fulton. I'd set her straight.

I wrapped my arms tighter around myself. "Yes."

She turned to Belinda and lifted an eyebrow as though waiting for confirmation.

Belinda glanced down at the porch and remained silent.

Detective Martinez shifted her weight. "I think I'm going to need you to come down to the station."

I gasped. "*Now?*"

She shot a glance through the window behind me. "No," she said regretfully. "I'm sure I'd get an earful if I took you down now." Her gaze swung between the two of us. "And I want you to come too."

Belinda's eyes flew open. "Me?"

"I think we need to dig deeper into your mother-in-law's death."

Belinda stiffened. "We'll be bringing our attorney."

The detective bobbed her head around and said in an accusing tone, "Well, if you think you *need* one . . ." She grinned and started for the steps before she stopped and glanced over her shoulder. "Oh, and it's not a wake."

I gave a tiny shake of my head. "What?"

She turned her whole body around to face me. "You said you were at your mother's wake. She was buried this afternoon. Wakes are the vigil before a funeral, but then your mother didn't want one."

My head swam. "How do you know what my mother wanted?"

Her eyes lit up. "You just have to know who to ask. And my apologies, I was at the funeral, but thought it best to not go through the receiving line."

I stared at her in horror. "You didn't even know my mother. Why would you come?"

"Funerals are interesting. You can learn all sorts of things." A mischievous look filled her eyes. "Lots of family secrets."

I tried to hide my reaction, but it wasn't one of my most convincing performances. Belinda put her arm around my back.

Detective Martinez gave us a mock salute. "I'll see you both at one *tomorrow*."

chapter
two

As Detective Martinez sauntered down the porch steps with a happy little skip, Belinda grabbed my elbow and tugged me inside.

My nerves had been plenty frazzled *before* Detective Martinez showed up, and our encounter had nearly pushed me over the edge.

What had she meant about family secrets?

Ignoring the twenty-five or so people who were still mingling on the first floor of my mother's house, Belinda dragged me into my mother's home office and shut the curtained French doors. "What did you tell her?"

"Me?" I nearly screeched. "You're the one who told her about Roy. Now she's jumped down a completely different rabbit hole."

"Sit," she said. My thoughts were so garbled that I thought she'd uttered an uncharacteristic curse word until she pushed me down into one of two wingback chairs in the office. Once I was settled, she walked out without another word, shutting the door behind her.

I wondered if she'd given me an adult time-out, but less than a minute later, she was back with Colt in tow. My stomach fluttered when I saw him—something I tried to ignore.

Colt Austin was a very fine-looking man who was very aware of his looks. He was tall and built enough to strain the shoulders of his department store dress shirt. His dark blond hair was styled, giving him a movie star look, and his bright blue eyes drew you in, but when he sang . . . well, he was like a male version of a siren. Women loved Colt Austin, and for a long time, Colt Austin had loved them back. But he'd told me last week that things had changed for him. He didn't want anyone else—just me.

He held an unopened bottle of whiskey and two glasses, and Belinda was carrying a tumbler of her own.

"It's that bad?" I asked as he shut the door with his butt.

He shot me a grim look. "I was saving this for later, to toast to your mother, but I thought it might come in handy now." He handed me both glasses, then nudged Momma's rolling desk chair closer to mine while Belinda sat next to me in the other wingback chair.

"We need to get our story straight," Belinda said, staring down at the glass she was cupping with both hands.

"There's no story to get straight," I said. "Momma refused antibiotics and then changed her mind. Nothing sinister about that."

"Not that story," Belinda said.

Colt had already unscrewed the whiskey and poured a generous amount into both glasses, so he turned to Belinda and poured a small amount into her glass. She downed it, then grabbed the bottle from Colt and poured until the tumbler was half full.

I stared in shock at my prim and proper sister-in-law. Dressed in a tasteful black dress and three-inch black patent leather pumps, her hair perfectly coifed and makeup understated, she looked like she should be nursing a glass of white wine, not tossing back whiskey.

"I'm not surprised she came by," Colt said, then took a sip of his drink. "But I thought your mother's death would buy you more time."

"You expected Detective Martinez to come by?" I asked in surprise.

"Not her specifically," Colt said. "Honestly, I expected Frasier or Bennett."

Detectives Owen Frasier and Brady Bennett.

I supposed it had been shortsighted on my part *not* to expect it this soon. Of course they wanted to talk to me. It didn't take much digging to figure out that Rowena Rogers had been linked to over half the people who had been killed in the last few weeks—and I was linked to them too. But it was Detective Martinez's final dig that bothered me the most. She'd been at Momma's funeral. While it had been open to the public, it still felt wrong that she'd been there. I felt violated. But that wasn't the only reason it troubled me . . .

Had she heard me shouting toward the woods after everyone had left except for me, Colt, and the funeral home staff? Had she figured out I had been shouting at my father, a man everyone presumed either dead or long gone?

"It's okay, Magnolia," Belinda said, obviously reading my expression. "You've spent the past two days preparing for your momma's funeral. Colt and I have discussed it, but we didn't want to worry you."

"Does she really think we know something, or is she just fishing?" I asked. My shaking hand sloshed the liquid in my glass.

Belinda turned to Colt, and he took a second before saying, "I think it's a bluff. Talkin' about Lila's death was a good way to throw her off and buy us more time."

I shook my head. "You purposely mentioned Roy to throw her off?"

Belinda made a face. "Hardly. I was caught off guard. But we need to make sure we're prepared next time."

"Do you think we left anything behind at Savannah House?" I asked. My hand was still shaking, so I started to put the glass down. Colt stopped me, putting his hand over mine and lifting it to my lips.

"I brought this for a reason. Take a drink. Or two."

I shrugged off his hand and took a healthy sip, still trying to decide what to do about him.

Turned out I wasn't immune to Colt's siren abilities, but he'd betrayed me.

For the last month, I'd told him multiple times that I was certain my father would never have willingly abandoned me, my mother, and brother. That he must be dead. Come to find out Colt had been working for my father the whole time—for the last three years, in fact—spying on Momma and Roy and me, after my return to Franklin, and reporting back to my father. He'd been coerced into it, and it was something he deeply regretted. According to him, he hadn't reported to my father since last week, after Emily Johnson's murder, but I still had trouble fully trusting him. I needed to prioritize my emergencies, though, and Detective Martinez and my interview at the station took precedence.

As I lowered my glass, Colt said, "We got out of that basement in a rush, but I think we're safe."

"My blood . . ." The gunshot graze wound on my arm began to throb, the pain triggered by the memory of that night.

"Never hit the floor. It landed on your dress and then my shirt. And the gunshots weren't from either of our guns, so we don't have to worry about any bullets or casings being tied back to us."

I gave him a pointed look. "If your gun had gone off, would they have tied it back to you?" I'd suspected his gun hadn't been in his name.

His expression turned blank. "No."

I nodded. "So there's nothing to tie us to that basement."

"Fingerprints," Belinda said with a shaky voice. "My fingerprints are on the door leading to the wine cellar and staircase."

A worried look flashed across Colt's face, but it disappeared as quickly as a summer storm. "Didn't you have a wedding there a few weeks ago?"

My lips parted slightly. How did he know that?

Belinda was giving him the same look, and he turned sheepish. "We all know that I was working for Brian Steele." The look in his eyes suggested it pained him to admit it.

I was quiet for a moment. I'd been so busy over the past nearly forty-eight hours I'd barely had time to think over the details of what Colt had really done for him.

"You've been there before," Colt said quietly, staring down at his glass. "There's a good reason for your prints to be down there." He turned to me. "Did you touch anything?"

"The staircase handrail. Mostly upstairs."

"I think you'll be okay. You never touched anything in the room." He took another drink, then said, "We have to consider that there may be witnesses. People saw all three of us at the ball. Did they see us all leave? And who saw us when we came back upstairs? Maggie had blood on her dress and my shirt tied around her arm, and I was just wearing my jacket. Sure, we went out the back, but we need to have a story to explain it. Just in case."

"That's easy," Belinda said. "Magnolia got a call from the hospital, and she was so upset she ran into something that cut her arm. You didn't want her to ruin her dress, so you used your shirt because you were in such a hurry to leave."

I almost commented on how quickly she'd come up with that story, but it occurred to me that she'd been living with my abusive brother for years. She was probably used to coming up with excuses. Instead, I said, "She's going to wonder why you didn't leave with us."

"How about this?" Colt said. "Brady acted pretty cold toward you at the ball, and he gave you shit for kissing me. We can say it upset you, we got into an argument, and that's how you got hurt."

I gave him a stunned look. "Are you suggesting that I pretend *you* hurt me?"

"No. But maybe it made you more careless. You know people lose themselves in the heat of the moment. We can say that's why we left. That way if they compare when the hospital actually called to when we left the ballroom, we won't have to worry about the time discrepancy."

I considered it for a moment. "Yeah, I guess that would work."

"Plus," Colt continued, "our run-in with Brady strengthens our alibi. People planning to commit murder don't usually take the time to talk to a jealous ex-lover. Especially if he's a cop."

He had a point.

The office door opened and I jumped, feeling guilty when I saw Tilly, Momma's best friend and business partner, standing in the doorway wearing her bright purple dress. Just like Momma would have wanted.

"You started drinking without me?" she asked, sounding hurt.

"Maggie was a little too overwhelmed," Colt said. "She's been wound up since Saturday night, and it's been a long, stressful day."

Tilly nodded, looking exhausted herself. "I never expected everyone to stay so long, but I can send them all home."

"No," I said as I got to my feet. I took another big gulp of whiskey, ignoring the burn, then handed the now-empty glass to Colt. "I'm fine now."

He grasped my wrist, staring up into my eyes. "You're not fine, Maggie. You don't have to go back out there."

"Yeah, I do." I shook him off, put the glass on the table since he hadn't taken it, and looped my arm through Tilly's.

Colt had been right. I wasn't fine by a long shot, but Tilly needed me. I knew she was feeling Momma's loss as acutely as I was . . . no, if I were being honest, probably even more. She'd been around for so much of my childhood, she felt like a second mother. I couldn't abandon her now.

I stuck by her side for the next hour as our guests dwindled. Since I'd been mostly estranged from Momma for the past ten years, it was a gift to hear so many stories about how she'd touched people's lives. She'd been as tough as nails, the kind of woman who never took shit from anyone, but she could be a loyal friend to someone in need.

When the last guest finally left, Tilly started to pick up what was left of the half-empty trays of food—Belinda and Colt had already cleaned up most of them—but I grabbed the plate of deviled eggs from her hand and set it back down on the counter. "How about we have that drink?"

Tears filled her eyes, and she nodded.

My throat burned and I wrapped my arms around her back, pulling her into a tight hug. To my dismay, she began to sob.

Belinda and Colt rushed over, and Belinda rubbed Tilly's back as she continued to cry into my shoulder. After a good twenty seconds, she finally started to settle down, and Colt put his hand on her arm. "Let's go sit down."

She nodded and pulled loose from my embrace. When he started to lead her to the sofa, she said, "Let's sit on the deck." Then she glanced back over her shoulder. "And don't forget the whiskey."

I grinned at her through my own tears. "Okay."

Belinda got the bottle and put it on a tray, and I added four glasses, then held the door open so my sister-in-law could carry the tray outside. Colt had already gotten Tilly settled into a comfy wicker chair, and he was starting a fire in Momma's fire pit with the gas starter.

After Belinda set the tray on a table, she started pouring drinks and I handed them out. By the time I got to Colt, he'd finished prepping the fire and was sitting on the loveseat. He set the drink down and reached out to me, and I hated myself for caving and sinking in next to him. Belinda slipped into the house and returned with an armful of afghans to throw over our laps. Leave it to my sister-in-law to think of the small details.

We sat in silence for nearly a minute. Tilly and Belinda watched the fire in silence, and I snuggled into Colt, resting my head on his chest. His arm curled around my back and settled on my hip. It was almost comfortable enough to make me forget.

"Lila would have hated this afternoon," Tilly said with a laugh. "She hated when people made a fuss over her."

"Remember when we threw a surprise birthday party for her two years ago?" Colt asked, chuckling. "Jesus, she cussed a blue streak. I thought Belinda was going to lose her shit."

Belinda sat up straighter. "I confess I was taken aback since she was threatening to do vile things to the person who'd organized the party."

"I presume that person was you?" I asked with a grin.

Tilly shook her head. "She would have never hurt a hair on your head, Belinda. She loved you like a daughter."

"I loved her too," Belinda said in a tiny voice.

"Hey," Colt said in a tone that suggested he was just warming up with Lila stories, "remember when we catered that wedding at the bride's backyard up in Belle Meade, and it started pouring down rain out of nowhere?" He turned to Belinda. "It was hilarious because Lila had been going on and on about how the bride was a total bridezilla . . . What was her name? It was some flower . . . Petunia?"

Belinda smiled. "Poppy. And she just wanted everything to be perfect."

"She was a terror," Tilly said. "Admit it."

Belinda made a face. "Okay, she was a terror."

They all laughed, and I managed a small smile.

Colt glanced down at me. "Lila had done nothing but gripe about this bride *for weeks,* and then it started to rain out of *nowhere*—"

Tilly lifted her hand. "No rain in the forecast at all."

"But Lila had personally created this immense appetizer display in an effort to placate the bride . . . and it was sitting outside."

I grinned. "Of course."

"The rest of the reception was under a tent," Belinda said with a hint of defensiveness.

Colt grinned. "Lila started yelling obscenities—right during the ceremony—which they were rushing through to get out of the rain. I thought Belinda and Tilly were going to crap their pants."

"I'd had to convince the bride that the Belles were the best, most professional caterers in Middle Tennessee," Belinda said.

Colt winked. "More like we were the only ones who could tolerate her."

A grin tugged the corners of Belinda's lips. "Maybe."

"Lila recruited me to hold a plastic tarp over the arrangement until the storm moved on five minutes later," Colt said. "But before saving the appetizers, she taught the flower girl and ring bearer a few new four-letter words."

Belinda held up her hand. "The videographer swore he could get those out of the video of the wedding."

The story was hilarious, and so true to my mother, but while I'd loved hearing so many new stories about her tonight, it hurt. I'd missed all of this, and there was no going back. That made me incredibly sad.

Colt's body sank into mine. "Lila was something else," he said, his tone quieter. "Nothing will be the same without her."

"No," Belinda said. "Our world will be a whole lot duller without her."

Tilly looked like she wanted to say something but remained silent.

After a beat, Colt lifted his glass up. "To Lila."

I lifted mine too. "To Momma." My voice broke.

Belinda's arm rose with her glass in her hand. "To the woman who was gracious enough to become my mother even before I married Roy."

Tilly lifted her glass and stared at us all as she took a big gulp. Then she said, "To my dearest friend. Who was an utter fool."

The three of us stared at her in shock, but she turned her attention to me. "We both know she was keepin' secrets about the past from you, girl. She made me promise to never tell you while she was alive. But she's dead now, and part of me thinks she willed herself to die sooner to save you."

My mouth dropped open in shock.

"Tilly!" Belinda gushed.

"You know how stubborn she could be," Tilly said.

"She's right," Colt added. "Lila Steele was one of the most stubborn people I ever met. She claimed it was her Sweet Briar, Alabama roots, but I never believed it. She could have been born in Buckingham Palace, and she would have turned out just as ornery."

26

Tilly held her now-empty glass out, and Colt refilled it with a larger pour than Belinda had given her before. She took another drink, then sat back. "You ready to hear the ugly truth, Maggie Mae? Because once you hear it, there's no turning back."

No. I wasn't anywhere near ready, but then again, I'd never be ready to have the rest of my childhood memories ripped to shreds.

chapter three

Your momma knew how much you worshipped your daddy, and she never wanted you to find out the truth about him."

I took a breath. "What truth is that?"

"First, your daddy was unfaithful."

I didn't react. I'd already known about that. Sure, Rowena could have lied about their affair, but I'd believed her.

"If your momma had one weakness, it was good-lookin' men, and your daddy was mighty handsome back in the day. Lila Brewer was tough as nails with the rest of the world, but your daddy was her kryptonite. He made her do stupid things."

"Like what?" I asked, thinking about the good-looking man sitting beside me.

"All through college, since the day I first met her at our freshman orientation, your momma had big plans to go into publicity in the music industry. She was fixing to move to L.A., but then she met your daddy at the beginning of her senior year, and they got serious real quick."

I shook my head. "Her degree was in communications. The few times I'd asked her what she'd planned to do with it, she'd told me she'd wasted her time on a worthless piece of paper. Why didn't she go to L.A.?"

"Your father. He'd decided that Nashville was booming and he had a better chance of making real money here."

"And Momma *agreed?*"

She pushed out a breath. "We all have our vices, and turns out your father was hers." She gave me a sympathetic look. "Sorry, Maggie, I know how much you loved your daddy."

My stomach threatened to expel the half sandwich I'd eaten earlier. I had to be careful about what I said to Tilly. She had no idea what I'd unearthed, and it would be safer for her if she went on not knowing. She might not have new information, but I was willing to listen to her version to see if she knew something I didn't. "I've come to realize that I viewed Daddy through the eyes of a child," I finally said, trying to keep the bitterness out of my voice. Rowena Rogers had told me the same thing the afternoon before she was murdered . . . probably by *him.* "I'm an adult now, and my eyes are wide open."

She studied me, the flames in the fire pit jumping between us. She looked like she was trying to gauge how much I could handle.

"I want the truth, Tilly. No matter how bad. I *need* the truth. All of it."

She nodded and took another drink. "I was never a fan of your daddy's, and it's safe to say he wasn't a fan of mine. He may have snowed your momma, but he never fooled me. After we graduated college, your momma and daddy lived together in a little house in Leiper's Fork. I'd gotten a job at the Grand Ole Opry Hotel in lower management, but your momma was struggling to find something, and *her* mother—God rest her soul—was givin' her a fit. She'd racked up nearly eighty thousand in student loans, and she was working at Target."

I winced.

"So I got her a job at the hotel. It didn't pay much, but it was better than Target. Your daddy didn't like it because he thought I was a bad influence on her."

Belinda chuckled. "It was usually the other way around."

"Right?" Tilly laughed. "He claimed the drive was too far, and he wanted her closer, but we both knew that was a load of poppycock. Especially after she saw him at one of the hotel bars with a woman."

"Was it a client?" I asked.

"He claimed as much, but when your momma asked later about how much she'd invested, he said she'd decided to use someone else because of Lila's reaction to her."

"I take it she threw a Lila fit," Colt said.

"Something like that," Tilly conceded with a wry grin.

"Are you sure it wasn't a client?" Belinda asked. "I know the Opry Hotel is huge, but it still seems pretty stupid of him to take the chance that Lila would see him."

"More like arrogant," Tilly said. She paused. "I'm not proud of this, but I found out the woman's name and did some poking around. She was an art dealer from New York, and she was in town to sell some paintings to a local businessman. I found them together in her room in a state of undress. He had the nerve to accuse me of impropriety for using my position as manager to catch them." She shrugged. "And catch them I did." She tugged her blanket higher. "Well, he was none too pleased and wanted to complain to management. I told him that could be arranged. I'd call Lila and let him complain to her. He shut up real quick."

"And Momma and Daddy weren't married?" I asked. "Why didn't he just break up with her?"

"He had the balls to tell Lila that he loved her and that he'd never cheat on her again."

"That was a lie," I said.

She looked surprised. "You found out about Tiffany?"

I gasped. "*Tiffany?*"

She grimaced. "I guess there was more than one after that."

"Who was Tiffany?"

"She was the fiancée of one of his younger clients. Tripp Tucker."

Tripp Tucker. I couldn't have been more shocked. "The singer who used to look up to Daddy like a father?"

31

She nodded. "Tripp didn't take it well, and neither did your mother. She almost left him that time." Tilly sat back in her seat. "She wasn't surprised your daddy had betrayed her again, but she *was* surprised he'd betrayed Tripp. That boy was like a son to him. Out of all those country music boys he used to bring home, he loved Tripp the best." She gave me a sad smile. "Even though Tripp had filed that lawsuit, your daddy still defended him, saying business was business."

I shook my head. I didn't remember any of that, but I'd been a child at the time. There was a lot I didn't remember from back then. "I wonder if Tiffany was before or after Rowena Rogers."

"Rowena Rogers? Your mother swore he wasn't sleepin' with her. Are you sure?"

It was a relief that Tilly didn't seem to know Rowena was dead. The names of the victims had been released that morning, but she'd probably been too caught up in the funeral to pay any attention to the outside world. I lifted my glass to my lips and took a slow sip. "Oh, I'm very certain."

I was struggling to process this new information about my mother. This was so unlike the woman I had known. Granted, Daddy was a completely different man than the version of him who'd existed in my head, but he'd left home when I was fourteen. I'd worshiped him with a childlike innocence. But my mother . . . although I'd lost almost ten years with her, I'd always wholeheartedly believed she was a woman who didn't take shit from anyone. I found it hard to accept that she'd tolerated so much from the one man whom she was supposed to be able to trust above everyone else.

"I don't bring this up because I'm trying to paint your momma in a bad light, Maggie Mae," Tilly said. "I have a purpose."

I sat up, inching away from Colt. There was no doubt he was a player, although I knew the women he'd slept with had been empty hookups. I wasn't immune to the pull of that kind of thing—my relationships in New York City had been about as deep as a kiddie pool—so I couldn't judge. When you felt hollow inside, you were always looking for something to fill the void. Was it foolish of me to think Colt could change when my father, the man Colt had worked for, had made a fool of my momma again and again?

Was this a case of like mother, like daughter?

"I need to hear the truth, Tilly," I choked out. "No matter how ugly."

She downed her glass, then held it out for Colt to refill. "When your momma found out about Tiffany, she kicked your father out for a week and hired an attorney to file for divorce."

"What made her change her mind?" I asked.

"The fact that he was a person of interest in a murder."

I nearly jumped out of my seat. "*What?* Who was murdered?"

"*Tiffany.*"

"Tripp's fiancée?"

"Yep. Tripp was a person of interest too."

"What about Tripp suing Daddy for losing all his money?"

"The lawsuit was already underway when she was murdered. All the more reason for your daddy to be a suspect. He actually dropped the suit a few months later, saying Tiffany's death made him realize he needed to focus on the important things in life."

"So who killed her?" Belinda asked.

"A drifter. He got life with no parole. But by the time they arrested the drifter, your momma and daddy had worked things out."

I stared at Tilly in disbelief. "Last week, Momma told me all about Tripp suing Daddy, but she never said anything about him being a person of interest in a murder."

"Years from now, I doubt Colt or Belinda will mention that you were a person of interest in two murders," she said defensively. "Your daddy didn't do it, so why would she? It was something they tried to put behind them."

It made sense, but I still found it alarming.

"How did she die?" Colt asked, his voice tight.

"Stabbing," Tilly said. "He mutilated her."

I sank back into the loveseat as the blood rushed from my head.

Colt turned to me and took my hand as he looked me in the eyes. "Slow, steady breaths, Maggie."

"What's goin' on?" Tilly asked.

Belinda released a strangled sound and said, "Emily . . . she was stabbed to death."

"Oh dear . . ." Tilly's voice trailed off, and I could tell she felt guilty.

I leaned forward, my elbows on my knees. "Tilly, you didn't realize, and it doesn't matter if I'm upset—I want to know. I *need* to know." I took a shaky breath. Momma had no doubt worried my opinion of her would change once I found out the dirty truths about our family's past. The proud, strong woman I'd known would surely have hated that thought. There was only one reason she would have insisted on this show of honesty . . . "I think you're right. Momma knew that keeping everything from me was putting me in danger."

"*What?*"

Damn my internal censor, or lack thereof. "Tilly, I'm fine."

"I thought Geraldo Lopez was your only danger."

"And Geraldo Lopez is dead," I hedged. "So I'm safe, but I still need to know what you know about Daddy's business partners."

She hesitated, then said, "Not much. He and Bill James were partners before you were born. Lila was sure Bill had killed his first wife while she and your daddy were away on a trip. They were having work done in the basement while they were gone, and her gut told her that Bill had buried her under the concrete floor. Your momma even made an anonymous call to the police, but nothing came of it."

Momma had told me this same story last week when she'd taken me to the very house, which was now owned by Bill James himself. The filing cabinet in the basement had been full of paperwork about his past business venture with my father, a failed land project called the Jackson Project. During our somewhat break-in—my mother still had a key since she'd lived in the house—my mother had brought up a good point: Why would Bill James buy a house that had never been his if he didn't want to live there or rent it out? It was definitely suspicious. Especially since the house had burned down that very night, and the news had called it arson. "And did you believe her? Do you think his wife was buried under the basement floor?"

"I wouldn't put it past him."

Belinda shivered.

I remained silent. I'd thought so too until I'd talked to Bill at his house last Saturday. I wasn't willing to bet my life that he hadn't done it, but I was far from sure.

"Who else did he work with?" I asked.

"Your daddy got a lot of clients through Max Goodwin. His high-end ones anyway."

Momma had told me that too.

"When he started the Jackson Project, he acquired a bunch of new cronies. That's where he picked up Geraldo Lopez and the elder Christopher Merritt, the accountant. Also Walter Frey, the real estate attorney, and Steve Morrissey."

"And Rowena Rogers and her husband," I added. Except for Bill and my father, all of them were dead now. "That's it? No one else?"

"That's not enough?" Colt asked.

Tilly was quiet for a moment. "There was one other. In the beginning."

That caught my attention. "In the beginning? Who?"

"Eric Duncan. He was the one who introduced your daddy to Bill James. Your parents were hosting a barbecue, and Eric brought Bill. Eric and your daddy were friends from college, and Eric was working with Bill at Merrill Lynch. Well, Bill and your daddy hit it off right at the start, but your momma didn't like Bill or his wife one bit. Nevertheless, your daddy decided he was gonna go into business with Bill. Or rather, with Bill and Eric."

I stared at her in disbelief. "Why haven't I ever heard of him before?"

"He didn't last long. In the end, your daddy and Eric had a falling-out."

"What happened to him?" Colt asked, perking up.

"I don't know. He left around the time your parents were married, and I never heard what happened to him after that."

"Why wouldn't Momma have told me about him?"

"I don't know. Maybe she didn't think it was important."

I doubted that was true. Momma had told me about the barbeque, but she'd failed to mention that the friend who'd introduced Daddy to Bill had been in their original partnership. That seemed like a purposeful omission.

Tilly shifted, and I could see that she was still holding back.

"There's something you're not telling me, Tilly," I said.

Colt leaned his elbows on his knees. "Why did Eric *really* leave?"

She grimaced.

"I'm gonna find out, Tilly," Colt said in an ominous tone. "So save me the effort and just tell me."

I couldn't help wondering how he'd find out. By contacting my father? One of his other sources?

Tilly pushed out a breath. "He sexually harassed your mother."

"What?" Belinda said.

Tilly took another drink. "Your momma had quit her job at the hotel to work for your daddy's business with Bill and Eric. One day it was just your momma and Eric in the office, and he nearly raped her. She kneed him in the balls and got away, but your daddy nearly beat him to death. Bill pulled your daddy off him and kicked Eric out."

"Did they press charges?" Belinda asked.

"No," Tilly said, lifting the glass to her lips and taking a generous gulp. "Bill convinced your father it would be in the best interest of the company to keep it quiet."

"And Momma agreed to that?" I asked.

"Not at first, but Bill finally convinced your daddy—and your daddy could convince her of anything." Her mouth tilted up on one side. "Well, after an argument. But your momma had been wanting to buy a house—*this* house—and Brian promised to put in an offer if she'd agree."

I shook my head. "I can't believe any of this. This is not the woman who raised me."

Tilly stared at me with sad eyes. "Your momma became the woman she is now after that day." She took another drink. "Well, I guess the woman she was." Tears filled her eyes. "She swore no man would ever hurt her again."

"And yet he did," I said. "And she kept forgiving him."

She nodded. "But part of her died every time." She paused. "Your momma was upset when he disappeared, but I suspect part of her felt relieved. That's why she remained distant toward you, Maggie. You were hurting so much, and your momma felt so guilty for feeling relieved that she could hardly look at you." She took another drink. "And Roy, he always felt like your daddy loved you more, and he was probably right. When Brian disappeared, I think he took it as proof that your daddy didn't love him enough to stay. Maybe he even felt a little guilty for the enjoyment he took in watching you suffer. Especially after you insisted your daddy was dead when everyone else was sure he'd run off with Shannon Morrissey."

"And what did Momma believe?" I asked. Tears clogged my throat, which pissed me off. My father didn't deserve any more of my tears.

"In the beginning, she was sure he was dead. She knew how much he loved you—more than his own life—so she knew he'd never leave you."

And yet he had. He was probably still in Franklin, waiting for God knew what. But Tilly didn't need to know that. "They're both dead now, and I'm an orphan. Even Roy doesn't want me." But I couldn't help thinking how alone my brother must feel. I had Colt and Tilly, but as far as I knew, he had no one. Even his wife was here with me instead of being with him.

But then again, that was *his* doing, and nothing could condone the way he'd treated Belinda.

As if she could read my thoughts, Belinda reached over and took my hand. "You're not alone, Magnolia. You have me. I promise."

"I'm here too, girlie," Tilly said. "I've known you since you were minutes old. Now that you're back, you aren't getting rid of me that easily."

Colt put his hand on my shoulder but remained silent.

I wiped a tear from my cheek. "Sorry for my moment of self-indulgence, Belinda. I know my father was to blame for your parents' deaths."

Her parents had invested their life savings in the Jackson Project, and they'd lost everything. The car accident they'd died in had been deemed a murder-suicide.

"I never really knew any better," she said with a small shrug. "Most of my memories of them have faded. You just lost your momma. Give yourself a break. Let yourself grieve."

I gave her a sad smile and Colt pulled me close again, stroking my arm. Fool that I was, I leaned into him and took the comfort he offered.

We sat in silence for a half minute before Tilly said, "One of the mourners at the funeral told me that Bill James is missing. I bet he ran off with all that missing money."

"You mean the million Daddy supposedly stole when he ran off with Shannon Morrissey?" I asked. I was pretty sure Daddy had stolen that from the Savannah House basement last Saturday night.

"No. The millions from the Jackson Project."

I stared at her in confusion. "Wait. I thought they went bankrupt."

"They did, but your momma was sure your daddy and Bill hid away several million before it did."

"Why didn't Bill take the money before now?" I asked. "Or why didn't Daddy take it when he left fourteen years ago?"

"Your momma heard your father talking to Bill on the phone late one night, a few months before he disappeared. He was talking about ten million dollars they'd squirrelled away in an annuity they'd hidden from the investors and the partners in the Jackson Project. Your daddy was arguing with Bill that he had a right to the annuity even though he'd given up his partnership and Bill was the sole owner. He disappeared soon after that." She gave me a stern look. "It's been twenty years. That annuity's ready to cash in."

My mouth dropped open. Was that the *real* reason my father was back?

Colt's hand shifted to the back of my neck, and he began to gently rub.

"Did you make an appointment with your momma's attorney tomorrow?" Belinda asked.

"I have to work tomorrow."

Tilly gave me a sympathetic look. "You don't have to work tomorrow, Maggie. I've still got the catering school helping out."

"No, at Alvin's shop."

All three of them looked at me like I'd lost my mind.

"You know Alvin doesn't expect you to go back to work tomorrow," Belinda said.

"He'll be pumping you for information, Mags," Colt said. "You know what a gossip he is. I think you should call him and tell him you need more time off."

I sat up and turned to look at him. "Just because you've kissed me a dozen times doesn't mean you have the right to tell me what to do, Colt Austin."

His eyes went round and his body stiffened. "You're right, Magnolia. I don't have any right to tell you what to do, but I'm worried about you."

What was wrong with me? My emotions were ping-ponging back and forth over him, and I was giving him—and myself—whiplash. Tears filled my eyes. "I'm sorry I'm such a bitch right now."

The guarded look in his eyes dropped. "Maggie, your momma just died, and you've had a lot happen in a very short period of time. Maybe you should take a few days to grieve."

Tilly and Belinda nodded their agreement.

"Magnolia, why don't you go fill your momma's big tub and take a long bath?" Belinda suggested. "That might help you relax."

"And stare at her shampoo and conditioner in her shower?" I pushed through my tear-clogged throat. "It will just drive home the fact I wasted ten years I could have had with her—ten years I'll never get back."

"Magnolia . . ." Belinda got up and perched on the edge of the loveseat I was on, reaching her arms out to me.

I hesitated. If I let her hold me, I'd fall apart—and I was pretty sure I wouldn't go back together the way I had been. Then again, maybe that was a good thing. The old Magnolia Mae Steele was a mess. I needed a stronger Magnolia to face the rest of my quest. But what if the pieces fit together wrong and I ended up a shattered, spineless fool?

But my tears had started, and there was no stopping them. My first sob hiccupped out, and I reached for my sister-in-law, terrified of what would happen when the dust settled. But I couldn't think about that now. She wrapped her arms around me and held tight as I sobbed and sobbed until I was light-headed, and there weren't any tears left.

As I settled down, I realized that Colt was now sitting in Belinda's chair. I rested my head on her shoulder as she rubbed soft circles into my back.

"I'm sorry," I said when I realized her shoulder was wet.

"Magnolia," she gently chided. "You buried your mother today. There's no reason to apologize."

I glanced over at Tilly. "How are you doing?"

She slugged back the rest of her whiskey. "I've had more time to come to peace with it than you. I've known this was a possibility for over a year."

"But preparing for something and actually facing it are two very different things, Tilly."

Tears flooded her eyes, and she gave me a sad smile. "My life will be far emptier now, but I'll survive. It's been a long day. I think I'll go and get ready for bed."

"You're still staying here tonight, aren't you?" I asked. She'd come home with Colt, Belinda, and me on Saturday night. We'd all felt the need to be close after leaving the hospital, and she'd been sleeping in Momma's room.

"I'm too tired to go home." She lifted her tumbler. "And a little too tipsy to drive. I'll stay tonight, but I think I should go home tomorrow."

"You can stay as long as you want, Tilly."

She stood and placed the afghan on her chair. "And I appreciate it, sweet girl, but your momma's gone. It's time for me to deal with that."

I stood and pulled her into a tight hug. "I need you, Tilly, and I think you need me too. You're my momma now."

"I'm always here for you, Maggie Mae. Always."

"Likewise."

She started to walk inside, then stopped and turned around. "I forgot. When I was answering the door earlier, I found a magnolia blossom on the doormat."

I froze. "What?"

"It wasn't a bouquet or a flower arrangement. It was just a single flower. I would have almost guessed it blew off a tree onto the porch, only there aren't any magnolia trees close by."

Colt's eyes widened, but Tilly seemed oblivious. "I put it in a bowl of water on the kitchen counter. It was too beautiful to throw away."

I nodded, unable to find the words to answer.

She gave one last wave and walked inside. As soon as Tilly disappeared from view, Belinda tugged me back down on the seat next to her.

"I take it there's a reason you're freaking out right now."

"It's from the killer, isn't it?" Colt asked.

I lifted my shoulders into a tiny shrug. "I don't know." I dug my phone out of my pocket and checked the screen. "No messages." But I couldn't ignore the fact that if the flower *was* from the serial killer, he'd skipped texting—his usual form of communication—and left two things for me in one day. My magnolia necklace and now an actual magnolia.

"Maybe you should call Brady," Colt said, worry in his eyes.

"And tell him what? Tilly found a flower on the front porch? There's nothing he can do."

"The front door's locked, isn't it?" Belinda asked.

"Yeah," I said. I'd checked it multiple times. I offered them a half-smile. "Even if it was from him, there's nothing we can do. We need to worry about more pressing matters—it's time to come up with a game plan."

chapter four

I grabbed the whiskey bottle and refilled my glass. I was going to need more alcohol in my system to get through this. I didn't even know where to start, but then I decided to start at the beginning. "Did either of you know about any of that? That Daddy and Bill had another partner in the beginning?"

"No," Belinda said.

"Not a clue," Colt added.

"And his affairs?"

They both remained silent.

"Belinda, did you know about the possible ten-million-dollar annuity?"

She was silent for a moment before she finally nodded. "Roy's been digging into the history of the investment firm. He always thought there was more to the Jackson Project than was made public, but the last I heard, he hadn't found anything concrete."

I gave my head a tiny shake. "Roy's digging into the Jackson Project?"

"He's been secretly investigating Bill."

"What?"

She poured herself more whiskey. "That's why he's working there, Magnolia. To dig up dirt on Bill and your father."

My ability to feel shocked—by anything—should have been blunted by the last week, and yet it hadn't been. This was the last thing I'd expected her to say. "Did Momma know?"

"No," she said bluntly. "No one knew except for me."

"But . . . why?"

"He was friends with Christopher Merritt—the son, not the father. They met at a party shortly after Roy and I started dating. You wouldn't think they'd have much in common. Roy was in his early twenties and just out of school, working as a DJ and sound engineer, and Chris was an established accountant with a family." She took a sip of her drink and sat back on the loveseat. "Don't underestimate Roy. He didn't just do weddings. He worked with some of the best recording artists. He was slowly building his career, but one day Chris just disappeared. The police said he'd had an affair with Rowena Rogers, then took off out of shame." She turned to me. "The first time I 'officially' met her was on Saturday night. When you ran into her before, I had no idea it was her."

"I didn't know either," I said. "Not until I went to her house on Saturday afternoon. I don't believe for one minute that she was having an affair with Chris Merritt."

Belinda nodded. "I don't believe it either. But there was no dissuading the police from their theory."

"Like Daddy," I said.

Colt shot me a guilty look, but I ignored it.

"Roy took Christopher's disappearance hard," Belinda said, shifting to the side and tucking her legs underneath her. "He and Chris had been meeting every week or two for breakfast to talk about their dead fathers' involvement in the Jackson Project. Even though their fathers had been the ones to swindle people, Chris and Roy felt like they'd been stuck with a poisoned legacy. They felt a need to make things right. If there was hidden money, they wanted to find it and return what they could to the investors."

None of this sounded like Roy at all . . . not the angry, unstable guy I knew.

Belinda continued, her words starting to slur. "Chris was trying to find the annuity—he suspected the same thing your momma did. He called Roy and told him that he'd found something. They were supposed to meet to discuss it, but Chris disappeared."

"Geraldo Lopez?" I asked.

She lifted her shoulder into a slow, uncoordinated shrug. "Roy was sure the answer was hidden in the apartment Christopher kept in Nashville. The lease was coming due, and Chris's wife didn't want anything in it, so Roy told her that he'd take care of the stuff for her."

"It's in Momma's garage," I said.

48

"He'd hoped he would find something useful, but he never did."

"Was the ceramic dog in Chris's apartment?"

"What ceramic dog?" Belinda asked.

"The tall Dalmatian," I said. "The one you saw in my trash. The one Geraldo Lopez was looking for." I paused. "Did Roy know about it?"

She shook her head, confusion filling her eyes. "I don't know."

"Did Roy know about your parents?" I asked. "Did he know about your plan to get revenge?"

She hesitated and guilt filled her eyes. "Roy promised to help me get some closure, but the deeper he got in the firm, the more he changed. He'd never been what you would call a gentle man, but he became mean and violent."

"You stuck with him for your revenge?" I asked in disbelief.

"I loved him in the beginning, Magnolia. Roy could be hard, but he had his tender moments. He took his promise to help me very seriously. And he loved me. Or at least he used to."

"Which brings us back to Detective Martinez," Colt said. "If the two of you are going to meet with her, you need to have similar stories, but they shouldn't be identical."

Belinda lifted her glass to him and said in a snotty tone, "You would know how to handle getting questioned by the police, wouldn't you?"

Colt's mouth pressed into a thin line.

I'd always suspected Belinda's animosity toward him had to do with his previous brush with the law, and her comment seemed to confirm it.

"He didn't do it, Belinda," I said. "You were right—he did have a record, and it was sealed, but Daddy was behind the whole thing."

"Maggie," Colt said, sounding exhausted.

Belinda remained silent, so I decided to press the issue. They were the two people closest to me, and I hated the tension between them. If I could make her understand, she might forgive him for whatever sins she thought he'd committed.

"That's how he roped Colt into working for him. He was arrested on bogus charges. While he was in the Franklin jail, Daddy visited him and told him his charges would be dropped if he agreed to be his spy."

She looked like she was about to say something, but the expression on her face told me she'd thought better of it. "I know that part," she finally said.

It was another reminder that even sweet Belinda had lied to me, and plenty.

Colt shifted in his seat. "You still need a plan for tomorrow."

Belinda looked close to tears. "We'll just go with your story, but it might not come to that. We won't be answering any questions without our attorney present."

"I can't afford an attorney." I started to panic.

Colt slipped his hand in mine. "You have Lila's money, Maggie."

"Roy said she was broke."

"I'm sure there's enough to pay for an attorney."

"I have more than enough," Belinda said, her voice slurring even more. "My *nest egg*. My rainy-day fund. The money I was saving to leave Roy."

I shot a glance back at Colt before turning to Belinda. "I'm not taking your money, Belinda." I lowered my voice. "Are you still leaving Roy?"

"He doesn't want me back."

That wasn't the answer I'd expected. Did she really want to go back?

She stood up, a bit wobbly. "It's been a long day, and tomorrow I'm going to regret drinking all that whiskey."

I stood up and gave her a hug. She clung to me and then let me go, looking exhausted. "I loved Lila, and her death is hitting me hard. I'll be better tomorrow."

"Okay." I moved out of her way and watched her go inside and head up the stairs. "Maybe I should go with her," I murmured.

"I need to talk to you first, Mags."

I sat down in Belinda's seat, sitting across from him, and nodded for him to continue.

He rubbed his thumb over the back of his other hand. "Where do you and I stand? At the cemetery, you seemed okay, but tonight . . ."

"Up until this last week, I never would have suspected Daddy had cheated on Momma, let alone so many times."

He leaned forward, resting his elbows on his thighs. "I didn't know anything about that. I promise."

"But you knew Daddy was alive."

His eyes hardened. "That man has controlled my life for three years, making me do things I never wanted to do. He took everything from me. My freedom, my ex-girlfriend." He paused. "Maggie, you have to trust me. You are better off without that man in your life. You were better off thinking he was dead."

"That was *my* decision to make, Colt."

"I know, Mags. I'm sorry." I could see that he was, but was he sorry for keeping it from me, or was he sorry he'd gotten caught?

Like my father.

I started to get up, but he tugged me down next to him. "There's something else we need to talk about." He paused to see if I'd protest, then continued. "We need to talk about the serial killer."

I pulled my arm free and wrapped my arms over my chest as I shivered.

"Is Brady Bennett still helping you?"

That was a good question. The situation with Brady was tense, and he was the only one in the police department who knew I had a connection to the serial killer. He'd seemed a little off the last few times I'd seen him, and his go-it-alone approach to finding the serial killer didn't feel right. Then again, he had plenty of reason to feel slighted. The morning of Momma's death, I'd told him I didn't want to date him, and later he'd seen me kiss another man. Even so, he'd come to the funeral, and he'd indicated he still wanted to work together.

Colt's eyes narrowed when he picked up on my hesitation. "You don't trust him to protect you?"

"I don't really trust anyone right now."

52

He hesitated. "Do you trust me?"

That was another good question. I knew Colt cared for me, but I was still struggling with his monumental betrayal. I didn't answer.

He gave a sharp nod and determination filled his eyes. "I understand, Mags. I do. And I promise I'll earn your trust back."

I really hoped so. I needed him more than I'd expected.

He stood and reached for my hand. "Let's go to bed." Then he paused. "Do you want me to sleep on the sofa?"

While Tilly had been sleeping in Momma's room, Belinda was staying in Roy's old room, and Colt was sleeping with me in my room. I was plagued with multiple nightmares every night, and he helped calm me down whenever I woke with a start.

"No," I said, feeling weak like my mother. I should send Colt away, but I needed him and I hated both of us a little bit for that.

I headed upstairs to get ready for bed, while Colt put out the fire in the fire pit. I was already in bed by the time he came up smelling like smoke. He went into the bathroom and took a shower, but I was still awake when he climbed into bed next to me wearing a T-shirt and athletic shorts.

He reached for me and pulled my head to his chest. I felt safe in his arms, but it was a false security. A serial killer was after me, and we'd just spent an hour talking about my father's affairs and hidden millions.

"Why are we still looking into Daddy's past?" I asked, resting my hand on his chest. I couldn't ignore that my insides began to tighten and heat up, but I had more important things to deal with than my attraction to Colt. "I think I should be looking for the serial killer."

Colt's body tensed and he put his hand under my chin, tilting my face up so he could search my eyes. "You need to stay as far away from the serial killer as possible. Tell me the truth, Maggie—can Brady still be trusted to protect you, or do you think he'll let his personal feelings get in the way?"

"I'm not sure."

"Then you stay as far from his investigation as possible," he said. "When was the last time you heard from the killer before the magnolia?" I'd told Colt everything over the weekend, needing to unburden myself.

I considered lying to keep from worrying him, but I was tired of lying. "This afternoon at the funeral."

Colt bolted upright. "What? What did he say?"

I sat up too and turned to face him. "Brady gave me a necklace last week, a magnolia pendant. I lost it, but the killer somehow got ahold of it. He was at the ball Saturday night, and he sent me a text with a photo of the necklace. Our table at the ball was in the background."

He looked pissed. "Why am I just now hearing this?"

"Because Belinda semi-kidnapped me to trap my father, then Rowena and her goon were killed, and then Momma died. Honestly, I forgot about it. But today at the funeral, the director handed me the necklace, saying it had been found on one of the seats."

Fear filled Colt's eyes. "The serial killer was at your momma's funeral?"

"I guess so."

"I need to get you out of town."

"What are you talking about?"

"A sadistic serial killer is playing with you, Maggie. I'm not going to let you hang around and see what he has planned next. You refused to leave before because you didn't want to miss out on time with your mother, but we buried her today. It's time to make you safe."

"What about Belinda? The killer threatened to hurt her if I told Brady about him. If he finds out . . ."

"You told Bennett last week, and nothing's happened."

"Not true. He killed Emily while I was staying with Brady, and I'm pretty sure he did it to remind me to keep my mouth shut."

"Emily had been asking around about why you left ten years ago," Colt said. "Maybe she found something that made the killer nervous."

I'd considered that too, but there was no denying he'd sent me a text at around three in the morning—after her time of death—to let me know he'd left me a warning.

"I'm tired of running away, Colt. I ran away ten years ago, and I don't want to run anymore."

Colt looked scared. "Then you shouldn't be alone. You need someone with you at all times."

"What I need is a new gun. I still haven't replaced the one that was stolen out of my purse." My eyes narrowed as a new thought hit me. "Do you think Daddy stole the gun and the bag of gold out of my purse the night Lopez attacked me?"

"Why would you think so?"

"Roy wasn't at the fundraiser because he was at a dinner in Nashville, but I thought I saw him in the shadows," I said. "I know now that it was Daddy."

His eyes widened. "Your father was at the art fundraiser?"

I nodded.

He wiped his hand over his face. "I don't know what the fuck is going on, Maggie, but I don't like any of this. Come away with me."

"No. I have to see this through."

"The serial killer isn't going to let you go this time, Magnolia. We both know that flower was from him. That's called escalation, and it's not good."

"We're going to stop him." I sighed and tugged him down to the pillows, letting him wrap an arm around me and hold me close.

He leaned down and kissed me—tentative, as though testing the waters. I kissed him back but with hesitation. I wanted to forgive him, especially since the proof of his concern for me was so evident, but I kept thinking about my mother and how she'd forgiven Daddy again and again. I didn't want to be that woman.

His lips left a trail of kisses up my cheek and to my temple. "Go to sleep. I'll be here. I won't let anything happen to you."

Even though he couldn't promise any such thing, I closed my eyes and soon drifted off to sleep.

chapter five

The next morning, Colt and Belinda both tried to talk me out of going to work at the Rebellious Rose, insisting that I needed more time, but I knew sitting around Momma's house would only make me feel worse. I was nowhere near ready to start going through her things, and if I sat around, my mind would dwell on the stuff of my nightmares.

Work was the best thing for me.

Tilly had gotten up before all of us to go check on her dog before she headed to the catering kitchen. Belinda was the next to leave, and after trying—and failing—one last time to get me to call in to work, she insisted she'd call me after she talked to an attorney. We'd agreed we would only go to the station if the attorney advised it.

As soon as he and I were alone together, Colt gave me a worried look. "I don't want to leave you," he said.

"In fact, you're a mess. Do you know how many nightmares you had last night?"

"Four."

"That's right. Four nightmares that made you wake up crying and screaming. You need to give yourself a break, Maggie."

After each one, Colt had held me close and wiped my tears, assuring me I was safe. I knew his request came from a place of genuine concern, but I was still determined. "You have no idea how much I appreciate that you lost sleep for me."

"Mags, I'd stay up all night if it would make you feel better. That's not the point."

"I know, and that's what makes me appreciate you even more, but that man has stolen too much of my life. I want to go work for Alvin this morning. I need to. It will take my mind off everything." Then I reached up on my tiptoes and gave him a soft kiss on the cheek. "Thanks for being patient with me."

"Thanks for giving me another chance."

Colt left and I finished my coffee before heading downtown. As I made the drive, it occurred to me that I still had clothes and things in my apartment behind Ava Milton's house. I needed to fit a visit into my schedule.

I pulled into the parking lot behind the shop and looked around for anything suspicious. When nothing popped out, I got out of my car—my pepper spray in hand—and headed for the back door to the shop, coming to an abrupt halt when I saw Brady get out of his car parked several spots down.

"Magnolia," he said, walking toward me.

59

Startled, I put a hand on my chest to slow my racing heart. "Brady. You scared the crap out of me." I didn't bother asking him how he knew my schedule—he seemed to make a habit of it.

"You shouldn't be out here alone, Maggie."

And we both knew why, but I doubted the killer would go after me at ten o'clock in the morning in a downtown Franklin parking lot. I felt like he would toy with me more. But then again, what if I was wrong?

Brady stopped a few feet in front of me. Wearing dress pants, a button-up shirt, and a dark tie, Brady Bennett looked like a very attractive catch. And maybe he was, but there were too many red flags. Too many things that didn't add up.

But couldn't I say the same thing about Colt?

I gave my head an involuntary shake and dropped the pepper spray into my purse, trying to jolt my thoughts back to the serial killer. My mind drifted to the files I'd seen in Brady's apartment. All of those murdered women . . .

Then I realized that while I'd seen their photographs, I didn't know anything about them. They were nameless, tortured dead women to me, and that felt very wrong and impersonal. They deserved better. "How were the other women taken?"

His eyes widened. "*What?*"

"The women he killed. How did they disappear?"

My question seemed to momentarily stump him. "Uh . . ." He glanced at the building before shifting his gaze back to me. "Melanie Seaborn, the woman you . . . saw . . ." He lowered his voice and compassion filled his eyes. We both knew what he wasn't saying—*murdered*. "She was a nurse. She never showed up for her seven a.m. shift at the hospital."

Her face from that night appeared in my head, and I swallowed my rising nausea and panic. Until now, I'd never considered what she'd been like outside of the confines of that basement, let alone the fact that she'd had a life—a job, friends. Maybe even a spouse or boyfriend.

I nodded, trying to control my rising hysteria. I needed to get more information out of Brady— something I could only do if I stayed calm. "When was the last time she was seen?"

"Leaving the hospital the day before. Around four in the afternoon."

"She lived alone?" I asked.

He cleared his throat, clearly uncomfortable with the direction this conversation was taking. "Uh . . . yeah."

"And the others?"

"I'm not getting into this now, Maggie. Not here."

That was fair, not to mention he didn't necessarily have to tell me anything. It was all official police business. Sort of. "Then why are you here? Why aren't you working with Detective Martinez?"

He looked caught off guard by my question. "She was on vacation last week when I got assigned the Emily Johnson case, so my boss gave me a temporary partner and moved her to a new case. Why do you ask?"

"Because she came to Momma's house last night while we were still entertaining mourners."

His back stiffened. "What did she want?"

"She wanted to know if I knew anything about the murders in the basement of Savannah House the night of the masquerade ball."

Some of the color bled from his face. "She didn't tell me she was going to see you."

"She wants me and Belinda to come to the police station at one."

He took a second to ask, "Are you going?"

"Not unless Belinda's attorney says we should."

"You have *an attorney*?"

I narrowed my eyes. "After the last two times I was interrogated at the Franklin police station, I thought it best to have someone with me who is actually concerned about my rights."

"She thinks there's a connection to you." The pained look in Brady's eyes confirmed that he got my dig. He'd been present during my last interrogation. His partner had treated me like I was garbage, and he hadn't intervened. I still held a tiny grudge.

"I guess so. Her questions were vague, but she said she was at Momma's funer—" Oh . . . how could I be so stupid?

I gave him a look of disgust. "But you already knew that. You were there too."

He had the good sense to remain silent.

I pushed out a sigh, feeling the weight of the world on my shoulders.

"What do you know about the murders Saturday night, Magnolia?" Brady asked in a low voice.

I narrowed my eyes. "You're not going to read me my rights first?"

He groaned, sounding pissed. "I'm trying to *help* you."

"Like you helped me when you told your partner about our talk in the coffee shop? Because frankly, *Detective* Bennett, I could do without that kind of help."

He looked embarrassed. "You know I didn't have a choice."

I heaved another sigh and rubbed my forehead with my fingertips. "I believe you. But who's to say you won't find yourself in the same position in a few days? Whatever I tell you could get me hauled into the police station for questioning or, worse, arrested."

His face hardened. "Have you committed a crime?"

"Does it matter if I *haven't?*" I asked in a short tone. "Seems to me plenty of the members of the Franklin Police Department rearrange the facts to fit their theory, truth be damned."

"That's not true," he protested vehemently.

"Isn't it? You told me yourself there's at least one dirty cop on the force. Isn't that why we're keeping it secret that the same man who killed Amy and Emily left that scar on my leg?"

His eyes flew open, and he glanced around to see if anyone was close enough to have heard my proclamation. Thankfully, the lot was empty of other people.

How could I have been so careless? I wasn't thinking straight. My nightmares had left me exhausted.

"Maggie," he said in a low tone. "I promised you that I would protect you, and my promise still holds, whether we're together or not."

"Has the FBI shown up yet?" I asked. "You said they were coming last week."

A grimace tightened his lips. "The agent got called to a more pressing case."

"They can do that?"

"They only have so many agents." He paused. "Are you really with Colt Austin?" His obvious disgust tainted his words.

"That's none of your business, Brady."

"Is that why you're not wearing my necklace anymore?"

I opened my mouth to tell him about the necklace—how the killer had found and returned it and I could barely stand to look at it now—but I didn't want to get into any of that. Instead, I said, "Don't make me hurt you any more than I already have."

He looked taken aback, but he let the subject drop. "Does he know about the serial killer?" He sounded worried. "Does he know the danger you're in?"

I hesitated, then decided to tell him the truth. "Yes."

"And you're here alone? He's not with you now?"

I lifted my eyebrows. "You think I need a bodyguard? If I were with you, would you be taking me back and forth to work?"

"As a matter of fact, yes," he said, looking adamant. "You're in danger, Maggie. You're not taking this seriously enough."

Part of me wondered if he was right. Maybe I should tell him about the killer's latest messages—his "escalation," as Colt had called it—but something held me back. I took a breath, then asked, "You obviously didn't know about your former partner wanting to question me and Belinda, so why are you here, Brady?"

His face softened. "I wanted to check on you. I'm worried about you. You've been through so much this past month. How are you handling your mother's death?"

Call me a fool, but I believed he was being genuine. My shoulders relaxed. "As well as can be expected, I guess. I knew she was dying, but I didn't expect it to happen so soon."

"I'm sorry. I know it has to be hard for you." He shifted his weight. "Honestly, it's hard for *me* to believe, and I barely knew her. I just saw her last week at the restaurant, and then she was in the hospital. Dying."

"Her immune system was weak. It didn't take long." But then, he already knew that. I'd told him in the hospital, the morning before she died.

"I'm fortunate to still have my parents, so I have no idea what you're going through, but if there's anything I can do, please let me know."

"Thanks," I said, surprised at how earnest he sounded.

"In fact . . ." His voice trailed off, but he held my gaze. "I think you should move back into my apartment." When I started to protest, he held up both hands in a defensive move. "Maggie, hear me out."

I closed my mouth and wrapped my arms across my chest.

"This isn't some pathetic attempt to get you back. You can stay in the guest room. In fact, you should take a temporary leave of absence from all your jobs and hole up there until I can find this guy."

"So your answer is for me *to hide?*"

He looked confused as to why I so obviously thought this was a bad idea. "It's not permanent."

"No."

"Maggie, if you'll just—"

"No. I'm not hiding. I did that ten years ago, and because I hid, more women have died. I'm done hiding."

"You said you blocked it out ten years ago, so how could you have come forward?"

"I could have gone to the police and showed them my cut. They could have helped me remember. They might have found *him.*"

Conflict waged in his eyes before he finally said, "Do you think they would have believed you?" When I didn't respond, he continued, "After you insisted that your father was dead, do you think they would have believed you?"

My mouth dropped open as if on a hinge, but I quickly shut it.

Regret washed over his face. "You might have gotten someone who was sympathetic, but you also might have gotten someone who wrote you off as a hysterical teenager. It would have been a crapshoot." He gave me a sad smile. "You were right to run. You saved yourself, and there's no harm in protecting yourself now."

"By hiding like a coward?"

He took a step closer and a fierce look filled his eyes. "You're not a coward. Don't even entertain the thought."

I closed my eyes. It was tempting to hide in Brady's fortress of an apartment with its security and alarms. I'd be safe there—or at least I'd *feel* safe—but I'd also be running from my problems. *Again.* I was tired of running. "I have to go into the shop before I'm late."

"So you won't stay with me?" he asked, sounding disappointed.

"Did you really think I would?"

I decided to make my break for the shop, but the second I started to sidestep him, he moved to block my path.

"Wait," he said.

I stared at his chest, then lifted my gaze to meet his.

"If you insist on traipsing around like nothing's wrong, then I want to give you something. It's in my car." Without waiting for me to respond, he put his arm around my lower back and steered me in that direction.

"What is it?" I asked, but I didn't resist. There was no denying that I felt safe when I was close to Brady, like no one would dare mess with both the police detective and the man. Too bad I'd screwed it all up by sleeping with him last week.

What was wrong with me?

"I need to show you." He opened the passenger door and waited.

I looked up at him and gave him a wry grin. "Is this when you take me to your apartment against my will and lock me up for my own good?"

He grinned back, but it looked sad. "If I thought I could get away with it, I'd probably give it a shot."

"I can't go anywhere, Brady. I have to go inside to work."

"We're not going anywhere. I need to give you something, but I don't want to do it out in the open."

"Okay . . ." I'd only been half teasing about the kidnapping thing, but I got into the car anyway.

Once I was inside, he closed the door and walked around to the driver's seat, climbing in next to me. I started to get nervous when I saw his car keys in his hand, but he inserted the key into the glove compartment and opened it up, revealing a small handgun. He grabbed it and held it over the console, resting it on his palm.

"I take it you know how to use one of these?"

Shocked, I lifted my eyes to his expressionless face. "Yeah."

"I want you to carry this. Just in case."

Here was the solution to my gun problem. Brady was the last person I'd expected to provide it. He still held it on his palm, waiting for me to take it, but I hesitated.

"When was the last time you fired a gun?" he asked.

"Uh . . . when my dad showed me how to use *his* gun."

"So a good fourteen years ago?"

I nodded, finally picking up the weapon. My hand had a slight tremor.

"When do you get off work?"

"At three, but if Belinda's attorney says it's okay for us to meet with Detective Martinez, we're supposed to be there at one."

"I'll take care of Maria. Will you let me take you to the range for target practice this afternoon?"

"Uh . . . yeah." Anyone who walked around with a gun should know how to use one—that was just common sense.

"Thank you. You have no idea how relieved I am." He put the gun back in the still-open glove compartment, then closed and locked it.

"I still don't understand why you're doing this," I said, clasping my hands together in my lap.

He searched my face with a look of frustration. "I've never made any secret of the fact that I care about you, Maggie. Just because you got scared because we were moving too fast doesn't mean I stopped caring."

"Brady . . ." I needed to nip that idea in the bud. "It wasn't that."

He grabbed my hand and tenderly held on to it. "You are in no position to make any decisions about *anything.* Just accept that I care about you and want to make sure you're safe. Nothing devious about that, right?"

"No." But something still felt off. Brady was an exceptionally good-looking man who probably had a dozen women dying to go out with him. Why was he so persistent about dating *me*? But maybe he was just the hero type, and it would be a blow to his ego if something happened to me now that he'd appointed me his damsel in distress. I refused to believe he wanted to date me because of my YouTube ignominy.

"Good," he said with a grin. "Now that that's settled, I need to talk to you about something else."

I was sure he was about to press me about the murders at Savannah House, but instead he said, "I know this is hard, but I really need you to take me to that house in the woods."

My skin crawled and I involuntarily sucked in a breath. "What do you hope to find? He murdered that woman . . ." No. She had a name, and she deserved my respect. "*Melanie* ten years ago."

"There might not be anything there, but maybe there is. If it helps us find the killer, then it's worth the effort."

So *this* was his real reason for being here. He'd been hounding me to take him to the house for nearly a week—even yesterday at the funeral—and until now I'd managed to avoid it. While I doubted there would be any evidence left after a decade, I knew he still needed to see it. I just didn't feel comfortable going out there again. "Have you told Owen about the connection yet?" I asked. "That there's a serial killer on the loose?"

"He's got enough to deal with right now."

I straightened. "What's going on with Owen?"

Brady hesitated. "Once the connection between Walter Frey and Geraldo Lopez came to light, the department decided to look into how he handled the Walter Frey murder. Especially since there was a possible connection to the case his uncle had worked on."

"The cell phone . . ." When I'd discovered Walter Frey's body behind the bar where we'd arranged to meet to discuss the night of my father's disappearance, I'd seen a cell phone and a list of names clutched in his hand. But Owen had never mentioned a cell phone in his report, and the phone hadn't been listed as evidence.

"Yeah." He paused, then said, "You'll likely be interviewed by someone in the department about that too."

I was going to be interviewed for *two* separate investigations? "Why?"

"To make sure your story lines up with his."

"He must be crapping his pants right now."

"To put it mildly."

I took a breath, only then realizing I'd been holding my hands so tightly my fingernails were digging into my palms. "Are you here to coerce me to stick to a script?"

"No. You need to tell the truth."

"But Owen—"

His eyes hardened. "Tell the truth, Maggie."

"Are you two at odds?" I wasn't sure why that bothered me so much, especially since as recently as last week I'd believed Owen was trying to kill me. The thing was, Rowena Rogers had admitted that Owen's uncle had been caught in the middle of my father's investigation and had been innocent of wrongdoing. For some reason, I felt like I owed it to him to make sure he didn't suffer because of my father too.

"That's neither here nor there. You need to tell the truth."

I pressed my lips together, purposely not committing one way or the other. "When will they contact me?"

"They know your mother just died. Unlike Maria, they might wait until the end of the week."

"What do they think happened?"

"Just tell your side of the story. That's all you need to worry about."

I was more confused than ever. "But you told Owen I just stumbled upon Walter Frey's body, not that I'd arranged to meet him at the bar. What do you want me to do about that?"

"Keep up that story, but tell them the truth about everything else."

"But—"

"Just trust me on this, Maggie."

I really wanted to trust him, but he was making it difficult. It was like he was hanging his best friend out to dry. Why?

He looked out the windshield and grinned slightly. "Alvin's watching us right now. You're going to get a buttload of questions about what we've been up to."

Brady was right. Alvin was a notorious gossip. "I need to go inside."

He opened his door and was out in a flash, intercepting me as I got out of the passenger side of the car. "I'm going to walk you to the door. Don't leave until I pick you up at three."

I shook my head. "Brady . . ."

"Maggie. Please. Don't fight me on this. I'm trying to protect you."

I found myself saying, "Okay."

He smiled as we started walking toward the back door. "If you get off sooner, let me know."

"Okay."

His smile spread, and for some reason I found it unnerving. He stopped at the back door and turned to face me. "If anyone comes in that worries or frightens you, call me. Even if you think it's nothing."

"That seems extreme."

"A serial killer is sending you personal messages. Anything short of putting you under witness protection doesn't even broach extreme." He bent over and kissed my cheek. "Stay safe." He opened the door, waited until I was inside to shut it, and then walked away.

chapter
six

What were you and the delicious-looking detective talking about in his car?" Alvin said the moment Brady started to walk away.

I gave him a sly look. "I'm surprised your lip-reading skills failed you."

His grin turned lopsided. "You were too far away."

My eyes widened. I'd been joking. "He was offering me his condolences."

"He couldn't do that in the parking lot?"

I lifted my shoulder into a coquettish shrug. "A girl doesn't share all of her secrets." I suddenly hoped Colt didn't drop by to see me today. How would I explain *that*?

Alvin turned serious. "I was sorry to hear about Lila. She will be dearly missed."

I swallowed the lump in my throat. "Thanks, Alvin."

The bell on the front door rang, announcing a customer, and another one soon walked in. I spent the next few hours keeping busy—which was exactly what I needed, but around noon I got a call from Belinda that brought me back to my troubles.

"How are you doing?" she asked as soon as I answered.

"Fine. Keeping busy."

"Have you gotten anything else strange?"

I knew she was thinking about the magnolia blossom. "No. Nothing."

"Would you tell me if you had?"

I almost said no, but I needed to stop acting like I was in this alone. The problem was too big for me to solve without help. "Yeah. I would."

"Thank you." I heard the smile in her voice. "That means a lot to me, but that's not the only reason I called."

"I take it you've talked to your attorney."

"Yeah, but apparently Detective Martinez postponed our meeting."

Brady had come through, but how had he arranged it? "That's good news, I guess."

"Yeah. She'll let us know when it's rescheduled."

"Okay. Thanks for taking care of that, Belinda."

"It was no problem. You'll be home at your momma's for dinner?" she asked.

Tilly had a catering job tonight. I knew I should help, but I couldn't bring myself to walk into the kitchen and face the staff. "Yeah. I'll be there."

"See you tonight," she said.

Alvin gave me a questioning glance after I ended the call. We'd never discussed personal phone calls while working, and for the most part, I didn't take them, usually resorting to texting on the sly.

"Just Belinda checking on me," I said as I stuffed my phone into my pocket.

He nodded and gave me a sympathetic glance. "You know you didn't have to come in today, Magnolia. I could have gotten someone else to cover."

"No. I want to be here. Really. I need to work, Alvin."

"Let me know if it gets to be too much, okay?"

"Okay."

Another customer walked in, and I soon lost myself in my work again. Another hour passed, and when the back doorbell rang, Alvin looked toward it with an appreciative glance. "It seems to be the day for Franklin's finest to drop by."

I'd been helping a woman choose the right finger for an antique ring she was looking at, but I glanced over my shoulder and saw Owen walk inside.

"Is there anything I can help you with, Detective Frasier?" Alvin asked.

"I'm just looking," he said. "Thanks, Alvin."

I kept track of Owen out of the corner of my eye while I finished helping the woman and rang her up. As soon as she headed for the door, Owen made a beeline straight for me.

I walked around the counter and led him to the back of the shop. "I was going to call you," I said in nearly a whisper. His brows lifted, and I added, "For multiple reasons."

He pretended to study a silver candlestick as he said in a low voice, "You've talked to Brady?"

"This morning."

He glanced out to the parking lot. "We shouldn't talk here."

I opened my mouth to ask why, then closed it. He was right. "I get off at three, but Brady's picking me up."

Surprise filled his eyes. "I thought you were with the musician now."

"Who told you that?"

"Brady."

"He's not picking me up for anything romantic." But it *was* personal, and I wasn't sure I should tell him the reason.

He studied me for a moment. "Tell him you can't make it. You and I *really* need to talk."

"He's going to want to know why, and I'm tired of lying. What if I can get off at two? That's only forty minutes from now." When he hesitated, I said, "I don't owe you a damn thing, Owen. Take it or leave it. You're lucky I'm meeting you at all."

His eyes darkened. "You're right, but we can't be seen together. I took a chance coming here as it is."

"Why did you?"

"I wasn't sure you'd take my call."

He had a point. We'd never considered each other friends. More like adversaries. "And the call would show up on both of our bills, providing proof that you'd called me," I added as the thought hit me. "Where do you want to meet?"

"My apartment. No one will think twice about both of our cars being parked there."

"Okay. What's the address?"

He frowned. "You can't plug this into your GPS, Magnolia. No trace. Turn off your phone. Turn off your OnStar if you have it."

"My car's way too old for that. Just tell me the address, and I'll keep it in my head." I gave him a sly look. "All that script memorization pays off."

He told me his address and gave me directions. "I think it goes without saying that no one can know about this. Not even Brady."

"Yeah. I know."

He walked out the back door without another word.

"What did Franklin's second hottest detective want?" Alvin asked.

"Brady told him to check on me." I needed to ask Alvin to let me off early, but I couldn't ask yet. It would look too suspicious.

"That Brady Bennett is quite the catch, Magnolia."

"Yeah . . ." I knew I should tell him I wasn't with Brady, but I didn't feel like getting into it. I had enough to deal with.

Another customer came in and I moved to the back of the store, casting a glance out at the parking lot. I didn't see Owen's car anywhere—I figured he must have left—but I didn't see any other ominous signs either.

Alvin started chatting with the customer about the unusually mild April weather we'd been having, and I refolded some napkins that had been tossed onto the folded pile. Twenty minutes later, my boss was at the cash register straightening the paper bags as a customer walked out the door with her purchase.

"Alvin, would you mind if I leave early?" I asked. "I'm so exhausted. I'm not sure if I'll make it until three." Not a lie. There were dark circles under my eyes that all the concealer in the world couldn't cover up.

"Of course, Magnolia. You go home and rest."

"I hate leaving you like this."

"Things have slowed down. I'll be fine."

"Thanks, Alvin." I grabbed my purse and headed out the back door with my pepper spray in hand, glancing around first to make sure there wasn't anyone lurking behind any of the cars.

Owen's apartment was north of the Galleria Mall, so it took me about fifteen minutes to get there from downtown. It was a newer complex, and it looked like it must cost a near fortune in rent. After parking in the lot in front of the building next to Owen's, I took the elevator to the fourth floor—the top floor—and found Owen's apartment halfway down the hall. I rapped on the door, and it opened within seconds.

"Magnolia. You came," he said in surprise.

"Like I said, I wanted to talk to you too."

He stepped out of the way and let me in.

The apartment had an open floor plan with the kitchen by the door, the living area straight ahead, and a small balcony that overlooked the pool. Owen gestured to his sofa, and I sat down while he sat on the perpendicular loveseat.

I decided to take the offensive. "Brady told me that your superiors are looking into how you handled the Walter Frey murder case. They figured out the connection to your uncle's case."

He sat back, resting his hand on the arm of the loveseat. "Honestly, I'm surprised he told you."

"He warned me that someone from the department would contact me with questions about what happened." I paused. "Brady knows I saw the cell phone and paper. And we both know that you said you didn't find them."

He remained silent, his expressionless face giving nothing away.

"I asked Brady what I should say when they question me, and he told me to tell them the truth."

If Owen was surprised, he didn't let on. "And is that what you plan to do?"

I decided to take a chance, probably a stupid one, but a chance all the same. "I met Rowena Rogers last weekend."

His eyes widened. "Are you confessing that you know something about her murder?"

"No. I'm confessing that I met with her last Saturday afternoon. I wanted answers, and I knew she had them."

"Have you told Brady this?"

"No. Only one other person knows about it, and not everything."

Suspicion filled his eyes. "So why are you telling *me*?"

"Because you and I are more alike than you realize, Owen. We both want the same thing."

"To clear your father?" He released a bitter laugh. "You're wrong there."

"I've given up on clearing my father's name. The deeper I dig, the worse he looks."

"Then what do you want, Magnolia?" he asked in a snide tone.

I couldn't blame him. I had the power to destroy his career. I understood his suspicions. "I want the truth, Owen. I want the dirty, nasty, smelly, rotten truth."

"Even if your father comes out smelling the worst of them all?"

"I already know he will."

That surprised him, not that I could blame him. He knew I'd been looking to clear Daddy's name just last week. "What made you come to that conclusion?"

"Rowena was one of the people who helped me see the light." My expression softened. "She knew about you, Owen, and she knew about your uncle."

His eyes widened.

"She said your uncle had no part in any of it. He was just caught up in the whole thing." I looked him in the eye. "Your uncle was innocent."

"I already know that," he said in frustration and stood. He walked into the kitchen and grabbed two glasses from the cabinet. "I don't have much to drink," he said. "I have a bottle of wine—left over from my old girlfriend—scotch, beer, and water."

"Water." Even if it hadn't been early in the day, I was too tired to drink anything alcoholic, not to mention I was supposed to meet Brady to shoot the handgun he was giving me. I couldn't show up with alcohol on my breath.

He filled one glass with ice and water, then poured himself scotch.

I knew he needed time to work through this, but I was meeting Brady in forty-five minutes, and it was hard to resist the urge to hurry Owen along. He walked back into the living room and set the glass of water on the coffee table in front of me.

"Owen, I think we can help each other. I've become privy to information about what happened fourteen years ago. You want answers, and so do I. What if we pool our information?"

He sat on the loveseat and took a long drink of his scotch. "What I have is official information."

"And I have information I suspect *you* don't have. You'll never get it out of Rowena Rogers. She's dead." I paused. "But I have conditions."

He took another drink, then said in a dry tone, "Of course you do."

"Anything I tell you stays between you and me. No Brady. And you can't use anything against me legally."

"I can't agree to that."

"Then I guess we're wasting our time." I grabbed my purse and stood. "Let me know if you change your mind and want to talk."

I started toward the door, and Owen called out, "Magnolia. Wait." But he didn't sound happy about caving.

Wearing a grim expression, I turned around to face him. "This is a big decision. Why don't you take some time to think about it?"

He didn't answer.

"As a sign of good faith, I'm going to tell whoever interviews me that I didn't see a cell phone."

He set his glass on the coffee table and stood. "Why would you lie?"

"What purpose would it serve to tell the truth? We both know who killed Walter Frey, and I know you're a good cop. But I *do* want to know one thing."

"What?"

"I want to know why you took it. To get information to help you clear your uncle's name?"

He didn't answer, but I wasn't surprised. To do so would incriminate himself, and he still hadn't decided if he could trust me.

"Believe it or not," I said, "I might understand your motivations. Think about it and give me a call. But get a burner." I turned and reached for the doorknob, suddenly wondering why Brady had a burner phone. I spun back around. "Do you already have a burner phone?"

"No. If I did, I would have used it to call you instead of coming to the store."

"Why would Brady have a burner phone?"

"He doesn't." Shock washed over his face. "Wait. He has one?"

It was my turn to remain silent.

He shoved his hands into his pockets and moved closer. "Aren't we a fine pair. Both full of secrets, and neither of us willing to trust the other."

I decided to take another risk. "I saw the files you brought Brady last week."

His eyes flew wide. "He showed you?"

"No. I found them myself. He'd hidden them."

"Why would you look for them?"

"Because I saw the photos spread out across his table. He thought I was asleep, so he probably thought it was safe to look at them. I recognized one of the women."

"Amy Danvers?"

"No. I didn't see her photos until after I found the file. I recognized Melanie Seaborn."

He cocked his head and asked skeptically, "How do you know Melanie Seaborn?"

I took a few steps closer and stared up into his face. "Look at the timelines, Owen."

Then I turned around and walked out the door.

I was halfway to the elevator when Owen stepped into the hall. "Magnolia. Wait." When I ignored him, he followed, reaching me as I pushed the down button. "You think you can drop a bombshell like that and *just walk away*?"

"You don't trust me, and I don't trust you. I don't know how we're going to get around that, but we need to find a way. Let's both take some time to think it through." I punched the button multiple times.

"What do you know about Melanie Seaborn's death?"

I tried not to react. Just hearing her name made me want to burst into tears. The elevator door opened, and I started to get in, but Owen grabbed my arm and held tight.

I shot him a glare. "Let go of me."

"Not until you tell me what you know about Melanie Seaborn."

"Let go of my arm, Owen."

"Does Brady know?"

The elevator doors started to close. I jerked out of his hold and pushed the doors back open. After I stepped inside, I turned around to face him. "I have nothing to lose here, and you have everything to gain. Think this through."

The doors shut, but I could still see his angry face.

He'd call me. It was only a matter of when.

chapter seven

Brady was already sitting in his car in the parking lot when I pulled in, and the look on his face told me he wasn't happy. I parked three spots away from him, and as soon as I put the car into park, Brady was standing next to my driver's side window.

I rolled it down and he leaned over with an irritated look. "Where were you?"

Lifting my chin, I said in a no-nonsense tone, "I had to run an errand."

His mouth pressed into a thin line. "I thought you were working until three."

I gave him an unapologetic stare. "I got off early."

"To run your errand," he said with a blank look.

"It's none of your business where I went or what I did. I'm here. I'm fine. Let's do this." I realized I ran the risk of pissing him off, but his attempts to control me were getting on my nerves. I needed to set some boundaries and hoped his concern for my safety won out.

His eyes darkened, but he didn't press the issue. "I'll drive you there." He reached for my door handle, but it was locked.

I didn't unlock the door. "How about I just follow you?"

He stared at me for several seconds. "Why don't you want to get into the car with me?"

I groaned and rubbed my forehead. "That's not it, Brady. We're not together, but I *would* like for us to stay friends. However, that's never going to work if I feel like you're suffocating me."

His jaw set and a vein began to throb in his forehead. "What part of you being in danger do you *not get*?"

"Then why haven't you told anyone else in the department about my involvement?"

"I've already told you—"

"That someone is corrupt and you're protecting me." It felt even more bogus now than the first time he'd said it. "Look, Brady, I don't want to fight with you. I'm being practical here. Aren't you working today? What if you get called in while we're there? I can't tag along with you. I need my own car."

He frowned. "You're right. Fine. Follow me, but I'll text you the address in case we get separated."

An hour later, I walked out of the gun range with the gun in my purse, feeling a lot more confident about using it. Brady walked me to my car, and when I reached the driver's side door, I glanced up at him. "I don't have a permit. Isn't that a problem?"

"We're not going to worry about that right now. The important thing is that you can protect yourself," Brady said. "If you need to use it, we'll deal with the rest."

"Aren't you risking your career by doing this?"

He reached up and tucked a strand of my hair behind my ear. "I care about you, Maggie. I promised you I'd protect you. I take that seriously."

I reached up and grabbed his hand. He'd been professional inside the gun range, so this shift caught me off guard. "You can't do that, Brady."

He pulled his hand loose. "You're right. I'm sorry."

I took a step away and opened my car door. "I need to go home."

"To your apartment?"

"*Brady.*"

"I just need to know where you are in case you need me."

"I'm staying at Momma's house with Belinda."

"And Colt." His tone made it clear he didn't approve.

I shot him a glare.

He lifted his hands in self-defense. "Sorry. That was out of line. I suppose I should be grateful you have two people with you."

88

My cell phone began to ring as I got into the car, and I left my door open in my haste to pull it out of my purse. "I've got to go, Brady. Thanks for everything."

"We still need to go out to that house, Maggie," he said, staring at me with an intense gaze.

"Not tonight." I didn't recognize the number that had popped up on my caller ID. Had Owen gotten a burner? Was he calling me to accept my proposal?

Brady looked like he was about to say something, but I closed the door, answering the phone as I started the car. "Hello?"

"Magnolia Steele?" a man asked. I didn't recognize his voice.

My heart lurched in my chest. Was this someone from the police department? "Yes?"

"This is Wilber Wimple, your mother's estate attorney. Do you have time to stop by my office today?" I'd expected him to call me earlier, and I sure hadn't expected to hear this much urgency in his voice.

"It's already after four, Mr. Wimple," I said. "Wouldn't you rather wait until tomorrow?"

"Your brother has already called me twice today and is very . . . insistent. I'd like to read the will as soon as possible."

I couldn't hide my surprise. "Reading of the will? Isn't that something you just see in movies and on TV? I found Momma's will on her desk."

"That was her old will. I have her new one."

"What? She has a *new* will?"

"Given the circumstances, it would be best if you could meet me at my office at five. Can you be here?"

"Uh . . . yeah," I said.

He told me his address, which I committed to memory, and I immediately texted Belinda after we hung up.

I have a 5:00 meeting at Momma's lawyer's office. Roy will be there. Can you come?

She responded within seconds.

Her attorney already contacted me. I'll see you there.

Neither of us was ready to face my brother, but at least we would be together.

Brady was next to his car, still watching me, so I gave him a tiny wave as I backed out of the parking space, trying to figure out what to do for the next forty-five minutes. I decided to go to Starbucks to get a cup of coffee and look up everything I could find on Eric Duncan.

I didn't have my laptop, but I did have a nearly fully charged smart phone. I went inside and ordered a cappuccino, then sat at a table and typed in *Eric Duncan Tennessee*. Might as well start with the basics.

The first results revealed a computer science professor, a real estate agent, and a doctor. It wasn't until the third page that I found the man I was looking for—Eric Duncan, a financial planner in Murfreesboro.

I searched for his LinkedIn account and found that he owned his own small firm with only three employees. He'd worked at a few other places over the past thirty years, and there, at the bottom of the list, he'd listed his first investment job—JS Investments, co-owner with Brian Steele and Bill James.

Staring at the photo of the man who had tried to rape my mother, I wondered what I was doing. Why was I diving down this rabbit hole? Sure, my father was lurking around and Bill James had disappeared, but my father had his precious gold. What did I care if there was a multi-million-dollar annuity? All the other players were dead. I needed to concentrate on more important things . . . like evading a serial killer. But I couldn't deny that the two were somehow connected. But how? Was all this sleuthing really helping?

I glanced at the time and saw I had ten minutes to get to the attorney's office. Normally, it would be a five-minute drive, but I worried it might take longer with rush-hour traffic.

I pulled into Wilber Wimple's parking lot at 5:03, and hurried into the office. The receptionist was expecting me and ushered me into a conference room down the hall. I had expected to see Belinda and Tilly sitting at the table, but to my surprise, Colt was sitting between them. Had Tilly gotten someone to cover for her and Colt for the catering job tonight? My brother sat at the end of the table, to my left—as far from the others as he could get. The look on his face told me he planned to destroy me.

An older man stood up at the opposite end of the table. "Magnolia?"

"Yes," I said as I walked toward him with my hand extended.

"Wilber Wimple," he said, shaking my hand with a limp grasp.

"Sorry to be late," I said as I took a seat, sitting directly opposite Colt. "I'm still not used to traffic. It's gotten a lot busier in Franklin since I left."

"For God's sake, Magnolia," Roy snarled. "You've been back for a fucking month. You should know about the traffic by now."

Belinda gasped at his curse, and Mr. Wimple tugged at the knot on his tie, clearly uncomfortable.

"Forgive my brother," I said in an affable tone. "My mother would be horrified."

"How the fuck would you know what would have horrified our mother?" Roy asked, his words slightly slurred. Had he been drinking? "You barely knew our mother. I was the one who stayed and helped her pick up the pieces after you left. Just like dear ole *Dad*."

I looked him in the eye. "I know. And I will regret that for the rest of my life, Roy, but this is not the time or place. You're making Mr. Wimple uncomfortable."

Roy shot the older man a glare. "I'm sure you've heard plenty of family drama, Mr. Wimple. What's one more?"

The attorney cleared his throat and gave me a strained smile as he picked up the file in front of him. "As you all know, you're here because Lila created a new will a few weeks ago."

I looked at him in surprise. When I'd returned to Franklin a month ago, Momma had told me that I was getting the house, something she hadn't shared with Roy. Why had she created a new will? Presumably she'd still planned to give me the house. Just last week, she'd told me that she wanted to add me to the deed so I could skip probate. A task we hadn't completed.

"This is preposterous," Roy bellowed, picking up a small stack of papers in front of him and waving it at the attorney. "As I told you on the phone, I have her will right here."

"And was that will signed two years ago?" the attorney asked.

"Yes . . ." Roy suddenly sounded less certain.

"Then it's null and void. The will in my hand is her second, which she had drawn up after she signed that one."

Roy's mouth dropped open, and his hands clenched the top of the table. "Second? And what does this new will say?"

Mr. Wimple's hand shook as he picked up the paper. "I think I need a glass of water." With that, he got up and walked out of the room, shutting the door behind him. I wouldn't blame him if he ran and didn't come back.

Roy turned to face me. "What the hell did you do, Magnolia?"

"I didn't do anything, Roy. I swear."

"Did you know about this new will?"

I shook my head. "No. She told me some details right after I came back, and last week she told me that she'd made arrangements for her funeral, but I had no idea there was a new will."

Roy shifted his glare to Tilly. "What do *you* know, Tilly? What the fuck are you even doing here? This is for *family*." He spat out the word as if it were poison.

"Tilly *is* family, Roy," I said in a sound resembling a growl. I reached my hand across the table toward her, and she stretched her arm to take my hand and squeezed. "She deserves to be here just as much as you and me."

"What about him," Roy said, flippantly waving his hand at Colt. His eyes narrowed as he stared at me. "Fucking him doesn't make him family, Magnolia."

Colt released a guttural sound and his face reddened. "You can take all the potshots you want at me, but leave Tilly and Magnolia out of it."

Roy released a bitter laugh. "Who would have thought Colt Austin actually gave a fuck about anything other than himself?"

I jerked my head toward Colt and held up my hand. "I can handle this."

"She's already got you on a leash," Roy said. "Colt Austin domesticated. Has hell frozen over?"

"Enough, Roy," Belinda said in harsh rebuke. "You're making this more difficult than it has to be."

He turned his attention to Belinda. "My lovely wife. It's good to be reminded of where your loyalties *really* lie."

Her expression softened. "Roy . . ."

The door opened and Mr. Wimple walked back in with his glass of water. His hands were still shaking, and he looked like he would rather be at the dentist getting a root canal than sitting here facing my brother.

His receptionist followed him, a cell phone in her hand, and took a seat in a chair by the still-open door. Presumably she was there to call 911 if Roy got out of hand.

I truly hoped it wouldn't come to that.

Mr. Wimple took a big sip of his water, set the glass down on the table, and pulled various papers out of the file folder.

"What are you waiting for?" Roy demanded.

"Stop challenging him, you fool," Tilly said. "Calm your ass down, and he'll get started."

Roy looked slightly chagrined as he leaned back in his chair, assuming a less predatory stance.

Mr. Wimple lifted his double chins and took a deep breath. "We're here to read the last will and testament of Lila Mae Steele, but she's written a letter for me to read first."

I clasped my hands under the table. I'd stopped breathing at the word "letter," I realized, and I forced myself to start again.

The attorney opened a sealed envelope, unfolded the papers within, and began to read. "If Wilber is reading this to you, then I'm dead. I hope I left on my own terms and that I didn't give you too much grief in the end, although maybe a little. I'd like to think I went out with a bang instead of a whimper."

Tears filled my eyes. It was such a Momma thing to say.

"Roy and Magnolia, I'm sorry I left you orphaned, although I think you both have figured out by now that your daddy's not dead."

The receptionist by the door gasped, but Mr. Wimple didn't look all that surprised by her statement. If anything, he was more worried about our reactions. But Roy sat in his chair unfazed.

"Magnolia, I know you're dead set on finding out the details of what happened to your daddy, but it all comes down to a simple truth: he loved you—you were the most precious thing in his life—but it wasn't enough. It's not your fault, girl, so don't you accept that mantle. I learned years ago that the love he felt for me wasn't enough either. It took me a while to let it go, but I finally did and found my happiness elsewhere. You need to find yours, Maggie. We find it in the people in our lives, not in our possessions or our accomplishments. You have people who love you dearly. Lean on them. Trust them. Let them heal your heart, because Maggie Mae, your heart has been broken time and time again, by both your father and me, and for that I'm eternally sorry. My job was to protect you, and I failed miserably. I'll carry that guilt to my grave and beyond. But don't you accept the guilt of thinking you weren't enough to hold your father here. That's his burden to carry. Not yours."

Unshed tears made it difficult to see the table, and I was grateful I'd sat opposite the people I cared about rather than beside them. If any of the three people facing me on the other side touched me right now, I'd shatter to pieces, and at this moment, I needed total control.

"Roy," Mr. Wimple continued. "My son. My love. My joy. My sorrow. Your father claimed your sister, and I claimed you, and yet I was never enough. Your father left a void that couldn't be filled, and for that I'm sorry too. I know why you went to work for Bill James, and you need to let it go. Your bitterness is making you unhappy, son, and it's slowly poisoned you to the good things in life. Your anger has gotten the better of you, and you're losing everything important to you because of it. Your father's not worth your time and energy, Roy. The best punishment you can give him is to let him go."

I cast a glance to my brother, whose gaze had dropped to the table. His Adam's apple bobbed as he swallowed, trying to keep his emotions in check.

"Belinda," Mr. Wimple read, "I've loved you like a daughter. I knew you lost your parents as a child, and I tried to fill that void, just as you tried to fill the void Magnolia left in my heart. We weren't perfect, the shapes didn't quite fit, but it was enough to ease my sorrow. I can only hope I was as much comfort and joy to you as you were to me. I hope you know that when Magnolia returned, she didn't replace you. My heart was big enough for you both." Mr. Wimple took a drink of water. "Thank you for welcoming Magnolia home with open arms and an open heart, even at the risk of upsetting your husband. You're a beautiful woman, Belinda, both inside and out, and I am a better person for having known you."

Belinda dabbed her eyes, looking down at the table.

"Colt," Mr. Wimple read, glancing up at him then back at his paper. "I'm sure you're wondering why you're here, but you've been an important part of my life for the last three years. The day you walked into our catering kitchen asking about a job, I looked into your eyes and knew I could trust you, even if you didn't trust yourself."

I glanced up at Colt. His jaw was tight and his hand clenched the side of the table. I knew what he was thinking—that he'd betrayed her trust and used her. Colt had thought the world of my mother, so I knew her uncharacteristic kind words had to be difficult for him to hear.

The next thing Mr. Wimple read surprised us all.

"But I knew what you were doing, boy. I knew the whole time."

Colt's eyes widened, and he looked across the table at me in shock.

"I always knew that when push came to shove you would do the right thing. Take care of my girls, all three of them. They need you more than ever now."

Tears streaked down Colt's cheeks, and he brushed them away as he tried to swallow.

"Tilly," the attorney read. "My rock. My dearest friend. My greatest love. You were there from nearly the beginning. I'm sure you were there until the end. I'll miss you the most, but life will go on without your cranky, self-centered friend. Go find someone who will love you better than I could manage. You deserve better than me, Tilly. You deserve the world."

Tilly shook her head and silent sobs racked her body. Colt reached over and pulled her into a sideways hug.

Mr. Wimple took a drink, and I was sure he was done with the letter, but he took a breath and said, "Roy, I'm about to say some things that will be hard for you to hear, but you need to hear them anyway." The attorney gave my brother a worried look. "I know you hold your sister responsible for so many things, but you need to let that go. You need her, and she needs you. You have a common enemy now, and he will storm the castle. You need to batten down the hatches. Trouble's coming, and you need your sister. Never forget that I love you, even from the great beyond."

Mr. Wimple set the letter down, and my shell-shocked brother stared at him, aghast.

"That's it?" Roy demanded.

"To the letter," Mr. Wimple said.

"What the hell does she mean that trouble's coming?"

The attorney shrugged. "I don't know. This letter was sealed and only to be opened after her death. Are you ready for me to read the will?"

I turned toward Roy and he looked at me in a daze. "What does that mean, Magnolia?"

"I don't know. Is she talking about Daddy? I know he's still here. Do you think he'll try to lay claim to anything?"

The vulnerability on his face morphed into hard lines and a rigid jaw. "She had him declared dead years ago. He has no right to *anything*."

Just because he had no right to it didn't mean he wouldn't try.

Roy turned away from me, giving his attention to the attorney. "Read the will."

Mr. Wimple nodded, then said, "I, Lila Mae Steele, declare this to be my last will and testament. I revoke all prior wills and codicils."

A tingle ran down my spine. I had a very bad feeling about this.

"I have two living children," Mr. Wimple continued. "Magnolia Mae Steele and Roy Michael Steele. To Roy, I bequeath seventy percent of my seven-hundred-and-fifty-thousand-dollar insurance policy, a total of five hundred and twenty-five thousand dollars. The other thirty percent will be used to pay off debts incurred before death and during probate. Whatever is left will be given to my daughter-in-law, Belinda Steele."

Belinda's eyes widened in shock. I was caught off guard as well. Roy had led me to believe Momma was practically destitute.

"To Tilly Bartok, I bequeath my half of Southern Belles Catering, but if Magnolia ever shows an interest, I request that she be given twenty-five percent ownership."

Tilly wiped fresh tears off her face as she glanced over the table at me. "Of course. It's yours if you want it, Maggie Mae."

I nodded, tears burning my throat.

"To Colt Austin, I give the contents of my safety deposit box. You'll know what to do with it."

Colt's eyes jerked up to meet mine. What was in the safety deposit box? Was it something that would help us fight Daddy?

Mr. Wimple glanced up. "Mr. Austin, I have the key to the safety deposit box and the information you'll need to get into it."

Colt nodded.

"To Magnolia, I give my jewelry, a smaller fifty-thousand-dollar life insurance policy, and my car. I also give her my house and all of its contents."

I glanced at Roy, trying to gauge his reaction. His face was still hard as granite, but his hand had clenched into a tight fist. He was not happy about this, probably out of principle. There was no doubt he'd gotten the larger portion. The house couldn't be worth more than four hundred thousand, and that was on the high side.

"Anything remaining or not covered here will be shared equally by my two children." Mr. Wimple set the will down and gave an anxious scan around the table. "The rest is legal jargon. Are there any questions?"

Roy looked up with pure rage on his face. "I protest."

Mr. Wimple blinked and grabbed the edge of the paperwork with a tight fist. "Protest what?"

"I refuse to accept this will. My mother wasn't of a sound mind two weeks ago. The cancer or chemo or *something* affected her brain. She would never have done this."

"Done what?" I asked in disbelief. "Given me the house? Given Tilly the business? Given Colt her safety deposit box? You still got the majority of her money. What exactly are you *protesting*?"

"You!" he shouted, getting to his feet. "You have ruined everything, Magnolia!" He balled his fists and looked like he was about to lunge for me.

chapter eight

Colt was instantly up on his feet, his chair flying out behind him and hitting the wall with a loud thud. "Don't even try it, Steele," Colt said through gritted teeth. "*I will take you down.*"

My brother pointed his finger at Colt as he turned to Mr. Wimple and his receptionist. "Did you all hear that he threatened me? I should press charges."

The receptionist had hopped out of her chair and looked like she was about to make a call.

"For what?" Tilly demanded, her face turning red. "For protecting your sister? You threatened *her* bodily harm."

Mr. Wimple looked like he was about to have a stroke.

I had to get this under control. "How do you feel cheated, Roy?" I asked in a calm voice.

A vein pulsed in his forehead. "I want the house. *It's mine.*"

I realized his eyes were dilated. Was he on drugs? Momma had suspected he wouldn't be happy to hear this news, but his reaction seemed miles beyond reason.

"You have a house, Roy," Tilly said. "And it's a whole lot more suited to you than your momma's house. Why not just let Maggie have it?"

"She doesn't deserve it." To my surprise, his voice broke. He sat back down in his chair, looking close to panicking. "I need that house."

I shot a questioning look to Belinda. She looked torn and moved to Roy's side, squatting next to him, no small feat since she was wearing a pencil skirt. "Y'all go on out to the waiting room," she said, giving us a worried look. "I'm going to talk to Roy."

None of us moved.

"I don't think that's a good idea," Colt said. "You can talk to him, but I'm staying by the door."

Belinda frowned. "I can handle this, Colt."

My brother was furious, but he also looked profoundly sad. Despite how bad things had become between us, my heart twisted to see him so broken.

"No offense, Belinda," Tilly said, "but we've all seen the results of you handling things. I'd feel a whole lot better if Colt hangs around."

I expected Belinda to look offended, but she looked resigned instead. "I need to talk to Roy. Alone." She looked up at me. "Magnolia. Please."

My brother was like a ticking time bomb. If she could talk some sense into him, it might be worth the shot. I grabbed Tilly's arm. "Let's go into the waiting room. We'll leave Colt outside the door."

Tilly reluctantly agreed, but Colt's body was tense as he stepped into the hall. I glanced back at my brother, and Belinda mouthed, *thank you*.

I walked out hoping I'd made the right decision.

I cracked the door behind me and stopped, waiting to see if I could eavesdrop on their conversation. I had a hard time dredging up any guilt over it. I was too worried that Roy would hurt his wife.

The receptionist stood in the hallway next to me and whispered, "Maybe I should call the police."

I had to admit that I was considering it myself, but we'd had enough drama over the last few weeks to last a lifetime. "Let's see if she can get him to calm down."

Colt's full attention was focused on what was going on in the room. From the soft—and, sadly, indecipherable—murmuring, it seemed to be going well, until I heard a loud thud and Roy shouting, "I knew you'd take her side!"

The receptionist started to dial 911, but I put my hand over hers and said, "I have a friend in the police department. Let me call him." I cast a glance to Colt, who was still staring through the crack in the doorway to the conference room. I was pretty sure he hadn't heard me. Should I give him a warning?

Instead, I walked toward the waiting room and pressed Brady's speed dial, wondering if I was doing the right thing.

He answered on the first ring. "Maggie? Are you okay?"

"Yeah. I'm fine, but I might need your help. It's my brother."

His voice hardened. "Is he harassing you?"

"In a way." I paused. "We came to Momma's attorney's office for the reading of the will."

"And he was unhappy with the results."

"Yeah. Belinda's in the conference room with him right now, trying to talk reason into him, but I think he's either been drinking or on drugs."

"Give me the address." His voice was tense. I gave it to him; then he said, "Get your sister-in-law out of that room. I'm close enough to be there in five minutes."

"Thanks, Brady." I stuffed my phone back into my purse as I headed back down the hall. Colt was still in the hallway, which I took as a good sign, but as I got closer I realized the door was now shut.

"Why is the door closed?"

Colt gave me an exasperated look. "Belinda closed it. I was sure she was heading to the door to leave, but she shut and locked the door instead."

Why would she do that? "It sounds quiet in there now," I said.

"Too quiet."

I pressed my ear to the door and heard absolutely nothing. "What do you think they're doing?" I whispered.

He started to say something, then stopped himself. "I don't think you want to know my opinion."

I took a step back in surprise. "Why?"

"Because you're not going to like it."

I crossed my arms over my chest. "Go on."

105

"Belinda married Roy for a reason, Maggie."

"You heard what she said. She used to love him."

"Maybe, but you know she probably started dating him because she knew his father was Brian Steele?"

I'd already come to that conclusion. She'd been working with Roy on a plot to bring my father down, so it wasn't a leap to assume she'd befriended my brother with that plan in mind. She'd always told me she had both a reason for staying and a plan for leaving, so that fit too. Besides, it was too big of a coincidence to believe that she'd just happened to meet and marry the son of the man she held responsible for her parents' deaths. "So what do you think's going on now?"

"I think Belinda's convincing him that she's still part of his plan. She may not be living with him, but she's still on board." He leaned closer. "Hell, she's living with you. She's really close to you right now."

My eyes widened. "You think she's living with me to spy on me?"

He scrubbed his hand over his face. "Honestly, Mags, I don't know who to trust anymore."

"Do you trust me?"

His gaze held mine. "You're the *only* person I trust at this point."

Right or wrong, I trusted him more than anyone else in this mess. I'd trusted Belinda until she'd held a gun to my head at Savannah House. While I'd never believed she would shoot me, she'd put me in a dangerous situation. In light of everything, it would be stupid to disregard Colt's opinion. "Why would she be spying on me?"

"Maybe Roy has decided he wants that annuity for himself."

"That's crazy. I'd never even heard of it until last night. How would I know anything about it?"

"You've done a damn good job of upsetting the apple cart, Mags. You've found the missing gold, unmasked Geraldo Lopez, and flushed out Rowena Rogers. If I was betting money on who would find it, I'd bet on you."

"I don't give a damn about the annuity. I'm done with anything to do with my father and the stupid Jackson Project."

"If you say so." The look he gave me suggested he didn't believe it for a minute.

I almost contradicted him, but another thought fought for my attention. "Did Momma ever hint that she was leaving you what's in her safety deposit box?"

He shook his head. "Never."

"Do you know what's in it?"

"I'm guessing it must have something to do with your father."

"It's pretty coincidental, isn't it? But there was no reaction from Roy. I would have expected him to put up more of a fuss," Colt said. "Instead, he threw a fit over you getting the house. Why?"

"Good question."

I heard voices behind me, and one of them belonged to Brady. "I'm looking for Magnolia Steele."

Colt's grin fell. "What the hell is *he* doing here?"

"I called him. The receptionist was about to call the police, and I didn't want to stir up trouble. We have enough to deal with."

"You know that's exactly why Roy's gotten away with so much shit. I loved Lila like a mother, but she made excuse after excuse for that man. If he had to man up and face consequences for his actions, maybe he'd see a reason to change. Instead, you all coddle him. It's bullshit."

I started to protest, but closed my mouth. Colt was right.

Colt's gaze lifted over my shoulder, and his expression hardened. "On second thought, I'm glad you called Bennett. There are a few questions I'm dying to have answered." He gave me a half-smile that was anything but friendly. "Pun not intended."

"Maggie," Brady said from behind me. "Are they in this room?"

I turned around to face him. "The door was cracked open, but Belinda closed and locked it while I was calling you."

Brady rapped on the door with his knuckles. "Belinda, it's Detective Bennett. I'd like for you to open the door."

There was a moment of silence before she called out, "Just a minute."

Then I heard a loud crash, and Brady and Colt tensed before the door opened. My brother appeared in the opening with one hand on the door frame and the other on the partially open door, blocking our view into the room. "This is private, Detective."

Brady stood his ground. "I want to see your wife, Mr. Steele."

"She's fine."

"And yet I still want to see her."

Belinda pushed Roy's arm away so she could stand next to him in the doorway, as if they were a united front. "I'm fine, Detective Bennett." She shot me her version of a glare, keeping her gaze on me. "When did you arrive?"

"Just a few minutes ago," Brady said in a calm voice. "Mr. Wimple was disturbed by your husband's behavior."

"And he knows you personally?" Roy asked in a dry tone, his eyes trying to focus on Brady's face.

"Mr. Wimple preferred to handle this discreetly rather than call a patrol car, which might have ended in an arrest and unwanted publicity."

"How thoughtful of *Mr. Wimple*," Roy said, his gaze on me.

"Mr. Steele, do I smell alcohol on your breath?" Brady asked with a blank expression.

"What business is it of yours?"

"Did you *drive* here, Mr. Steele?"

Roy lost some of his bravado.

"I'd like for you to take a sobriety test," Brady said.

"And if I refuse?"

"That's your right, but if I see you get behind the wheel of a car, I'm going to haul your ass down to the station for a Breathalyzer test. And I promise it *will* make the news."

"You can't do that."

Brady's eyes narrowed. "Try me."

Roy took a step closer, his jaw clenching. "Do you have a problem with me, Detective?"

"I have a problem with any man who takes out his frustrations by physically abusing women."

Roy's face was inches from Brady's. "Where's your proof, Detective?"

"I saw plenty of proof on Magnolia's body," Brady said, looking like he was just barely restraining himself. "I saw the bruise on her arm a month ago, and just a few weeks ago, I saw the outline of *your hand* on her face."

Belinda gasped, and Colt rushed forward with a low growl, but Brady blocked him. "That won't help anything, Austin."

"You don't know that it was me," Roy said. "You have no proof."

Brady gave Colt a shove back before turning to face my brother. "I have Magnolia's word. And we won't even start on the bruises you've left on your wife."

Roy remained silent.

Brady's eyes darkened. "I abhor bullies, and you, Mr. Steele, are the walking definition of a bully. I guarantee you that if you ever lay a hand on your sister again, I will toss your ass in jail with the biggest, meanest cellmates I can find."

"Are you threatening me, Detective?"

Brady's head tilted slightly to the left while he held my brother's gaze. "Yes. I most definitely am."

The two men had a staring match for a few seconds, broken when Belinda put a hand on Roy's arm. "Roy, let's go."

Roy violently shrugged his wife off his arm. "I'm leaving this shitshow."

He started to walk out of the room, but Brady blocked his path. "I suggest you call an Uber."

They had another momentary standoff, which Belinda again ended. "I'll take him home."

My stomach twisted. "I don't think that's a good idea, Belinda."

She gave me a pleading look. "I'll be fine, Magnolia."

"She'll be fine, Magnolia," Roy sneered. "Go home to your new house you didn't earn. You were too busy lying flat on your back, screwing directors and producers to do porn on Broadway."

I sucked in a breath. I knew Roy didn't think much of me, but his insults still hurt.

Colt wrapped an arm around my back and pulled me away from my brother.

"That's right, Magnolia. Let a man save you again."

Something in his tone caught my attention. What did he mean by *again*? I jerked away from Colt and moved closer. "What does that mean?"

Colt reached for my arm, but I stepped out of his reach, moving between Brady and Roy. "What does that mean, Roy?"

An ugly smile spread across his face. "You're a lucky, lucky girl, Magnolia. Did you ever stop and ask yourself why?"

The blood rushed from my head as he moved past me toward the waiting room.

Belinda hurried after him, and part of me knew I should stop her, but the rest of me was trying to stave off a panic attack.

"Maggie?" Colt asked in a worried tone, crouching to look into my eyes.

I stared at him in horror.

My brother had been there that night. He'd been in that house of horror.

chapter nine

Colt tried to reach for me, and I pulled away in panic.

Fear filled his eyes. "Mags, it's been a rough afternoon. Why don't you sit down?"

I couldn't move. I could barely breathe.

He reached for me again, but I jerked away like a wild animal caught in a trap.

Distantly, I heard Brady's voice, Roy's belligerent yelling, and Belinda's soothing tones. Nothing they were saying registered.

Tilly appeared in front of me, casting a glance at Colt and then back at me. "Maggie, we're going to sit down, okay?"

I didn't answer, but I didn't shrink away as she reached for me. I let her lead me back to the conference table and lower me into a chair. She sat in a chair in front of me while Colt stood behind her, watching me with concern.

"Do you want a drink of water?" Tilly asked.

I shook my head as tears filled my eyes. Roy had been there. He knew what had happened that night. I was sure of it. It explained why he'd hidden my bloody clothes, but what had he seen? What did he know? Why hadn't he told anyone?

I felt a hand on my shoulder, and I jerked away, terror threatening to engulf me. Brady was next to me, and he lifted two hands in surrender before lowering to a crouch beside me.

"Talk to me, Maggie. What did Roy mean about you being a lucky girl?"

My chin trembled and my body began to shake.

My brother had witnessed at least some part of my nightmare, and until now, he'd never said a word.

"She's in shock," Brady said as he shrugged off his jacket. "I'm going to put this on your shoulders to warm you up. Okay?"

I looked over at him, knowing I needed to answer him, but I couldn't get out the words.

"Maggie," Tilly said with a tear-filled voice. "You're scarin' me, sweet girl."

I knew I should put her fears to rest, but I couldn't make the lie—*I'm okay*—come out. Tears clogged my throat, and I felt close to a hysterical breakdown.

My brother knew about my encounter with the serial killer.

I knew he couldn't *be* the killer. He'd been fourteen at the time. Too young. Too scrawny. The killer had been tall and strong—strong enough to pick me up and carry me kicking and screaming down the stairs like I was a rag doll. Plus, the killer had spoken to me, and not in my brother's voice.

No, Roy wasn't the killer, but I was positive he knew who was.

"What happened?" Tilly asked Brady. "Did Roy threaten her?"

"No, he said she was lucky, then asked her if she ever wondered why . . ." He studied me with narrowed eyes, followed by a dawning look of horror that told me he'd guessed the truth. "*Shit.*" He tore out of the room as if his pants were on fire. "Colt, take her home and lock the goddamned doors!" he shouted as he ran down the hall.

"What was that about?" Tilly asked.

Colt seemed to finally understand what was happening, and he reached for me with a new urgency. "Mags. Let's get you to your momma's house."

"What's going on?" Tilly demanded.

"Brady thinks Roy is going to drive home after all," Colt said. "He's going after him to catch him in the act. He wants me to lock the doors in case Roy shows up at Lila's house." His lies were delivered so smoothly I couldn't help wondering how many of them I'd fallen for. How many more he'd try to slip past me.

I knew Brady was going after Roy to find out what he knew, but my brother would never tell him anything. He'd go to his grave before he'd confess.

Colt finally convinced Tilly that I was just overly tired, and while Brady was likely overreacting, it was still a good idea for me to head home. She agreed, though the worried look didn't leave her eyes. Colt found my keys in my purse, and I was sure he saw the gun inside, but he didn't comment on it as he led me out to my car and deposited me in the passenger seat. I leaned back against the headrest, my mind filled with images from that terrifying night. Had Roy been there the whole time? I didn't think so, but when had he shown up?

When Colt pulled into Momma's driveway, I stayed in my seat, still in a fog. Did Roy hate me enough to wish the killer had killed me too? To hope he'd come back for me now?

My door opened, and Colt helped me out and supported me all the way to the front porch. As I waited for him to unlock the door, I realized I was still wearing Brady's jacket on my shoulders.

As soon as we were inside, Colt locked the door, and I stopped and put my hand on the wood. Once upon a time, I had believed it could keep out the monsters. Instead, it had locked two of them inside with me.

"Mags, let's go sit down. Are you hungry? We have some leftovers from yesterday."

I shook my head, but didn't say anything as I sat on the sofa.

Colt paced in the kitchen and eventually brought the whiskey bottle and two glasses to the living room, setting all three on the coffee table. He sat next to me and poured whiskey into both glasses before handing one to me. "Drink. It'll help with the shock."

I did as he asked because I wasn't sure what else to do. I was still stuck in my head, in that night, reliving

116

every horrifying moment and trying to figure out where my brother fit in.

We sat like that for some time, Colt watching me like he was worried I'd fling myself out the window. Eventually, probably about twenty minutes later, there was a knock on the door and Colt jumped off the sofa to answer it. I heard the door opening and then Brady's voice. "How is she?"

"Not good. She hasn't said a word. I'm worried. Maybe I should take her to the ER or something. Did you find him?"

Brady paused. "Yeah. Let me talk to her."

I watched Brady walk toward me, and I could tell from the look on his face that he hadn't gotten anything out of my brother.

"Maggie. Can I sit next to you?"

I didn't answer, still clutching the half-empty glass of whiskey to my chest.

He took my silence as permission and sat next to me, taking the glass from my hand and putting it on the coffee table. "I found Roy at his house. Belinda drove him home. I grilled him about that night ten years ago, but he claimed to know nothing about what happened to you."

I finally found my voice, but it sounded far away. "He's lying."

"I know, but I've got no reason to haul him in and question him."

Tears filled my eyes.

"You need to stay away from him. I think you should file a restraining order."

117

"Belinda," I whispered.

His eyes hardened. "Was there the whole time and heard every word. I offered to bring her back here, and she chose to stay." He paused as though he was considering his next words carefully. "I'd like to question Belinda. Martinez is dying to question you both. Maybe I should question her about what *she* knows about that night."

I shook my head. "No. She doesn't know anything more than what I've told her." I didn't think I could handle it if she did.

"She might—"

"No."

"Maggie . . ." He looked upset as he watched me. "I'm so sorry."

I didn't answer. What was there to say?

"Roy wants the house," Colt said.

Brady turned to him in confusion. "What?"

"Lila gave Maggie the house. Roy lost his shit when he found out. Not in a *I want her toy because she has it* kind of way. More like he wants this house for something specific." Turning to me, he said, "What if Roy took something from the serial killer and stored it in this house?"

Brady stared at him in bewilderment.

"It can't be that," I said. I wasn't sure my fragile psyche could handle the thought of something belonging to the serial killer being hidden in Momma's house. "Well, it doesn't matter. Roy can have it. I don't want it."

"Bullshit!" Colt shouted. "Your momma wanted you to have this house, and I'll be damned if I stand back and let your brother bully you into giving it to him."

Brady turned back to face me. "Colt's right. If nothing else, you shouldn't be making any major decisions right now. Let this settle for a few weeks, hell, a few months, before you decide."

I didn't respond, but I could see the wisdom in his words. I was in no shape to make a decision about anything.

Brady took a breath. "I want you to get a good night's sleep, and tomorrow we're going to that house. I have to see it, Maggie."

"What house?" Colt asked.

"*The* house," I said, my voice hoarse.

"Wait." Colt shook his head. "The house where she was attacked? *Have you lost your fucking mind?*"

"No. I need to see it."

"Then pull up Google Earth and have her point it out." Colt clenched his fists at his side. "She's not going out there with you."

I gave him a pointed stare. "Last time I checked, Colt Austin, I was still capable of making my own decisions."

"*Maggie*—"

"I'm not discussing it one way or the other now," I said. "Not tonight."

Brady nodded. "Fair enough. Do you work tomorrow?"

"I'm cleaning Ava Milton's house tomorrow morning."

Both men's faces contorted in shock, but Brady's expression quickly turned to anger.

"The hell you are," he said. "You said cleaning her house was part of your rental agreement. You're not living there."

"He's right," Colt said. "Besides, after the way you dissed her at the masquerade, she's liable to kick you to the curb if you show up."

"A deal's a deal. I'm going," I said. There was a whole lot more to it than my dedication to our agreement. Ava Milton knew about just about everything in this town, and I needed to find out what she knew about my brother. Besides, I needed to pick up my stuff from the apartment anyway.

"Maggie," Colt sighed out.

"What part of me making my own decisions do you not understand, Colt?" I demanded.

"I'm just worried about you."

"And I appreciate it, but this is something I need to do." I glanced at Brady. "I know neither of you understand it, but I don't care. I'm going."

Brady's mouth pinched into a thin line. "Maria's going to make you come in for questioning tomorrow."

"About the murders at the ball?" Colt asked.

"Yeah," Brady said, his back still to Colt. "Just treat it like it's no big deal, and they'll let you go."

"What do you mean treat it like it's no big deal?" I asked. My mouth dropped open. "Do you think I killed those people?"

"No."

"But . . . ?"

He looked me in the eye. "I know you know something about it."

I remained stock-still.

Brady stood, and when he looked down at me, his eyes had gone cold. "You're an actress. Play a role. You were missing from the ball for a good twenty minutes before you left with a bloody arm. Tell her you were screwing Colt in the bathroom. If she knows anything about your arm, tell her you cut it while he had you pinned to the wall, but I doubt she'll know, so wear something to cover it up like you did today."

He knew about my bloody arm? The blood rushed from my head, and I felt faint. My mouth dropped open and I started to say something, but I didn't know what to say. How closely had he been watching me?

Brady turned to Colt. "If anything happens to her, I'll hold you personally responsible. And there will be consequences to pay."

"Brady!" I protested.

But Brady didn't even flinch; he held Colt's gaze, waiting for a response.

Colt tensed, but he didn't look as angry as I had expected. "I won't let anything happen to her."

Brady gave a sharp nod and then headed for the door.

"Your jacket," I called after him.

"You can give it back to me when we hike out to the house tomorrow."

He walked out the door, and Colt followed him and locked it.

121

"I don't even know where to start," he said, still in the entryway.

"Then don't."

He walked into the living room and sat down in the chair next to me. "He thinks you know about Rowena's murder, but he's telling you to lie about it?" He shook his head. "Scratch that. He *knows* we're involved. You heard what he said." He gave me a pointed look. "There's no way he could know all of that unless he's been following you."

I didn't answer.

"What's his endgame?"

"I have no idea."

"I know he wants you, but risking his career for a..."

I shot him a glare. "Choose your next words very carefully, Colt Austin."

"Risking his career for a *friend* seems extreme."

"Agreed," I said in defeat.

"I'm not sure you can trust him."

Tell me something I don't know. "Unfortunately, he's my only ally in the Franklin Police Department, so I have no choice." At the moment. I still hoped Owen would come through.

"Be careful, Mags. This is a very dangerous game."

I picked my glass back up and took a big swig. Apparently dangerous games were what I did best. And it looked like I'd just kicked it up a notch.

chapter ten

I didn't sleep well. Roy lurked in my dreams, and I woke up over a half dozen times. Colt was there every time, but I felt like I was using him. After the fourth time, I confessed my guilt, but Colt assured me that he wanted to be there.

I was eager to have a morning away from anyone who had witnessed my meltdown the night before. Shame rushed through me when I thought about my reaction. I'd worked so hard at being strong. Would I ever be able to put a permanent end to my panic attacks?

Normally, I would've thought I was certifiable for looking forward to a visit to Ava Milton's house, but today was different. Ava usually left me to my own devices when I cleaned, but if I played my cards right, I'd get to spend some extra time with her this morning.

I hadn't heard directly from the killer for nearly thirty-six hours, but I knew it was just a matter of time.

My apartment was above the detached garage behind Miss Ava's century-old house, only a few blocks from downtown. I parked in the spot Miss Ava had assigned me—in the driveway behind the house—then walked up to the back door that led to the kitchen. I'd planned to knock, but Miss Ava had seen me coming, as usual. She opened the solid wooden door and stared at me through the screen door.

"I'm surprised you had the nerve to show up," she said in a snippy tone.

"A deal's a deal," I said as I stopped about ten feet from the door.

"Don't you have paperwork to deal with regarding your mother's death?"

"Already taken care of." I held on to my purse strap and maintained eye contact. "My mother was an organized woman. Are you going to let me in?"

Her steely eyes narrowed. "Why are you really here, Magnolia Steele?"

"To clean your house, Ava Milton." I used a little more sass than I probably should have given the situation, but Ava gained part of her power through intimidation, and I refused to let the woman intimidate me. I'd been terrorized in a basement by a serial killer. That put everything else into perspective.

"You were rude at the masquerade ball," she said.

"So you only want milquetoasts cleaning your house?" I quipped.

Her chin lifted slightly, and I knew I'd pushed her too far. "I always knew you were an insolent girl."

She started to shut the door, but I said, "I'm here to bargain with your favorite kind of currency."

The trajectory of the door reversed, and she opened it wide enough to show the left side of her face. "What does that mean?"

I had more information than I intended to share with her, so the real question was what would be enough to get her to cooperate. "Honestly, I'm surprised you're shortsighted enough to turn me away after everything that happened at the masquerade ball. Especially since Rowena Rogers was murdered days after I asked about her," I said. "And then there's the fact my father's business partner has since disappeared."

She remained silent.

"You told me your career was using information. I'd think *you*, of all people, would want to get as much information as you could."

"Who's to say I don't already know?"

"Then send me away, but you'll regret it before I'm inside my car."

She opened the door a little wider. "Why would I presume you know *anything*?"

"I guess there's only one way to find out."

The door swung open, and she disappeared into the kitchen. I took that as a sign that I was invited inside.

She was standing in front of the coffee maker, pouring coffee into a white mug. There was already one next to her on the counter, so I knew she'd poured this one for me. She handed it to me with a defiant look. "Start talking."

"I was thinking we could arrange a barter," I said, taking the cup. I opened the refrigerator and pulled out a carton of cream.

She frowned. "I'm listening."

I poured cream into my coffee and put the carton back into the fridge. "I talked to Rowena on Saturday morning."

"Does that mean you're a suspect in Rowena's murder?"

"No." Not technically. "Have you heard who is?"

She smiled, but it wasn't friendly. "Is that the information you want to barter for?"

"No," I said. "Consider this part a friendly exchange."

Miss Ava snorted. "So you and I are friendly now?"

I sat down at her kitchen table and took a sip of my coffee. "We've had our moments."

"You're far too presumptuous, Magnolia Steele. Far too confident."

"And maybe that will be my downfall," I said in a dry tone, "but at least I'll fall informed. I'm sure you've told yourself the same thing many times over."

Ava stared at me with steely gray eyes that were still sharp and observant despite her age—sixties, on the low end, but I'd begun to suspect she was in her seventies. "Why are you still digging?" she asked, tilting her head slightly as she watched me. "Surely you have your answers by now."

I'd thought so too. Now I wasn't so sure.

While I was desperate for information on my brother, I knew I needed to butter her up first. Besides, there were plenty of other things I wanted to know.

Brady had been assigned to Emily's murder, so he was officially working the serial killer case—whether the department knew there was one or not—but I was more likely to get information from Ava Milton than he was, not to mention I didn't quite trust him. I needed to use it to my advantage, especially since the whole thing was like a giant spider web, and at the moment, I was the only one standing in the center.

I gave Ava a cold, hard stare. "Miss Ava, I've only just begun digging."

To my surprise, she broke out into a full-on belly laugh. When she finally settled down, she dabbed at the corners of her eyes and sat down across from me. "There's never a dull moment with you, Magnolia."

"I suppose life is pretty dull when you know everything," I said. "And I suspect it's been a long time since someone surprised you."

Her grin was genuine. "Maybe not as long as you think."

"What do you know about Eric Duncan?"

She tried to hide her reaction, but I'd caught her off guard. "He was a partner of your father's . . . back in the day. One of his first partners."

"And do you know why he left?"

"Eric Duncan had a serious case of wanderlust— with his eyes *and* his hands. I wasn't surprised when he left your father's partnership, but I was surprised when his son became your father's client."

127

I couldn't hide my reaction. "What?"

She grinned and her eyes lit up with victory. "You didn't know?"

"Obviously not. Why would Eric Duncan's son choose Daddy as his financial planner?"

"Because Clint Duncan was an up-and-coming singer. His first big hit earned him a large royalty check. Max Goodwin coerced Clint into hiring your father."

Clint Duncan. His name struck a chord. I remembered one of his huge hits from when I was a kid—"Baby, You're Mine"—but I'd also seen his name in one of Miss Ava's newspaper clippings. There'd been a photo of Clint and Daddy at a fundraiser. But it made no sense that Clint would hire Daddy when his own father was a financial planner, especially since the rival planners were likely enemies. "I bet that didn't go over too well with Eric."

Her grin spread and her eyes sparkled with mischief. She loved this. She took a sip of her coffee, her pinky extending from the cup. "It seems to me that I'm the only one doling out information here. When are you going to start dishing it?"

What to tell her? I should have come up with a better plan before I started this game. "Rowena admitted to having an affair with my father. She said he took off with a one-million-dollar investment. She put cameras up in my apartment in an attempt to get it back."

Miss Ava released a harsh laugh. "If you're going to feed me false information, then this deal is pointless."

"And what part of that is false?" I asked defiantly.

"Rowena didn't put those cameras in your apartment, Magnolia, though it doesn't surprise me that she tried to take credit for it." She tutted, as if chastening a naughty toddler. "And after I was kind enough to grant her access to them . . ."

She was admitting that *she* had done it. Only, she wouldn't have done it herself, would she? My blood turned icy. Had *Colt* installed the cameras? I knew he'd installed security cameras before, and he'd done all kinds of odd jobs for Rowena. But why would he point the cameras out if he'd been the one to install them? It didn't make any sense. I needed to let it go for now. I had more important issues to deal with. "Why would *you* put cameras in my apartment?"

"Why not? I knew you were full of information, and I wanted it."

"You wanted the gold."

Her answer was a wide grin.

"You put the cameras in after Geraldo Lopez was killed," I said, reassuring myself that she hadn't spied on me for long.

Her eyebrows rose playfully, or as playfully as Miss Ava could achieve.

She could be trying to psych me out. Maybe I could flush out the truth. "Rowena thought I had the gold, but if you installed the cameras *before* Geraldo Lopez broke in, you must have known better. He stole it from me."

"Not all of it. There was another bag."

There it was—confirmation that she'd watched me pull the remaining bag of gold out of the wipes container hidden under the kitchen sink. I needed to pull myself together. I should have known by now that Ava Milton was ruthless. "That bag was stolen too. From my car." No need to tell her about the one Colt'd had evaluated. After all, we no longer had any of it.

"You should have gotten a safety deposit box. Or buried it in my backyard."

"Why would you want one million in gold?" I asked.

"Why *wouldn't* I?" she asked.

That made no sense. Robbery seemed beneath her. Why would she give Rowena access to the cameras if Miss Ava wanted the gold for herself? Then it hit me— she was trying to flush out my father too. "Now neither of us has it."

"That's because Bill James does," she said.

"And why do you think *he* has it?"

"He confronted Rowena in that basement. He shot her, and I know you witnessed it."

How did she know we were down there? "And now you're feeding *me* erroneous information," I said. "Bill James didn't kill Rowena, and he definitely doesn't have the gold."

Surprise flickered in her eyes. "*You* have it?"

I laughed. "You're more concerned with who has the gold than with who killed Rowena?"

"Why would *I* care who killed Rowena?"

I lifted my eyebrows.

"So who has the gold?"

"I think you know." I held her gaze. "My father."

She sat back in her chair, and her gaze turned cloudy. "So he's really back? You've seen him?"

Not in the basement, but I had no doubt he'd been there. "I saw him two days ago."

A knowing look washed over her face. "He stayed for your mother's funeral." She pushed out a breath wearily. "He really did love her, in spite of his philandering."

I had serious doubts about that, but I kept my thoughts to myself. I decided to throw her off again. "What do you know about the serial killer?"

Her reaction lasted no longer than a blink, so quick that someone who didn't know her wouldn't have noticed. "What serial killer?"

"The man who killed Emily Johnson. And Amy Danvers." My gaze focused on her. "And Melanie Seaborn."

Her face slightly paled. "Amy Danvers killed herself."

"Did she?"

Miss Ava paled even more.

"There were more," I said. "Unfortunate women whose names I don't know, but they're still just as dead. All starting twenty years ago."

She didn't respond.

"It has something to do with Daddy, but I can't find the connection."

"You think I know it?" she asked, sounding belligerent.

"Why did you hire Colt?" I asked.

"You think I'm sharing the terms of my employment of Colt Austin with you?"

"I think you're scared of the serial killer."

131

She didn't answer.

"What do you know about my brother?" I asked.

She looked startled. "A woman could get whiplash talking to you."

"What do you know about my brother?" I repeated.

"He's working for Bill James. He married Belinda Germaine last year. He's an alcoholic and an abuser."

"What else?"

Her eyes widened slightly. "Is there something else I *should* know?"

Was she bluffing? I looked at her for a long moment, weighing her sincerity, before deciding that she seemed genuine.

"Who do you think the serial killer is?" I asked.

"If I knew, he would already be arrested." She took a sip of her coffee, but her hand shook slightly.

"The serial killer has something to do with my father."

"Maybe Brian Steele is the killer. He was accused of murder before," she said, some of her attitude returning.

"A drifter was arrested for Tiffany Kessler's murder." Seventeen years ago.

"But did the drifter really commit the murder?" she asked. It was a good question. What if Tiffany Kessler's photo had been in Brady's envelope? Aside from Melanie, I hadn't looked at the names. Couldn't bring myself to.

On the surface, it didn't look good for my father, but I would have recognized Daddy's voice in that basement, and as much as Roy seemed to hate Daddy, I doubt my brother would have kept *that* a secret.

And yet there was no denying the murders had taken place at weirdly specific intervals, ones that matched up with major events in Daddy's life.

"I have reason to believe he didn't do it," I finally said, "but someone who knows him has been killing those women. It started twenty years ago, around the time the Jackson Project imploded. There was another murder seventeen years ago, after Tripp sued Daddy, and fourteen years ago, when Daddy disappeared. Then ten years ago . . ."

What had happened ten years ago?

I'd graduated high school.

Daddy must have come back for my graduation. The revelation was enough to almost tip me over in a dead faint.

". . . and this last month," I finished, my voice softer.

"And three years ago," Miss Ava said in a strained voice.

"Three years ago?" I asked, jerking my gaze to hers. Brady hadn't mentioned a murder three years ago, but if there had been one, it might have coincided with Chris Merritt's disappearance. "What murder?"

She drew in a deep breath before a grim smile lifted her lips. "Maybe you don't know as much as you think." Before I could say anything, she asked, "Do you think your father has been in town for the last month?"

"I don't know. Why?"

She remained silent, and I stood and took my coffee cup to the sink.

"Are you ready to get to work?" Miss Ava asked.

"Yes. I definitely am." I rinsed out the cup, then walked out the back door.

chapter eleven

I knew I should clean my things out of my apartment, but it was hard to care about a couple of suitcases full of belongings. I headed straight to Belinda's office instead. I was worried about her, but I was also hurt.

I found her in her reception area, creating a new display table with gold-rimmed china plates and crystal goblets.

She looked up at me as I walked in the door. Setting the goblet in her hand on the table, she said, "Magnolia, are you okay?"

I didn't answer as I walked toward her, stopping only a few feet away.

"I suppose I owe you an explanation," she said, absently smoothing out the wrinkles in her cream-colored linen pants.

"Is that what you want?" I asked. "Do you want *him*?"

She glanced down at her shoes. "It's complicated, Magnolia."

I tried to stuff down my pain. "I understand why you took him home—I do—but . . ." It was none of my business why she stayed with him. As hard as it was to accept, it was her choice. "I need to know what happened after you left."

"I drove him home, Magnolia," she said indignantly. "He didn't drink and drive."

I spun back around to face her. "I'm talking about *after* you took him home."

"You're upset with me for leaving you alone?"

"No . . . about the serial killer."

She shook her head, slack-jawed. "What are you talking about?"

I hesitated. "Did Brady come to your house?"

"Yes, and he warned Roy to stay away from you."

Was she lying to me? She looked genuinely confused.

"Belinda, I'm talking about the fact that Roy knows something about what happened to me ten years ago. He knows about the serial killer."

"How would Roy know about the serial killer?"

"You heard what he said to me. He told me I was lucky and asked if I ever wondered how I got that way."

"That could have meant anything," Belinda said in frustration. "It's a stretch to assume it had anything to do with the serial killer. Brady must be grasping at straws."

136

"What did Brady say to Roy?"

"I told you. He warned Roy to stay away from you or he'd arrest him."

"Were you with Roy the entire time he spoke with Brady?"

"No. Brady said he wanted to talk to him about something else. They exchanged looks and Roy told me to go inside."

Brady claimed to have discussed everything in front of Belinda. One of them was lying, but which one? "How long were they outside alone?"

"I don't know. Maybe a couple of minutes? I barely had the alarm turned off and my purse put away before Roy came inside."

I had no idea what to believe. I desperately wanted to believe Belinda, but things weren't adding up with her *or* Brady.

"I think Roy knows something," I said. "Momma told me Roy hid my bloody clothes."

Her face paled. "What?"

"The day after my graduation . . . She said Roy hid my bloody skirt."

"How did your skirt get bloody?" she asked. While Belinda knew I'd had an encounter with the serial killer, I hadn't told her all the gory details.

I'd worn yoga pants to clean Miss Ava's house, so I grabbed the waistband and jerked them down to mid-thigh, showing Belinda and anyone walking past her office my black panties.

"Magnolia!" she shouted, turning away. "What are you doing?"

"Look at it!" I pointed to the scar on my leg. "*This* was why my skirt was bloody."

When she realized I wasn't going to pull my pants up until she looked, she slowly turned around and then focused on my leg. "Is that a scar?"

"This is the scar I told you about Saturday night. The serial killer cut it into my skin to remind me to keep my mouth shut. Emily had one too. So did Amy."

"Is that why they asked me if she was a cutter?" Belinda asked in bewilderment. Then things started falling into place. "The killer . . ."

I pulled my pants back up. "Roy knows something about the killer. Either he was there in that house, or he saw the killer dump me at the edge of the woods, but he knows *something*."

She slowly shook her head. Her eyes were wild. "No, Magnolia. He doesn't know anything."

"Think about it, Belinda. I was in that basement and lived through that hell, and the only way my mind could handle it was to block it from my memory. What if Roy saw something? How did *he* process it? What if he's abusive because of that night?"

"That's crazy!" she shouted. "Roy doesn't know anything about the serial killer!"

"Are you sure?" I asked quietly. "Are you willing to bet your life on it?"

She started to say something, only to close her mouth before a word came out.

"I think the killer has something to do with Daddy," I said. "Last week, Brady said he thought there was some connection, and I think he's right. As best as I can tell, this all started twenty years ago, when the Jackson Project failed. Three years later, Tripp Tucker's fiancée was murdered."

"You think it was Tripp Tucker?"

"What if he did it and blamed Daddy?"

"So he killed random women?" She sounded incredulous.

"*Were* they random?" I asked. "No one other than Brady has connected the deaths." Hopefully the FBI would show up soon and help catch this guy.

She was quiet for several seconds. "So tell Brady what you're thinking. Let him investigate it."

Except one of them was clearly lying, and I didn't know which one of them to trust. "Why didn't you come back to Momma's house last night?"

She looked surprised by the sudden change in topic. "Roy needed me."

"He needed you," I said in a flat voice.

She sighed. "I know when you look at Roy, all you see is an angry man who lashes out. But he wasn't always like that, Magnolia. He used to be happy."

"That's his problem, Belinda. Not yours."

"It *is* my problem. I've made him unhappy."

That just pissed me off. Colt was right—we all needed to stop coddling Roy. "You are not responsible for my brother's happiness. Roy is responsible for his own happiness."

Belinda looked down at the floor. "I made him take that job, Magnolia," she said, her voice just above a whisper.

I shook my head. "What are you talking about?"

139

She looked up at me with tear-filled eyes. "I made him take the job with Bill James."

"No. You said he took it to find out the truth of what happened to Christopher Merritt."

"He did, but I encouraged him to do it. He knew about my parents, and he hated your father. He saw it as a way to get revenge."

"Then it was his decision, not yours."

"He didn't want to do it. I pressured him into it."

I wasn't sure how to handle that. Roy had told me that he'd groveled to get Bill to hire him—something that seemed to have humiliated him. Had Belinda really coerced him into it?

"Did he hit you back then?" I asked, sounding more accusatory than I'd intended.

"No! That only started over the last year and a half. Only once before the wedding, and he swore he'd never do it again." Her voice trailed off, and she sounded embarrassed. "He's just under so much pressure, and I haven't been supportive—"

I held up my finger and wagged it at her. "Oh, hell no. Don't you do that. Don't you *dare* accept responsibility for his abuse."

She fell silent.

"So now what?" I asked. "You stay with him forever? Until he doesn't feel so much pressure?"

"He's not like you, Magnolia. He doesn't have anyone like you do."

Her thought echoed the one I'd had the night of Momma's funeral, but I didn't feel sympathetic anymore. "And whose damn fault is that? You deserve better than him, Belinda. Momma begged you from her deathbed to leave him."

"Don't you bring your momma into this," she said, tears rolling down her cheeks. "She didn't understand."

"*I* don't understand. Help me understand."

"If I leave him . . . I have no idea what he'll do."

"And what does that mean?" I asked. "You don't know what dry cleaners he'll use to press his shirts? You don't know how he'll figure out what to eat for dinner? You don't know how much he'll drink if you're not there to monitor his intake?"

I saw a flicker in her eyes that suggested I wasn't far off with that one.

"You don't know what he'll do to manage his temper?" I asked. "You don't know who he'll use as his new punching bag?"

Humiliation filled her eyes, and while I was sorry for hurting her, I wasn't sorry for what I'd said. I suspected she was worried about the last two, but if Roy was that much of a loose cannon, he shouldn't be left to his own devices. And she definitely shouldn't be monitoring him. He needed professional help.

"Belinda, you can make excuses for him until the cows come home, but I'm never gonna buy a word of it, and if you were in my shoes, you wouldn't buy it either. And you *know* that."

More tears spilled down her cheeks, but she didn't contradict me.

"Just like Roy has to want help and has to want to change, you are the only person who can help yourself," I said. "I love you, and I'm here for you, but it's up to you, Belinda." Then I turned around and walked out of her office. She didn't call me back.

I had no idea what to do. I was devastated about Belinda, but I knew it was true. I couldn't help her until she was ready to be helped. And I couldn't trust her until I figured out the source of the inconsistency between her story and Brady's.

Who could I turn to? Of the people who knew enough to help, I trusted Colt the most, and yet there was no getting around the fact that he'd been tangled up with my father (willingly or not).

My phone rang with a number I didn't recognize. "Hello?"

"Magnolia Steele?" I recognized the voice. Detective Martinez. "We need you to come to the police station right away for an interview."

"An interview?" I wasn't in the mood to deal with her right now. "That's funny," I said in a flippant tone, "I don't remember applying for a job at the Franklin Police Department."

"You might think you're cute, Ms. Steele, but I assure you that you're not. If I don't see you in an hour, I'll send a patrol car to pick you up."

I wasn't sure if that was an empty threat, but testing her didn't seem like a good idea. "I can't wait to see you, Detective Martinez. I'm passing Starbucks on the way. Can I pick you up a drink? You seem like a Caramel Macchiato kind of girl. Nonfat?"

What the hell was I doing? But I was pissed at the world right now and apparently setting it on fire.

I'd psychoanalyze myself later.

"Sure, Ms. Steele," she said in a saccharine voice, "you can get me something. A confession. See you in thirty minutes now." Her cheerfulness was unnerving.

Good Lord, I was stupid.

I considered going in and asking Belinda if she'd gotten a call too. We were supposed to share an attorney, but I had a feeling I should leave her alone for the time being. Let her sit on what I'd said. Besides, I'd had an attorney with me on my first interview at the police station, and a fat lot of good it had done me. Emily had practically turned into a statue and left me to my own devices.

I could do this on my own.

I decided to walk to the police station to buy some time. I needed to take Brady's advice and play a role. I was good at playing roles, but I'd gotten too comfortable in Franklin. I'd started being myself, which might be the most dangerous thing I could do.

As soon as I walked into the police department, I headed up to the reception window, big as I pleased. My role was an innocent woman with nothing to hide, but this wrongly accused woman I was playing was no passive wallflower. She was tired of taking shit, and she wasn't going to take it anymore.

Essentially, she was me . . . with less knowledge.

I suspected this wouldn't go over well.

The receptionist picked up her phone. Moments later, the door to the back opened and Detective Martinez walked out wearing black pants and a white button-down shirt—it wasn't a blouse because there was nothing feminine about it. She was dressed for police business. And the way she held the door open, her back ramrod stiff, her head slightly turned so her gleaming eyes were trained on me, told me her current police business was taking me down.

"Well, well, well," she said. "If it isn't Magnolia Steele ready to give me my confession." She looked me up and down, taking in my yoga pants and fitted T-shirt. "You just walk out of a Pilates class?"

"You really ought to try it," I said with a whole lot of attitude. "It'll do wonders for your figure."

Her eyes flashed with vengeance.

Well, if I was going down, I was leaving a scorched earth behind me.

She seemed to recover slightly and gestured to the back. "Right this way, Ms. Steele."

I walked through the door, past a few desks, then down a hall into an interrogation room. The same one she'd used when Brady had called me and asked me to come in for questioning, although he was conspicuously absent this time.

I took the same seat I'd used before.

She followed me in, shutting the door as she chuckled. "You seem familiar with the drill."

I crossed my legs and stared at her, trying to keep my face emotionless. Her statement didn't need a response.

"What have you been up to, Magnolia?"

"Have we moved on to first names, Maria?" I asked with raised eyebrows. "I'll be sure to update our relationship status on Facebook."

A grin spread across her face, but she didn't look amused. "Why the hostility? What are you trying to hide?"

"*Hide?* Maybe I'm hostile because I don't like you. You showed up after my mother's funeral while I was still entertaining mourners. I'd just buried my mother, Detective, and your attitude was callous and cold. And maybe I feel inconvenienced at being forced to come down here at your whim," I said. "Maybe I had plans this morning. Dealing with estate issues is messy business." Little did she know.

"You know what else is messy?" she asked, sitting in the chair across the table from me. "Murder."

"That seems like your area of expertise, Detective Martinez, so I'll take your word for it."

"Oh, but you've witnessed a murder or two, Magnolia," she said matter-of-factly.

"Have I?" I asked, sounding bored. Finding two dead bodies wasn't the same as witnessing a murder. "I think I'd remember something like that."

Detective Martinez leaned forward. "You're telling me you've completely blocked it out?"

Ice slid down my spine, but I reminded myself she didn't know anything about that night ten years ago and quickly covered any possible reaction. She was trying to get me to break on Rowena Rogers's murder. "Blocked out a murder? I must have if I don't remember it."

She looked pissed. "So you're saying you don't remember when Geraldo Lopez was shot?"

"*Geraldo Lopez?* Of course I remember Detective Frasier shooting him," I said, shaking my head in confusion. "But I didn't consider it murder. Dr. Lopez was about to slash my face with a knife. Detective Frasier shot him to protect me."

"Detective Frasier ended his life with his gun. We call that murder."

"You're charging Detective Frasier with *murder*?" I asked incredulously, then instantly regretted breaking character. But Detective Martinez didn't seem to notice.

"Our internal investigation has determined that Detective Frasier acted appropriately in the line of duty. But the death certificate still states the cause of death as murder by gunshot wounds."

What was she hoping to prove? "Why am I here, Detective? I don't think you want to question me about the night Geraldo Lopez died."

"Maybe I do. Were you two friends?"

"I met Dr. Lopez briefly at my father's office when I was a child."

"Not Dr. Lopez. Detective Frasier."

"No, but we're acquaintances."

Her eyebrows rose. "How so?"

"Through Brady . . . Detective Bennett. I met Detective Frasier outside the police station when I dropped by to see Detective Bennett. Then I saw him again at a bar called the Kincaid. I was there singing with Colt Austin, and Detective Bennett was there with friends. Detective Frasier was one of them. After we left the stage, Detective Bennett invited me to his table."

"Did you talk about the case at all?"

"Which case?" I asked. "Dr. Lopez hadn't broken into my apartment yet."

146

"The Walter Frey case. You were the one to discover his body. Surely you met Detective Frasier during the investigation of that case."

"When Detective Frasier arrived at the murder scene—the Walter Frey murder scene," I added to be clear, "he seemed to have his hands full. Detective Bennett was there, so he took my statement."

"You never talked to Detective Frasier about the Walter Frey case at all?"

"When we were at the Kincaid, I asked him if there had been any progress, and he said he couldn't talk about it."

"And that's it? He never called you? Never dropped by to see you?"

"What is this?" I asked, getting irritated. I needed to derail this fast. "If Detective Frasier is interested in dating me, perhaps he should man up and call me himself."

Detective Martinez was getting pissed. "He doesn't want to date you."

"Then why all the questions about whether or not he called me or dropped by to see me?"

"We're trying to determine if there was any irregularity about the Frey murder investigation."

"That sounds like a Franklin Police problem. Why involve me?"

From the look on her face, I was pretty sure Maria Martinez would shoot me dead if she thought there was a remote chance she could get away with it. "As I said, we're trying to determine if there were any irregularities.

When you found Mr. Frey, did you notice anything unusual?"

"I found a bullet hole in his head," I said in a dry tone. "I consider that unusual."

She waited a second. "Did you see anything else?"

"I was too busy freaking out that I'd found another dead man to notice anything else."

"Did you see a cell phone?"

"Yeah. My own. The bartender found me right after I stumbled upon Mr. Frey's body. He had my purse. I got out my phone and called Detective Bennett."

Her eyes lit up. "And why did you call Detective Bennett instead of 911?"

"You want the truth?"

She held her hands out from her sides—a *Eureka!* gesture—and gave me a fake-friendly smile. "At last. That's why we're here."

"I called Brady because of the way your department treated me after I found Max Goodwin's body. I was utterly traumatized and received no sympathy whatsoever. Instead, you treated me as a suspect. I wasn't over the trauma of *that* ordeal, so when I found Walter Frey's body, I panicked. I didn't think I could handle those accusations again, so I called Brady." At least all of that statement was true.

"What made you think Detective Bennett would help?"

"Because I knew he would be less likely to automatically consider me a suspect."

"Why?"

"*Why?* Because he told me that he had believed I was innocent of Max Goodwin's murder."

"How did you have his number?"

"After Amy Danvers's death, Brady made it clear he was interested in dating me. He gave it to me." But that wasn't true. He'd given it to me before that, but it didn't seem prudent to tell her so.

Surprise filled her eyes. "Detective Bennett said he wanted to date you?"

"Are you *serious*?" Was she messing with me? According to Brady, half the department knew I'd lived with him for nearly a week, which meant his partner had to know.

The scowl that covered her face was so deep, I suspected she'd have permanent lines. "Have you dated Detective Bennett?"

I resisted the urge to cross my arms; I knew that would make me look like I was on the defensive. Instead, I rested my hands in my lap and said in a bored tone, "I'm not sure what my personal life has to do with Walter Frey's murder investigation."

"Are you or are you not dating Detective Bennett?"

"I most certainly am not."

She watched me for several seconds as though trying to determine if I was lying. "Why does your brother think you killed your mother?"

"He doesn't. Like we told you the other day, my mother had a DNR. She was tired of fighting cancer after three years of chemo, especially since the doctors had told her there was nothing more they could do for her. So when she came down with an infection, she refused antibiotics. My brother and I both tried to convince her to change her mind, but she refused. Roy told the nurse he was going to contact his lawyer. Momma changed her mind the next day—" I paused when my voice broke. "But it was too late, and she died that night."

"Why did your brother blame you?"

"Because he couldn't believe our mother would voluntarily leave him. He had to blame someone, and I've always been his favorite scapegoat."

"Did you go to the masquerade ball?"

She was employing my whiplash technique, but I was ready for her. "The answer's still yes. I attended with Colt Austin. I wanted to stay at the hospital with my mother, but she insisted that I go. She missed seeing me dressed up for prom, so she insisted I dress up for the ball so she could take photos."

She made a face that suggested I'd mentioned something interesting to her. "Aww . . . Colt Austin. He works at your mother's catering business?"

"Yes."

"Are you romantically involved with him?"

"I'm not sure how that's pertinent to this discussion."

She grinned, but there was danger in her eyes. "Answer the question anyway."

"At the risk of sounding cliché, it's complicated."

"And what makes it complicated?"

I gave her a deadpan look. "Shouldn't we be painting each other's nails while we discuss our relationships? Is there anything you'd like to share about yours?"

"Answer the question, Ms. Steele. What makes it complicated?"

"My mother died five days ago, Detective Martinez. It seems like a bad time to make a decision about dating someone."

"And yet he's living with you?"

"Colt Austin isn't living with me."

"Then why has he spent every night with you since your mother died?"

"And how would you be in a position to know that?" I asked. Had she been spying on me?

Her grin was confirmation enough. Why would she put so much effort into knowing who was staying at Momma's house?

"Colt is a friend. He's been my friend since the night I moved back to Franklin. He worked for my mother and her partner for three years. He was close to them both, so he took my mother's death hard. We're both dealing with her loss, and neither of us wants to be alone." I tilted my head. "Not that it's any of your business."

"So you attended the ball with Colt Austin. How long did you stay?"

"I'm not exactly sure, but we left early. And since I know you'll undoubtedly want to know why, it's because we had a disagreement. Colt didn't like the way I reacted to seeing Brady at the ball."

"You saw Detective Bennett at the ball?"

"He attended with his mother."

"And what was your reaction?"

I was treading on dangerous ground. "I was unnerved and slightly embarrassed," I said. "I'd had a

151

brief relationship with Brady, and I was there with Colt days later. The last thing I wanted to do was hurt Brady."

Her eyebrows shot up. "You were with Brady Bennett romantically? You dated?"

Why was she acting so surprised at the thought of a connection between us? "Yes. But like I said, it was very brief. I'm not sure you could call it dating."

"And what would Detective Bennett call it? A hookup? A one-night stand?"

The door behind her opened and Brady walked in with a dark look on his face. "I'm sure she'd call it the beginning of a relationship."

chapter twelve

Detective Martinez's eyes went round as she turned to face him, and I couldn't hide my look of surprise either.

"Brady," she finally said. "I don't think you should be in here."

"I'm not going to let you humiliate Magnolia on my account." He shot me an unreadable look before he turned back to his partner and took a seat in the chair next to her. "Magnolia had my number because I gave it to her after the Max Goodwin case was solved."

That was a lie, and we both knew it. He'd given it to me before he knew I had any connection to Goodwin. At the time, he'd worried that I was acting skittish because I was a domestic abuse victim.

Had he been watching from the other side of the mirror? He must have been, considering the way he'd timed his entrance.

Brady continued, "There was no conflict of interest at that point. I told her I was interested in seeing her again, and she was understandably reluctant. But she called me a couple of weeks later in a panic and said she'd found a body. She sought out my help because she was terrified of being harassed again. I went to the bar and called Owen since he was on call that night. Since Magnolia was already nervous about trusting the Franklin police, Owen and I decided she'd feel more at ease if I took her statement. We figured she'd be more likely to give a full account of what happened if she wasn't worried about being named a suspect."

I watched him in shock.

But he ignored me and continued his stare-down with his partner.

Her face reddened and she looked close to waling on Brady. "This is not the time and place to give your statement, *Detective*."

"It seems like the perfect time and place. Once again, Magnolia is being treated hostilely by our department, which means we're in danger of losing the trust I've worked on rebuilding. I'm in here hoping to salvage what might be left."

Detective Martinez leaned back in her chair and asked incredulously, "And why would we give a shit if we have her trust?"

His eyes narrowed and his jaw clenched. "Are you really that shortsighted, Maria? Perhaps we should leave the room and discuss it."

They had a stare-off for a good five seconds before she broke eye contact, swearing under her breath. "This isn't your interview, Bennett. Get out."

"I've been working on this case for over a month, Maria. I'm staying."

There was no hiding my surprise or my pain. I'd thought Brady had come in to save me embarrassment, but he was acting like he'd been using me the entire time. Was he lying to his partner, or had he been lying to me? What agenda was he working toward? My emotional turmoil clearly showed on my face, because Detective Martinez's annoyance had turned to thinly concealed glee.

Brady turned to me with an expressionless face. "Ms. Steele, I'm sorry you had to find out this way."

I wanted to believe this was all an act for Detective Martinez, but even if it was, something wasn't right with Brady. He lied too well for a detective, and how could I ignore the fact that he and Belinda had very different stories about his chat with Roy? And I couldn't help but remember that Momma hadn't liked him.

I wasn't sure what to believe, and my emotions were too raw for me to process it.

I got to my feet. "I'm done."

Detective Martinez stood and blocked my path. "You're not done until I say we're done."

She stood about three feet in front of me, and we were about eye level. She didn't intimidate me, and I wasn't even playing a role right now. "Are you arresting me?"

"Do I have a reason to arrest you?"

"Detective," I forced out, tears stinging my eyes. "Is your mother still living?"

"That doesn't have anything—"

"Is she still living?" I demanded. "It's a simple question."

"Yes," she conceded.

"Are you close to her?"

She looked like she was about to protest, but she said, "Yes."

"My mother and I were so much alike we butted heads for my entire childhood. We spent the past ten years mostly estranged. But when I came home a month ago, we both decided to try to work on our relationship during the time we had left." My voice broke. "I thought I had more time. I thought I had months. I wasn't ready to let her go." My voice broke again. "My mother died five days ago, and I'm beyond devastated. And now I'm finding out Detectives Bennett and Frasier have been using me for some type of investigation . . ." Having gotten over my initial shock, I didn't for one minute believe Brady had gotten close to me for an investigation, but he *had* insisted on getting close to me for some other reason. It was all too much to process.

I took a breath. I would *not* fall apart now. Not here. I wouldn't give either of them the satisfaction. "If you have an ounce of compassion left in you, then please get the hell out of my way."

To my surprise, she stepped to the side.

I reached for the door, refusing to look at Brady, then walked out and headed straight for the exit.

156

No one stopped me as I descended the steps. I had no idea where I was going, only that I was headed back downtown.

It was no surprise when I found myself at the catering business. Colt was helping Tilly with inventory today. I held myself together until I walked through the back door and saw the two of them going through a pile of produce and groceries while Tilly held a clipboard.

Tilly took one look at me and worry filled her eyes. "Maggie? You okay?"

I shook my head and a tear escaped down my cheek. "I need to talk to Colt for a moment." I shot him a look before turning back to Tilly. "I'm sorry to steal him, but this is important."

"Of course!" Tilly said as she walked toward me and pulled me into a hug. "Let me know if you need anything." Then she released me and headed up the stairs to the office.

I heard the door close as Colt moved in front of me. I could tell he was anxious, unsure of what I needed. "What happened, Maggie?"

I wasn't going to lose it yet. I needed answers. "Why are you staying at Momma's with me?"

Pain filled his eyes. "I know why you're hesitant to trust me, and if I could change what I did, I would. I'm trying to prove to you that you can."

"Why are you with me, Colt?" I demanded.

Confusion washed over his face. "I told you."

"No. Not really. Why are you with me?"

He reached for me, putting his hand on my arm, and when I didn't push him away, he pulled me into an

157

embrace. I remained stiff, but that didn't deter him. "Because I'm falling in love with you, Magnolia," he said, searching my face with pleading eyes. "And the thought of losing you because of what I did terrifies me. I know I should give you space, but even if you weren't in danger, I'd be afraid to leave you alone. I'm worried that you'll decide you don't need me and I'll lose you forever." He took a breath. "I deserve to lose you, Maggie. I know that. That's why I'm so terrified. You have every right to kick me out of your life, but I haven't felt this way about a woman in a very long time, and I *know* we could have something special."

I wasn't sure what to believe. I'd never felt so alone in my life, which was saying something since I'd spent the ten years I'd lived in New York holding everyone at arm's length. More than ever I wished Momma was still alive. I trusted her opinion of people, and I needed her advice more than ever. She'd believed in Colt in spite of knowing about his arrangement with Daddy. Why?

I started to cry. "I can't take one more person using me."

His hand slid up to my upper back and his hold tightened. "Mags, what happened? Why are you so upset?"

"Tell me you won't hurt me," I said as I broke from his embrace and took a step back. "Tell me you're not using me."

A war waged in his eyes. "I wish I could tell you that I'll never hurt you, but I can't." I started to back up more, but he reached for my arm and held me in place. "Let me finish. *Please.*"

158

I nodded and jerked out of his hold.

"I can't promise that I'll never unintentionally hurt you, but I promise from this moment onward to always tell you the truth, no matter how hard it is for the both of us."

Could I really trust him? I only knew that I wanted to.

"Maggie. What happened?"

"I went down to the police station to talk to Detective Martinez."

"About the murders on Saturday night?"

"It never got that far," I said. "She asked questions about how I knew Owen and about the Walter Frey investigation."

"What did she do? Why are you so upset?"

I could tell him about Brady, but what good would it do? He'd never really trusted Brady, and while he wouldn't say *I told you so*, he really couldn't do anything to help me. Besides, it would be weird for him to comfort me about *this*, and I had no idea what to think. I suspected Brady had been playing a part to get his partner to leave me alone, but the smooth way he'd lied to someone he knew well seemed like further proof that I couldn't trust him. "I think everything's caught up with me. Especially after I told off Miss Ava this morning."

He grinned. "I would like to have seen that."

I gave him a wry smile, but another thought flitted through my head, and my expression turned serious. "Why did she hire you two years ago?"

Dread washed over his face. "Mags . . ." I was sure he wasn't going to answer, but he took a deep breath and said, "*I* approached *her.*"

"Because of my dad?"

"Yeah. I think he knew she was snooping, so he told me to get close to her."

"And how did you manage that?"

"Christopher Merritt had just disappeared, and I played on her fears that your dad would go after her too."

"Ava Milton doesn't seem like the type who can be easily played."

"She's not. And it took some time. I met her at a party, while I was bartending, and I flirted with her."

"That's disgusting."

He shrugged, but he didn't look happy. "I told her to give me a call if she ever had any issues that she needed a man to deal with."

"She fell for that?"

"Not entirely. But someone tried to break into her house, and she contacted me to keep an eye on her place for a few weeks."

"So that's why you were there at night?"

"Yeah . . ." He sounded confused. "It didn't take long for me to figure out that Ava's not the skittish type. I think she made up the break-in so she'd get a chance to figure out what made me tick."

"I take it you continued a *working* relationship with her after that," I said in a disgusted tone.

He grimaced. "I never slept with her, if that's what you're implying, but yeah, I did things for her. She knows everything about everyone, Maggie. And I learned all kinds of things through her."

"Which you promptly delivered to my father."

He hesitated, then grabbed a metal barstool and dragged it over to me, going on to position a second one within a couple of feet from mine.

Once we were both seated, he nodded. "Yeah," he said. "I told him things. But not everything."

"Why did Miss Ava go to *you*? Do you think she knew you worked for my father?"

"Honestly, I don't know."

"I eavesdropped on the first Bible study I helped with. The one right after Walter Frey's murder. One of the women said Ava had dealt with a messy business two years ago and that it had spawned two more issues."

He hesitated, then said, "I helped with the two other issues."

"And what were they?"

"They weren't related to your father or Christopher Merritt. She has multiple businesses and rental properties, and she had an issue with one of the businesses. She tried to handle it her usual way, and when it didn't work out, she had me deal with the outcome." He paused and guilt washed over his face. "I'd rather not say how I took care of it. I'm not proud of it."

"Why did the woman insinuate it had something to do with Walter Frey and Christopher Merritt?"

He shook his head, looking genuinely confused. "Maybe because one of the issues was violent."

"I deserve better than these bullshit vague answers, Colt," I said in a hard voice.

161

"I know." He ran his hand through his hair. "You can't tell anyone what I'm about to tell you, Magnolia. You have to swear."

I frowned. What was he going to tell me? But I wanted to know badly enough that I was willing to make a blind agreement. "Yes. I swear."

He took a breath and then slowly blew it out. "She pissed off a customer, and he retaliated by showing up at the *spa* a few days later. He roughed up an employee and told her to give Ava a message."

"A *spa*?" I asked incredulously.

"You're a smart girl," he said in a dry tone. "Read between the lines."

"*A brothel*?" How ironic that she'd worried it would ruin her reputation if too many men dropped by my apartment. Then again, I suspected she would want any stink of impropriety far, far from her home.

"That's an old-fashioned term."

I was stunned speechless. "But . . . Miss Ava . . . she's . . ."

"So prim and proper? What better way to get information than when men are their most vulnerable?" he said, not sounding happy.

"What did she have on you?" I asked.

"I never used her services," he said in disgust. "I only did her bidding."

"So she had an unhappy customer and he hurt one of her . . ."

"Escorts. Yes." He smirked. "It was an escort service. They accompanied men to parties, events, and so forth. It was up to them if they slept with the guys.

162

Totally legit." He gave me a theatrical wink. "But let me just say it was expected they would put out."

"But I suspect you won't find Ava Milton's name on the business license."

"Exactly. But this one guy got pissed when he realized the information he'd given his date had fallen into Ava's hands. Most people had no idea there was a connection, but somehow he figured it out."

"And what did you do?"

"I roughed him up a bit and told him if he ever hurt another girl, I'd cut off his dick next time."

"Why didn't he have you arrested?"

"He didn't know it was me. I wore a ski mask."

I didn't say anything for a moment. "Who was the guy?"

"Maggie, this has nothing to do with your father."

That perked me up. "Who was it?"

He grimaced. "Clint Duncan."

I gasped.

"This had nothing to do with your father, Maggie," he repeated with more insistence. "Clint's a dried-up and bitter man who lashes out at the world. It was a coincidence."

I wasn't sure I believed in coincidences anymore. I studied him carefully as I asked my next question. "Did you know Ava planted the cameras in my apartment?"

He stared at me for a moment, shock washing over his face before fear replaced it. He sucked in a breath. "I didn't plant them, Maggie. I swear on Lila's grave. I didn't do it, and if she'd made me, I would have told you immediately."

"But you *did* tell me immediately," I said. "When we went into the apartment after Lopez's murder. You saw the cameras right away and rushed me out of the apartment."

"I didn't know, Maggie!"

Something caught my attention then—something I'd almost missed. "You said if she'd *made* you do it. Despite being my friend, you would have put cameras in my apartment if she'd insisted."

His eyes widened, but he didn't answer.

My chest constricted and I got off the stool. I knew I was onto something. "What does she have on you?"

He continued to stare at me.

"Why are you still working for her?"

"I'm not. The last thing I did for her was to get you to move into her apartment."

"And you never once thought it might not be in my best interest to move in there?" I asked in an accusatory tone.

He ran a hand through his hair, his eyes full of panic. "You wanted answers, Mags, and I knew Ava had them. I figured it was a win-win situation."

Anger was pumping through my veins instead of blood. "And you never considered that maybe you should be honest with me? Say, 'Hey, Ava Milton wants you to move into the apartment over her garage. I don't know why—maybe she wants to know what you know about your father—but you can learn a lot from her too?'"

His eyes turned glassy, and his mouth parted as if he wanted to say something. He stayed silent.

"Nothing?" I asked in disbelief. "You say nothing?"

"You're right. She has something on me."

"What?"

He didn't answer.

"You swore you would be honest with me, Colt. You swore no more lies."

"This isn't a lie, Magnolia. I'm just not answering."

"My life is in danger, and you're still refusing to be honest with me."

He was slow to respond. I stared up at him, narrowing my eyes. "I want you to take me to the safety deposit box my momma left you right now."

He still didn't answer.

I gasped and took a step backward. "You've already been."

He took a step toward me. "Maggie . . ."

"What was in the box, Colt?"

"If you'd just listen . . ."

"The only thing I'm going to listen to right now is what you found in that box."

The defeat in his eyes nearly killed me. "I can't tell you."

"Can't? Or won't?" I hated that my voice broke. When he didn't answer, I shook my head. "Does Ava Milton know?"

His gaze dropped. "No."

"Well, *that's* a shocker." I was being ugly and hateful, but I didn't care. After everything, he was still hiding things from me. For all I knew, he hadn't stopped making reports to Ava.

I turned and hurried up the stairs. When I got up to the office, Tilly was sitting on her desk chair, staring at my mother's empty desk with tears on her cheeks.

I wasn't sure how much heartbreak I could take.

She glanced up at me and dabbed the corners of her eyes. "Don't be so hard on him, Maggie."

"He's kept some pretty massive secrets from me, Tilly," I said defensively. "He won't even tell me what was in Momma's safety deposit box."

"Maybe he has a good reason, sweet girl." Her chin quivered. "His heart is breaking too."

"He was working for my father, Tilly, reporting what we were doing to him."

"I know." She took a breath. "Your momma knew too. But she also knew he was a good man trapped in an impossible situation, and she spent the past three years trying to make him a *better* man. And it's worked, Maggie. For the first time, his focus is on someone other than himself, and that person is you."

"He's still keeping secrets from me."

"And you're still keeping secrets from him."

The words felt like a blow, but there was no denying she was right about that.

"I need to take a few days off to think," I said. "I know I'm supposed to help—"

Tilly held up her hands. "I've got enough help. You take as long as you need."

"About my part of the business . . ."

She shook her head and stood, walking toward me. "It's here if you want it; otherwise, I'll buy you out, but it's too soon to talk about that. You need to grieve,

Magnolia. You need to mourn your momma." She tugged me into a hug and I relaxed into her, resisting the urge to cry. I was done crying . . . at least for now. I'd let myself cry later.

I pulled free and kissed her cheek. "I'm here for you too, you know."

"I know." A sad smile spread across her face. "I know." Then she gave me a tiny shove. "Go home. Go do what you need to do."

I reluctantly turned and headed for the door.

"Maggie?" I turned at the waist to face her, and she looked even sadder than before. "Don't run off without telling me, okay?"

My chin quivered and I ran back to her, offering her support this time. She thought I'd leave town like I had last time. "I won't. I swear."

She nodded and pulled away, wiping a stray tear from her cheek. "Look at the two of us. Lila would have hated this."

I laughed, but it was bittersweet. "I know. That's what makes it so great."

Tilly gave me an ornery grin. "You're terrible."

"I am my mother's daughter."

Her smile fell. "That you are."

I really left then, because I knew I was making her even sadder. Colt was pacing when I reached the bottom of the stairs.

I lifted my chin. "I'm giving you one last chance to tell me what was in that box or what Ava has on you. Just one. You pick."

"I can't."

167

I expected that answer, but something hurt deep in my chest. "I can't see you right now."

A resigned look filled his eyes. "Are you staying with Brady?"

"I'm a grown-ass woman. I don't need a man to protect me."

"No, but it wouldn't hurt to have someone with a big-ass gun," he snipped back.

"I have my own big-ass gun." I opened the back door and stomped out into the parking lot, half-expecting Colt to follow me. Hoping he'd follow me.

He didn't.

His secrets were more important than keeping me.

chapter thirteen

I wasn't sure what to do or where to go, so I just got in my car and drove. It felt right when I found myself in the cemetery a half hour later. Momma's grave was a rectangle of dirt with a small metal plaque marking the spot. Flowers covered half of it. As I approached her grave, I nearly laughed at the thought of how pissed she would have been to see them. Ever practical, Momma had hated cut flowers.

"Why kill something just because it's beautiful?" she used to say. "It's selfish to take it for yourself and not share it with the rest of the world."

I sank to the ground as I remembered a talk I'd had with her a few months before high school graduation. My school had held a Valentine's Day fundraiser where students could buy roses and send them to other people—a friend, a secret crush, a significant other. I'd been upset because my boyfriend at the time, Tanner, hadn't sent me any roses. All my friends' boyfriends had sent *them* flowers. When Tanner figured out that I was upset, he showed up at my house after school with two dozen long-stemmed red roses, but I was still pissed. My attitude irritated the snot out of Momma, and she lit into me after he left.

"Is it wrong to want my boyfriend to send me flowers?" I demanded through my tears.

"But you didn't really want your boyfriend to send you flowers, now did you?" she asked. "Because that boy brought you more flowers—and better-looking ones at that—than the ones he would have sent you at school, and you *still* aren't happy. You wanted those flowers for the wrong reasons, Magnolia."

She was right, but I couldn't bring myself to admit it at the time, because when she put it that way, it seemed petty and trite, and I felt entitled to my outrage.

Some of Momma's bluster faded, and she sat down next to me on the sofa and took my hand, waiting until I looked up at her to continue. "There's a reason for the phrase beauty is more than skin-deep, Maggie. You're a beautiful girl, but don't let your looks get in your way."

I bristled and tried to pull my hand away. "Are you calling me shallow?"

"No, Maggie. Listen." It was her tone that got through to me—soft and tender—so unlike the woman who'd raised me. "This isn't even about Tanner's roses." She paused. "I know you're tenderhearted, even if all those teenage hormones are getting in your way, but what I'm about to tell you is a lifelong lesson, so listen good, okay?"

I nodded.

"There are people out there who will use you for your looks. And they'll use their own looks and charm to hurt you. Lucifer was a beautiful angel, the most beautiful angel of all, and look where that got him."

My lips parted in surprise. Was she comparing me to Satan?

Her hand tightened around mine. "You have to be more wary than most. Men will want you because of your beauty, but many of them will only want you for your looks and not what's deep inside you—a pure and loyal heart. When your looks fade, those men'll be gone, just like the roses Tanner brought you. You're a good girl, Maggie . . . when you're not getting in your own way."

"What's that mean?"

"It means that you worry too much about what other people think than about being true to yourself. The Maggie I knew two years ago would have shrieked with happiness at those two dozen flowers, instead of pouting about not getting a half-wilted rosebud at school." She put her free hand under my chin and tilted my face up to meet her gaze. "Magnolia Mae Steele. Ignore the naysayers, and be true to yourself."

I gave her a watery smile. "And stay away from Lucifer because he'll drag you to the fiery pits of hell."

She grinned. "I knew you were a bright girl, but just remember Lucifer's not wearing a name tag. Be wary of all pretty men who seem too good to be true." Sadness crept into her eyes. "Because they usually are."

Now, sitting on the ground next to her grave, I realized the sadness in her eyes had been put there by my father's betrayals. "Oh, Momma. I know you were warning me, but why weren't you more direct?"

"Speaking to graves, are you? Makes me rethink working with you."

I whipped my head to the side and found myself looking up at Owen. I got to my feet and held his gaze. "How'd you find me?"

"It wasn't hard. I was pulling into the parking lot behind the catering kitchen while you were pulling out. I followed you. When I saw you sitting here, I decided to give you some space."

"Are you going to work with me?"

"I'm considering it. We need to work out a few terms first."

I nodded. "Agreed."

"I heard about your showdown at the station with Detective Martinez."

I lifted my shoulder into a half-shrug. "Is Brady really working with you?"

"You mean did he and I come to some sort of agreement with the Walter Frey case? No. He was the one who suggested taking your statement. I told him that I thought he might be too close to you to get an accurate statement, but he blew me off."

More lies from Brady. "So why did he take my statement?"

"Because he was worried about you. I believe that part is true." He shifted his weight. "I thought he was just trying to hit on you, but after our chat last week, I pressed him for his real reason, and he admitted you'd arranged to meet Walter Frey to talk to him about his involvement with your father."

Had Brady been playing me even back then? "Is Brady working some big case related to my father? Did he get close to me just to gather information?"

Owen shook his head. "He was blowing smoke up Maria's ass, but there are rumors that . . . well, she suspects you're back in town to do your father's bidding. She thinks the timing of the deaths and your return are too closely linked to be coincidental."

"What does Brady think?"

"That you're caught in the middle."

"And you?"

He hesitated before pushing out a breath. "I'm prone to fall in line with Brady on that one." But he didn't look happy to admit it.

"But you're not working together on that theory?"

"Brady is uncharacteristically tight-mouthed on the subject, and he seems obsessed with the Emily Johnson case." He held my gaze. "Brady asked me to pull Amy Danvers's and Melanie Seaborn's files after he started the Johnson investigation. You left town at around the same time Melanie was murdered. What's the link?"

I shook my head and gave him a tight smile. "Sorry, Owen. We need to work out some details first."

He tilted his head to the side. "I'm listening."

"I'm an anonymous source as far as you're concerned. No one knows you're getting this information from me."

He grimaced. "I'm not a reporter, Magnolia. It doesn't work that way."

"Don't you have informants?"

"Yeah, but they still have to testify if it comes down to it."

"No offense, but I don't trust your department. I didn't even trust you until a few days ago."

"Why do you trust me now?"

"As I already told you, Rowena Rogers told me your uncle was innocent and you are too."

His eyebrows lifted. "She referred to me by name?"

"No, but she was very specific. She knew all about you."

He took a second to process my words. "And you didn't kill her?"

"No. Of course not. Why do members of the Franklin Police Department keep accusing me of murder?"

He lifted a hand in surrender. "It had to be asked, but do you know who *did*?" When I didn't answer, he asked, "Do you know *anything* about Rowena Rogers's murder?"

When I still didn't answer, he sighed and ran a hand through his hair.

"What exactly do you propose here, Magnolia? What's your endgame?"

"To clear the reputations of your uncle and Shannon Morrissey. To stop a serial killer."

That caught his attention. "A serial killer? Was Brady onto something?"

"I meant what I said. If we're going to help each other, anything I tell you has to be kept a secret. You can

174

use what I tell you. I can lead you to places and give you information, but I want my name left out of it."

He scowled. "How am I gonna explain to everyone how I knew where to go?"

"Your great intuition." I held his gaze. "When I say you can't tell anyone, I mean *anyone*. No Brady."

"He and I aren't exactly seein' eye to eye these days."

"Maybe so, but you've been friends for years. I suspect you'll make up. And you can't tell him."

"Fine. I won't tell him. But you can't tell anyone you're working with me either."

"I don't have anyone to tell, so you're good." The reminder of just how alone I was sent a spike of pain through me.

"What about that musician you've been singing with? The one who works for your mother?"

"He works for her partner now, and we're taking a break."

A hint of a grin lifted the corners of his mouth. "You have the shortest relationships of anyone I know."

I lifted my chin and gave him a haughty glare. "Since this is a working partnership, I don't see how that concerns you. If it helps explain how you got the information, I can call and leave you 'anonymous' tips," I said, using air quotes.

He really grinned this time. "I think you can just tell me, and I'll go from there."

"How are you going to fit this in with your regular work?"

"That shouldn't be a problem since I'm on administrative leave."

"What?"

"Internal affairs has some questions about my handling of Walter Frey's murder . . . and a few other things. That's why I heard about what happened in the interrogation room. I was summoned to the station to get the good news about my unpaid vacation."

"Is it normal to suspend someone over that?"

"No. Let's just say there are some people who don't want me there."

"And if you were to figure out the identity of a serial killer?" I asked with raised eyebrows. "Would that help you keep your position?"

"You really think there's a serial killer?" he asked.

"Surely you looked at the files you pulled," I said.

"I pulled two files for him—one was murdered ten years ago, and the other had committed suicide. Seems like a stretch."

I blinked. "Wait. *What?* Only two files? Then where did he get the other ones?"

He looked startled. "What other ones?"

"There were at least four other murders, Owen, and Brady has files on all of them."

Owen scowled. "We need to see those files."

"Do you think Brady will hand them over to you?"

"No." He paused. "But you can get them."

"*Me?*"

"You were staying at Brady's apartment, so you know how to get in, and you know where he was hiding it. You're the logical choice."

"You're kidding, right? I can't break into his apartment. Why don't you just ask him about it?"

176

"No way. Like I said, he and I are at odds at the moment. He'll never tell me."

"So we just jump to breaking and entering? I thought you were a cop!"

"Trust me, if Brady finds you in his apartment, he won't consider it breaking and entering." He looked me over, and for a second I thought he was going to walk away and say none of this was worth the hassle, but a grudging look of acceptance twisted his face and he pushed out a sigh. "Come on. You've got some files to steal."

chapter fourteen

My car was more memorable than his dark sedan, so we agreed to ride together. My car needed to be parked somewhere, so I drove it back downtown and parked behind the catering kitchen.

I opened Owen's passenger door, but he immediately said, "Get in the back. I don't want it to look so obvious that we're working together."

As I climbed into the backseat, I found myself hoping this decision to work with Owen wasn't a big mistake.

We were silent during the ten-minute drive to Brady's condo, but when he pulled into the parking garage, I started to get nervous. "How do you know Brady won't be home?"

"He never goes home during the day."

"But you do?" I asked.

"Not usually. Meeting you was a special circumstance."

"You have no problem working against your friend?"

Owen parked in a spot and turned around to face me. "I don't want to think of it that way. I have no intention of getting him into trouble. It's just that he and I have different priorities right now." He paused. "You're willing to work against him. Is this the revenge of a woman scorned?"

"This isn't any type of plot against Brady," I said, slinging my purse strap over my shoulder. "I trusted him until last week, when I realized certain things weren't adding up. I need answers, and I'd hoped he could help me find them, but now . . . I'm not so sure his cold case obsession explains his connection to the serial killer cases. I think it's personal."

Owen's eyes narrowed. "Cold case obsession?"

"Brady told me that he'd discovered Melanie Seaborn's murder in a cold case club. She had the same mark on her leg that Emily Johnson had. And Amy Danvers."

"What mark?"

I watched his face. "I think it would be easier to show you. Let me go see about those files."

Then I opened the car door and got out. I was nervous during the short elevator ride to Brady's floor, and when it stopped, I looked to make sure no one was around. The hall was empty—not that I'd ever seen anyone around, come to think of it.

Brady had given me a key, and I hadn't given it back yet. I started to put the key into the lock, then stopped and knocked on the door just in case he was home. I had no idea what excuse I'd use if he opened the door, but I figured it would be better than walking in on him without warning.

When he didn't answer, I unlocked the door and quickly closed and locked it behind me. I headed straight for the closet where I'd found the files, but the packet wasn't where I'd originally found it—on the top shelf of his coat closet in a basket of hats and gloves. I wondered if it would be in the apartment at all. What if he'd taken it to the police station? But the night Owen had brought Brady the packet, they'd both acted like it was a hush-hush transaction. I'd bet money it was still in his apartment. Then again, he'd put the envelope in the closet to hide it from me. Now that I wasn't here, he could keep the files in the open.

The envelope wasn't out in the open either, but several minutes later, I found it hidden under his socks in his underwear drawer. I dumped the files out of the large envelope on Brady's neatly made bed and flipped through the pages, my gut clenching when I saw the photos. I quickly stuffed them back inside. My heart couldn't take seeing the suffering those poor women had endured.

I was heading for the front door when my phone buzzed with a text. I checked the screen and sucked in a breath. The message was from a number I didn't recognize.

Brady's on his way up. Get out now.

Shit.

180

As I tried to figure out how I could possibly escape unnoticed, it barely registered that Owen must have taken my advice and gotten a burner phone. Thankfully, I had a large purse, so I stuffed the envelope inside as I went out into the hall. I had just gotten the front door closed when the elevator doors opened and Brady appeared.

"Maggie?" he asked in seemingly genuine shock. "What are you doing here?"

I forced a fake smile, putting all my Broadway power behind it. "Sorry for just dropping by like this, but I decided to take a chance. I guess I almost missed you."

"After this morning in the interrogation room, let's just say I'm surprised to find you here."

"Yeah . . . well . . ." I was determined to find out everything I could, so I might as well do a little more digging while I was here. "I wanted to talk to you about that."

He stepped beside me and unlocked his door. "Can you come in for a few minutes? I'm not staying here long. I just needed to pick up something."

Oh, crap. I hoped it wasn't the envelope in my purse. I had no idea what he'd do when he found out it was gone, especially since I was the only likely suspect. Maybe Owen could photograph or photocopy the pages and return the package before Brady noticed. "Yeah," I said when I realized he was holding the door open and waiting for an answer. "That's why I came by. To talk to you."

"It might be better not to do it in the hallway."

I stared up at him, searching his face. Brady had lied to me. Multiple times. Maybe it was naïve, but I still couldn't believe he'd hurt me. He'd always seemed genuinely concerned for my welfare. "No. Inside is probably better."

I walked over the threshold again, grateful I'd been so careful during my search for the files. There was no visible evidence that I'd just been in here.

Brady gestured toward the sofa. I sat down on one side and he sat beside me, leaving a respectable distance between us.

"I need to explain about this morning," Brady said, reaching for my hand before he stopped himself. "Maria's like a barracuda. She would have been relentless. When I heard she had you in the interrogation room, I watched to see what she was doing. I saw enough that I decided to put a stop to it."

"I had it covered, Brady."

"I know, but we've had so many setbacks . . . I couldn't stand watching her tear you apart because of me. I'm sorry."

"Did you really befriend me to get close to me for an investigation?"

"No! Maggie, you know I didn't. When we met at the deli, I had no idea who you were. You know I was interested in you well before I found out about your involvement in any of this."

Call me crazy, but I believed that to be true.

He pushed out a breath and leaned forward, holding my gaze. "I've never made any secret of my interest in you, Maggie. There's no conspiracy there. I made up that story to get Maria to lay off you."

"And she's not going to figure out that you bluffed?" I asked, trying to control my irritation. There were so many contradictions in his story, so many lies and so much misdirection. I was tired of tiptoeing around the truth. I was tired of buying into his stories. I wanted answers. "I want the truth, Brady. Will you please just give me the damn truth?"

His mouth parted in surprise. "What are you talking about?"

"I talked to Belinda this morning. She told me about your confrontation with Roy, and her story and yours are completely different."

His forehead wrinkled. "What did she say?"

"I want your version again."

He sat up straighter. "I went to their house and—"

I lifted my hand. "Hold up right there. How did you know where they lived?"

"I'd already looked it up. The night you stayed with Belinda. I wanted to know in case you called and needed help."

Once again, Brady had information about me that bordered on stalkerish. Last week, he'd seemed aware of my every move, something he'd covered for by saying half the police department knew we were together. Maria Martinez had proved that was a lie.

He waited for a moment to make sure I was satisfied, and I gave him a slight nod to continue. "When I got there, I confirmed that Belinda did drive home; then I asked him what he meant by his statement. He pleaded ignorance and said he was just stirring up shit. When I asked him if he knew anything about the night you disappeared, he said he knew you'd gone out in the woods to screw your friend's boyfriend." His mouth twisted to the side. "Only, he wasn't so delicate."

"And where was Belinda?"

"She was there the whole time. She protested that Roy couldn't have known anything because he wasn't even at your momma's house that night."

I frowned. "Technically, he wasn't. He was next door at his best friend's house." But how would Brady know that if he were lying?

I felt sick to my stomach. "Did Belinda go inside at any point?"

"Yeah. At the end, but by then I was telling Roy to stay away from you."

I nodded. Why would Belinda lie? Had Roy told her something about that night—something she didn't want me to know? I wasn't sure my heart could handle that.

Time to address the other issues. "When you told Detective Martinez that you'd been trying to establish trust between us for a case, what were you referring to?"

He looked worried but didn't hesitate to answer. "She thinks you're in town because of your father. She's convinced he's biding his time until he comes back to collect money stolen from the failed Jackson Project. So I let her believe I had gotten close to you to determine your role in that."

Little did Brady know . . . "So is she working with Owen? Doesn't he believe the same thing?"

"No. She and Owen don't get along. She firmly believes Owen's uncle was dirty, so she doesn't trust him."

What a mess.

"Has Roy bothered you? Has he tried to contact you?"

"No." My mind was on his partner and what she'd hoped to achieve. Catch me finding that annuity? Pulling one million in gold out of a ceramic dog? "Why didn't you want me to cover for Owen?" While I didn't trust Brady at this point, it was better to stick with the devil you knew. If Brady waved any red flags bearing Owen's name, I would have to rethink my brand-new partnership. "The real reason. Are you two having issues?"

"I didn't want to put you in a difficult situation. There are too many lies and half-truths going around. I think it's time for the truth to come out."

"Okay." But he still wasn't being honest. I considered pressing him on how he had *really* tracked my movements last week, but I doubted he'd tell me. Better to let him think I was falling for his excuses. I considered using this opportunity to ask him about Emily's case, but if he had information he could share about the serial killer, I was pretty sure he'd tell me.

I stood. "I need to go check on Tilly."

He stood too, keeping his distance. "I really need to go out to that house, Maggie."

"I'm not sure what Tilly has planned for me," I lied. "Can I tell you when I have a free hour?"

"Yeah." But the disappointment in his voice was undeniable.

I started toward the door, which Brady opened for me.

"Do you trust Owen?" I asked.

He nodded. "I'd trust Owen with my life." He gave me a questioning look. "Why?"

"I'm trying to figure him out. Thanks." I headed out into the hall, and Brady walked me to the elevator.

"Do you still have that gun in your purse?"

I nodded. "Yeah."

"If you need to use it, shoot to kill, Maggie."

I tasted bile on my tongue. "I hope to God I never have to use it."

"Me too."

The elevator doors opened and I walked inside and turned around to face him, wondering how I could ever have believed he represented comfort and safety. Just one more reason to question my judgment, which wasn't good since I was putting all my eggs in a new basket named Owen Frasier.

I hoped I wouldn't regret it.

chapter fifteen

Owen was sitting behind the wheel of his car, leaned back, but he popped up straighter when he saw me approaching him. I opened the back door and slid in, barely getting the door closed before he started pulling out of the parking space.

"I take it from the fact that you took so long that you saw Brady."

"Yeah. Thanks for the heads-up. That could have been bad."

"How did you explain being there?"

"I had enough time to get out into the hall. I told him I'd shown up to talk to him about what he said to Martinez this morning."

"And he bought it?"

"There was nothing to buy. I really did want to talk to him about it. He corroborated what you said about Martinez thinking I'm back in town because of my father." I leaned forward and put my hand on the back of his seat. "Brady says he trusts you with his life."

Owen tensed. "Way to drive the knife of my betrayal deeper, Magnolia."

"Do you think he's guilty of something?" I asked.

"Not exactly, but I think he's gotten in deep with something he doesn't want to be involved in."

I considered it for a moment. "I think so too."

"So why do you want to work with me?" Owen asked.

"Because you're not emotionally entangled with me. And because I need someone I can trust implicitly." I leaned forward more, catching his eye. "But if you betray me, Owen Frasier, you will spend the rest of your short life regretting it."

He nodded with a grim look. "And if I find out you've made all this shit up to get even with Brady over some lover's spat, I'll personally run you out of town."

I gave him a grim smile. "We're a fine pair."

He glanced toward the digital clock, and I reflexively did the same. 1:25. "I need to find out what you know. Do you have time to go somewhere and talk?"

"I've got all the time in the world, but we need to go somewhere outside of Franklin. Can you make sure we're not being followed?" I wasn't taking any chances.

"Someone might be following you?"

It was time for me to let him know what he was getting into. "You know that serial killer we were talking about?"

Owen swerved his car into a strip mall parking lot, jerked the engine into park, and whipped around to face me. "What the fuck, Magnolia?"

"That's why I really left town ten years ago." My throat tightened, and I forced out the next words. "I witnessed Melanie Seaborn's murder."

Some of the color left Owen's face, and I could see he was struggling with whether or not to believe me, but he simply turned around and faced the front, put the car into drive, and took off.

I figured he was taking me back to my car, but he headed south—out of Franklin—frequently checking his mirrors. We sat in silence for ten minutes until he pulled into a diner.

He opened his car door. "I'm hungry. Let's get something to eat."

I followed him inside. He chose a table in the back, and it was late enough that the lunch crowd had already left. The nearest person was halfway across the restaurant.

He slid into a booth seat facing the door, and I sat across from him.

"We should be good here," he said. "Debbie closes the diner at two, so we'll have privacy."

"She won't kick us out? That's twenty minutes from now."

He shrugged. "She knows me. She closes for a few hours and starts her dinner prep. She lets me hang out in a booth and work on paperwork. She won't care."

A woman who looked to be in her forties came out and headed for our table. There was a huge smile on her face, and she did a double take when she noticed me.

"Brought a friend today, Owen?" She had a hopeful note in her voice.

He laughed. "Stop with the matchmaking, Debbie. This is business."

Her brow lifted. "You don't usually bring anyone but Brady here for business."

He grinned, but I could see it was slightly strained. "This case needed a little more privacy than usual."

She nodded. "Well, let me take your orders, and I'll let you get to it."

I grabbed a laminated two-sided menu. Owen, who'd clearly been here enough times to know the menu by heart, ordered a Reuben sandwich, fries, and tea, and I ordered a salad and water.

Debbie headed to the kitchen, and Owen took a deep breath and then said, "How did you happen to witness Melanie Seaborn's murder?"

"You decided to jump right in, huh?"

"Sounds like we have a lot to talk about," he said. "Might as well get to the heart of it."

"Shouldn't we wait for Debbie to bring our drinks first?" I asked. Once I started this story, I wasn't stopping.

"Good idea," he grudgingly said.

The few seconds of silence that followed were so tense, I found myself breaking it. "How long have you been coming here?"

"We're not here to make small talk, Magnolia."

"I'm about to tell you some very difficult things, Owen. A little bit of small talk would help put me at ease."

Guilt flooded his eyes. "You're right. I'm sorry. It's easier to dislike you."

190

His words hurt more than I'd expected. "Why?" I asked. "Why do you need to hate me?"

"Because of your father."

I didn't respond. I understood why he would feel that way, but it renewed my reservations.

"I was wrong, Magnolia," he said softly. "Your father left when you were barely a teenager. You had no say in what he did, and unlike Maria, I don't believe you're helping him now."

"So you believe he's alive too?" I asked.

"I know you don't believe it. Brady told me you were on a mission to prove he'd been murdered."

"I don't believe that anymore."

His eyes flew wide. "Have you been in contact with your father?"

"Not in the way you think."

His guard was back. "Does Brady know?"

I shook my head. "No. I only just found out my daddy's still alive, and Brady's been giving mixed signals lately. I know he wouldn't intentionally hurt me, but I don't totally trust him."

The hangdog look on Owen's face told me that he felt much the same way. "I'm going to need details."

Debbie walked out with our drinks, and I clammed up. She set them down and said, "I won't be back out for another ten minutes, so holler if you need something before then."

"Thanks, Debbie," Owen said.

When she was back in the kitchen, I leaned closer. "I'm about to give you a ton of information. We still haven't worked out what you're going to give me in return."

"What do you want?"

I took a moment to think it through. "I think I need protection."

He nodded slowly. "Does Brady know about your connection to the serial killer?"

"He was the one who figured it out."

"What does that mean?"

"The killer gave me a scar to remind me to never talk about that night."

He looked surprised and took a moment before he asked, "Why do you think the killer's after you now?"

"He keeps sending me texts."

"Holy shit." He sat back and rubbed his hand over the top of his head. "And Brady knows?"

"Yeah, but he says he won't officially make a report about it because he's afraid of dirty cops."

Pain flickered in Owen's eyes. "He didn't tell me."

I almost said I was sorry, but the sentiment would seem empty coming from me.

He pushed out a huge sigh and got out a small notebook and pen. "Maybe you should start from the beginning."

I nodded. He was right. But it was still hard to open up to him.

After several long seconds, he said, "Magnolia. I'm sorry we got off on the wrong foot, and I'm sure my past animosity is making it difficult for you to trust me with your traumatic experience, but I promise I'm on board now. I'll do what I can to help you."

"What about Brady?"

"If you're really being harassed by a serial killer, he should have reported it. Or, at the very least, told me. The question is why didn't he?"

"I was hoping you would know. There have been a lot of red flags with him," I said. "The burner phone. Knowing where I am all the time. The fact that he hasn't told anyone about what I witnessed. The FBI not sending an agent after all."

Owen held up a hand. "Whoa! What's this about the FBI?"

"Brady said he'd contacted them about the serial killer. And last week, he told me they were sending an agent. But when I asked him about the other day, he told me they didn't have the manpower to send someone."

He shook his head with a worried look. "I don't know anything about an FBI agent."

"So he lied?" I asked.

"Not necessarily." But there wasn't much conviction behind his words. "Maybe we should start with the files first; then we can ease our way into your story," he said in a soft voice. "By the time we finish, maybe I'll have proved that I'm not a total asshole and you'll trust me more."

I gave him a grudging grin. "That's a big maybe."

He laughed. "No wonder Brady likes you. He's used to getting what he wants and never having to work for it. I can see you keep him on his toes."

"Do you think he's bad?" I asked quietly, my stomach churning at the thought.

"No, Magnolia. Like I said, I think he's caught up in something that's spiraled out of control, and he's in too deep to ask for help."

I took a moment to absorb that. It rang true to me, though I had no idea what it might mean. "I want to tell you everything, Owen," I finally said, "but I need to tell Owen Frasier, the nephew of Gordon Frasier, not Detective Frasier. Can you separate the two?"

"In the interest of transparency, I feel that I should tell you that I might not be Detective Frasier much longer, so it might be a moot point."

"I need your assurance anyway."

He studied me for a moment before meeting my eyes and holding my gaze. "Magnolia Steele, everything you tell me is friend to friend." Then he extended his hand across the table.

I hesitated. How many friends had I acquired since I'd come back to Franklin only to find out that they had secret agendas of their own? At least I knew exactly where Owen stood. I grabbed his hand and shook. "Friend to friend."

He dropped my hand and offered me a genuine smile. "Let's get to work."

I pulled the envelope out of my bag, but after I placed it on the table, I kept my palms on it, holding it down. I wasn't ready . . . not yet. "I haven't seen much of this. The night you brought Melanie's and Amy's files over, Brady stayed up to look at all of these. When I woke up a few hours later, he was still looking at them, at well past three in the morning. I asked if he'd been up all night, but he told me he'd gone to bed and gotten up to look at them again. I have no idea if he was being truthful or not. I saw a few photos on the table and something about one of them looked familiar. It didn't immediately strike me that they were all dead, more that they were naked. At first, I thought he was looking at porn. But it all happened so quickly. He gathered them together and told me to go to bed, saying he'd be in there soon. But I kept thinking about those files, and after he was asleep, I got up and found the envelope in his hall closet. I took it to his guest bath and dumped it out and started to look it over, but it all hit so close to home . . . and then I saw Melanie's photos, and I knew it was her."

"And you said they were connected by a mark?" Owen asked.

"Yeah, a backward C with a line through it."

"Like a brand?" Owen asked with a frown.

Why had I never thought of that? Anxiety swamped my head. "Exactly like a brand."

"If Brady knew about your connection to the case, it helps explain why he latched on to you so fast," Owen said. "He seemed so protective so quickly."

But he hadn't known until last week, and he'd been protective weeks before that. Literally since the first time we'd met.

Owen gave me a sad smile, putting his hand lightly over mine. "We'll face this together, Magnolia."

"That's exactly what Brady told me."

That gave him pause. "In all fairness, I'm not taking this to the department either, so maybe you'd feel better sticking with him."

I shook my head. "No. I already told you that I like that you aren't emotionally involved with me. I need someone more clearheaded."

"I'll try my best to be that person," he said, holding my gaze.

I lifted my hands and let him tug the envelope across the table. I rested my hands in my lap and glanced at the single other guest in the diner, the man halfway across the restaurant from us, as Owen dumped the contents on the table.

"This is all kind of a mess," Owen said.

"What does that mean?" I asked, turning back to face him.

"Brady's usually neat and organized. This is unlike him."

My mouth dropped open as I saw the haphazard way the papers and photographs were stacked. "He never looked at it again." I lifted my gaze to Owen's. "I was looking at the photos in the bathroom, and Brady somehow figured out what I was doing. He unlocked the door and found me. I had gotten some of the papers and photos stuffed back inside the envelope, but he cleaned up the rest. If it's all unorganized, that must mean he never looked at it again, right?"

His mouth twisted to the side. "Yeah."

A shiver ran down my spine. "It's like he wanted me to see them."

He didn't protest at first, but after a few seconds he said, "Now, that's a stretch."

"Brady had seen my scar the night before. He reacted to it but didn't say anything. He was very curious about where I'd gotten it. Maybe he couldn't *tell* me there was a connection between me and the serial killer, so he planted those files so I'd make the connection."

"Again, it's a stretch," Owen said. "He could have pressed you more. I've seen the man in an interrogation room. He has a way of winning people over and getting them to share things no one else would share."

The blood rushed from my head.

Owen cringed. "I'm not suggesting what he told Maria was true—that he befriended you to get information."

It was impossible for me to consider that possibility right now, so I just shook my head. "I must be mostly immune to whatever charm Brady possesses. I had way too many secrets for his liking, even if he told me he'd be patient about getting answers. He saw my scar, and I refused to tell him about it. Of course, Emily was killed hours later, and she supposedly had the mark too."

Owen's eyes narrowed. "You're not suggesting that Brady's the killer, are you?"

"No. There's no way he could have gotten out of bed, left to kill Emily, then come back in time to get 'woken up' by the call to go to her murder scene. And he seemed freaked out the next morning—like he'd just made the connection. He came to find me at Ava Milton's because he was terrified the killer had found me. There's no faking that kind of worry and fear."

"Good, because secrets or no, he's not capable of doing something like that." He glanced down at the pile and picked up one of the photos. Not Melanie. I'd tried to avoid looking at them last week, but there was no ignoring them now. Tears clogged my throat.

"Good God," Owen muttered as he looked at another photo. "I'm guessing the wounds weren't postmortem."

"I read a few of the reports," I said in a broken voice. "They all had the same cause of death: blood loss. I think he slashed Melanie Seaborn's throat, but only after he cut her many, many times first. He was punishing her for something—something she said she didn't do, but I didn't hear what it was. At the end, she kept saying she was sorry." I paused. "But I had a concussion, so a lot of what I remember is blurry and fuzzy."

Owen's gaze lifted to mine. "You were in the same room? You saw the entire thing?"

"I have no idea how long she was there. I was running from my best friend's boyfriend. I'd caught him cheating and taken an incriminating photo, and he chased me deep into the woods. It was raining and I was drenched, and I found a deserted house and went inside. I'd lost Blake by then. I thought I heard a woman scream under the floor, but it was storming, so I wasn't sure. Then a man came out of the basement and dragged me down the stairs. The woman, Melanie—" I choked on her name, "—was tied to the rafters with her arms over her head. She was only wearing her bra and panties, and her body was already covered in slashes."

Owen looked grim.

I took a second to regain control before continuing. "He tied me to a metal pole, and then he realized who I was. He called me by name."

198

"He called you *Magnolia*?"

I nodded. "And my last name too. He slammed my head into the pole, and I lost consciousness for a while, but I could hear the woman screaming and saying she hadn't done it. The man came back to me and threw my dress up. He cut that mark into my thigh and told me that if I said anything to anyone, he would kill my mother and brother and make me watch before he killed me too. Then he killed the—Melanie. Her screaming suddenly stopped."

"How did you get away?"

"I have no idea. I passed out, and when I came to, I was at the edge of the woods behind my mother's house."

"He let you go," Owen said in amazement. "Why?"

I shook my head. "I don't know, but he told me if I was a good girl, he'd let me go."

"Did he force himself on you? Or coerce you into doing something?"

I studied him for a moment. "Are you asking if he raped me? No. It felt like he was letting me go for personal reasons."

"Then you might be right about the connection to your father."

"Yesterday, I asked Brady how Melanie had been taken. He said she was a nurse and hadn't shown up for her shift the next day."

Owen looked surprised. "A nurse. Do you think she was connected to your father somehow?"

"I have no idea. Two weeks ago, if you'd told me that my father had been unfaithful to my mother, I would have called you a bald-faced liar. Now I know that he likely had *at least* three affairs. Maybe she was another one of his liaisons."

"You said you think he's alive?" Owen asked.

"I'm pretty sure I saw him at Momma's funeral. In the trees at the edge of the cemetery. I waited until everyone left and shouted at him to leave me alone."

Owen looked shell-shocked.

"This is where I need to make sure you're really keeping this to yourself," I said. "There's a risk of incriminating myself."

He turned even more serious. "You have my word."

"I'm 99.9% sure that Daddy killed Rowena Rogers."

chapter
sixteen

His mouth sagged; then he recovered enough to ask, "Did you see him?"

"No, but he did it to save me, so I'm sure it was him."

"In the basement of Savannah House?" he asked.

"Yeah. Rowena found out that I had Daddy's gold. She sent her goon to tell me to deliver it to her last Saturday night."

"Gold?"

"It's what Geraldo Lopez was looking for in my apartment," I said, suddenly feeling exhausted. It felt good to tell someone else who might help me, but it was also emotionally draining. "I'd found it days before, hidden in a ceramic dog in my mother's garage. Momma didn't even know it was there. My brother had moved the entire contents of Christopher Merritt's Nashville apartment into her garage, telling her the items belonged to a friend who'd been transferred to Hong Kong."

"*What?*"

"I told you I know things." It was a smug statement, really, but I didn't sound smug. If anything, I sounded defeated. So many secrets. So many destroyed lives.

"Who told you this? Your mother? Your brother?"

"My sister-in-law. Belinda. My brother won't tell me anything." I shook my head. "Except at the will reading, he was upset I got Momma's house, more upset than he should have been." Then I told him what Roy had said, or rather what he'd implied, and Belinda and Brady's differing accounts of the confrontation that had come later.

He was quiet for a moment. "How well do you trust Belinda?"

"Before last week, implicitly. Now . . . I don't know." I told Owen about Belinda's parents, and how she blamed herself for Roy's abuse because she'd encouraged him to work for Bill. I considered not telling him the rest, but we'd made an agreement, and I planned to see it through, so I went on to tell him that she'd held me at gunpoint to draw my father out of hiding.

"And you *don't know* if you trust her?" he asked as though I were insane to consider it.

I supposed he had a point, and yet Belinda was more than the mistakes she'd made. "She's a good person who made a few errors in judgment."

"Errors in judgment that could get her arrested."

I gasped. "You swore that—"

"Calm down, Magnolia," he said with a frown. "I'm not telling anyone, but you need to think about what you just said. If your sister-in-law risked your life, do you really want to trust her?"

"She had her reasons."

"And she could still have them. You did say that she stayed with your brother last night."

He was right.

"And the musician?"

"Colt?"

"Yeah. Him. How's he involved in this?"

"He's not up for discussion, Owen."

He looked irritated, but his expression softened. "Sorry. I realize it isn't easy to share these things."

Which made me realize that I was spilling out my life story and he'd hardly shared anything. "Why are you so certain your uncle is innocent?"

"I thought you believed Rowena Rogers."

"Yes, but what made *you* decide he was innocent?"

His shoulders rose as he took a big inhale. "I saw how the accusations ripped him apart. How he let it define him, even after he quit the force. He's an old man now and still bitter. I just never thought someone who was guilty could let his department's betrayal rip him apart like that."

"So you became a cop to avenge him?"

"No, more like to show them they could damage one Frasier, but they couldn't destroy us all." A wry grin twisted his mouth. "Which is funny since I'm about to lose my job."

"Only, you don't seem devastated by the thought."

He chuckled. "Let's say that I've been bucking the status quo for years now. I would have been kicked out ages ago if not for Brady. He's the sensible one." His smile fell. "If you have to choose between Brady and Belinda, Brady's the safer bet."

I wasn't so sure about that, but I figured it didn't matter. I wasn't counting on either one of them right now.

Debbie emerged from the kitchen carrying two plates, and I gestured to the photos. "Debbie's coming out."

Owen picked up the pile, flipped it over, and began to stuff the papers back in the envelope.

"Y'all doin' okay?" she asked as she set our plates down. "Let me get you both some refills; then I'll let you get back to it."

"So why are you so interested in clearing your uncle's name?" I asked after she left. "You're about to hang up your badge."

"It was never about me. It was more about helping Uncle Gordon get his pride back. I figured that I could help him get closure by proving that your dad was shady." Then, as if realizing what he'd just said, he grimaced and added, "Sorry."

"That's one of the reasons I'm here with you now, Owen."

Debbie returned with a pitcher of tea and water and refilled our glasses before heading back into the kitchen.

"You didn't go to the police after you woke up in the woods?" Owen asked as he set the envelope down at the end of the table.

"No, I completely blocked out what happened in that house."

His brow furrowed in a thoughtful look. "How did you explain the cut on your leg or your concussion? To your mother or yourself?"

"I didn't. I was covered in mud from the rain, which helped disguise the blood on my clothes, and Momma thought I had a hangover, which explained my vomiting the next morning. But I knew I had to leave Franklin, so I bought a plane ticket to New York City. Every time I even thought about coming home, I had a panic attack." He started to say something, so I added, "The only reason I came back a month ago was because I was humiliated, homeless, and broke. Otherwise, I wouldn't be here at all."

"But you're still here. You could have gone back."

"I found out my mother was dying. And then I decided to dig into my father's disappearance. You know I never believed the story about how he'd run off, so I was dead set to prove it wasn't true. Now . . ." I paused. "Now, I'm trying to figure out his connection to the serial killer, because I know there is one. Every time something big happened with my father, the serial killer struck."

Owen glanced down at the envelope.

"The file showed that there were murders twenty, seventeen, fourteen, and ten years ago. And now these recent ones," I said. "Twenty years ago was the Jackson Project, and Daddy being accused of murdering Tripp Tucker's fiancée was seventeen years ago." I paused. "If you've investigated him, you knew about that one."

He nodded.

"That coincided with his lawsuit with Tripp. Then fourteen years ago, he ran off."

"And ten years ago?" Owen asked.

"I think Daddy came back for my high school graduation."

"Holy shit," Owen said. "What if your father is the killer?"

"My father is a lot of things, but I know he loves me. He saved me in the Savannah House basement. Besides, I would have recognized his voice."

"We need to go out to that house," Owen said. "The one where you witnessed the murder."

"Brady's been trying to get me to go out there since last week, and I keep putting him off."

"Why?"

"Because it scares the crap out of me. When my memories of that night returned, I went out there to see if it was real. It's still there—and still abandoned—but I couldn't bring myself to go down into the basement. But I also didn't go with him because I don't trust him. Still, I'm not sure how I feel about going out there with you and leaving him hanging."

"Then go with him."

I narrowed my eyes.

"I'm serious. We've both established that Brady's not the kind of guy who would hurt you. That way he'll see it, and you'll get him off your back."

"You don't want to see it?" I asked.

"I'll see it. You can see it first with him."

"I'm only going one more time, and that's one time too many."

"Fair enough."

I toyed with the lettuce on my plate, suddenly losing my appetite.

"You said the killer has been texting you."

"Ever since I got back into town." I told him about all of the texts, including the warning that had specifically targeted Belinda. Plus the magnolia blossoms, the necklace Brady had given me, and the dead cat he'd left on Momma's porch. It had looked like my childhood cat.

"So the killer has some connection to your past?" Owen said. "Maybe it was a professional relationship that was also personal. Someone who visited your father at home."

"Bill James came over," I said. "And Momma said that Tripp Tucker used to come over for dinner. Apparently several of his other young, up-and-coming country music clients used to come over too. I don't remember any of them, but I was also pretty young."

"Did your father ever host dinners for other clients? Your mother was a caterer. It stands to reason he would invite people over to impress them with your mother's cooking."

"I don't remember, but I can ask Tilly, Momma's best friend. There's something else too." I held his gaze. "Daddy and Bill James had another partner in the beginning. Eric Duncan. Tilly told me that Daddy and Bill kicked him out of the business because he tried to rape Momma."

"Did they file charges?"

"No. They decided to keep it quiet." I paused. "And there's one more thing—Eric's son, Clint Duncan, hired

Daddy as his financial consultant instead of using his own father. He was an up-and-coming country star, and Daddy handled his money. Tilly said he was one of the guys who came over too."

Owen looked interested in that one. "So Eric could have been pissed at your father for stealing his son as well as his career. I'll look into it." He took a bite of his sandwich. "I also need to pull the names of the victims to try and figure out the connection—if there is one—to your father."

I shuddered. "I don't want to look at those photos again."

"I'll take care of that part, but after I look at them, we need to return them."

I groaned. "Not it."

"Brady and I aren't getting along right now."

"Neither are we, yet I sucked it up and got the file. You get to replace it. I found them in the bottom of his underwear drawer."

He didn't look happy, but he didn't protest.

"So now what?" I asked.

"After we finish, I'll take you back to your car and go through the files. You'll go home, lock your doors, and hide."

"That's it?"

"What did you think you were gonna do? Go interview people with me? Your part is done now."

"So I'm just supposed to sit around and *wait*?"

He gave me a look that suggested that was exactly what he expected me to do.

"I need to know what you're doing, Owen. You're going to look at the files, but why don't I investigate the women too?"

He gave me a wary look. "What are you suggesting?"

"Look, it only makes sense for both of us to work on this. You can do the police detective stuff—"

"I'm on leave, Magnolia. I won't be doing *police detective stuff*. Not officially."

"Fine. If you want to get technical," I said, "then you do the dangerous stuff, and I'll do the desk stuff like internet searches."

He considered my suggestion for several seconds. "That's actually a good idea."

I gave him a smug look. "I have a few."

"I'll take another look at the files and pull some names and other information for you."

We were silent for a few moments while he ate his sandwich. I picked at my salad, my stomach a mess with nerves.

Owen pulled out the envelope. "If you're done eating, I'll pull that information from the files."

I set my napkin on the table. "Yeah. Go ahead. I think I'll go to the restroom while you have the photos out."

I had no desire to ever see them again. I slipped out of my seat and headed to the hall behind Owen.

I took my time in the restroom, rolling my eyes when I checked out my appearance in the mirror. I looked rough, but I wasn't trying to impress anyone. I tried to take enough time to ensure Owen would be finished by the time I got back to the table.

When I walked out of the restroom, he heard the door squeak and turned around to glance at me. "Ready to go?"

"You're finished?"

He stood and laid some cash on the table, then handed me a page from his notebook. "Their names and information."

"Thanks." I tucked into my purse and pulled out my wallet. "How much was my part of the bill?"

He waved me off. "Don't worry about it. If you were a real informant, I'd pay you somehow. I got off easy with lunch."

"Well . . . thanks."

We headed out to his car, and I got in the backseat again. We were silent for most of the ride, but when Owen parked in the lot behind the catering business, he turned back to look at me. "I just can't help thinking about the reason your father's back. I think there's something to the theory of the serial killer flushing him out, but why? Do you think he's really back to collect an annuity?"

I stared at him, knowing something was off, but I couldn't quite pick up on what. "Uh . . . I don't know. He hasn't tried to contact me, so I know that's not his reason."

He nodded. "Thanks for your help, Magnolia. Maybe you should get a burner phone too. Make it less likely anyone can tie us together."

"Yeah," I said absently. "Good idea. Thanks again, Owen."

"Thank you. You've given me hope for the first time in years."

I got out and watched him drive away, wishing I wasn't feeling the exact opposite.

chapter
seventeen

Part of me wanted to drive straight to the airport and fly as far away from Franklin as I could get, farther than New York this time. Maybe I'd go to Vietnam, like Colt and I had discussed, and lie on those beautiful beaches, but I quickly dismissed the idea. It wouldn't be the same without him . . . and he was still harboring secrets. Instead, I drove to Momma's house and locked myself inside. Too bad it didn't feel as safe as it had a month ago.

Then again, Tilly was right—I had secrets of my own. What if whatever had been in that safety deposit box had something to do with the woman Colt had loved and lost? The one who'd turned away from him after my father had arranged for his arrest. But how would Momma have found it?

I set up my laptop and started searching for the names on the list that contained limited information about each murder. I started with the case from twenty years ago—Stella Hargrove. The top reports were that her body had been found in Hendersonville, Tennessee. She'd been twenty-five, single, and a receptionist at a Baptist church. They'd suspected the church janitor for a short bit before ruling him out. Stella hadn't had a boyfriend or enemies. The police had been stumped.

The next case was Margarie Turnwell, who'd been killed fourteen years ago. She was from Elizabethtown, Kentucky, and her body had been found a week after her disappearance. The news reports said her boyfriend had been a suspect, but he had an alibi and the police couldn't arrest him. However, the family had been very vocal about their suspicions of him. She was an elementary school teacher, but she'd recently lost her job. The article didn't say why, but it did have a quote from the boyfriend saying she'd gone to Nashville the week before to visit a friend and suggested something had happened there. The police said they had followed up his lead and found nothing.

The next case was Melanie, and I wondered why I'd never looked her up before. Because pretending she'd never really existed made it more tolerable somehow? Brady was right. She'd been a nurse at Vanderbilt, and her body had been found in Clarksville. News reports said the police had concentrated their efforts on finding a drifter who had supposedly been seen hanging around the hospital, but they'd never found him. Just like Tripp's Tucker's fiancée . . .

I wondered why no one had made a connection between the cases before given the distinctiveness of the cut, but the two close to Nashville had been a decade apart, and the one in Kentucky was far enough away to escape notice.

There was only one more name on the list—Amy's. I didn't bother looking up her information. I'd been searching the internet about her death ever since Brady had confirmed she was one of the serial killer's victims.

Except something was missing. When I'd first looked at the files in Brady's bathroom, I'd seen a report for the murder seventeen years ago. Why wasn't there any mention of it on Owen's list?

Had Tiffany Kessler been the second serial killer victim after all? She and Amy and, to some degree, Emily had all been connected to people who'd been part of the Jackson Project.

I sent Owen a text to his burner, asking if there had been a file for seventeen years ago, but when he didn't respond right away, I did a search for Tiffany Kessler. News reports about her murder popped up. The one detail I remembered from the report was that the body had been found outside of Jackson. Sure enough, Tiffany's body had been found in Jackson, Tennessee, which was about one hundred and thirty miles west of Nashville.

Tiffany had been found outside of Jackson. The Jackson Project. The blood left my head, and I took a moment to let my equilibrium settle.

That couldn't be a coincidence. I needed to talk to Tripp Tucker.

I searched his name in connection with Tiffany's, and reports popped up from the time of the murder, saying that the country star was grieving the loss of his fiancée. He'd offered a reward to anyone who came forward with information about her abduction and murder. There were other reports from the Jackson, Tennessee, police department saying they were working with the Brentwood Police—where Tiffany had lived with Tripp—and while they had a few persons of interest, they weren't releasing any names. My father's name wasn't in any of the reports, but with people like Ava around, his name had surely made its way into the rumor mill.

The drifter both Tilly and Ava had mentioned had been arrested two years later, after he was caught trying to pawn her engagement ring at a store in Nashville. His trial had lasted only a few days, and he'd been sentenced to life in prison with no parole.

I doubted that the internet would give me Tripp Tucker's contact information, but I searched anyway, surprised to see that he was the guest of honor at a dinner in Brentwood tonight—a dinner I knew Southern Belles was catering.

It was time for me to dust off my waitress uniform. I was going back to work.

Tilly worked up a protest when I walked in through the back door of the catering kitchen wearing my serving uniform. Her mouth dropped open and she put a hand on her hip. "I thought you were taking the night off, so why on God's green earth are you dressed up like a server?"

"If I stay in her house for five more minutes, I'm gonna go batshit crazy," I said, walking past everyone to see what they were up to. It looked like they were about to load the vans.

"That still doesn't explain the uniform."

"We all know that's where my true strength lies—in serving. I'll still help out in the back, but I want to help serve too."

Colt hadn't been in the room, but he came walking down the stairs and did a double take when he saw me. "I thought you were taking the night off."

"Changed my mind."

He took a few steps toward me and placed his hand on my uninjured arm. "Are you sure you're feeling up to it?"

"Yeah," I said softly, staring up into his worried eyes. "I need to keep busy."

"Mags, about this afternoon . . ." He stopped and swallowed, his Adam's apple bobbing several times. When he spoke, his voice broke. "I want to tell you, but I can't."

"I know," I said. I'd thought about it off and on all day. If the contents of the safety deposit box had something to do with the woman he'd lost—the only reason I could think of for him to stay silent—I understood his need to protect her. Just like I'd protected him from Owen. I still didn't one hundred percent trust him, but I understood.

He gave me a small nod. "I don't want to lose you, Maggie. After I see this through, I'll tell you everything."

He started to pull away, but I grabbed his wrist. "After you see what through? You're not talking about this mess with Daddy, are you?"

I was sure he wasn't going to answer, so I was surprised by the slight shake of his head. "No."

"I think I understand," I said, "but we won't work if you have some huge secret hanging over you."

Defeat filled his eyes, and he started to pull away, but I dug my fingers deeper into his flesh.

"But I'm willing to wait. I'm willing to give you some time to see it through, but I won't wait forever, Colt."

"That's more than I can ask for."

"Until then, we need to just be friends. We make pretty good friends, don't you think?"

A sad smile lifted his lips. "Yeah. We do. Now let's get to work."

It was a good thing I'd decided to come in—a couple people who were supposed to help from the culinary school had come down with food poisoning after making a bad batch of oysters earlier that morning, so now Tilly was short-staffed.

We got everything loaded into the vans, and Tilly filled me in on the menu for the night—a three-course meal consisting of a house salad, roasted rosemary potatoes and chicken with asparagus, and cheesecake for dessert.

"Are you sure you're up to serving tonight?" Tilly asked with a worried glance.

"Are you worried I'll stir up trouble?" I asked with a sly grin.

"Well . . ." She shook her head, and I already knew she'd cave. "Your momma would be having a fit right about now."

I laughed. "All the more reason to do it, don't you think?"

"That's my girl."

We didn't have to drive far. The dinner was being held in one of the banquet rooms at The Factory. Our task was to make the industrial-looking space cozier and more inviting. Once we reached the location, we quickly got the tables set up and decorated with cut flower centerpieces and candles. Then Colt and another part-time employee began setting up bars at opposite ends of the hall.

A half hour before the event, I told Tilly I was going to light candles. Instead, I made a beeline for Colt.

"I'm surprised you didn't mention the new alarm system," he said.

"What alarm system?"

"Me and a buddy of mine set up an alarm system at your momma's house this afternoon." He gave me a sheepish look. "I know I should have asked permission first, but you were upset and needed space . . ."

"I was pretty preoccupied," I managed to choke out. "I guess I didn't notice. Wouldn't I have set off the alarm?"

"No. It's not turned on yet." He pulled out his phone and opened an app. "Everything's digital. There are sensors on the doors and motion detectors inside. Here. I'll turn it on now." He pushed some numbers on the key pad and showed me the screen. "When we finish,

I'll download the app onto your phone and show you how to work it."

I swallowed the lump in my throat, nearly speechless. "Thank you."

A warm expression filled his eyes. "Gotta keep you safe, Mags."

"Tell me what you know about Tripp Tucker," I said.

He glanced up in surprise. "Tripp Tucker?" A knowing look washed over his face. "He's gonna be here tonight, isn't he? That's why you really came."

"What do you know about him?"

Colt pulled two bottles of vodka from a box. "I know he had a hit album, or more accurately three hits on his album, and his second album sold like dog shit. He didn't take it well and blamed your father when he lost his money."

"Did you know about his fiancée's murder before Tilly mentioned it?"

"I'd heard rumors, but I don't know the details. I know Tilly said she was stabbed."

"Colt. I think she was killed by the serial killer."

"I considered it too, but what about the arrest?"

"What if he was falsely accused? You of all people know that's possible. They caught a man who tried to hawk her engagement ring at a Nashville pawn shop two years after she died. It doesn't mean he killed her."

A grim look washed over his face.

"I think she was victim number two," I pressed. "Seventeen years ago. Found outside of Jackson, Tennessee." I moved closer. "*Jackson*."

His eyes flew wide. "The Jackson Project." He glanced toward the still-empty guests-of-honor table. "What do you hope to do tonight?"

"Talk to Tripp. Find out what he knows."

He started to protest, then stopped. "For God's sake, Maggie, be careful."

"Tripp didn't kill her."

"You don't know that. He hated your father for losing his money and for sleeping with his fiancée. What if you're waking a sleeping bear?"

I leaned closer and whispered, "If Tripp Tucker is the serial killer, then the sleeping bear has already been awakened. Besides, we're in a public place. He won't do anything here."

"No. But he might do something horrible later." He turned even more serious. "This isn't a game, Maggie. When was the last time you heard from the killer?"

"Monday. Just the necklace and flower. No texts. Nothing since."

He studied me for a moment. "Just be careful. *Please.*"

I nodded, then flicked the lighter in my hand. "I told Tilly I was lighting candles. I need to get to work."

Tonight's dinner was being held to honor people who'd helped a popular children's music charity over the previous year. Tripp wasn't the only one who was being honored, which would hopefully make it easier to talk to him.

Once all the candles had been lit, I headed to the kitchen and helped Tilly and the others plate the salads.

I convinced one of the servers to let me serve the section that included the table for the guests of honor, and she was more than willing to comply since one of the honorees was notoriously cranky.

Tonight, Melisandre Bowers, the widow of country music legend Rock Bowers, was in top form. "The lettuce in this salad is wilted," she said as I set the bowl in front of her.

The lettuce wasn't wilted—Tilly would rather die than serve salad with wilted lettuce. But I plastered on a smile and said in the sweetest voice I could muster, "Let me take care of that, Ms. Bowers."

Since I'd given her the last bowl, I made my way to the kitchen to refill my tray. Before heading back to her table, I fluffed up her salad, leaving it in the same bowl, and added it to the tray. I made sure she got the just-fluffed salad.

She gave me a withering glare. "You should have served this salad to begin with."

It was a struggle to keep a straight face. Tripp Tucker was sitting several place settings to her right. He had been cautiously eyeing me since I'd first approached the table with drinks. I suspected he knew who I was, given that I'd been in the media, and he probably kept on top of those things. I was certain his apprehension was over whether I recognized *him*, and if so, he might be worried I wouldn't be too friendly after his major public falling-out with my father.

But he caught my eyes and grinned as I handed him a salad from my tray.

I grinned back and made a point of dramatically rolling my eyes. I needed to get into his good graces, and she *had* been ridiculous.

He chuckled as I moved on.

Melisandre was just as cantankerous when I served her the second course, claiming her chicken was cold even though it was steaming on her plate.

I served everyone else at the table, then took her plate back to the serving kitchen and stuck her chicken in the microwave.

Tilly gasped in horror. "What on earth are you doin', child?"

"Ms. Bowers claims her chicken is cold. I'm heating it up."

"Her chicken is cold?"

"No, Tilly," I said, offering her an apologetic smile. "Ms. Bowers is just a bitch."

"Magnolia!"

The microwave dinged, and I grabbed the chicken breast with a pair of tongs and set it back on the plate. "Don't worry, Tilly. I won't embarrass you or the Belles."

"That's not what I'm worried about," she muttered.

"I didn't overheat it. I promise."

She just shook her head and turned back to her plating job.

As I expected, Melisandre accepted the new chicken, and Tripp flashed me another grin.

After I served everyone in my section, I headed over to Colt and stood next to him, watching the table of honorees.

222

"How's it going over there?" Colt asked.

"I'd love to wring Melisandre Bowers's neck," I said with a sweet smile.

Colt laughed, the sound warming something inside me. For some reason, an image popped into my head: me and Colt sitting on a sofa watching TV—nothing exciting—his arm curled around me and the two of us laughing. The peace and happiness I felt at the thought scared me. I'd never thought of a future with anyone else before, not a real one. Sure, I'd thought about what life would be like with Brady, but it had never seemed real. It had seemed like an escape. A fairy tale with a guaranteed happily ever after. This *felt* real, but what were the chances that Colt and I would actually get to have that happy future? Slim to none.

His smile fell. "Maggie? You okay?"

I shook off my moodiness. It wouldn't help anything. "I'm fine. It's been a long day."

"Did you have to go back to the police station?"

"No." I scowled, watching the honoree table. Melisandre was frowning. "But I wouldn't be surprised to find Detective Martinez around the corner waiting for me, which might be a nice reprieve at the moment."

I headed to the table and smiled down at the grumpy woman. "Can I do something for you, Ms. Bowers?"

"The asparagus is limp."

The asparagus was stiff as a board on her plate. "I'm so sorry to hear that," I said in a grim voice. "Would you like me to get you a new serving?"

"No. Just take the plate away if you're going to serve cafeteria-quality food." Then she waved her hand in a flourish.

I picked up the plate as Tripp turned his attention to the surly woman. "You must dine with kings and queens in extravagance, Melisandre," he said in a teasing tone. "I found the chicken to be tender and juicy and the asparagus cooked perfectly." He looked up at me. "Please give my compliments to the chef."

I nodded, thankful for his intervention. "Tilly will be pleased to hear it."

The other guests murmured about how much they were enjoying their meals, but Melisandre shot daggers at me. I hadn't been the one to object to her assessment, but I'd made an enemy nonetheless. I couldn't bring myself to care.

After I cleared all the plates away, I served the strawberry cheesecake, and Melisandre surprised me by not complaining. Then again, my mother's recipe for cheesecake left little room for complaint. A memory popped into my head of the first time my momma had tried to teach me how to make this cheesecake—and failed miserably. A burning lump filled my throat.

I still had my tray, although now empty, but I headed down the hallway toward the bathrooms instead of the serving kitchen. After I rested the tray against the wall, I began to pace. Would it always be like this? Would the thought of her always bring me to tears?

"Are you okay?" a man asked.

I spun around to face him, expecting to see Colt even though it didn't sound like him. Instead, I found myself face to face with Tripp Tucker.

I wiped the tears from my cheeks. "Uh . . . yeah. I'm fine."

"Don't take it personally," he said, moving a couple of steps closer. "I've known Melisandre for fifteen years now, and she's never nice to anyone."

I forced a smile. "I don't care about that old goat." Realizing what I'd said, I covered my mouth with my fingertips. "Crap. I shouldn't have said that."

He laughed. "My philosophy is to always tell the truth."

I nodded. "And do you follow your own advice?"

"For the most part."

"And how many women have you pissed off that way?"

He rubbed his cheek as he fought a grin. "We won't talk about that part." The amusement left his eyes. "Seriously, Melisandre's been miserable for years. Complaining is her only happiness in life, so you've given her plenty of joy tonight. It seems wrong for you to be crying."

I shook my head and rolled my eyes. "I'm not crying over her, you fool."

His eyes widened, but he laughed. "I should be more careful about dispensing advice. If you're not upset about her, then why are you crying in the hallway?"

I realized he felt a little familiar, like a forgotten pair of shoes in the back of your closet. I couldn't remember anything specific about him, but I was certain he'd been at our house when I was a kid—and not just because I'd been told as much.

He was watching me, waiting for an answer, so I said, "My mother died this past weekend. While I was serving the cheesecake, I remembered it was one of the first things she tried to teach me to bake. I failed miserably at it."

His smile fell. "Is your mother Lila Steele?" He grimaced. "Sorry. *Was.*"

So he *did* know who I was.

"She still is," I said with a half-shrug. She would always be my momma even if she was no longer with me.

A war of emotions played out on his face before he finally said, "Do you remember me?"

"No. But I know you're Tripp Tucker. And I know you used to come over to our house when I was a kid. If I'm honest, something feels really familiar about you."

"You really don't remember me?" he asked in surprise.

I shook my head. "Nothing."

He studied me for a moment as though assessing me. "You used to love taunting me," he said with a sad grin. "You were smart as a whip even back then. Joking around with you was one of the many reasons I loved going to your house."

"I'm sorry that I don't remember you," I said, meaning it.

"It's probably for the best." He glanced over his shoulder at the room behind him, then back at me. "You were on Broadway. What are you doing serving bitches like Melisandre lukewarm chicken?"

I pointed my finger at him with a grin. "First of all, that chicken wasn't lukewarm. Tilly would rather die than serve lukewarm chicken. And second, my mother was a partner in the catering business. Maybe I'm claiming my inheritance."

"Not likely. Not about the chicken, but the claiming your inheritance part. You were always meant for great things, Magnolia Steele."

I shrugged. "For my mother, owning a catering business was a great thing."

"That was her. This is you." He leaned his back against the wall. "Do you know the greatest lesson I learned from your father?"

"To trust no one?" I asked sarcastically. "Or to keep your friends close and your enemies closer?"

"Surprisingly, I don't think that was pointed at me," he said. "When you were younger, your father could do no wrong."

"I was a child," I said bitterly. "I was an idiot."

He grimaced. "I take it you've heard some of the hard truths about your father."

I didn't respond. It was obvious enough.

"No, surprisingly, the greatest lesson he taught me was to be true to myself." He rolled his eyes. "It seems crazy now, especially after it all crashed and burned. But your truth is yours, Magnolia. You shouldn't follow someone else's, or you'll only end up unhappy."

I gave him a skeptical look. "My father taught you that?"

"In the beginning, before he became jaded." His mouth twisted as he focused on the wall behind me. "Or

227

maybe he was always jaded, but he used to be better at hiding it."

"Do you think he killed Tiffany Kessler?" I asked, trying to gauge his reaction. I needed to know what he thought of my father.

He looked startled, then said, "I didn't see that question coming."

I knew I should have worked my way up to that, but I was tired of tiptoeing around the truth. "I'm sorry, but my father lied to me, and it sounds like he lied to you too. I want the truth."

"I loved Tiffany," he said, his voice cracking with emotion. "I had no idea she was sleeping with your father."

"Are you sure he was?" I asked. "I know he had affairs, but I've since found out that he didn't sleep with Shannon Morrissey. Maybe he didn't sleep with your fiancée."

He made a face. "Oh, they slept together. Trust me on that."

"But do you think he killed her?"

"Not directly."

"What does that mean?"

"I found out about their affair because I came home and heard Tiffany on the phone, begging your father to leave your mother for her. He refused and Tiffany threatened to tell Lila about their affair. Brian threatened to destroy her if she did."

I felt like I was going to throw up. "So why don't you think he killed her?"

"Because I don't think he was capable of such a thing."

"Then how . . . ?"

"Tiffany and I got into a fight and she left. She never came back. They found her body several days later." His voice broke. "Of course, your father and I were both suspects, and we were both eventually cleared, but I blamed myself, and I blamed your father. She was the love of my life, and I've never gotten over her."

I nearly protested that he always had a new woman on his arm in the pictures that ended up in the tabloids. Shoot, he had one here tonight, a woman who looked younger than me, and Tripp had to be over forty, even if he didn't look it. But I knew better—people tried to fill loss in all kinds of ways. The fact that he was photographed with multiple women only drove his statement home. "I'm sorry."

He shook his head. "You didn't have anything to do with her death."

"But I reminded you of it."

"It happened a long time ago." Only, the look on his face suggested a hundred years wouldn't heal his wounds.

"I'm not sure the guy who was arrested for her murder actually did it."

He looked taken aback. "Why do you say that?"

I hated to press the issue since I'd clearly upset him, but wasn't pressing the issue the point of being here? "Because I don't think she was the only one."

The color left his face. "What does that mean?"

229

"Other women have been murdered. The same way Tiffany was killed."

He looked shaken, and it took him a moment to form a response. "The police never told me that."

"I don't know if they've made the connection. Until this month, the deaths have been years apart. Miles apart."

Tripp shook his head. "No. You're wrong. The police were certain they had the right guy."

"I think there's a connection to my father. She was found outside of Jackson. You lost money with the Jackson Project."

A vacant look filled his eyes and he sat on his butt, his legs stretched out in front of him. "The others?" he said, reaching up and grabbing my arm. "What's their connection?"

I squatted next to him, feeling guilty for dredging this all up for him again. "I don't know yet. I haven't checked."

"Maggie?" Colt's worried voice caught my attention.

I looked up to see his panicked face, only then realizing how strange Tripp and I looked. We were both sitting on the floor, and he was holding my arm. "I'm okay."

I started to stand, but Colt strode over and reached out a hand to help me up. When I was on my feet, he wrapped an arm around me and put himself between Tripp and me. "What's going on here?" he asked, his full attention on Tripp.

Tripp got to his feet and stared at Colt's arm around my back. His gaze lifted to my face. "I need to get back.

It was great catching up, Magnolia. Let me know if you want to talk again."

Tripp walked back into the hall, and Colt turned his attention to me, studying me with worried eyes.

"I don't think Tripp did it."

"Tell me about it later. We've got bigger problems, Mags. Detective Martinez is here looking for you."

chapter eighteen

Y ou have to get out of here," Colt said.

My back stiffened. "I told you—I've finished running."

He grabbed my wrist and tugged. "Then I'm dragging you out of here because she's got evil in her eyes, Mags. She's out to get you."

I released a nervous laugh. "Do you know how paranoid that sounds?"

"After everything that's happened, you think *that* sounds paranoid?"

He pulled me out of the back door and into the parking lot.

"I don't have my car."

"I called an Uber, but you're not going home." He pressed a key into my hand. "The Uber is taking you to my apartment. It's apartment 301. Tilly and the rest of us are covering for you, so stay there until I finish up. I'll come get you, and we'll figure out what to do next."

A car pulled around the side of the building, and Colt guided me toward it and opened the back door.

"Colt . . ." I said, looking up into his eyes. I'd given him grief over something that was obviously personal, and yet he was putting himself on the line to help me. Again. "About this afternoon—"

"Stop right there. You had every right to be upset, and I'm going to explain some of that after I get done here. Call me if you need me."

I threw my arms around his neck. "Thank you."

He gave me a short kiss on the lips and broke loose. "You need to go. Now." Then he pushed me into the backseat and shut the door.

The driver took off, and Colt watched for a moment before he went back inside. As I reached for the phone in my pocket, I realized I didn't have my purse. Hopefully Colt or Tilly would remember to grab it, but right now I felt naked without the gun hidden underneath my wallet.

Since Colt had ordered the Uber, I had no idea where I was going. I was surprised when it headed toward Brentwood. The car pulled into the parking lot of a luxury apartment complex, then pulled around to the back and stopped outside a door.

"This is it?" I asked, looking up at the building. I'd always pictured Colt living in a dive.

"Building 4," he said as if I'd lost my mind.

I got out and headed inside. There was an elevator, but I decided to take the stairs to buy more time. Colt had always told me I couldn't come to his apartment because he had roommates. How would they react to me just showing up?

When I walked up to his apartment, I knocked on the door, not wanting to walk in and surprise anyone, but when no one answered, I used the key Colt had given me. I'd expected to find thrift store furniture, not furniture that looked like it had come out of Restoration Hardware.

"Hello?" I called out in case one of Colt's roommates was home. I headed down a short hallway to check out the bedrooms. I found a home office with a desk and a computer and a bedroom with a nice furniture set and masculine bedding.

Colt didn't have any roommates.

I knew he'd told me a lot of white lies as part of his cover, but this seemed like a huge one. Colt worked for the Belles and some part-time musician gigs. The way I saw it, he didn't make enough money to cover the rent in this place.

Had my father paid for this?

The thought made me sick. I'd ask Colt when he showed up.

I headed into the kitchen and opened the fridge, fully aware that I was snooping. His fridge was mostly empty, with the exception of a carton of eggs, a bottle of ketchup, and several bottles of beer and water. I grabbed one and found a bottle opener in a drawer, then looked out of the living room window, taking in the view of the parking lot, which was full of nice cars—further confirmation that this apartment was outside of Colt's budget.

So *this* was why he'd never wanted me to come here. He'd always told me his apartment was off-limits, even when I was in danger. But I suspected there was also more to it—Colt Austin was a charmer who thought on his feet, so he could have come up with some believable explanation for living here. No, I was pretty sure he had been hiding something else from me, and I would have bet money there were clues in his home office.

Feeling like a traitor, I went into the second bedroom and flipped on the light. At first glance, there wasn't anything obvious. No papers. No bulletin boards. The desktop computer was password-protected, and the user name consisted of letters and numbers: A12M36. I knew there was no way I'd guess the password, so I didn't waste my time trying. I opened the closet doors and found some men's clothes that didn't look like anything Colt would wear—dress shirts, pants, and ties. A few khakis and polos, and two pairs of jeans. Had a former roommate left these behind?

I walked past a guest bathroom and headed into the other bedroom and opened the closet. The clothes in there were 100% Colt—jeans, T-shirts and Henleys, and plaid button-down shirts. His bathroom was cleaner than expected, and his shampoo and conditioner were in the marble-tiled shower.

I hadn't been sleeping well and I was exhausted, so I went back into the bedroom and lay down on the bed, feeling comforted because the pillows smelled like Colt. I'd drifted off to sleep, but I woke up about a half hour later when I heard a male voice outside the bedroom.

"—I know you want your cut," the man said, "but the money doesn't arrive until tomorrow."

It wasn't Colt, but the voice sounded familiar. Suddenly it hit me.

It was my father, talking to someone on the phone.

"I told you I'd make good and I meant it. We're almost there now. Be patient."

So he really was here for the annuity. Who was he making good with? Bill James? He seemed like the likely source.

My breath stuck in my chest and I froze, thankful that I was hiding in the dark. Tears welled in my eyes. For fourteen years, I'd been sure this man was dead, but he'd been in town since the Arts Council fundraiser and hadn't made a single effort to contact me. What would I do if he walked through that door and found me in here?

"What the fuck are you doing here?" I heard Colt call out from the living room.

"I pay for this place, in case you've forgotten."

"You said you were leaving," Colt said.

"And I will, but I'm not ready to go yet. I thought you were staying with Magnolia," my father said.

Was Colt still reporting to him? Colt had sworn that he hadn't been in contact with my father since he'd heard about Emily's murder.

"How do you know that?" Colt asked. "You have someone following me?"

"Don't flatter yourself," my father said. "I've had someone following Magnolia." He paused. "I thought you said she was done with the cop."

"I never told you any such thing," Colt said, sounding pissed. "I'm done answering to you."

"And what about Delilah?" my father asked. "Are you willing to risk her life?"

I gasped and sat up. Had my father just threatened someone's life? Was Delilah the woman Colt had lost when my father had screwed up his life?

"For three years, I've done what you asked. I've done things that keep me awake at night. But I draw the line at hurting Magnolia. Physically or emotionally. She deserves better from the both of us."

"You have no business sleeping with her, Austin. You don't deserve her."

"You lost the right to decide anything about her life the night you left fourteen years ago. You broke her heart for your selfish greed. *You're* the fucker who doesn't deserve her."

"She's out of your league, Austin. She's going to leave you when she finds out about Delilah, and she *will* find out about her, because I'll make sure that she does."

"Do you really hate her that much?" Colt asked in dismay. "She just lost her mother. Her brother treats her like shit, and you're about to dick around with her life. Again. *Leave her the fuck alone, Steele.*"

"She's my daughter. You have no right to tell me what to do."

"If you care about her at all, then for the love of God, leave her alone," Colt said, his voice getting closer.

"Where is she now?" my father asked. "You're supposed to be watching her."

"I told you I'm done reporting to you. Do your worst, Steele. Magnolia is my priority now."

My father laughed. "Oh, my God. You're in love with her."

Tears stung my eyes. This was not the man I remembered from my childhood. I'd known that, of course, but it felt different to actually witness it.

"Maybe I am," Colt said, his anger rising. "What she went through would have destroyed most people, yet she has overcome it. She's an amazing woman—she's strong and brave and so damned resilient, but you don't know any of that because you traded her for money. Guess what, Steele? You lost."

"When this is all settled, I'm going to reach out to her. But not yet. It's too soon."

"That's where you're wrong," Colt said, outside the bedroom door. "You're too damn late."

I slid off the bed and padded across the floor into the bathroom. My heart was breaking, tears were flowing down my cheeks, and I was trying to figure out whether I should let my father know I was here. I heard the bedroom door open. Then the closet door.

"You forget that this is my apartment," my father said from the bedroom.

"No, Brian," Colt said, "I'm aware of it every fucking day, but the contract has *my* name on it, so while you might have paid for it, legally it's mine. But don't you worry—I'm moving out. Find someone else to be your minion."

"She's only with you because she needs someone," my father taunted. "When she gets back on her feet, she'll dump you so fast your head will spin."

"You might be right, but I'll take every minute I can with her until she realizes she can do a hell of a lot better than me." The bathroom door opened, and the light flipped on. Colt walked in, and his eyes went wide when he saw me. But he quickly recovered and shut the door. He turned on the sink faucet and then pulled me to his chest and wrapped his arms around me, holding me close.

"Maggie," he whispered into my ear. "I'm so sorry."

I buried my face into his chest, trying not to sob and give myself away.

"When I came home and found him and no sign of you, I was terrified." He held me tighter. "Thank God you're okay."

I was far from okay, but I knew what he meant.

"What do you want to do?" he asked. "Do you want to confront him, or do you want me to get rid of him?"

I had so many things I wanted to say, but I wasn't sure I could handle it. Yet I'd waited fourteen years for a chance to see him. Was I really going to throw it away? "I don't know," I answered honestly.

He kissed the top of my head. "That's okay. I'm going to go finish packing. If you decide to come out, you do it, okay? If not, I'll get rid of him."

"But how will you explain coming in here and finding me and not telling him?"

Anger contorted his face. "I don't give a single fuck what that man thinks of me. If you change your mind, come out. I have your back."

I nodded. "Thank you."

He squeezed me and let me go. After he flushed the toilet, he grabbed his shampoo and conditioner out of the shower. He turned off the sink faucet, then turned off the light and opened the door.

"What the hell were you doing in there?" my father asked.

"You want a play-by-play of my bathroom experience?" Colt asked sarcastically. "I knew you were controlling, but that takes the cake."

"Where's Magnolia, Colt?"

"That's not my job anymore."

"You've spent the last four nights with her. It sounds like it's still your job. You just haven't given me a report."

I cringed at the reminder.

"I thought you claimed she's in danger," my father said.

"She *is* in danger. You just refuse to believe it."

"Rowena is dead. Geraldo Lopez is dead. And so are Neil Fulton and Walter Frey, although he was not a threat to her. Bill took off. There's no one left to hurt her."

"What about the serial killer?"

"Serial killer?"

Without even thinking, I walked out of the bathroom and faced my father for the first time in fourteen years. "Hello, Daddy. You have a hell of a lot of explaining to do."

chapter
nineteen

My father's mouth dropped open, and he quickly tried to cover his shock. "Magnolia."

He was standing by the door to the hall and took a step toward me. He looked older—more gray in his hair, a few wrinkles on his face. The man I'd known had been my hero. I'd looked up to him, literally. But I was taller now, and from where I stood in the bathroom doorway—a good eight feet between us—I didn't have to look up to him. We met eye to eye, and he wasn't the great man I'd wanted him to be.

He reached out a hand, but I backed up into the bathroom doorway. "Don't you dare try to touch me."

Sympathy filled his eyes. "Magnolia, I didn't realize you were here."

I didn't answer.

Colt stood next to his bed and an open duffel bag, a shirt in his hand. His hand tightened, and he looked ready to spring into action.

My father took another step closer, but dropped his arm to his side. I was shocked by the vulnerability on his face. "This wasn't how I wanted our reunion to go."

"Obviously," I said in the snottiest tone I could muster. The lump in my throat pissed me off. This man didn't deserve any more tears from me.

"Let's go out to the living room, and I'll explain to you what I can."

I considered arguing with him for the sake of making this more difficult, but I didn't feel like having this discussion in the threshold of Colt's bathroom.

I gave him a hard stare, which he took as agreement. He turned around and walked into the living room.

Colt watched me with a worried look. "Do you want me to stay in here?"

I knew I should do this on my own, but I didn't trust the man in the other room. Part of me was scared to be alone with him. "Can you come out? Don't do anything, just . . ."

He moved closer and put his hands on my shoulders. "Just be there on standby in case you need me to intervene?"

"Yeah."

"Of course, Maggie."

I turned around and walked out of the bedroom. He was waiting for me in the living room, standing by the front door.

"Have a seat, Magnolia," my father said, gesturing toward the sofa.

I stood in the entrance to the hallway, my anger surging. How dare he try to tell me what to do? "Let's get this perfectly straight," I said in an icy tone. "*I* am in charge here, not you. *I'll* be asking the questions and *you* will be answering, so why don't *you* have a seat, *Brian*."

He flinched at the mention of his name. "I understand that you're upset, Magnolia—"

"Shut the fuck up." I didn't raise my voice, but my harshness made him flinch again. "If *you* want to sit down, then by all means, do so, but don't you dare try to manipulate me any more than you already have."

His face softened. "I know how it looks."

I narrowed my eyes. "What part of shut the fuck up do you not understand?"

Anger tightened his jaw. "I'm still your father, Magnolia."

"*My father* died fourteen years ago. You are *not* my father. But again, let me make this perfectly clear, you are not in charge. If you push me too hard, I *will* walk out."

A hint of a smile lit up his eyes. "You won't. You want answers too badly."

I turned to look at Colt, who was standing in the middle of his kitchen. "I'm ready to go."

"Magnolia," my father protested, sounding like a parent trying to reason with a toddler.

Colt moved toward my father, who was still standing in front of the door. "Magnolia wants to leave."

My father was the same height as Colt, and the two men stood face to face.

My father didn't budge and a smirk covered his face. "This is a nice show, Colt, making Magnolia think you're on her side, but give it up. She's not leaving yet."

244

I walked over to Colt and stared up at my father. He was so cocksure that I was bluffing. So used to charming people and getting what he wanted, he was certain I'd bow down at his feet too. And why wouldn't he be? I'd been just like the rest of them.

But not anymore.

"So you refuse to get out of my way?" I asked with a whole lot of attitude.

"I recognize your need to feel in control," my father said with a patronizing smile.

Brady had said nearly the same thing to me weeks ago, and it had caught me off guard then just as much as it did now.

A look of triumph filled his eyes, reigniting my anger. I pulled my phone out of my pocket and took several steps backward.

Uncertainty washed over my father's face. "What are you doing, Magnolia?"

I unlocked the screen. "I'm calling someone who would *really* like to see you."

"Roy doesn't want to see me."

"Oh, I'm not calling Roy," I taunted.

My father lunged for me, but Colt blocked him.

"Magnolia, stop that right now!" my father shouted.

I had my contacts pulled up. "Yes, *Daddy*," I sneered, "I want to feel in control, and *you* did that to me. You fucked up my life, several times over, and I now need whatever control I can get whenever I can get it. Get away from the door, or I'll call a police detective who would love to have a chat with you too."

He clenched his hands at his sides, and his face contorted with rage. This wasn't going the way he wanted, and he was struggling to accept it. Turned out I wasn't the only one who wanted control. "Where do you want me?"

"I don't give a shit where you stand or sit, as long as you aren't blocking the door."

He walked over to the sofa and sat down. When he looked back up at me, his rage had faded and his face was awash with sadness. "This isn't how I wanted this to go, Magnolia." He shot Colt a glare. "She shouldn't be here. She was never supposed to come here."

Colt's gaze was deadly. "I had my reasons."

He didn't want my father to know about Detective Martinez.

I crossed my arms over my chest. "I'm here. Get over it. You may have orchestrated your exit fourteen years ago, but you're not orchestrating this. Not this time." My voice broke, pissing me off again.

His expression softened, making him look more like the man I'd called Daddy. He patted the sofa next to him. "Maggie. Come sit by me."

"I don't want to be anywhere near you. Let's talk this through."

Colt walked over to the dining room table and grabbed a chair. He set it in the middle of the living room and then moved back into the kitchen, leaning his butt against the counter as he kept his eyes on my father.

My father kept his gaze on me, smiling softly. "You've grown into a beautiful woman, Magnolia."

I remained silent as I sat down in the dining chair, trying to keep my emotions in check. Two weeks ago, I would have been overjoyed to be sitting across from him, but I'd found out too many awful things. Too many hard truths. "You've seen me before now."

"Not up close."

"You were there the day Colt and I were singing outside the Rebellious Rose. You were close then."

He shook his head. "I wasn't there." The confused look on his face told me he meant it.

I cast a quick glance to Colt, who was wearing a poker face.

Then who the hell had been watching us? He'd worn a baseball cap, pulled down low enough to hide his face. I hadn't pointed him out to Colt, and at the time I'd thought I was overreacting, but now I wondered. Especially in light of everything else.

"You've had Colt watching Momma and Roy. You must have had someone watching me in New York. Was it someone I knew?"

He gave me a sad smile. "I had to make sure you were safe, Maggie."

"So it *was* someone I knew." I racked my brain, trying to figure out who it could have been. "Did you have someone here before Colt?"

"No. Not here. After Christopher Merritt disappeared, I thought it best to keep an eye on your mother and brother. Just to make sure they were safe."

I understood what he was saying. "But you had someone watching me in New York long before that. How long?"

"I didn't know where you'd gone at first. I was panicked. Your mother was very tight-lipped about it."

"You were in contact with Momma?" I asked in dismay.

"No, I meant she wasn't telling people. My usual sources didn't know."

"Was Ava Milton a source?" I shook my head. It didn't matter. "Who was the person in New York? Or was there more than one?"

His eyes pleaded with me. "Maggie, what does it matter? It's only going to hurt you."

"It matters *to me*. Answer the damn question."

His shoulders slumped slightly, and he gave me a reluctant look. "Your friend Jody. Then, when she left to tour with *Wicked*, the director."

"Griff?" My ex-boyfriend. The man who'd cheated on me and then kicked me out of his apartment. After the shock faded, I realized it made a sick kind of sense. According to Colt, my father had known I was coming back before I'd shown up. But the news about Jody hurt a lot worse. She'd been there since nearly the beginning. She'd been my roommate. My best friend. The one person I'd always turned to. And it had all been a lie.

Tears filled my eyes, and I hated myself for giving my father the satisfaction of seeing me hurt. Had nothing in my life been real? Had he orchestrated everything and everyone? "Did you tell Griff to kick me out?"

"It was time to come home, Magnolia."

I stood and put my hand on the back of the chair. "I worked my ass off to get that role."

"And you got it, Maggie. I let you have that victory, but it was still time to come home."

"You *let* me have it?" I couldn't stop the tears this time. "You paid Griff to give me the role?"

"I wanted my baby girl to have her dreams. I love you."

I gaped at him. I hadn't earned that part. Never in my wildest imagination had I suspected him of manipulating my life to this extent. My entire life was a lie.

I turned to Colt. "I can't do this."

His eyes looked glassy as he nodded.

I turned to leave, putting my hand on the doorknob, then stopped. If I left before I got answers, I was letting him manipulate me. Again.

I took a deep breath and turned to face him. "Congrats. You're an excellent puppet master, but that's not love. Love is holding your wife's hand as she's dying. Love would have been comforting me after I was kidnapped and terrorized at knifepoint. Love is *being there*, you fucking asshole."

"Held at knifepoint?" He looked furious as he turned to Colt. "When did this happen?"

"You ask *me*, not him," I said. "I'm standing right here."

My father turned back to me, fury contorting his face. "When did this happen?"

"You lost the right to know. You should have been here."

"I'm here now. *When did this happen?*"

I gave him a defiant look. "You can ask from now until the end of time, and I'll never answer you. You lost the right to know the day you abandoned me."

Then understanding widened his eyes. "The night of your graduation. What happened?"

I pointed at him. "Shut your mouth." I took a breath to try to regain control. "Your job is to answer my questions, not make observations."

He sat back on the sofa and waited, but the look on his face suggested he was humoring me.

"Did you kill Tiffany Kessler?"

He did a double take. "Why would you ask me that?"

"*Obviously* because I want to know if you killed her."

Disbelief washed over his face. "No. Of course not. They arrested the man who killed her."

"Tiffany's body was found outside of Jackson. Tripp was suing you over the Jackson Project." I quirked an eyebrow. "Sense a trend? Think someone might have been trying to send a message?"

He stared at me in disbelief. I'd managed the impossible—my father appeared visibly shaken.

"Never put it together before?" I asked. "I thought Brian Steele was smarter than that."

He didn't answer.

"What do you know about Melanie Seaborn?" I was proud of myself for asking him that without breaking down.

He shook his head. "What is this game?"

"Did you know her or not?" I demanded.

"No. I don't know her."

"What about Stella Hargrove?"

"Are these women you think I had affairs with?"

"Did you know her?"

"No!"

"Margarie Turnwell?"

He pushed out a frustrated breath. "I don't know any of these women, Magnolia. Why are you asking?"

"But you knew Tiffany," I said with a sneer. "You knew her *very* well."

My father looked defeated. "I won't discuss Tiffany with you. You're my daughter. I don't expect you to understand."

"Try me."

He pushed out a breath of frustration. "I loved your mother, but it was a different kind of love. I needed passion and fireworks, something I never had with Lila."

"Then you should have divorced her."

"I couldn't because I would have lost you."

"So instead you just threw me away a few years later. If you'd divorced her, at least I would have seen you on the weekends." I shook my head. "Don't lie to me. You never cared about me, not really. You were quick enough to trade me for money, and let's be honest, you were counting on me to help cover up your escape by telling everyone you'd been killed. Rowena told me as much. You made me look like a *fool*."

He leaned forward, resting his elbows on his thighs. "I cheated on your mother. I made mistakes. I admit that. But that had nothing to do with me leaving, Maggie."

"Then why did you leave?" Rowena had told me her version, but I wanted to hear it from him.

251

"You've clearly looked into the Jackson Project. Bill and the others never forgave me after it fell apart. They all blamed me when the smaller investors came to them, demanding their money back. I realized they were plotting against me."

"Because you were stealing money from your investment firm."

Frustration wrinkled his brow. "I was a co-owner until the Jackson Project failed. Then I signed away my rights as partner to Bill to help save the firm—no one wanted to invest their money with the man who had lost *millions*. But Bill and I had an agreement that even though I wasn't a legal partner, he would still treat me as a partner in every way, and that included money. But he started hiding money from me. Bill was cheating *me*. I decided I was tired of playing his scapegoat. I was going to get what was mine."

"So you started stealing money, got caught, and then ran off. Money was more important than your family."

"Maggie, I know you don't want to hear this, but your mother was glad to be rid of me. And as for Roy . . . that boy never liked me."

"He still felt abandoned."

He was quiet for a moment. "I'm sorry for that. Mistakes were made."

I released a bitter laugh. "Mistakes were made. That erases all the bad things you did."

"No, Maggie. It's me admitting to some fault in this."

"*Some* fault in this?"

"I was going to bring you with me."

The blood rushed from my head. "What?"

He sat forward on the sofa. "I loved you so much I couldn't imagine leaving you behind. I even paid to get you a fake identity. Bought you a plane ticket. I had packed a bag of your clothes."

I was stunned at his revelation. "So why didn't you take me?"

"It would have been too dangerous for you. And I realized I'd be taking you away from your mother and your brother and Maddie and everything you loved about your life."

The irony was that I'd lost them all anyway. I wasn't sure how I felt about his admission. What would I have done if he'd spirited me away fourteen years ago? As much as I hated to admit it, I probably would have gleefully followed him.

I'd been an utter fool.

"That's not the only reason," Colt said with a sneer. "It would have been harder to hide with a fourteen-year-old girl. Maggie would have missed her mother, and she might have given you away by calling her. Don't make it out to be something noble. That decision was selfish too."

My father turned a hateful glare at Colt. "This is none of your business, Austin. Stay out of it."

But Colt was right. My father was still lying to me. It was what he did, plain and simple.

"So you're back for the annuity?" I asked in a snotty tone. "I heard you on the phone telling someone to be patient. That you were getting the money tomorrow. You don't have enough money?"

He scowled.

"You must have plenty of funds if you could afford to pay Griff to make me the lead in *Fireflies at Dawn*."

"Magnolia . . ." He sounded frustrated.

"But I guess there's never enough money for greedy men."

"That's enough," he said in a harsh tone.

"Is it?" I asked in defiance. "I don't really think it is." Something came back to me. "You said it was time for me to come home. Why?"

"Your mother. She needed you, and you needed her."

I felt like I'd been punched in the gut. "You knew she was dying?"

"Of course I knew."

"How?" Then it hit me. *Colt*. I shot him a glance, but he refused to look at me.

"Why did you pick Colt?" I asked. "I know you had him arrested on bogus charges so you could force him to work for you. You must have bribed someone to make that happen. Why go to all that trouble? There are plenty of people who would have taken the job willingly."

"I had my reasons."

"Colt quit answering to you last week. Are you going to punish him for it?"

My father looked at him. "I haven't decided yet. His work is done, but he can't seem to let part of it go."

"You had no problem with Griff sleeping with me," I sneered.

My father turned to look at me. "Griff didn't deserve you either, but he didn't love you. He never expected to keep you."

I shifted my gaze to Colt, but he still refused to look at me.

"Why are you here now?" I asked. "Is it really the annuity?"

"I have my reasons."

"How does Gordon Frasier play into this?"

He looked confused. "Gordon Frasier?"

"The cop who was investigating your disappearance."

He shook his head. "I was already gone, Maggie. I didn't pay any attention to what happened back here for nearly a year. Every day I woke up wanting to come back. Wanting to tell you I was sorry. If I'd seen something upsetting, I might have come back and ruined everything. I couldn't let that happen."

"Am I supposed to feel sorry for you?"

He looked taken aback. "No. Of course not."

"Where did the gold come from?"

He smiled. "I knew you'd find it. That ceramic dog was the key."

"When did you put it in Christopher Merritt's apartment?"

"I didn't. I put it in the garage about a year ago." A wry smile spread across his face. "I knew about your mother. I was already making plans for you to come home."

I jerked my head to face Colt. "Did you know that?"

He shook his head, his eyes wide. "No, Maggie. I swear I didn't."

I turned back to my father. "You still didn't answer about the gold. Where did it come from, and why did you hide it for me to find?"

"The gold was Bill's. He'd become obsessed with hoarding gold. So I took it to taunt him. I knew the others were conspiring against me, so I told Geraldo Lopez I'd give him one million in gold if he'd tell me what he knew. He told me, but he still conspired against me."

"He told me it was his."

He grinned. "Technically, he was right. Stupid me only asked for information in exchange for the gold, not loyalty. When I found out he'd betrayed me, I moved it. It wasn't where I told him to look. But he still wanted it."

"So you had two reasons to send me back," I said. "Momma and your desire to stir up trouble with the people who were left."

"I knew they'd all freak out once you came back. And that Lopez would think you knew something. Especially since you were there in his office when we negotiated the exchange of the gold. He told me the details of their betrayal while you sat in the chair."

"You risked my life—both then and now—to piss off your old partners?"

"Magnolia," he said in a patronizing tone. "I knew you were safe then. None of them would hurt a child, and Colt was watching you after you came back."

"Geraldo Lopez almost killed me. And then Rowena Rogers."

He frowned. "I admit I didn't expect it to go that far. I knew they'd all get paranoid after Max Goodwin was murdered, but—"

"Wait. You knew Dr. Lopez would kill Max Goodwin?"

"Magnolia, *I* killed Max Goodwin."

I took a step backward. "*What?*" Did that mean . . .

I'd asked Lopez if he'd killed Steve Morrissey, and he'd said he wasn't going to confess to anything. He hadn't confessed because he hadn't done it. My father had been at the fundraiser that night; he'd pulled the trigger.

My father got to his feet, anger making his face hard. "He disrespected you in New York. He dared to proposition you, knowing you were my daughter. He did it to spit in my face. That was why he was the one who had to die first."

I stared at him in disbelief and then turned to Colt to gauge his reaction. I took some comfort from seeing the horror in his eyes. He hadn't known either.

"But I was a person of interest!" I protested. "I was almost arrested!"

"I would never have let it get that far. That's why I killed Neil. I made it look like someone in the industry killed them instead of you."

I couldn't believe he was being so matter-of-fact about this. "Why did you kill Amy Danvers? She was completely innocent. The police think she killed herself!" I'd believed Lopez had killed her too, but he'd never admitted to that either. Only that Amy's suicide note had inspired faking his own kidnapping.

"I didn't kill her."

"Then who did?"

"I don't know."

"The serial killer," Colt said.

My father turned stoic. "There is no serial killer. I'm not a serial killer."

He thought we were talking about his partners' deaths. How many had he killed? Maybe *he* was a serial killer too. "How can you be so sure about that?" I asked.

He continued to give me a blank look.

"You also killed Steve Morrissey," I said flatly, stating it as fact.

"I was trying to flush out Lopez. I knew he'd faked his kidnapping."

"How many people have you killed?" I asked in horror.

"Only the ones who were necessary."

I took a step closer to Colt. "And who else is necessary?"

My father looked amused. "You're worried about Colt." His grin spread. "He's safe. I have other ways to make sure he stays quiet."

I wasn't taking any chances. I slowly shifted, blocking as much of Colt from my father as I could. "Delilah?"

My father nodded.

"And what about me? Aren't you afraid I'll tell someone?"

"No. I'm your father. You won't tell anyone."

He shouldn't be so sure about that.

"What's your endgame?" I asked. "You're here to get the annuity, exact some revenge, and then what?"

"I want you to come with me when I leave."

"*Where?*"

"Somewhere far from here. We'll have plenty of money to live on. You'll never want for anything again."

"And if I don't want to go?" I asked.

He gave me a knowing look. "You will. You've missed me, Magnolia. You've spent the past month looking for me." He took a step closer. "I'm so proud of you. You were determined to find me. Now that you've found me, you're not going to let me walk away." The crazed look in his eyes scared me.

Colt put his hand on my shoulder and squeezed. "I think you should go, Steele."

"That's not your decision, Austin. In fact, you've done your job, and now it's time for you to leave Magnolia alone."

I pointed my finger at my father. "You don't get to decide that. Don't you try to tell him to leave me alone."

"Magnolia, you don't know—"

"Stop. I'm not fourteen anymore. I'm a grown woman and capable of making my own decisions." I clenched my fists at my sides. "Colt's right. It's time for you to leave—and not just this apartment. You need to leave Franklin and never come back."

"I'm not done here, Magnolia, but when I am, you'll come with me so we can rebuild our family." With that, he headed to the front door and left.

Colt ran over to the door and threw the deadbolt. "As soon as he pulls out of the parking lot, we need to leave too."

"Do you really think he'll come back?"

"No. He's not who we're running from at the moment."

"Then who?"

"Detective Martinez. She has a warrant out for your arrest."

chapter twenty

W*hat?*"

"She told Tilly she was there to arrest you, and Tilly told her off."

"Why didn't you tell me at the dinner?"

"Because I didn't want to tell you something like that and then shove you in a car."

He was right. It was probably better this way.

My phone was still in my hand. I unlocked it and started to call Owen—his number was already pulled up and ready to call—but then I realized he was on leave. I doubted he would know anything. I pulled up Brady's number and stared at it for several seconds before I placed the call. I didn't trust Brady, but I would bet money that he didn't want me to be arrested.

"Magnolia? Are you okay?" he asked as soon as he answered.

"Why is Detective Martinez going around telling people she has a warrant out for my arrest?"

"*What?* On what charges?"

"I don't know. I don't think she was forthcoming when she showed up at the dinner I was working."

"She tried to arrest you in front of the guests?" he asked in horror.

"No. It never got that far. So I'm guessing you *didn't* know . . ."

"I didn't know, or I would have warned you. Where are you now?"

"Oh, no," I scoffed. "I'm not telling you that."

"Maggie, you have to trust me. I'm on your side."

"Find out what she wants to arrest me for. Then call me back." I hung up.

Colt hurried to his room, and I went back to the window, watching my father emerge from the front door of the building. He walked up to a dark sedan and stopped next to the driver's door. He lifted his hand in a wave as he glanced up at the window, smiling at me.

I stepped back in horror, realizing I'd done exactly what he'd expected me to do.

"Has he left yet?" Colt asked.

"He just reached his car. He looked up and waved. He knew I'd be watching."

Colt wrapped an arm around my shoulders. "Don't let him mess with your head, Mags. It's his specialty."

After finding out that he'd been manipulating my life, it was hard not to let it mess with my head.

"Why does Martinez want to arrest you?" Colt asked, looking out the window.

"Brady said he didn't know."

"Do you believe him?"

"I don't totally trust him, if that's what you're asking."

"Do you trust me?"

I gave him a hard stare. "I trust you more than anyone else at this point."

"Why do I get the feeling that's not saying much?"

I took several steps away from him. "So what's your plan?"

He scrubbed a hand over his face. "My plan was for us to stay at my friend Terry's house until we get this figured out. He's on the road with the Rascal Flatts. Martinez can find out my address, but I doubt she'll think to look for us there. Now, I'm starting to think we should go farther."

"Like where?" I asked. "Those beaches in Vietnam?"

"As a matter of fact, yeah," he said unapologetically.

"And let my father get away with literal murder?"

"Then tell Bennett about his confession before we leave. Martinez isn't the only one you need to worry about, Mags."

"Exactly. I don't want to leave the serial killer on the loose."

"In case you hadn't noticed, you're not the police. It's not your responsibility to catch him."

"If I leave, he might hurt someone else just to make me pay."

"Leave it to the police, Maggie. Bennett knows about it—let him take care of it."

"I told Owen too."

Colt's brow shot up. "When?"

"This afternoon. I told him almost everything."

"Why?"

"Because I don't fully trust Brady. And someone else in the police department needed to know."

"Why don't you sound happier about that?"

"Because Owen is on leave. He's being investigated for how he handled the Walter Frey case."

"So he's no help at all?" Colt asked.

I frowned. "I'm not sure."

The phone vibrated in my hand. Brady's name was on the screen.

"What did you find out?" I asked.

"She was lying, probably trying to scare you. She doesn't have a warrant for your arrest, but she does want to officially bring you in for questioning about the Savannah House murders. She's pissed at me for interrupting her questioning this morning, and she's taking it out on you because she knows it will piss me off."

"And she's your *partner*?"

"Maria has a temper, but she's a good detective. She'll cool down."

"And what am I supposed to do until then?"

"Tell me where you are, and I'll come get you."

"No." I hung up and turned to Colt. "I'm not running anymore. Take me to the police station."

"What? No!"

"She doesn't have a warrant out for my arrest. She only wants to question me."

"How can you trust that?"

264

"It's better than hiding." I grabbed his arm and tried to drag him to the door. "I'm not hiding anymore."

"And what are you going to tell her?"

"I'm not sure yet."

"It seems like you should have a plan before you march in there."

I shook my head. "No. I'll know what to tell her when she asks. Now let's go."

"Are you sure?"

"No. But it feels right, and that's all I can trust."

A half hour later, Colt and I walked into the Franklin Police Department, and I told them I was there to talk to Maria Martinez. I didn't know if she'd be there at ten o'clock at night, but I suspected she'd come in once she heard my name.

The receptionist took my name. As I suspected, she said Detective Martinez was out, but they'd let her know I was here.

"I don't like this, Mags," Colt said, casting a nervous glance toward the receptionist counter.

"You don't have to stay, Colt. I can get a taxi or Uber home."

"Is that where you're going after this? To your mother's house?"

"That's presuming Martinez lets me go at all," I said.

"What if she tricks you into admitting something you shouldn't?" Colt said. "Brady might not be able to save you from this."

"I'll take my chances."

Denise Grover Swank

"Magnolia," he pleaded. "*Please.*"

"You should go."

"No." Reluctant resolve filled his eyes. "I'm not leaving you."

"What if they want to arrest you because of what I tell her?"

"I'll take my chances."

About ten minutes later, the door to the back opened and Detective Martinez appeared, wearing a smug grin. "Well, look what the Colt dragged in."

"Oh, that was clever," I mocked. "I better be careful back there. Who knows what you'll trick me into saying."

"All I want is the truth, Magnolia. You shouldn't have to be tricked into telling it to me."

Colt gave me a dark look as I followed the detective back to the same interrogation room. I knew he was upset that I was riling her up, but I'd decided it was the best way to play her. Rile her up and throw her off. Hopefully I'd tell her enough that she'd leave me alone.

I sat in the same chair as last time and waited while she shut the door.

"Detective Bennett won't be saving you this time."

"Saving me?" I asked. "From himself? I thought I'd made it clear to both of you that I don't want to see him again."

"I meant saving you from *me.*"

"Should I be afraid of you, Detective Martinez?" I asked in an icy tone. "I thought we were both interested in the same thing. Justice."

"I'm interested in truth, Ms. Steele."

"Are you sure about that?" I asked.

Detective Martinez sat in a chair at the table in front of me. "Why don't you try me?"

"My father is here in town. I just saw him less than an hour ago, and he confessed to killing Max Goodwin, Neil Fulton, and Steve Morrissey."

She stared at me in disbelief, then burst out laughing. "And I'm Marie Antoinette."

I cocked an eyebrow. "Does that mean you'll be serving cake soon?"

"No. But I might be tossing you into a holding cell for giving me a false statement."

"See?" I said. "You're not interested in truth after all. Are you still wanting to know the truth about Rowena Rogers's murder? Ask my father about that too."

"So that's your statement about Rowena Rogers's murder?"

"I'm not here to confess," I said. "I'm not confessing to something I didn't do. I'm not sure my father killed her and the man she was with, but he's the most likely suspect."

"So I'm supposed to believe Brian Steele is here in Franklin, murdering people."

"Why is that so hard to believe?" I asked. "Wasn't the consensus that my father ran off with Shannon Morrissey fourteen years ago? Why couldn't he come back?"

"Why *would* he? Why now?"

"Revenge."

"Against who?" she asked.

"I'm guessing the people who wronged him." I thought back to my conversation with Owen that afternoon. "Gordon Frasier. Why did people think he was dirty?"

She released a short laugh. "This is my interrogation, not yours."

I rested my hand on the table. "Humor me."

"We had surveillance photos of your father meeting with Gordon Frasier before he disappeared."

"So? He was investigating him."

"No. Frasier wasn't assigned to your father until after his disappearance. He claimed he'd been following a lead from an informant, but the internal investigation determined there was no informant."

My father had lied. He knew Gordon Frasier. I shouldn't have been surprised, but the admission still caught me off guard, and Detective Martinez noticed. "My father led me to believe he didn't know anything about him."

Her smile melted into a grim line.

"It looks like you might be starting to believe me," I said. "Ask yourself this . . . Why would I lie?"

"To take the spotlight off yourself."

"Ahh . . ." I said with a contemptuous grin. "Haven't you heard that I *love* the spotlight?"

"You had the spotlight with Max Goodwin. And then with Geraldo Lopez."

"And now I'm back for a curtain call with the biggest surprise of them all. My father."

"You expect me to take your word for it that Brian Steele is here killing people for revenge?"

"My job is to tell you what I know. The truth. Your job is to decide whether to believe it or not. You want my statement? Here it is: I went to the masquerade ball with Colt Austin. We danced and Brady Bennett saw us. I'd slept with Brady days before, and he hadn't expected to see me there with Colt, let alone kissing him. Obviously our encounter didn't go well, and Colt and I had a disagreement. We left and went home to my mother's house. Shortly after we got there, the hospital called and told me to come in right away. As soon as we went to the nurse's desk, they told me that my mother had passed away."

The words sent a fresh pang through me. It occurred to me that if my father hadn't manipulated me to return to Franklin, I wouldn't have been here to make amends with my mother before she died. Did that mean I owed him for giving me one last chance with her?

What was I doing? I was excusing the things he'd done. That was the work of a master manipulator.

"What do you know about Rowena Rogers's and Kent Wentworth's deaths?"

"I've told you what I know. It's up to you what you do with it."

"That's it?" she asked.

"Yes." I started to get up, but something compelled me to sit back down. "No."

She watched me expectantly. "No?"

"There's something else we need to discuss."

"Go on." She struggled to contain her excitement. Did she think I was going to recant and confess? She was about to be disappointed.

"My father killed Max Goodwin and Neil Fulton, but Amy Danvers supposedly killed herself and wrote a confession. If she didn't kill them, why would she have confessed to something she didn't do?"

"She *did* kill them," Detective Martinez insisted.

"But what if she didn't? Who killed *her*?"

"We can play what-if all day," Detective Martinez said. "But what's the point?"

"Amy had a cut on her leg. A *C* with a slash through it. Ask Brady about Emily Johnson."

"And how would you know anything about Emily Johnson? How would you know about *any* of this? Were you using Brady for information?"

I cocked my head. "I thought *he* was using *me*." I stood again. "That's all I have to say. Am I free to go?"

She watched me, her earlier cockiness gone. "Yes. You may go."

I made my way out the door, but as I headed to the reception area, I heard Detective Martinez ask someone to contact the Brentwood police about Amy Danvers's file.

chapter twenty-one

When I walked into the reception area, Colt was anxiously pacing. I headed straight to the front door, and he followed on my heels.

We walked side by side to his truck, and as soon as we got inside, I said, "Take me to Momma's house."

"What did you tell her?" he asked, his hands tight on the wheel.

"That my father confessed to killing Max Goodwin, Neil Fulton, and Steve Morrissey, and that I highly suspect he killed Rowena Rogers and her special friend."

His body tensed and fear filled his eyes. "What have you done, Magnolia?"

"I told her the truth."

"He's going to kill you."

"No," I said as I stared out the side window. "I don't think he will."

"He might kill me," he said quietly.

I reached over and grabbed his hand, threading his fingers with mine. "No. That won't be happening either." I squeezed his hand. "She didn't believe me, but I asked her if Amy didn't kill those men, then who did?"

"What have you *done*, Magnolia?" he repeated.

"I've tried to get yet one more of Franklin's finest to find the serial killer."

"This is dangerous."

"It's been dangerous. I'm just speeding the end along."

We were silent for the rest of the short drive to Momma's house—my house now. Colt looked around before he let me get out of his truck to go inside. He locked the front door behind us and set the alarm, then walked through the house, making sure no one had snuck inside to lie in wait.

After declaring the house safe, he opened the fridge and pulled out a half-eaten pie and two forks. He set it on the kitchen table and patted the spot next to him. "I have some things to tell you."

"You think it will go better with pie?"

He gave me a sad smile. "Everything goes better with pie."

I couldn't help but smile back. "True enough."

I poured two glasses of milk and set them down on the table, then took the fork he offered and sat down at the end of the table next to him.

"Whatever was in Momma's safety deposit box had to do with Delilah, didn't it?" I asked.

"Yes." He dug his fork into the French silk pie and took a bite.

"She was the woman you loved. And lost."

He took another bite.

"I understand that you have things you want to keep private, but there's no judgment from me, Colt. I know you aren't perfect. Maybe that's why I feel so connected to you. Because we get each other."

"It's more than that, Magnolia. And what I found in that safety deposit box both frees Delilah and curses me."

I dug my fork into the pie and forced a grin. "From what I saw, my mother had plenty of curses for you. She didn't need a safety deposit box for that."

The corner of his mouth tipped up. "True enough." Then he turned serious. "Your mother found out the truth, both about who Delilah really is and how to free her."

I set my fork on the table and asked quietly, "Who is she, Colt?"

His gaze lifted to mine. "You asked why your father chose me. Delilah is the reason."

"He had something on her too, didn't he? Something made up to hurt her?"

"Maggie, I'm scared this is the one secret that will be too much for you. The curse part."

"Then I really need to know, don't I?"

He turned to look out the back window and nodded.

"Did you love her?"

"Yes."

I took a second before I asked, "Do you still love her?"

He chuckled, but his eyes were sad. "No. I let her go the day she turned away from me."

"There's a difference between letting someone go and not loving them anymore."

He grimaced and gently said, "I guess you would understand that all too well."

"Yeah." I picked up my fork and took another bite of pie. "Did you purposely intend to hurt me with this secret, Colt?"

"No, Maggie. I swear. But I won't be the only person you might be upset with after you find out the rest."

"Momma? Daddy?"

He didn't answer, just took another bite.

"I can handle the truth, Colt. Look at all the truths I just learned from Daddy. I'm sitting here eating pie instead of freaking out and sobbing in the corner."

He reached over and cupped my face, looking deep into my eyes. "I know. It only proves that you're stronger than me." Then he dropped his hand and scooped another bite of pie.

I almost countered his claim—he'd proven he was plenty strong—but I could see he was working his way up to saying something.

"Delilah was caught up in the mess your father created. If it came to light, she'd lose her teaching license."

"Teaching license?" I asked in confusion. "You said she was a waitress."

"She was. She waitressed while she was in college. She'd wanted to be a teacher her entire life, and after

274

graduation, she found a job as a first-grade teacher. We were talking about moving in together, and then I got arrested. Her school found out and rescinded their offer."

"Couldn't she have found another job? Someplace that didn't know about your false arrest?"

"No, because they arrested her as an accomplice."

"And a felon can't get clearance to teach," I said in defeat.

"That's right. She blamed me for it, but the irony was that we were both arrested because of her sister. Your father got a two-for-one special with Delilah. He got me to work for him and kept her sister in line."

Dread balled in my stomach and I forced myself to ask, "Who is her sister?"

He gave me a blank stare. "Belinda."

"*Belinda?* But she's an only child."

He shook his head. "Belinda came to Nashville after her grandmother died, and she brought her sister with her. Delilah was in college. Now they're estranged."

"That's why Belinda doesn't like you."

"Delilah blamed us both for nearly ruining her career and her life. Your father made sure to tell her why she'd been targeted. Your father threatened that he'd unseal her expunged records if I ever stepped out of line."

"And Belinda?"

He shook his head, releasing a bitter laugh. "She was to keep Roy in line."

I couldn't believe what he was saying. "Belinda knew you were working for my father the entire time?"

"She didn't know the details, but I'm sure she suspected."

"And she never told my mother?"

"Maybe she did. In the letter the attorney read, your mother said she knew."

"So what was in the safety deposit box?"

"Delilah's arrest report and plea bargain. And a deposition from a retired police officer who said he knew Delilah and I had been falsely accused."

"How did he know?"

"Because the arresting officer was still the retired cop's friend."

"Who was the retired cop?"

"Gordon Frasier."

I put my fork down. "Who was the arresting officer?"

"Robert Mahoney. Do you know him?"

"No."

"I had the *pleasure*," Colt said bitterly. "Let's just say I never want to see him again."

I grabbed my laptop from the kitchen counter and did a quick search for Robert Mahoney. "He was killed in a hit-and-run about two months ago."

"Right before you came back," Colt said.

Of course. But this proved Brady was right. There had been at least one dirty cop on the police force. Were there more?

"So Momma knew you were working for Daddy, figured you were being blackmailed, and somehow found out about the false charges. Who would have helped her look that up?"

276

Colt's eyes went round. He got up and ran out the front door, but before I could start to wonder where he'd gone, he returned with a packet in his hand. He pulled out the papers and started flipping through them. "Emily. She took his deposition. She sometimes did work as a public defender. She must have gotten access somehow."

"Even so, that doesn't explain how Momma got Gordon Frasier to give his statement in the first place."

"A couple of months before you came back, a man came into the office a couple of times to see your momma. But he came in through the back door." Colt pointed to my laptop. "See if you can find Gordon Frasier's picture."

I typed in his name. The top results brought up my father's disappearance, but when I clicked on the images tab, several photos popped up.

"That's him," Colt said. "That's the man who came to talk to your mother." He turned to look at me. "That could explain why Emily was killed. She was getting too close."

"And she'd been looking into my disappearance too. So we have Amy, who was blamed for Max Goodwin's and Neil Fulton's deaths, and Emily, who was looking into who framed you. Both crimes were perpetrated by my father."

"And both Amy and Emily were killed by the serial killer," he said.

I shook my head, feeling overwhelmed. "I don't know what to do with this, Colt."

"Me neither."

277

We sat in silence for a moment before I said, "This means you're free from my father. He has no hold on you now."

He looked mighty forlorn for someone who had just gained his freedom. "But where does this leave you and me?"

"You mean because of Delilah?"

"Yeah."

"I'm still not sure why you didn't tell me the truth this morning."

"I swore to Delilah I wouldn't tell a soul. But I called her after you left this morning and told her she was safe. She hung up on me." He rested his forehead on his hands. "I've spent the past three years doing your father's dirty work to keep her safe—all while she's gone on living a normal life—and she couldn't even say thank you."

"She didn't deserve you, Colt," I said softly.

He glanced up at me, lowering his hands to the counter. "*I* didn't deserve *her*." A look of self-disgust washed over his face.

I reached over and covered his hand with mine. "No. My way was the right one." I smiled softly. "Just remember I'm always right."

He chuckled and hope filled his eyes. "I guess I'd save myself a shit ton of arguments that way."

"I knew you were a smart man."

"Some would argue against that," he said wryly.

"Shut up and kiss me, Colt."

He turned his hand over and held mine, then stood, pulling me to my feet.

I walked around the edge of the table and put my hand on his chest while I stared up into his eyes.

He watched me with a now-serious face. His hand dropped mine and lifted up to caress my neck, his thumb brushing my jaw.

A shiver ran down my spine, and an ache deep inside of me began to grow.

He wrapped his other arm around the small of my back and tugged me closer until I was pressed firmly against his body. Then he leaned down, his mouth inches from mine, as his hand tilted my head back.

Impatient, I lifted onto my toes to press my mouth to his. He grinned against my lips, but then took control. I wrapped my arms around his neck as his tongue tangled with mine, making me forget all the horrors of this night, the past month. The past fourteen years.

"I want you," I breathed against his lips, then started to step backward, leading him upstairs.

He tugged me to his chest. "You're giving me mixed signals, Mags. Pulling away while you tell me you want me."

I grinned. "So you *don't* want to go upstairs to my bed?"

"You don't have to leave me for that." He put his hands under my arms and lifted me up.

I laughed and wrapped my legs around his waist and my arms around his neck. "Afraid I'll change my mind on the way up the stairs?"

A sexy bad-boy smile lit up his face. "I'm not taking my chances." He kissed me as he headed for the stairs, then lifted his head and grinned as he climbed.

My room was the first on the right, and he strode in, letting me slide down his body as he reached the bed. He sank one hand into my hair and gave me a long, leisurely kiss. When he lifted his face, he looked down at me with lust-filled eyes.

I reached for the top button of my shirt, but he pushed my hand down and started making quick work of the buttons. He spread my shirt open and rested his hands on my waist. Heat flooded my body and my breath increased, making my chest rise and fall. His gaze fell to my breasts as he pushed my shirt over my shoulders and let it drop. My bra was right behind it. His hands slowly skimmed up my sides, cupping my breasts.

He was still wearing his bartender's shirt. I unbuttoned his shirt, pausing every few seconds while he distracted me with his hands on my body. A confident grin spread across his face as I tugged off his shirt.

I rested my palms on his chest and let my fingertips trail over his pecs. My gaze lowered to his eight-pack abs.

"When do you have time to work out?" I asked in awe.

He laughed. "I'll tell you about my workout plan later." Then he pushed me down on the bed and leaned over and unfastened my pants. He pulled them off leisurely, teasing me—no, from the look on his face, I could tell he was teasing us both. Then he grabbed his wallet out of his pocket and pulled out a condom. He set both things on the nightstand before taking off his pants.

I reached for him, and he lay down next to me.

"You're perfect," he said, sliding his hand behind the back of my head and pulling my mouth up to his. His free hand roamed my body and the V between my legs, making me ache for more.

So why not take it?

I pushed Colt over onto his back, then straddled his waist.

His look of surprise and lust, tempered by a touch of amusement, gave me a thrill. I rested my hands on his shoulders and then lowered my mouth to his neck, kissing my way down over his sexy chest to his abs.

He grabbed my arms and tugged me up to his face, his lips reaching for mine. His lips and tongue danced with mine again until I rose up and snagged the condom off the nightstand.

"Impatient?" he asked, but I could see that he was impatient too.

I lifted a brow. "Complaining?"

He laughed. "Not a chance."

I opened the package and rolled it onto him, reveling in the feel of him beneath my fingers. Then he grabbed my hips and I guided him into me, closing my eyes as he filled me.

"Jesus, Maggie," he groaned, his fingers digging into my flesh.

He rolled me onto my back and pulled my leg up to his hip. He kissed me again as he drove deeper. I clung to him, each thrust pushing me higher until I shattered, calling out his name.

Colt gave one last thrust and collapsed on top of me, wrapping his arms around me and pulling him with me as he rolled onto his side. He kissed me again and then lifted his head. Brushing my hair from my cheek, he said, "I love you, Maggie."

I lifted my hand to his face, but I couldn't say it back. Not yet.

chapter
twenty-two

Y ou want to do *what?*" Colt asked the next morning.

"I'm going to go talk to my brother."

He shook his head. "No. We have no idea what he'll do. It's dangerous. *He's* dangerous."

"I have to talk to him."

"No, you don't. We'll find another way."

"Sorry, but you don't get a say in the matter." I got out of bed and headed into my bathroom. Colt followed me in.

I turned on the water for the shower and waited for it to warm up. Colt pulled my back to his chest. "Mags. This is crazy. What do you hope to find out?"

"What he knows about the night I was kidnapped. What he knows about our father."

"He won't tell you anything."

"I still have to try."

He spun me around and pushed my back up against the wall, kissing me until I was boneless and eager to stay in bed with him all day . . . but I didn't have that luxury. I was running out of time, and I knew it.

I wrapped my hands around his neck and looked up at his face. "You're really cute when you're all protective."

His brow shot up in mock offense. "*Cute?*"

I laughed. "Okay, *sexy*. But I'm still going."

He took advantage of the shower and our naked bodies to try to get me to change my mind, but I was determined to see this through.

After our shower, I asked Colt to go buy me a burner phone. He went out the front door, wearing nothing but his jeans, so I wasn't surprised when he came back a few moments later with a phone in his hand.

"You can use this," he said, handing it over with solemn eyes.

"You used this to communicate with my dad."

He nodded. "His number's in there if you want it."

I curled my upper lip. "I have no intention of calling that man." Instead, I looked up Owen's number on my phone, plugged it into the burner, and placed the call.

"Hello," was his tentative response.

"It's Magnolia."

"You texted me with your phone yesterday," he said in an accusatory tone.

"I know. But I've rectified the situation. There was nothing about Tiffany Kessler on your list. Was her file in the batch?"

"No."

"It was in there when I saw them at Brady's house. I wonder what it means?"

"I don't know." His tone softened. "I haven't learned anything else, if that's why you're calling."

"Well, I have plenty to tell you." I told him about talking to Tripp, Detective Martinez's attempt to scare me into compliance by showing up to "arrest" me, and my face-to-face meeting with my father. I held back the personal stuff, including my father's insistence that I leave town with him, but I told him about my father's admission that he'd killed three men and about the strange phone call I'd partially overheard—and my suspicion that it might have been with Bill. I finished my word vomit by telling him that I'd gone to the police station to inform Detective Martinez about my father's confession.

"But there's one more thing, Owen," I said. "Martinez said your uncle met with my father before his disappearance. Your uncle said he talked to him because of an informant, but there wasn't one."

"They were sure Uncle Gordon was on the take, but he wasn't."

"Are you sure?" I asked softly. When he didn't respond, I said, "Just remember that I was positive my father was innocent, but I was very, very wrong. Colt has an affidavit from your uncle that he knew a police buddy of his fabricated the charges against Colt Austin and his ex-girlfriend three years ago."

"How would he know that?"

"Good question, but the affidavit is signed and notarized."

"Who was the arresting officer?" he asked in a subdued voice.

"Robert Mahoney."

"He was killed a couple of months ago. A hit-and-run when he was off duty."

"A month before I came back to town."

He was still silent.

I'd given him enough to consider. "We have even more proof the serial killer is connected to my father somehow, but I have no idea what to do with that."

"Let me take care of it. I'm focusing on Tiffany Kessler's murder. I've discovered that Clint Duncan was also a suspect, so I plan on having a chat with him today."

That caught me by surprise. "Aren't you still on leave?"

"Technically."

I suspected that wasn't confirmation that he was allowed to do it, but Owen was a big boy and could determine his own lines to cross. "Let me know what you find out, and I'll do the same." Although it was pretty undeniable I was the one supplying ninety-five percent of the information . . .

"Be careful, Magnolia."

"Thanks." I decided not to tell him about my plan to check on my brother, which likely wouldn't fall under the *be careful* umbrella.

Colt had been sitting on a barstool at the kitchen counter, watching me pace while I'd talked to Owen. "Does the fact you didn't tell Frasier about your field trip to downtown Nashville mean you changed your mind?"

"Not a chance."

I did relent and agree to let Colt drive me up to Nashville, but I told him that he couldn't come up to Roy's office with me. He agreed initially, but from the look on his face as we walked into the lobby, I could tell he was going to put up a fuss about having to sit and wait.

I pulled him into a hug and smiled up at him. "Do you trust me?"

Bewilderment clouded his eyes. "Maggie, I have always trusted you."

My stomach was knotted with nerves, but I forced out a glib laugh. "I can think of a few times that wasn't true."

"We'll talk about those later," he said. "Let's go upstairs."

"Good try." I pushed him down into a chair. "I'll call you and put the phone in my pocket. That way you can listen to the whole thing, and if I say a code word, you can come up and save me."

A mischievous grin lit up his eyes. "Like a safe word?"

I laughed. "Sure."

"What's the code word?"

"I don't know. How about . . . bubbles?"

He grabbed my arm and tugged me closer for a kiss. "We'll give that code word a go later."

I pulled loose and shook my head. "Don't be so sure of yourself. We'll take this day by day." I was lying. I had no intention of getting rid of him.

"Then I need to step up my game," he teased. "And make sure you don't even consider cutting me loose."

"I'm looking forward to it." I walked toward the elevator and joined several people who were waiting for the doors to open.

My phone vibrated, and when I pulled it out of my purse, I was surprised to see Colt's name on the screen. I answered as I glanced back at him.

"Forgetting something?"

"I was getting to it."

Worry covered his face. "Be careful, Mags. Don't take any crazy chances, okay?"

"I won't."

The elevator doors opened, and I followed the small group inside, pressing the button for Roy's floor.

I slipped my phone into the front pocket of my jeans.

I was surprised that I was so calm as I walked into the office Belinda and I had broken into just last week. I stopped at the receptionist's desk and gave her a friendly smile. "Is Roy Steele in?"

She smiled back. "Yes, but he's really busy dealing with Bill's absence. Did you have an appointment? I don't see anything in his schedule."

I waved my hand in dismissal. "We threw it together kind of last minute, so maybe he forgot to tell you. I know where his office is, so I'll just see myself back."

I headed to the hallway without waiting for permission, but she didn't try to stop me.

Roy's office door was open, so I took a second to compose myself and then stepped into the threshold.

My brother was sitting at his desk, his head bent forward as he rubbed his forehead. Seeing him like this—

vulnerable and alone—made me feel a little sorry for him. I remembered how terrified he'd been when Momma was dying. Maybe there was still a chance to put what was left of our family back together.

Then I thought of our father and the hopelessness returned.

"Hello, Roy," I said softly.

His gaze jerked up and rage contorted his face. "What are *you* doing here?"

"I want to talk."

He reached for the phone on his desk. "I'm calling security."

"I'm only here to talk." As he put the phone to his ear, I said, "We can talk about the house. You want it, right? We can discuss that too."

He put the phone down and rested his hands on his desk. "I'll give you ten minutes."

I nodded and shut the door behind me, then sat in one of the chairs in front of his desk. I took one look at the fury in his eyes and my heart broke. "Why do you hate me so much?"

"That's why you're here?" he asked. "I thought you wanted to discuss something productive."

"When you offered me fifty thousand dollars to leave town, you told me that I'd always ruined everything. What else did I ruin?"

He pushed out a huge breath, then said, "I already told you, Magnolia."

"I stole the attention," I said. "Daddy loved me more than you, but after he left, Momma was too upset to give you enough love."

"You make it sound so petty," he said.

"You're not wrong," I said. "You needed love and attention, and I was high-maintenance. I'm sorry."

He stammered, clearly caught off guard. "I was alone."

"I know. I really am sorry." Most of his anger was gone, so I decided to plunge right in. "Were you there that night? The night of my graduation party?"

"You know I was spending the night at Tyler's house."

"Did you follow me into the woods?"

He didn't answer.

"You and Tyler used to love playing in the woods. You built that fort out there. Did you ever see an abandoned house?"

"What if we did?"

"Did you follow me out to that house, Roy?"

He drummed his fingers on his desk and refused to look at me.

"You did. We both know you did. You said so at the attorney's office."

"I never admitted to any such thing, but you sure sent that detective after me, didn't you?"

"He figured it out on his own," I said. "He knows about the killer." When he didn't say anything, I added, "What happened when Brady showed up at your house?"

"He was freaked out that I'd driven home, but Belinda told him *she'd* driven. As soon as she went inside, he told me he knew I'd witnessed something related to your kidnapping. He pressed me for details, but I told him he was crazy, and he eventually left."

Roy's description matched Belinda's, not Brady's. Why had Brady lied? To what end? To make me distrust Belinda and alienate myself from one of my allies?

"Roy, I know you hate me, but do you hate me enough to want someone to kill me?"

He closed his eyes for a long moment before blinking them open again. "A month ago, I told you to leave, Magnolia. I offered you all that money just to leave."

Oh, my God. "You were trying to protect me."

His chest rose and fell rapidly. "He said he'd kill you if you came back and told people."

I gasped. "Who?"

"I don't know who he is. He texted me."

"What did you see that night, Roy?"

He looked up at me with wild eyes. "I don't want to relive it again, Magnolia."

"Neither do I," I said, "but it replays in my mind every single night. Sometimes multiple times a night. I still have the scar." I took a deep breath. "We have to stop him. He's killed more people since he killed Melanie."

He tilted his head. "Who's Melanie?"

"The woman who was killed that night. Her name was Melanie Seaborn. She was a nurse."

Roy looked away, but his face had gone pale.

"She was only one of several, Roy. Tiffany Kessler—do you know about her?"

His eyes widened. "The woman Dad was accused of killing? He didn't do it."

"No. He didn't. The serial killer did."

"There's no serial killer. I would have heard about it on the news."

"Most people haven't put it together just yet. Brady knows. And now a couple of other cops know too, but that's it."

"Two victims, years ago," he said in a patronizing tone. "That doesn't mean we're dealing with a serial killer."

"Amy Danvers and Emily Johnson were killed by him too. And there were still more. The killer's been texting me too." I waited until he turned back to me with teary eyes. "I need to know what you know."

He shook his head. "I don't know anything."

"Please, Roy. I'm begging you. I need you to help save my life."

He swallowed and looked close to tears. After about ten seconds, I was sure he wasn't going to answer, but before I could say anything—or leave—he said, "I followed you out into the woods. I'd seen Blake go out there with some girl, and then you followed them. I wanted to see what was going on. I thought maybe I'd see you two having sex. If I was lucky, the three of you."

"Eww! You knew I was with Tanner."

He shrugged. "Once I got out there, I saw Blake running back toward the house. He didn't see me—I hid from him in the trees—but I didn't know where you'd gone, so I kept looking. It was raining, and I was about to give up, but then I remembered the abandoned house. I didn't think you were there at first . . . and then I heard the screams." He got up and started to pace. "The screams were coming from the basement, and I was about to go downstairs, but I saw a camera on the floor and picked it up."

I hiccupped a sob that came out of nowhere. I'd suspected something like this, of course, but to hear the confirmation was almost too much. "My camera. The one I used to take photos of Blake." Another sob broke loose. "I dropped it when I was trying to escape."

Roy continued to pace. "I took it downstairs that night. I took photos."

"Photos of what?"

"Everything."

I felt faint. "Where's the camera?" I finally choked out.

"It's in Mom's house."

"Is that why you wanted the house?"

He nodded and then walked behind me.

I stood and spun around to face him. "Why didn't you just get it? I'm sure you still have a key."

"Because it's not stuffed in some sock drawer, Magnolia," he said, sounding pissed. "I was smart enough to hide it somewhere it wouldn't get found."

"Where?"

"It's embedded in the fireplace in the basement."

I blinked, certain I'd heard him wrong. "What?"

He shot me a glare. "Remember those bricks that kept falling out of the basement fireplace? Well, Momma had it fixed about six months after you took off." He flung his arm wide. "You ran off and left me to deal with all of it."

"I'm sorry about that too, but I blocked it out for ten years. I didn't remember until I came home."

"Well, lucky you," he sneered.

"I was the one who had a giant *C* carved into her leg! I was the one who got a concussion."

"And I was the one who had to live in that house knowing what had happened in those woods."

"Why didn't you tell the police, Roy?"

"Why didn't you?" he shot back. "You were the one tied to a pole."

I released a gasp and sat down in the chair, worried I was about to faint. "You really saw it," I said, barely above a whisper.

"I admitted that I did."

"I know, but . . ." I covered my mouth with my hand, trying to get a grip. "I woke up at the edge of the woods," I said, my voice breaking. "The concussion knocked me out. I remember Melanie screaming up until the moment he killed her, and then everything was gone until I woke up next to our backyard. I have no idea how I got there."

"The killer carried you there."

My stomach roiled. "You saw it?"

"No. But he told me he would return you home. He told me to go home and wait there, but he said that if I told anyone, he'd kill you and dump you where no one would ever find you. And if I didn't keep quiet even after you came home, he'd kill both you and Momma."

I shot out of the chair, making it tip slightly. "You talked to him?"

"I was hiding on the stairs, behind the partial wall. He found me, but I hid the camera in my shorts pocket and he never saw it. The woman was dead and you were slumped against the pole. He knew who I was."

"He knew who I was too, but his face was covered, and I didn't recognize his voice. Do *you* know who it was?"

He shook his head. "No." But he looked so terrified I wasn't sure I believed him.

"Why did you keep the camera?"

"Insurance. In case I ever needed proof." Roy started pacing again. "Is that all?"

"Daddy's back," I said, watching for his reaction. His blank expression told me that he already knew. "I saw him last night."

"When you say you saw him, you mean in the shadows . . . ?"

"No, I mean we had a conversation."

He closed his eyes for several seconds this time. "You did *what?*"

"He didn't mean for me to see him. It just happened."

"It just happened," he sneered hatefully. "I've wanted to have a conversation with him for the last ten years, and nothing. Then you just happen to bump into him." His face turned red and he pointed his finger at me. "That's a crock of bullshit, Magnolia. It did not *just happen.*"

He was getting agitated, and now he was standing between me and my escape route—something else he had in common with our father.

"He just showed up and I . . ." I wasn't about to tell him that I'd been at Colt's apartment, which, by the way, had been paid for by our dear ole dad. "I'm sorry."

He clenched his fists and shouted, "Quit saying you're sorry!"

I took an involuntary step backward into the desk.

Roy advanced toward me. "What did he say?"

"He said a lot of things."

"What in particular?"

"I asked him about leaving us." My voice broke as I said, "I asked him why he did it."

"And?"

"He did it because he's a selfish bastard who loves money more than his family. I also asked him why he's back."

Roy laughed, but it sounded deranged. "I know why he's back."

"The annuity?" I asked.

He scowled.

"He's killed at least three people, Roy. Probably more."

"And they probably deserved it."

I gasped. "How can you say that?"

"The world is full of stupid people who get what's coming to them."

"Have you lost your mind?"

"No." He stopped in front of me with crazed eyes. "I'm thinking more clearly than I have in a long time."

Roy's office door burst open, and Colt stood in the opening, his chest heaving. He looked like he'd climbed a dozen flights of stairs. "Get away from her, Roy," Colt said breathlessly.

Roy laughed. "Or what?"

Colt strode toward him with murderous eyes. "Did you hurt her?"

I intercepted Colt and held him back. "I'm fine. He never touched me."

"I think you have all the information you need now," Colt said, starting to breathe easier. "Let's go."

Colt was right. I'd wanted to keep pressing him—something told me there wouldn't be a second chance—but Roy was acting unstable. He was either about to kick me out or literally strangle me, so we were pretty much done anyway.

Colt cupped my elbow and led me to the door, never taking his eyes off Roy. Then he hurried me out of the office. When we reached the elevator bank, the elevator was already there, thank God, and a woman was getting out.

Colt punched the button for the lobby just as Roy slammed through the door to his firm's reception area. The doors closed just in time.

We were both silent for several seconds before I said, "I take it you know what we're doing next?"

"It's time to rip apart a fireplace."

chapter
twenty-three

When we got to Colt's truck, I realized my phone was still in my jeans pocket. I'd never ended my call with him, although I suspected he'd ended the connection himself.

I pulled it out anyway as Colt opened the passenger door for me, and one look at the screen erased any satisfaction I felt over what I'd learned from Roy.

You've been a bad girl.

"Maggie?" Colt's voice was tight.

I held up my phone so he could read the text from the blocked number.

"Shit." He leaned closer. "It came through five minutes ago. Was he talking about seeing Roy?"

"Could be. Or it could be what I told Detective Martinez. Or seeing Daddy. Or talking to Owen. It could be all of the above." I stared at the words on the screen, trying to figure out which one he meant, but then I decided to stop feeling sorry for myself. The serial killer had threatened Belinda specifically in the past. She needed to know she was in danger.

She answered on the first ring. "Magnolia," she said, her voice sounding far away. "I'm surprised to hear from you."

"Belinda, I just got a text from the serial killer, and he's pissed. I'm worried he'll come after you to get to me."

"Oh!" She took a moment, then said, "I'm at the office right now, and I have clients back to back today. I also have a gun and pepper spray. I'm sure I'll be fine."

I was still worried. "Try not to be alone, okay?"

"I won't." She sounded sad. "I'm grateful you still care."

"You're my sister-in-law. Of course I care. But we really have to talk later." I paused, about to hang up, but I was tired of letting things lie. "I know about Delilah."

She didn't say anything for several seconds. "Colt told you."

"And Daddy," I fudged.

She paused again. "You talked to your father?"

"Yeah."

"Are you okay?"

A defensive part of me wanted to give a sarcastic answer. I felt so betrayed by her, but I still loved her. I wanted to give her a chance to explain before I made a final decision. "It was rough, but I'm okay."

"What did he say?"

I glanced at Colt, who was sending me a scowl. He obviously didn't approve, but I didn't care. I didn't answer to him. But he wasn't wrong. I couldn't fully trust

Belinda after everything that had passed between us. "I'll tell you about it later."

"I hate that we're at odds, Magnolia. I miss you."

"I miss you too. We just need to talk."

"Thanks for not giving up on me."

"How can I? Momma loved you too."

I hung up, then immediately called Tilly.

"Tilly, where are you?" I asked as soon as she answered.

"I'm at the catering kitchen. Why? What's wrong?"

"Are you alone?"

"We have that lunch today. We're about to load the vans. In fact, Colt's supposed to be here helping. Is he with you?" She sounded frazzled and at her wits' end.

Oh crap. I covered the phone, then whispered to Colt, "You're supposed to be helping Tilly with a lunch."

The look he gave me—full of guilt but not surprise—told me that he'd known. He'd been willing to miss it for me.

"Tilly," I said, "Colt had to drive me up to Nashville for an errand, but we're on our way back. Sorry to keep him for so long."

"Are you okay?" she asked.

"I'm fine, but I need you to be careful. Emily's killer is still on the loose, and I can't help but think he might hurt other people I love. If anything happened to you . . ." I swallowed the lump in my throat. "Just stay with lots of people today, okay? Stick close to Colt once we get there."

"I will, sweet girl. Just hurry up and get here so I can make sure you're safe too."

I hung up and turned to Colt. "Why didn't you tell me that you were supposed to work for the Belles today?"

He shrugged. "I knew you'd take off and talk to Roy on your own. And I'm not sure why you told her I'd come in. We need to find that camera."

"We set the alarm," I reminded him. "The cameras you and your friend installed outside the doors will show us if anyone tries to get in."

"I still think we should make that camera our top priority," he said.

Part of me thought so too, but it had waited ten years. It could wait a few more hours. Besides, I needed a short reprieve.

"You didn't have to come in there and save me," I said with attitude. "I was doing just fine on my own."

"I know, and I knew I risked pissing you off, but I don't regret it. I would much rather have shown up *before* he hit you than after."

"You don't know that he was going to hit me."

"I think we both know there was a very strong possibility. Your brother's been unhinged lately. Even more so since your momma's death."

I gave him a grudging nod. "You're right. Thanks."

A sexy grin spread across his face. "I love hearing you say that."

"Thanks?"

"Nope. That I'm right."

I couldn't help but smile, even though my guts were tumbling with anxiousness and fear.

We were quiet until we reached the interstate. Colt was the one who finally broke the silence, and I could tell he'd been stewing on the words for some time. "So, Roy saw everything happen that night . . ." He cast a glance at me. "How do you feel about that?"

"I haven't really had a chance to process it. Part of me is angry that he didn't try to save me, but what could he have done? He was fourteen. He was a kid with no way to defend himself. He could have left me there, but he stayed."

"Taking pictures," Colt said in an ugly tone. "Sick fuck. I think he liked watching."

My chest tightened and I forced out, "*What?*"

"Because he followed you out into the woods, hoping to watch you have sex. And because he kept the camera. Was it a digital camera?"

"Yeah. Why?"

Colt's upper lip curled. "I bet he looked at those photos over and over."

I gasped. "How can you say that?"

"Because Roy Steele is a sick fuck who likes abusing women. I saw the look in his eyes when he hurt you at that bar, Magnolia. He gets off on it. Maybe it all started when he saw the killer, but I guarantee you that he got off on looking at those photos."

"You don't know that. Besides, why would he let them brick the camera into the fireplace if he wanted to see them?"

"I bet part of him was horrified that he liked to look at them." His expression had turned grim. "Bricking it up into a fireplace seems drastic, don't you think? If he

302

really kept it for insurance, he'd want to keep it closer, more accessible."

"He was fourteen, probably fifteen by then. Most teenage boys aren't known for thinking things through."

Colt shook his head. "I still say it smells fishy. And if the camera's really in the fireplace, why would he freak out about you getting the house? Why not let the camera stay there forever? You never would have found it on your own. And why hide the entire camera, anyway? Why not just bury the memory card?"

"I don't know. Again, he was a teenage boy."

He shook his head. "I'm not buying it. He's worried about someone seeing what's on it, but not because of the evidence on there. He's worried about something else."

"Like what?"

"I don't know."

I shuddered. I refused to seriously consider what Colt was saying, mostly because I worried there might be some truth to it. "But he tried to save me when I came back to town. He gave me money to leave."

His mouth pressed into a thin line. "Maybe."

"What does that mean?"

"There's more to all of it. I can feel it."

I studied him for a moment. "Is there more that *you're* not telling me?"

He jerked his eyes to mine. "No. You know everything I know."

"If I find out you're lying to me . . ."

"I've told you everything. I swear." We were quiet for about a half minute before he asked, "So what do you want to do now? Maybe you should call Detective Martinez and find out if she's gotten anywhere."

I shook my head. "She wouldn't tell me anything. Brady would be more likely to share, but I don't want to call him. After what Roy told me, I know he was lying about his conversation with my brother. Belinda's story matches Roy's."

"Unless Roy and Belinda are trying to make you not trust Brady."

"You think they agreed to purposely lie to me?" I asked in surprise. "Why? To what end?"

"I don't know, Maggie. I don't know anything." His hands tightened on the steering wheel. "I still think we should leave town. Everything seems to be coming to a head. It's not safe for you here."

"No," I said firmly. "I'm not going anywhere. I need to see this through." I softened my voice. "But if *you* want to leave—"

His jaw tensed. "*No.* If you stay, I stay."

"Colt. If anything happens to you . . ."

His eyebrows shot up. "Do you really think I could leave you? I'm staying with you to the end, no matter what that means."

It was the *no matter what* that bothered me.

"So what next?" he asked.

I ran through my mental list. "We need to find the camera. Why don't you drop me off at Momma's house? I can try to find it while you help Tilly."

"No fucking way am I leaving you alone, even with the alarm system. You can come with me and help work the lunch. Then we'll smash the fireplace."

I didn't really want to be alone either, so I saw no reason to fight him on it. "Crap. I should have asked Roy about the Duncans. He might have told me something we could use."

"Do you really think there's a connection between Duncan and the serial killer?"

"I'm not ruling anything out, and apparently neither is Owen since he's checking on Clint Duncan today. There are too many things that tie the serial killer murders to Daddy to be a coincidence. It makes sense that it would be someone who holds a grudge against him. Seems to me that Brian Duncan has a lot of reasons to hate him."

"Or the serial killer could be working to *help* your dad. Amy's faked suicide covered up your father's murders."

"Yeah . . . but I'm not so sure. Daddy claimed he didn't even know about the killer."

"Asking Roy wouldn't have done you any good, so don't beat yourself up about it. I doubt he would have answered any more questions. He was already worked up past the point of reason. And what are the chances he was looking that far back into your father's past? Wouldn't he have focused on the Jackson Project to help Belinda get her revenge?"

"Not necessarily. Roy thinks our father wronged him, and I'm sure he thinks he's owed compensation. After Brady questioned him and Bill James at the office, Roy told me I was ruining everything. Sure, he might be interested in revenge like Belinda, but I'd bet Momma's house that he's more interested in that money."

"You could ask Belinda about Eric Duncan," Colt said.

"She was there when Tilly told us about him. If she knew anything else . . . anything she was willing to share, she would have told us on Monday night." We had another possible source of information, but she might not be so receptive this time. "I'm sure Ava knows more about the murders. Maybe she even knows how they're linked."

"She definitely knows about Tiffany Kessler, but I don't think she knows about the others."

Ava had mentioned a murder three years ago, but there hadn't been a file in Brady's packet of files. "What do you know about a murder three years ago?"

"Nothing. That would have been before I worked for her, and while I knew she was concerned about something that had happened in that timeframe, I didn't know any details."

I narrowed my eyes.

He lifted a hand in self-defense. "I don't know anything, Maggie, I swear. My number one priority is protecting you, and if any information I have from anyone could help you find the killer, I'd share it."

"What time is it?"

"Ten thirty. Why?"

"Because I'm not going to the catering kitchen with you."

He sat up straighter in his seat. "Where the hell do you think you're going?"

I smiled, but I didn't put any warmth into it. "I'm going to a Bible study."

chapter twenty-four

As I walked through the door into Ava Milton's kitchen, I knew I was jumping from the frying pan into the fire. After the way I'd handled our conversation the day before, I suspected she'd make a fool out of me, but the unlocked back door also seemed like an open invitation—or a dare. Probably both.

The kitchen looked messier than usual with unwashed pots and pans in the sink, but the table was covered with the usual display of food. I heard voices in the living room, and I walked toward it, the clicking of my shoes ensuring there would be no sneaking up on anyone.

Miss Ava was standing in the front of several rows of chairs, as usual, and she stopped talking as I approached the group and sat in a chair in the back. Her mouth sagged open with what appeared to be shock, a new sensation for her, I was sure.

A shudder rippled through her body before she said, "Magnolia Steele, what do you think you're doing?"

I crossed my legs and tried to look prim and proper. "I'm here for the Bible study, Miss Ava."

"You were not invited. You are not a member."

I lifted an eyebrow. "Do you want me to take notes to justify my presence like you had me do last week?" I looked around the room. "Is anyone else on the chopping block?" I focused my attention on a woman in the second row and pointed my finger at her. "Georgine, have you been stirring up shit again? I bet you're next." She was Miss Ava's nemesis and had challenged her at every opportunity at both meetings I'd attended. Miss Ava must have some reason for keeping her around.

Multiple gasps filled the room.

"Magnolia, will you kindly leave?" Miss Ava said in a tight voice. Her eyes were slightly bugged out, and her cheeks were pinker than usual.

"No . . ." I said, tilting my head to the side. "I have some old business to discuss . . . or is it new business?" I sat up straighter and held her gaze. "Maybe I should just bring it up between the two discussions. That way we can cover both."

Miss Ava's face started turning red.

"By all means," I said with a slight hand wave. "Go on with your meeting. I'll wait." When no one said anything for a few seconds, I said, "Oh. Did you just finish with old business?"

The woman next to me, an elderly woman named Ruth, turned to me with a downturned mouth and patted my arm. "Magnolia, are you feeling all right? Your mother died less than a week ago. It must still be quite a shock."

I gave her a sweet smile. She was one of the kinder members of the group. "Thank you, Miss Ruth. And thank you for the flowers you sent to the funeral. That was so sweet of you. I'll be sure to send you a thank you card once I have this whole serial killer situation under control."

Her mouth dropped open as if I'd tripped a lever, and the room filled with louder gasps than before.

"Serial killer?" Georgine burst out. "*What* serial killer?"

I shifted in my seat so I could see Georgine. "The one who killed Emily Johnson last week. And Amy Danvers a few weeks ago. And Melanie Seaborn ten years ago, Margarie Turnwell fourteen years ago, and Tiffany Kessler seventeen years ago. Twenty years ago, poor Stella Hargrove was the first victim . . . as far as I can tell." I cocked my head as I turned my attention on Miss Ava. "There was also a murder three years ago, but you forgot to give me details on that one." I glanced around with a sheepish look. "Sorry. Please let me know when it's my time to talk."

Thirty-two sets of eyes stared at me.

Good thing I thrived on attention.

"So does that mean it's my turn after all?" I asked sweetly.

Miss Ava seemed to get control of herself. "You've already hijacked the meeting, so by all means, carry on, Magnolia."

I stood and gave her a good-natured grin. "You know you want to hear what I have to say."

"You're wrong about Amy Danvers," Georgine said with a smug tone. "She committed suicide and wrote a note confessing to the murder of those two men."

"And that's exactly what the serial killer wanted you to think," I said, walking toward the front of the group where Miss Ava stood. "Only, I know for *a fact* that Amy Danvers didn't kill Max Goodwin and Neil Fulton."

"And how do you know that?" Miss Ava demanded.

I swung around to face her. "Because *my father* killed them."

The gasps were even louder this time.

"What do you mean your father killed them?" Miss Ava asked. "How do you know that?"

"Because he and I had this lovely chat last night—a real tête-à-tête." I glanced over my shoulder. "Georgine, in case you're wondering, that means face-to-face and private." She undoubtedly knew what it meant, but I couldn't pass up the opportunity to screw with Miss Ava's nemesis.

"And what was discussed in this supposed meeting?" Miss Ava asked, clearly flustered.

"Well . . ." I said with a hint of a drawl. "I can't tell you everything. Father-daughter stuff, you know, but I *can* tell you he told me that he killed a number of people. When I asked how many, he would only say they all deserved it. I think there might be more murders, but none of you have anything to worry about unless you think your name might be on my father's naughty list . . ."

310

Miss Ava's face paled.

"I knew you made a huge mistake by hiring her!" Georgine shrieked as the room broke out into chaos.

From the hysteria behind me, I suspected more than a few were worried they might be next on Daddy's list. The fact that over half of them ran out of the house confirmed it.

Miss Ava composed herself once more, placing her hand on her stomach as she inhaled deeply. Georgine was shouting at her, telling her she'd pay dearly for putting them all in danger.

Poor Ruth approached me, her hand shaking as she reached for me. "I hope you tell your father I sent the flowers for your mother."

Struggling to keep a straight face, I said, "I'll be sure to let him know." With that, she scurried out with the others.

What in God's name had these women done?

Only a handful of them had the gumption to stay, Georgine included. She seemed worried, so I suspected she'd be the most likely to cave.

I pivoted to face her. "There was a murder three years ago, around the same time Christopher Merritt disappeared. Who was killed?"

Her face paled. "She was Walter Frey's niece."

I resisted the shiver creeping along my spine. "His niece? What happened to her?"

"She was murdered in Florida."

"Florida?"

"She was going to college there. They never found the killer."

"Why did you think it had something to do with my father?" I asked, whipping around to look at Miss Ava.

"Because," Miss Ava said in a dull voice, "Walter received an anonymous text from someone who said he hoped his warning had been understood."

"What did the police say?"

"He never told them."

I shook my head in disbelief. "How did you find out?"

"A year later, Ruby told us. She was distraught because Walter was in trouble over some land deal and their daughter was getting married, and after all the trouble from the past . . . she was considering leaving him."

"And that's when you hired Colt. For protection. Did he know why?"

"No," Ava said, taking a seat in a now-empty chair in the front row. "I told him I'd had an intruder and observed how he handled it. I needed to know he'd protect me if the need arose."

"And you rented the apartment to me to find out what I knew about my father."

She nodded.

"I told you it was stupid!" Georgine shouted, agitated again. "You've only riled him up again!"

"How did his niece die?" I asked.

"Her throat was slit."

I expected as much, but it was shocking nonetheless. One more innocent woman brutalized for *what*? So many lives had been lost.

312

"My father didn't kill Walter Frey's niece," I said, hoping I was right. He'd seemed confused by the idea of a serial killer, and he'd flat-out denied any involvement in Amy's death.

"Then who did?" Georgine asked in a snippy tone.

"Look," I said, turning to face her again, "I just admitted that my father killed people. I have no reason to lie about this, and I'm trying to find out myself."

"Why aren't the police handling it?" another woman asked as she twisted the fabric of her shirt at the base of her throat. It took me a second to remember her name was Jackie.

"Because the police don't seem to be taking this seriously. I need to stop the man before he kills someone else." I leveled my gaze at Miss Ava. "I need you to tell me everything you know. No more games."

She glared at me, and Georgine shouted, "Oh, for God's sake, Ava! Let go of your stubborn pride!"

Miss Ava took a breath, then pursed her lips into a thin line. "Magnolia, take a seat. I'm straining my neck looking up at you."

I grabbed a chair from the other side of the aisle, plopped it in front of Miss Ava, and then sat facing her. "I'm tired of playing twenty questions. Just save us all a lot of trouble and spit it out."

Miss Ava tried to look offended, but it didn't take. She seemed too worried to pull it off effectively. "We all invested in your father's project," she said, her voice sounding deflated. "Some of us lost a lot of money. We wanted our money back."

I narrowed my eyes. "Yeah, I'm not buying that. Sure, you wanted your money back, but you're pretty vindictive. I suspect you wanted your money back, but only as a side dish to your revenge entree."

She pursed her lips and nodded her head slightly.

"How'd this group work?" I asked. "Christopher Merritt's and Walter Frey's wives were part of your group, not to mention Rowena Rogers herself. Didn't you see them as enemies?"

Miss Ava gave me a condescending smile. "You know the saying, my dear. Keep your friends close and your enemies closer."

Jackie sat down next to Miss Ava, and the older woman gave her a distasteful look, not that Jackie seemed to notice. "That's not who they wanted revenge on," she said.

"My father."

"We knew he was still alive," Miss Ava said, her attitude returning.

"So we laid a trap," Jackie said.

"You did no such thing," Miss Ava snipped. "*You* were no part of it."

A pouty look washed over Jackie's face. "I *voted* for it."

"And that's not the same thing at all," Miss Ava said.

"Look," I said. "I don't give a flip who voted for what. I want to know what you *did.*"

Miss Ava's sense of indignation resurfaced. "I will not stand to be spoken to in such an insolent manner, Magnolia Steele."

"Perhaps I should call my daddy," I said in a syrupy sweet tone. "And ask him who else is on his list."

She scowled and I was pretty sure I'd made an enemy for life.

"So," I prodded, "you all decided to plot against my father. I take it the partners' wives and Rowena were part of the plot."

"We knew he'd stolen that money, and we wanted it back. And sure enough, he took off with millions."

I gave her a look of disgust. "Why in the hell didn't you tell me that at the start?"

Her thin silver eyebrows rose. "Would you have believed it? Everyone knew you maintained his innocence when you were a child. I was determined to find out if you still believed it."

"Which was why you decided to keep an eye on me."

"And once you found out that I believed he was murdered . . ."

"I decided I could gently guide you toward the truth. Colt was supposed to help me, but he dragged his heels. That's why I needed the cameras."

"Gently guide me toward the truth," I mocked, but even as I said the words, I realized she was absolutely right. The evidence she'd presented me with—those old newspaper clippings, the small teases of information—had been the best way to hook me in and challenge my beliefs.

"Good job." I brought my hands together with one clap, startling the three of them. The only women still left. "Mission accomplished. We're all on the same page that my father is a thieving murderer. What's next?"

Ava's mouth opened, then closed.

"We were hoping to get you on our side," Jackie said. "So you'd help us."

"Only, we planned to be more conniving than that," Georgine said.

"Well, of course," I said. "That's a given since Miss Ava's involved."

Miss Ava scowled.

I held my arms out. "Phase one complete. I'm on your side. What's the plan?"

Georgine leaned closer. "We want you to find out where he's hidden the money."

"So you can get it back?" I asked.

"Of course."

I narrowed my eyes at Miss Ava. "What's the real plan? Not the one you fooled your friends with."

When she refused to look me in the eye, it hit me. "Oh . . . *I* was part of the plan."

Georgine looked confused. "Of course you were. You were supposed to find out how we can get the money back."

"Georgine," I said as though I was talking to a toddler. "Really? You believe that? Does that sound like Ava Milton to you?"

"Like I said, we were going to be a lot more conniving." She cast a glance at Miss Ava, who kept her eyes down.

The fact that she wouldn't look at me was freaking me out. "You wanted your money, and you also wanted to make him pay. So you were planning on blackmailing him by using me, but how?"

Ava looked up. "What does it matter now?"

"It matters a whole helluva lot. I want to know how far you were willing to go."

The defiance in her eyes told me she'd planned to go pretty far.

"Why's this so personal for you?" I asked.

Ava continued to hold my gaze and said, "Jackie. Georgine. The meeting's over. Leave."

They both blustered about the injustice of it all, but in the end, both of them got up and left.

Miss Ava continued her staring contest with me, and once it was just the two of us, she said, "Oh, Magnolia. You've been more fun than I expected."

"Yeah, I hear that a lot," I said in a flippant tone. "Now, why is it personal to you?"

"I don't have to tell you a thing," she said, lifting her chin.

I stood. "You don't, but I bet I can figure it out." I was certain this involved a some*one*—not a some*thing*— and I was willing to bet there was evidence of him or her somewhere in this house. I knew I wouldn't find it on the first floor. I'd spent enough time dusting her knickknacks and artwork to know it was all impersonal. That meant the information I needed was upstairs, so I headed for the staircase.

Miss Ava got to her feet. "And where do you think you're going?"

"Finding answers."

I expected her to follow me; instead, she headed toward the kitchen. I took that as a bad sign and pulled my phone out of my pocket to call Colt.

"Are you done?" he asked. "You ready for me to pick you up?"

"Not quite. I might need you to pick me up from the Franklin police station."

"Did Detective Martinez call you back in for more questions?"

"No, I might get arrested for trespassing. At least I think that would be the charge," I said as I reached the top of the stairs.

"What are you talking about?" he asked, sounding anxious.

"Miss Ava won't give me the answers I need, so I'm searching for them myself." I cracked the first door on my right, revealing a generic bed, nightstand, and dresser. *Guest room.*

"What are you doing, Maggie?" He sounded even more nervous.

"She was going to use me to get back at my father," I said, "not just to find information. I think she was going to do something drastic, like hold me for ransom."

"She told you *that*?"

"No, she didn't have to. I could see it on her face. I called her on it, and she definitely didn't deny it."

"That sounds pretty extreme. Even for Ava."

"I know, which means my father must have hurt her really bad." I poked my head into the next room. This one looked like her bedroom. Jackpot. There were photographs spread all across the room. "If I can find out how he hurt her, maybe I can help make it right."

"It's not your job to right his wrongs, Mags."

"I know, but part of me feels like I have to do it anyway . . . if nothing else, to keep her from having me kidnapped and held hostage."

"Don't joke about that."

"I'm not joking. I have to go. I'll tell you what I find." Then I hung up so I could focus on snooping.

Three photographs in elaborate filigree frames sat on her dresser. One was a black and white wedding photograph of an ecstatic young bride and groom. I didn't have to look very hard to see that the bride was Miss Ava, even though the genuine smile almost threw me off. She couldn't have been more than twenty. The next photo was of a young girl. Based on her dated clothes and her facial features, I placed her as Miss Ava's daughter. The third photo was of a young family—a couple and their daughter, who looked like she was around ten years old.

"My granddaughter," Miss Ava said behind me. Her voice cracked, and she cleared her throat before she said, "She was twenty-one when she died seven years ago."

A heaviness settled on my shoulders. "I'm so sorry. What happened?"

"She was murdered."

My heart skipped a beat as I spun around to face her. "How?"

"She was going to school out on the West Coast. She went out to a bar with friends and told them she was leaving with a man she'd just met. Said she'd get a ride home."

"She never came home," I finished, staring at the happy girl in the photo.

"No."

"She had multiple cuts," I said in a dull voice.

"The police kept that part quiet. They told the public she died of stab wounds."

My breath stuck in my chest as grief and guilt washed over me. "Did she?"

"You tell me," she said, her words laced with anger.

I set the photo on her dresser and took a step toward her. "This is *not* my fault." But as soon as the words left my mouth, I couldn't help wondering if that was a lie. What if I'd been brave enough to stay and go to the police ten years ago? What if I could have prevented her senseless death as well as the others'?

"But it *is* your father's."

"What makes you think that?"

"Because after her funeral, Steve Morrissey received a single white flower in the mail. Do you know what that flower was?"

I swallowed the terror rising in my throat. "No."

"A magnolia blossom. Only, the stupid fool didn't realize what it was. My granddaughter was killed to send him a message, and he didn't even understand it."

I felt light-headed, so I grabbed the edge of the dresser. "Oh God . . ." I waited a moment for my faded peripheral vision to return before I asked, "Why your granddaughter? Why send the flower to Steve Morrissey?"

"My son-in-law was Steve Morrissey's brother."

My mouth dropped open. "And the death in Florida? She was Walter Frey's niece?"

"There were rumors about him and her," she said.

Rowena Rogers had said the same thing, only she'd been a lot blunter. Incest.

Ava frowned. "I didn't put it together at first. I didn't even know about Steve Morrissey receiving that flower until his wife told me a few years later. And then Walter's niece was killed, and the warning he was given . . ."

"You put it together."

I sat down on the edge of her bed, my head still fuzzy. "You think my father did this. To what purpose?"

"Every single death is tied to seven of the nine original partners." She narrowed her eyes. "Everyone but your father and Bill James."

I blinked hard, trying to keep myself together. "What?"

"I looked into the murders you told me about. Every single victim has some tie to one of the nine original partners of the Jackson Project. A niece. An old—but significant—girlfriend. An old neighbor. Someone whose death would hit hard, yet a connection distant enough to evade the attention of the police. Only the people involved would understand."

I tried to catch my breath. So much premeditation . . . yet why was I surprised? I'd known there was a link. I just hadn't put it together on my own.

"What about Amy and Emily?"

"Amy was the daughter of a woman Max Goodwin actually fell in love with years ago, then lost to his philandering." The look in her eyes was full of both fear and pride. "She *may* have even been his secret daughter."

"You told her."

Her eyebrows raised slightly. "Excuse me?"

"You were the one who told Max Goodwin's girlfriend that he was cheating on her."

She lifted her chin, but she looked smug, not remorseful. "That's neither here nor there."

"How much do you actually know about people in this town?" I asked in disgust. "And who made you important enough to destroy people's lives?"

"I save them as well, you insolent girl. I do what is best for everyone."

"According to you and your rules," I countered. "What about Emily? What was her connection?"

"Emily . . . as far as I can tell, she wasn't related to anyone."

Then why was she killed? Because she got too close to the truth?

"So you're telling me that you think my father had something directly to do with their deaths?"

"Why would the killer send Walter a text saying he hoped he liked his warning and Steve a magnolia flower if it wasn't tied to your father?"

She had a point, but he'd seemed so surprised at the suggestion of a serial killer. And he wasn't the one who'd hurt Melanie. I'd been there, and apparently Roy had witnessed it too. So what was the serial killer's aim?

More to the point, who was he?

chapter twenty-five

My phone rang and I pulled it out of my pocket, cringing when I saw Brady's name on the screen. I knew I should share Miss Ava's information with him, but I suspected he was calling about my chat with his partner. In fact, it was nearly noon. I was surprised it had taken him this long to call.

Against my better judgment, I answered. "Hey, Brady."

"Magnolia, where are you?" His tone was short.

"I'm at Miss Ava's."

"*Again?*"

"It's Thursday. Bible study."

Miss Ava snorted.

"I need to talk to you ASAP."

"I'm not sure when I'll be done here. Can't you tell me over the phone?"

"You're done *now*. I'll be there in ten minutes."

I hung up, feeling anxious about Brady's insistence as well as how short he'd been. He had undoubtedly heard about the statement I'd made to his partner the night before. My trust in him was plummeting by the second, and I really wasn't sure getting into a car with him was a good idea. As I dropped my phone back into my pocket, Miss Ava looked pissed.

"You and I are *not* done," Miss Ava said. "We are far from done."

She must have heard Brady's side of the call. "Then you have ten minutes to finish it." Or less if I decided to bolt before Brady showed up.

She walked toward her door. "We're not having this discussion in my bedroom."

I followed her out of the room, then turned back and gave her photos one last glance before going downstairs. I was scared, and more than tempted to call Colt and beg him to run away with me and never come back. The revelations Miss Ava had shared with me were just so . . . heavy. So terrifying. But that smiling face of Miss Ava's granddaughter kept me rooted to this mess. She might not have died if I hadn't run before. No one else was dying because of me.

My phone rang again, and I recognized the number as the one Detective Martinez had used to call me the other day. I answered her call too.

"Magnolia Steele," she said in an icy tone. "We need to chat."

"I feel so popular today," I said in a fake-sweet voice as I descended the stairs.

"I'm not calling to bolster your ego. I need to talk to you more about the murders."

"Which murders?" I asked, feigning innocence.

"Just get your ass down here."

"Well, it just so happens Brady's on his way to pick me up. I'll have him drop me off at the station."

"Brady Bennett is picking you up?" Her tone suggested this was not something that should be happening.

"Do we have a bad connection? Is that why you're asking me to repeat myself?"

"You get down here by yourself. Or, better yet," she said, sounding a little flustered, "let me send a squad car."

My heart stuttered and I stopped at the bottom step. "Am I being arrested for something?"

"No, but do not get into a car with Detective Bennett. He has been instructed to have no contact with you."

I almost defended him, but I cut myself off. I needed to think this through a little bit more. "Thank you for the information."

"I'm serious, Magnolia Steele."

"And so am I, Detective Martinez." I hung up and continued to follow Miss Ava into the dining room, where she had begun to dismantle the food display on the table.

I could see why Brady wasn't supposed to have contact with me—it was surely a conflict of interest at this point—but why hadn't he told me to keep quiet about meeting him?

"So chummy with so many police detectives," Miss Ava muttered.

I stopped several feet from the table. "What does that mean?"

"It's surprising is all." She swung her head to glance at me. "But then everything about you has been a surprise."

I flashed her a smile. "You can't help but love me."

Her gaze met mine for a long moment, and then she abruptly turned her back and carried two platters to the kitchen. "You remind me of her."

I grabbed a plate half-filled with mini quiches and a decanter of orange juice and followed her. "Your granddaughter?"

She set the platters on the kitchen counter, and I did the same. "She was feisty. Not afraid of anything. At first, we figured that was why she was killed, because she had no fear."

"I have plenty of fear."

Her eyes lifted to mine. "Do you?" She turned away and headed back into the dining room. "The irony is that it wasn't her lack of fear that got her killed. It was something she had no control over."

She picked up two more trays, and I grabbed the last two plates and followed her.

"Would you really have used me to get back at my father?" I asked.

"I thought we had already established that I would," she barked, but the words sounded forced and full of false bravado.

"Are you still going to try to get your revenge?"

326

She studied me for several long seconds before she said, "You'll be the weapon of our revenge, just how we planned."

"What does that mean?"

"Your father still sees you as the teenage daughter who worships him. The fact that you're bringing him down will be the best revenge of all."

I almost argued that he knew I didn't still worship him, but he hadn't seemed to accept that. "Who says I'm bringing him down?"

"Going to the police station and telling Detective Martinez that your father confessed to killing three people is a great start to his downfall."

"I'm positive my father's not the serial killer, Miss Ava. He was taken by surprise, so it has to be someone who has known him for at least twenty years." I paused. "I need to know more about Eric Duncan."

"I don't know what more there is to know."

"Come on, Miss Ava. When I asked you yesterday, you said his son had hired my father as his financial planner, but you changed the subject when I asked you how Eric took it."

"He didn't handle it well at all. He vowed to get even with your father. He had a temper and he showed up at your father's office once and your home twice. The police were called." She paused. "One of the officers who showed up at your house was Gordon Frasier."

"The detective who handled Daddy's disappearance . . ."

"There are multiple connections to the Franklin Police Department," she said. "You're friendly with one of them."

"Brady?" When she nodded, I said, "How?"

"Eric Duncan is his uncle."

The bottom fell out of my stomach. "This town is like the six degrees of Kevin Bacon, only there are only two degrees."

"Eric Duncan is the brother of Brady's mother, Amanda. The families became somewhat estranged when Clint signed with your father. Clint's father refused to see him, so Brian had him spend a lot of time at your house."

"Like Tripp Tucker."

"Both of them looked up to Brian. He replaced their absent fathers."

"And after he lost all their money?"

"Tripp never forgave him, especially after what happened with his fiancée. Clint, on the other hand, never blamed Brian. He was a staunch defender of your father until he disappeared. And after."

"He might have believed the partners wronged my father."

"Possibly."

"Clint Duncan was an adult when he came to my house, and I don't remember him. Brady's not much older than me . . ."

"Clint was eighteen when he hired your father as a financial planner. His father, Eric, is a good ten or more years older than Amanda. They were never close, and

Brady's father couldn't stand Eric. When Eric disowned Clint, Brady's father tried to cut off all contact with him."

"Tried?"

"Amanda and the kids still saw her brother and his family at their parents' house on a few occasions. Brady knows both his uncle and his cousin."

There was no denying that Brady had a connection to the serial killer. He'd known about Melanie Seaborn's murder before starting at the police academy. Had he suspected his uncle?

The doorbell rang and I jumped. "That's Brady."

"He's here to take you to the police station?"

I gave her a look of impatience. We both knew she'd overheard my phone calls. "Detective Martinez said he's not supposed to have contact with me."

Her eyebrows rose. "And yet he's still here. He must *really* want to see you."

The doorbell rang again.

"What are you going to do?" There was a challenge in her eyes.

Ultimately, there wasn't much of a choice at all. "I've got questions and he's got answers." I pushed the swinging door open and headed into the living room, pausing only to scoop my purse up off the chair I'd left it on earlier. I was almost to the door when I heard Brady pound on it and shout, "Magnolia!"

I opened the door and relief filled his eyes.

"Why are you so worried?" I asked.

"There are a lot of people who don't have your best interests in mind, and I'm concerned for your safety."

There were so many red flags where Brady was concerned, but I still believed he was genuinely worried about me. "Your partner says you're not supposed to be talking to me."

Disappointment turned his mouth down. "Why didn't you tell *me*, Maggie? Why did you tell Maria instead?"

"I hadn't planned on it. I went in to talk to her, and it just came out. I'm sick of all the lies, Brady."

"You really saw your father?"

"Last night. It wasn't planned. I ran into him."

The hard look in his eyes softened. "Are you okay? I know that had to be a difficult reunion."

I nodded. "It was."

"He admitted to murdering those three people?" he asked.

I crossed my arms and leaned against the door frame. "Martinez says you're not supposed to be talking to me."

He scowled. "They don't like that you know things that haven't been released to the public."

"Did you get in trouble?"

"I told them you snooped and found my files." He cringed. "Sorry to throw you under the bus like that."

"Why?" I asked. "It's true. Like I said, I'm good and finished with lies." I tilted my head and looked up at him. "Brady, I need to ask you some things."

"Shoot."

I glanced over my shoulder at Ava, who'd joined me by the door and was avidly listening to our conversation. "Thanks for your help."

Her eyes hardened. "Bring him to his knees."

I gave her a grim smile. "I'll do my best." Then I shut the door behind me.

Brady forced a chuckle. "I hope she wasn't referring to me."

She'd been referring to my father, but I didn't correct him.

He had started down the porch steps, but I gestured toward two wicker chairs on the porch. "I'd rather talk here."

He turned on his heels to face me. "You don't trust me." He sounded hurt.

I didn't answer, and he glanced around before shifting his gaze pointedly to the front door. "Do you think discussing this here is a good idea?"

"No," I conceded.

"I'm not going to hurt you, Maggie. I think I've proven that time and time again."

He was right. Besides, I really did need answers. I followed him down the stairs, and he opened the passenger door.

"You really want to defy Detective Martinez?" I asked.

"Do you really think you should be alone?" he asked.

After the text I'd received this morning, no. I got inside the car, and Brady shut the door behind me before walking around and slipping behind the steering wheel.

"What exactly did your father confess to?" he asked as he backed out of the driveway.

"Not to the serial killings. He admitted to killing Max Goodwin, Neil Fulton, and Steve Morrissey. I'm sure he killed Rowena and her goon. I asked him how many people he's killed, and he gave me a vague answer. He said only the people who deserved it."

"What if he thought Amy Danvers deserved it?"

"He didn't kill her. But whoever is killing these women has known Daddy for at least twenty years and knows all the original partners in the Jackson Project."

"How do you know that?"

"Every woman with the exception of Emily has some personal tie to one of the partners. Seven of them."

Brady pulled to a full stop at a four-way intersection, then turned to gape at me. "How do you know that?"

"You already know?" I asked.

"You know I've been investigating the murders. But you're wrong. There were only five."

I shook my head. "You're missing two. Steve Morrissey's niece was killed seven years ago in California, and Walter Frey's niece was killed in Florida three years ago."

"How'd you find that out?" He groaned. "Ava Milton."

"Steve Morrissey's niece was Ava's granddaughter." I pinned my gaze on him. "She also told me something else. About you."

"That my uncle used to be your father's partner?" He cast a glance at me. "I can't believe she didn't tell you sooner," he said in defeat. "Ava Milton knows everything about the people in Franklin."

"Why didn't you tell me?" I asked, sounding more hurt than I'd intended.

"I had my reasons, Maggie. And I didn't want their connection to bias you against me."

"Why did you *really* get interested in Melanie Seaborn's murder?"

"I think my cousin might be the serial killer."

chapter twenty-six

Y*our cousin?*" I asked. "Why?"

"My uncle had a temper, and my father had seen enough of it that he refused to have anything to do with him. I hardly ever saw my cousin when we were growing up. But after Clint got his record deal, he wasn't on speaking terms with his father either. Things got worse when Clint turned out to be a one-hit wonder. Like any good washed-up singer, he drank heavily to get through the days. The year my grandmother turned seventy, she guilted everyone into spending Christmas with her. She even convinced Uncle Eric and my father to come."

I realized he hadn't turned left to head to the police department, but I didn't call him on it yet. I decided to see where he went.

"But tempers were short, and Uncle Eric and Clint got into it. Clint blurted out that if Uncle Eric pushed him hard enough, he'd meet the same end as 'that girl' last summer. My uncle shushed him, and everyone could tell that something weird had happened. Later, Clint was three sheets to the wind . . . again . . . and I was thirteen and too curious for my own good. So I asked him what he'd meant by that, and he said something about a dead girl outside of Jackson. His best friend's girlfriend."

"Tripp Tucker was your cousin's best friend?"

"Yeah. Later, I realized he was talking about Tiffany Kessler. I wondered if he'd had something to do with it, but then they arrested someone else and I let it go. Seven years later, I ran into Clint in a restaurant bar. He was drunk off his ass, and he called me over and asked me if I was still curious about murders. He told me to check up in Clarksville a few months before. So I did . . . and that's how I found out about Melanie Seaborn's murder."

"Did he admit to killing her?"

"No. Not even close to a confession. But the fact that he knew about a murder in Clarksville, which hadn't made big headlines, made me curious. So I started digging into both cases and realized they were remarkably similar. I joined that cold-case club specifically to submit Melanie Seaborn's case. The man arrested for Tiffany's murder was still in jail, yet there were similarities that weren't made public. I notified the FBI, but they weren't interested because of the conviction in Tiffany's murder. I decided I really liked investigating—when I told you that before, I wasn't lying—so I went to the police academy.

"I did more digging in my spare time, and discovered the case twenty years ago, after the Jackson Project fell to pieces. And a case in Kentucky fourteen years ago. Then there was nothing after Melanie. I thought it was done until Amy." He shook his head. "I had no idea I'd missed two."

"How could you have known about those? I'm surprised you found out about the one in Kentucky." I turned to scrutinize him. "Did you really call the FBI last week?"

His knuckles whitened as he gripped the steering wheel, but he didn't answer, which was answer enough.

I looked out the window, realizing we were heading toward my mother's neighborhood. Fear shot up my spine. "Where are we going, Brady?"

"We have to go check out that house, Maggie."

I shook my head adamantly. "No. I have to go talk to Detective Martinez."

"This is more important. There's a killer on the loose, whether it's my cousin or not, and something out there might help us catch him."

"But I told Martinez I was coming to see her. I need to tell her about Miss Ava's granddaughter and all the victims' connections to the Jackson Project."

"We'll go to the house first. Then we'll tell her everything we know."

I grabbed the armrest on the door as I started to panic. "No, Brady! I can't go out there."

He gently shook his head. "You've been full of excuses for over a week, Maggie. This is important."

"*Why?* What do you hope to *prove*, Brady?" I asked, nearly hysterical. "That your cousin did it or that he *didn't?*"

His face remained grim. "Just like you, Magnolia, I want the truth."

"If you're so interested in the truth, then why did you lie to me about Belinda after you followed Roy home the other night?"

"Why do you think it was a lie?" he asked, but he reeked of guilt.

I suspected my theory was correct—that he was trying to separate me from the people I trusted so I'd lean on him, but I wasn't about to get into it with him. "What's going on with Owen?" I needed to find out if Owen had contacted Clint Duncan. And I needed to tell him about Brady's connection and theory.

"What do you mean?"

"I know he's on leave."

"Maggie, he's not on leave. He quit."

"Quit? That's not what he told me."

He did a double take. "You talked to *Owen*?"

"Yeah, about the report, and he definitely told me he was on leave. He was at the police department when I was there giving my statement on Wednesday."

"He was there turning in his badge."

I wasn't sure what to make of that. If Brady was right, Owen had lied to me too. Was there *anyone* I could trust?

"It wasn't because of you, Maggie," Brady said, softening his tone. "He said he was tired of his uncle's shadow hanging over him all the time."

I'd sat with him at the diner . . . I'd told him my deep, dark secret . . . I'd broken into Brady's apartment to get him a file he had no business having. *Why?* I took

337

a second, then asked, "What did Gordon do after he quit the police force?"

"He got a job at a hardware store."

"What will Owen do now?"

"I don't know. Like I said, we're not getting along right now."

So I'd heard, but I wasn't eager to get in the middle of that. "I'm not going out to that house, Brady. I'm going to the police station to talk to Detective Martinez before she decides I'm the murderer." I held out my phone in my hand. "If you don't turn around right now, I'll call her back and tell her you're holding me hostage."

"Maggie. Why won't you take me out there?"

"Because I lived through a real-life nightmare in that house. The thought of even walking into those woods puts me on the edge of a panic attack. I know I have to go out there, but not now. I can't do it."

"You can do whatever you put your mind to. You're a strong woman. I'll be there, and you still have the gun I gave you, right?"

I nodded.

"Not to mention we'll be going in the daylight. Now's the perfect time to go."

He had a point, but I didn't like the way he was trying to force me into it. Still, I was wavering a little when my phone rang with a call from a familiar number.

"Hello, Detective Martinez," I answered.

Brady shot me a dark look as he turned into my mother's neighborhood.

"Where are you?" his partner demanded.

"I just left, and I'm on my way now. I should be there in five to ten minutes."

"That's what you said ten minutes ago."

"What can I say about this crazy Franklin traffic?" I hung up and turned to Brady. "Take me home so I can get my car and drive myself."

"Maggie . . ."

"I didn't rat you out, but I can if you don't let me get into my car and drive to the police station."

He was silent until he pulled into the driveway next to my car. "I know I sound like I'm on a loop, but we *really* need to go out to that house."

"Tomorrow. I'll go tomorrow, but now I'm going to the police station." When he didn't argue, I said, "I'll call you later."

He stayed in the driveway until I backed out of the space and headed to the police station.

An hour later, I walked out of the police station just as frustrated as before I'd walked in. Detective Martinez had been belligerent and suspicious of where I'd gotten my information. I'd told her about the victims' connections to the members of the Jackson group, including what I'd learned about Walter Frey's and Steve Morrissey's nieces, and gave her Ava Milton as my source. I'd also mentioned that I suspected Clint Duncan's involvement in the women's deaths, but I was careful not to bring any mention of Brady into it.

Colt had tried to call me five times while I'd been talking to Martinez, so I called him back right away as I walked out to my car.

"I'm sorry," I said. "I just walked out of the police station after giving them more information. This is the first chance I've had to call you back."

"I've been freaking out for the last half hour, Maggie. Are you okay?"

"I'm fine. Where are you?" I asked.

"We're almost done here at the luncheon. Then we're heading back to the kitchen. Did you tell her about the camera?"

"No. I told her everything I know about the victims so they can try to find the killer. Miss Ava gave me more information, but I don't want to get into it on the phone. I'll fill you in on all the details later, but they have some good leads, and Clint Duncan is one of them."

"Thank God." He took a second before he asked, "Did you tell her about witnessing Melanie Seaborn's murder?"

"No," I said quietly. "I don't trust her enough for that. But there is *some* good news. The Brentwood police have reopened Amy's case. They're looking at the comparisons between her and Emily's deaths."

"While that *is* good news, I suspect the serial killer isn't going to like it. Have you heard anything from him since this morning?"

"No."

"Well, to be safe, maybe you should wait at the police station until I leave here. Or better yet, go back in there and demand police protection."

"Martinez doesn't trust me for having all this information. If she could have found a reason for locking me up, she would have done it in a heartbeat. She's not giving me a guard."

"I'm scared for you, Mags."

I was scared too, but I wasn't hanging out in the police station lobby until Colt picked me up. I could only imagine what Martinez would do if she found me out there. "I'll be fine, Colt. I think I'll just head back to Momma's house. I have a gun and I'll lock myself in with the security system until you get there."

"Maggie . . ."

"I'm sure as hell not staying here at the police station a minute longer. I'm heading home."

"Okay, but Tilly knows something's up. Don't worry—" he interjected before I could protest, "—she doesn't know what's going on, just that you're upset. She wants me to take you away for the weekend." When I didn't say anything, he said, "Just think about it, okay?"

I was tired and weak, and to my surprise, I found myself saying, "Okay."

"Text me as soon as you're safe inside the house, and I'll be there as soon as I can."

I headed home, locked myself inside. After I texted Colt, I heated up leftovers for lunch. I carried the plate downstairs to the basement and studied the fireplace, trying to see where the bricks had been replaced. Whoever had repaired it had done a good job, but I could distinguish five newer looking bricks. That was where I'd start.

By the time I finished my lunch, I had convinced myself I didn't need to wait for Colt to start smashing bricks. I found a hammer in the garage, carried it downstairs, and started bashing. However, the bricks were a lot harder to tear out than I had expected.

The doorbell rang and I stopped mid-swing, my heart leaping into my throat. Then I realized the serial killer was hardly likely to ring my doorbell and politely ask to murder me.

I headed back upstairs, holding the hammer in my free hand as I turned off the alarm and opened the door. I was surprised to see Owen on my porch.

"Why are you sharing information with Maria Martinez and not with me?" he asked. "I thought we had a deal."

I put my free hand on my hip and dialed up the attitude. "And rumor has it that you're no longer a Franklin police officer."

"I can still help you find the truth."

"Then you really should talk to your best friend," I said. "He thinks he knows the identity of the serial killer."

"Who?"

I dropped my hand from my hip and lifted the hammer to rest upright on my shoulder blade. "The same person you told me you were investigating this morning. His cousin, Clint Duncan."

He froze and his face went slack with shock. Finally, he said, "Clint Duncan is Brady's cousin?"

"Go figure."

Owen frowned. "What's with the hammer? Self-protection?"

"A little home redecorating." But I was sure the brick dust on my jeans was a dead giveaway that I was up to something. "If you quit the force, then why are you still so interested in all of this?"

The corners of his eyes wrinkled with irritation. "You know why. Uncle Gordon."

"My father was corrupt. He admitted to killing people. It's only a matter of time before it trickles down to your uncle and clears him . . . or confirms his guilt."

Owen's scowl deepened.

"All that's left is the identity of the serial killer, and Brady thinks it's his cousin. So let me ask you one more time, Owen: Why are you here?"

He pushed out a groan. "Because I've got a head start on all of them, and whether I quit or not, investigating is in my blood. I've already interviewed Duncan, and now I've probably scared him. Ten to one he bolts. You're in the thick of this. Did you tell everything to Martinez?"

I frowned and dropped the hammer to my side. "No. I kept my own personal involvement to myself."

"So that means you don't trust her either."

I cocked my head. "What do you mean by *either*?"

"In addition to talking to Clint Duncan, I talked to Uncle Gordon about the officer who arrested the musician."

"You mean Colt?"

He curled his lip. "Yeah. Him. Uncle Gordon said Mahoney, the arresting officer, was in thick with Martinez. If Mahoney was dirty, what if she is too?"

Dread doused over me like a cold shower. "And she's the one I told everything to . . ."

"She might use it all, or she might suppress some of it." An earnest look filled his eyes. "If she's dirty, I want to nail her too."

"Too? Did you have anything to do with Mahoney's hit-and-run?"

His eyes flew wide in shock. "I can't believe you asked me that question."

"And yet, it's still sitting between us like a stinky turd—did you have anything to do with it?"

His face hardened. "No. And if you distrust me that much, maybe we should end this joint effort right now. I was talking about your father."

He'd talked to Clint Duncan, and I wanted information—especially if he was right and there was a chance the guy was going to bolt. I backed up and stepped into the entryway, giving him room to pass me.

He walked in and glanced around as he headed toward the living room. "What were you doing with the hammer?"

I shut the door behind him and turned on the alarm system. "Trying to find a camera."

He glanced over his shoulder and gave me a blank stare.

"I've got a lot to fill you in on, but first I want to hear about Clint Duncan."

He sat down in a chair while I sat on the sofa, sitting sideways and crossing my legs in front of me.

"Duncan was a suspect in Tiffany Kessler's murder, but he had an alibi, albeit a flimsy one. He and a friend were at a bar the night of her disappearance, but no one else could corroborate their story, and there was nothing tying him to the case. This morning I pinned him down, and he confessed he hadn't gone out to the bar."

My mouth dropped open. "How did you get him to admit that?"

"Probably by catching him by surprise years later. He swore up and down that he had nothing to do with her murder, but he was nervous."

"I'd probably be nervous if Martinez showed up on my doorstep seventeen years from now, asking me questions about my alibi the night Max Goodwin was murdered. And we both know I didn't do it."

He pressed his lips together. "Fair."

"What else did he say?"

"I asked him where he was ten years ago at the end of May, and he fumbled with an answer. It seemed like a better idea to focus on the more recent murders."

"Again . . . if someone asked me . . ."

"Agreed, but his nervousness was suspicious."

"What was his answer?"

"He said he didn't know for certain, that he often goes to his Alabama lake house over Memorial Day weekend, so he might have been there."

"And what about Amy's and Emily's murders?"

"No alibi. He said he was likely at home, writing music." When I gave him a questioning look, he added,

"He's a songwriter. A pretty good one from what I hear. He might not be performing them anymore, but others are. He's still making good money."

"So why would he screw that up by murdering women who had connections to the Jackson Project partners?" I asked.

"What connections?"

"I'll tell you in a minute. Finish your story first."

Owen narrowed his eyes at that, but he continued. "He claims he doesn't hold a grudge against your father. He says he let it go years ago, but his body language said differently. I can guarantee he hates Brian Steele." He paused, then said in a softer voice, "And he has no great fondness for you."

"Me?"

"He didn't come right out and say it, but when I asked him if he knew you, his body stiffened and he gave a flat answer that he didn't know you. It definitely suggested he didn't like you."

I resisted the urge to react, but it was strange to hear a man I didn't remember, one I hadn't seen since I was a kid, hated me for no good reason. "Anything else?"

"No, and there's nothing to hold him or charge him, but he's suspicious as hell. If *I* were working this case, I'd be asking all of his old friends about Tiffany Kessler's murder. I'd definitely be digging deeper."

"Why her case?"

"Because her cuts were more random and deeper than in the other cases. Her death was personal."

"In that case, it sounds more like Tripp would be a suspect," I said, shivering. I'd been alone with him the night before.

Owen shook his head. "Tripp had an alibi. He was on a radio show later that night, and the next morning he left for a business trip. But Clint spent a lot of time with Tripp and Tiffany, and the original report says he admitted to being in love with her."

"So if he hated my father and found out she'd slept with him . . ."

"The original report also says Tripp called Clint and told him about Tiffany's affair, then asked if he knew where she was. He denied seeing or talking to her." A cold look filled his eyes. "If I were a betting man, I'd bet the serial killer is Clint Duncan."

"I might be able to help confirm it," I said softly.

"What?" Then understanding filled his eyes. "You mentioned a camera."

First I told him what I'd learned from Miss Ava and Brady. Then I told him everything I knew about what my brother had seen and done that night. About the pictures on the camera, and how he'd bricked the camera up into the fireplace.

"Why would he do that?" Owen asked, puzzled.

"To hide it," I said. "He says he kept it as insurance, but it's odd that he put it someplace practically irretrievable."

"Agreed." He stood and looked at the fireplace. "Is this the fireplace? I can help dig it out."

"No, it's in the basement." I pointed to the hammer on the coffee table. "But that's pretty worthless."

347

He grinned. "I know better than to suggest that it's your lack of upper body strength. Maybe a flathead screwdriver would help chisel it out. Do you have one?"

"Yeah, in the garage."

I headed toward the door in the kitchen, and he called out, "A flathead is the one with the straight end, not the prong-looking one."

"I know what a flathead screwdriver is," I called back sarcastically as I grabbed one out of the toolbox. "I know a thing or two about tools."

Owen stood in the open doorway, watching me with a smart-ass grin and holding the hammer in his hand.

I gave him a sassy look. "I've dated a tool or two."

"It's no wonder Brady likes you," he said. "You're not his usual type."

My heart nearly stopped. "And what type is that?" I asked carefully.

"I don't know . . . easygoing, go with the flow. He calls the shots and they go along." He noticed my subdued expression. "Are you thinking he dated you because of this case?"

I didn't answer, but I held his gaze in a challenge.

"I can assure you that Brady lost his usual chill when he met you. He did *not* want to date you because of this case. It may have complicated things and made him more intense, but Brady is totally into you." He scowled. "Even with the musician in the picture. I think he's waiting for that guy to dump you."

"Wow. That's lovely," I said, walking back into the kitchen.

I started to close the door, but Owen grabbed the edge and stopped the swing. "Are these really Christopher Merritt Jr.'s things?" His interest seemed piqued.

I scanned the contents of the garage and pushed out a sigh. "They are. If you want to take a stab at finding something, go for it. Apparently my brother has already looked for the elusive evidence Chris supposedly found."

He looked like he'd rather head out into the garage than rip apart my fireplace, but to his credit, he shut the garage door.

Maybe I could trust him yet.

chapter
twenty-seven

W e tromped downstairs, and I showed him the few chips I'd dented into the bricks and handed him the screwdriver. Owen had just begun chiseling the mortar between bricks with the screwdriver and hammer when my phone rang with a call from Detective Martinez.

"Magnolia," she said when I answered, "I wanted to let you know that we brought Clint Duncan in for questioning, and we found some incriminating evidence in his home."

"What kind of incriminating evidence?"

"I shouldn't be telling you this, but since you were the one who tipped us off . . . He had photos of several of the murdered women as well as a map of Tennessee that had pins in the locations where their bodies were found." She paused. "Thank you for your help."

I closed my eyes, trying to let the news sink in. "Thank you for letting me know."

"Good news," I said to Owen as I set the phone down. "Martinez said they have Clint Duncan in custody. He had incriminating evidence in his house." I filled him in on the details.

Squatting in front of the fireplace, he sank back on his heels. "Well, I'll be damned." The look of relief and satisfaction on his face was contagious.

"Is it over?" I asked as tears sprang to my eyes.

"If he hasn't confessed, no. But if he's the killer, they'll find a way to make it stick. That victim board is pretty damn incriminating, so yeah, I think it's over, Magnolia." The compassion in his voice caught me off guard, but then again, he'd been a lot kinder and gentler after we'd made our truce yesterday.

No more looking over my shoulder. What would it be like to not live my life in fear?

"What do you want to do about the camera?" Owen asked after a few seconds, and I opened my eyes to face him. "If your brother took photos and got a good one of his face, it could help firm up the evidence against him."

"I want to get it out," I said. "Roy was so freaked out over it being found, I've been driving myself crazy wondering what's on there." But if we were going to submit it as evidence, I had to accept the possibility that my brother would get in trouble for having hidden it.

He got back to work, and after he had the third brick chiseled out, he said, "I think I see something."

I leaned forward, and sure enough, I could see the edge of something silver. "I think that's it."

He whistled. "It's a good hiding place. No one would have found it without knowing it was there."

"Good thing Roy told me." But now that I thought about it, I was surprised that he'd said anything. Why not keep the secret forever? Was he as ready to put this to bed as I was?

"No kidding."

It only took two more swings of the hammer on the angled screwdriver before the camera was fully exposed. Owen pried it out, then handed it to me. I glanced up at him in surprise, and he shrugged. "It's technically yours."

I took the camera and tried to turn it on, but it was hardly surprising when nothing happened. "It's been buried for ten years," I said. "The battery's dead. But I have another idea."

I hopped up and headed up the stairs. I tried to call Colt as I climbed, but his phone went straight to voicemail. I left a message, telling him that I had good news and he should call me back, and left it at that. This was too important to leave in a voicemail.

Owen followed, and I led him into the kitchen, grabbing my laptop on the way. I set it down on the counter and popped the memory card out of the camera and into the slot in my computer while he stood quietly to one side.

My hand shook so badly I had a hard time opening the icon for the camera. A folder full of mini photos filled my screen. I held my breath as I clicked on the first photo and started the slideshow. There was no preparing myself for what I was about to see, so I might as well jump in.

The first photos were of graduation, my friends and me still in our graduation gowns. We were smiling and so happy, and part of me wished I could go back and tell me not to follow Maddie's boyfriend into the woods that night.

I kept clicking and a dark photo filled the screen. I knew what was coming next. I'd taken these photos and the flash hadn't come on for the first one. Sure enough, the next photo was of Ashley Pincher giving Blake Green a blowjob. The next few photos were of the woods, photos I'd taken accidentally as I'd run from Blake that night.

Owen stirred behind me. "You don't have to look at these, Magnolia. Why don't you let me look for you, and I'll tell you what I find?"

I shook my head, but my voice quavered as I said, "No. No more hiding."

He put his hand on my shoulder. "If you change your mind, let me know. There's no shame in protecting yourself from this."

"Thanks."

The scene switched abruptly in the next photo—the basement of the abandoned house filled the screen. It was from the perspective of the stairs, where Roy had been hidden. A nearly naked woman was on the left side of the photo, wearing only her bra and panties. Her arms were raised over her head, but I couldn't see her face. On the floor to the right of her, a small figure was huddled against a metal pole. *Me.* The man with the hoodie stood between us, his back to the camera.

Owen drew a breath of shock as a shudder ran through my body. His hand tightened on my shoulder.

"Magnolia, you don't have to do this. Let me look at them. There's no reason to torture yourself."

I was so tempted to take him up on his offer, but I had to do this myself. I shook my head. Tears burned my eyes, and I blinked to clear my vision.

The screen changed to a similar photo. The next one showed the killer squatting on the floor in front of me with a knife in his hand.

Several others showed the killer cutting my leg with my skirt up to my lap. I swallowed my nausea. My brother had not only sat there and watched the killer torture me and Melanie, he'd taken photos—one after another. Seeing them hammered that fact home.

While none of the photos showed the killer's face, I'd seen enough photos of Clint Duncan to imagine it. My chest constricted and I felt the beginnings of a panic attack stirring.

A sharp knock landed on the door, and I jumped and slammed my laptop shut.

"Are you expecting someone?" Owen asked, sounding on edge as he reached for the gun in his shoulder holster.

"Maybe." I was expecting Colt but not this soon.

I heard the front door open, and Colt shouted in panic, "*Maggie!*"

I stood and walked around the corner to face him.

"Thank God," he said, relief replacing the panic in his eyes. Then he got a better look at me, and the agitation returned. "Are you *okay?*"

I nodded even though it wasn't true.

Colt's attention turned to Owen, who now stood behind me. "Detective Frasier. I wondered whose car was out there."

From the look on Colt's face, he hadn't just wondered—he'd full-on panicked.

"Austin," Owen said with a sharp nod.

The two men took each other's measure for several seconds before the beeping of the alarm caught Colt's attention. He finally caved, pivoting to punch in the code on the keypad and then shut the front door.

"You're home sooner than I expected," I said.

"Tilly cut me loose early. I wanted to get back to you. I saw I had a missed call from you," Colt said. "But you didn't answer when I called back, and I was worried. Especially when I saw the car."

"Sorry. I was . . . busy."

"With Frasier," was his guarded response, but I knew it wasn't aimed at me. "So what's the good news?"

"They have Clint Duncan in custody," I said. "They found a bulletin board with a map in his possession. Photos of the women were pinned to the locations where the bodies were found."

A guarded look of elation spread over Colt's face as he turned his gaze to Owen. "Does that mean Maggie's safe?"

Owen gave a slight nod. "He hasn't confessed, but when *I* talked to him, he acted guilty as hell. I suspect he is."

Colt bounded for me and pulled me into a hug, holding me close for several seconds before he mumbled into my hair, "Thank God."

I clung to him, not quite believing it was true.

"Did you come over to tell Maggie?" Colt asked, still holding me close as he looked over my head at Owen.

"No." Owen gave me a questioning look and didn't say anything else. He was probably wondering how much Colt knew about our arrangement.

"It's okay," I said. "Colt knows I've talked to you." Breaking free of his embrace, I gave him a reassuring smile. "Owen dropped by to fill me in on his interview with Clint Duncan. I was trying to get the camera out of the fireplace when he showed up. He helped."

I could see that Colt wanted to protest, but he wisely kept his mouth shut. Turning toward Owen again, he asked, "Did you find it?"

"We did," Owen said cautiously. "In fact, we were looking at the memory card on Magnolia's laptop when you walked in."

Colt's worry was back and his eyes widened. "Maggie? Are you okay? What did you see?"

Tears filled my eyes again and I started to shake.

Owen's phone rang, and he pulled it out of his pocket, frowning when he saw the screen. "Frasier," he said as he answered. His eyes darkened as he listened to the person on the other end of the line. Finally, he said, "I'll be right there." As he stuffed his phone in his pocket, he held out his hand. "I'm going to need to take the SIM card with me."

Bewildered by the request, I glanced up at Colt, who looked furious. "Do you want to give it to him?"

I shook my head, trying to hold myself together.

Owen started to walk toward the laptop, but Colt stepped around me to intercept him.

"Do you have a court order for that card?" Colt's jaw tightened, and the cords in his neck strained. "Because I guarantee you that's the *only* way you're walking out of here with it."

Owen's face reddened.

"You're no longer a cop, Owen," I said. "You turned in your badge yesterday. You have no right to it."

Owen rose to his full height, his demeanor changing from concerned, affable friend to police officer on the job. "I'm still going to need to take it to the station."

Colt moved closer. "You heard her. Time for you to go, Frasier."

For a second, I thought Owen might actually hit Colt, but he turned around to face me. "We're not done, Magnolia."

I held his gaze, wondering what had just happened. "I know."

Owen walked out the front door, shoving his shoulder into Colt's as he passed, but Colt just turned to watch him go out with a cold, hard stare. After he left, he shut and locked the door behind him.

"Are you okay?"

I nodded, but I was still shaking.

"What happened?" Colt asked, pulling me into his arms again.

"I don't know. He was fine until that phone call."

"So Frasier found the camera, and then you checked out the photos on your laptop?"

"Not all of them," I said in a flat voice.

"How much did you see?"

"My graduation. Some of the party. Ashley giving Blake a blowjob. Accidental photos of the woods while I was running." I took a moment, waiting for my heartbeat to slow down. "The basement."

Colt's arms tightened. "Oh God, Mags. They were on there?"

I nodded as tears filled my eyes. "Like I said, I haven't seen them all. The ones I saw didn't show his face, but I guess it doesn't matter anymore."

"Did you keep the card because you want to see the rest? You don't have to do this," he said, resting his chin on my head. "Let me look for you."

I wrapped my arms around his back and clung to him. "That's what Owen said," I whispered, dangerously close to losing it. "I'm sick of men trying to do everything for me."

"The key difference is that Owen wants to see what's on that memory card to serve some purpose of his own, and the only damn thing I care about is you."

"Are you sure?"

"Oh, Mags. I'll crush the damn thing and never look at it if that's what you want."

I started to cry, partly because the nightmare was on replay in my head, but partly because I believed him. He really would do that for me.

He led me to the sofa, and we sat down while I sobbed against him. The horror of that night wasn't only in my head now. The proof was also in those photos, and I wasn't sure I could handle other people seeing them. I was half-tempted to let Colt follow through on his offer to crush the card, but I knew I couldn't. What if Clint Duncan's face was in one of the photos? The police needed every shred of evidence to make sure any murder charges stuck.

Colt held me close, kissing the top of my head until I settled down.

"Did you see yourself in those pictures?" he asked quietly, rubbing slow circles on my back.

"Yes," I whispered.

He held me tighter. "I'm so sorry." His voice sounded strangled.

"It's not your fault."

"I know, but it still needs to be said. It kills me to think about you facing the aftermath of this alone back then. But you're not alone now. You can count on me all the way."

"We need to finish looking at those photos," I said, starting to sit up straight.

"Not right this minute. We'll do it when you're ready, okay?"

"Thanks." I pulled loose, then stood and went into the kitchen to get a glass of water.

"You need a moment alone?" Colt asked as he followed me.

"Yeah," I said, amazed that he understood my mixed signals. "Just for a few minutes."

"How about I go downstairs and check out the fireplace, then I'll be right back?"

"Thanks."

"If you need me or someone shows up, let me know."

I managed a grin for him, grateful that he was here with me and not Owen. "Go already."

He headed for the stairs, pausing to give me a long look before he stepped through the door and disappeared from sight.

I closed my eyes and took deep breaths, trying to focus on cute, cuddly kittens instead of the photos on my laptop.

I heard Colt coming up the stairs less than a minute later, and I couldn't help but smile. He hadn't been able to keep away for longer than that. Not that I minded. Maybe it meant I was weak, but I couldn't handle being alone right now.

"The mess isn't so bad," he said, standing in front of the garage door with the hammer and screwdriver in his hand. "He could have smashed it more."

"He seemed careful," I said, still standing at the sink.

Colt disappeared into the garage, and by the time he returned, I felt slightly more settled. "Why does Owen care what's on that memory card?"

I shrugged. "Curiosity? He seemed pretty thrilled to hear they had Clint Duncan in custody."

"I'm not sure what's going on with him, but it seemed personal." Colt studied me for several seconds. "I think we need to look at the rest of those photos. But I mean it, Mags. I'm willing to do it for you. There's no reason you have to live through it all again."

"No," I said. "I have to face my demons."

chapter
twenty-eight

I walked over to the laptop and opened the lid, then entered my password while I was still standing. My fingers shook so much it took me three times to get it right. Before, I hadn't quite known what to expect; now, I knew photos of my nightmare lurked on that laptop, just waiting to be brought out into the world.

"Do you want to sit?" Colt asked softly. "Or move the laptop somewhere else?"

I wasn't sure moving would help, and sitting would feel too confining. Maybe it was time to just rip off the Band-Aid. "No." I clicked the folder and started the slideshow from the beginning, hating that stupid girl in the photos who'd thought she had an entire life of normalcy ahead of her.

When the photos changed to the basement, I took a step back. Colt shot me a worried look but didn't reach for me. I would have shoved him off, and he clearly sensed that. It felt like the walls were closing in, trapping me with the laptop, but I told myself I could do this. I could see this through.

Colt held on to the back of the chair beside me, his knuckles white, and he let out a low sound like a growl when the sequence of photos showing the killer slicing my leg flashed across the screen. Roy had made sure to get plenty of photos of that, which made me think Colt might have been right about him too. Something was very wrong with my brother.

We'd reached the point where I'd stopped the slideshow earlier. The killer was standing with his back to the camera, the bloody knife in his hand. In the photo, my head was drooped forward and blood was running down my leg.

The next photos were of the killer moving toward Melanie, but his back mercifully blocked what he was doing.

I gasped aloud when I saw the next photo. The killer had turned around to face the camera dead-on, but his hood and the shadows hid his face. There were two more photos like this, with the killer getting closer and closer.

The next photo was totally black, but the next one was an image of my bloody and muddy clothes. The photo after it showed another set of clothes—hospital scrubs, bloody on the shoulder and the front.

"I bet those belonged to Melanie," I said. "She was a nurse."

Colt didn't say anything.

The image changed and it showed the basement, which was now empty except for the blood-stained floor.

There were multiple photos like this, then some more with the bloody clothes.

"Why would he bring those there?" I asked in a whisper.

"Because he's twisted."

I turned around, but Colt continued to face the computer screen. A few seconds later, he leaned over and pressed a few buttons and then closed the laptop. He headed out the back door to the deck, bracing his hands on the railing and leaning his head forward.

I watched him, wondering what he was thinking. Wondering why he'd walked away from me. I followed him and stopped in the open doorway.

"Colt," I said tentatively.

He turned to face me, his face contorted with anger and pain. "Clint Duncan's lucky the police have him in custody. I'd like to kill him."

I shook my head. "No." Maybe I should have given the memory card to Owen after all. Or Brady or Detective Martinez. I shouldn't have let Colt see it.

"I can't even imagine . . ." His voice broke, and he took a step toward me before stopping. "I want to hold you, but I'm scared to touch you. What do you want, Mags? What can I do to make this better?"

Tears stung my eyes. "I need you, Colt."

He was there in seconds, tugging me into his arms and holding me close, as if he never wanted to let go. "Please let me take you somewhere else. Anywhere. We'll give the memory card to the police, and we'll come back if they need us for anything." When I didn't answer, he tilted my head back so I was looking up at him. "I'm begging you, Maggie. You need a break from all of this."

Part of me knew I should stay, but I was exhausted and emotionally frazzled. And, truth be told, I wanted to get the hell out of Dodge. If only for a little while.

"Tilly . . ."

"Will give us her blessing. She already told me to take you away. *Please*, Maggie."

"Okay."

He kissed me hard, holding me so tight I could barely breathe. "We can't let your father know."

"Agreed." But that shouldn't be an issue. I had no plans to see him, and it was clear he and Colt weren't on good terms. With any luck, the police would bring him in next. "Where do you want to go?"

"Vietnam seems too extreme, but let's keep with the beach theme and go to Hawaii or the Caribbean."

I smiled. "Sounds good. You pick."

But if we were leaving town, there was one more loose thread I needed to tie up. I went upstairs to figure out my clothes situation and called Belinda. When she didn't answer, I left a message.

"Belinda, it's Magnolia. The police have caught the killer, so Colt and I are leaving town for a short break." I paused. "Momma loved you like a second daughter, and she wants you to be happy. I want to make us right before I go. I love you. Call me back."

I couldn't bear to leave things as they stood with Belinda, and after seeing those photos, I was really worried about her. Roy was sick and becoming increasingly dangerous. I couldn't leave her without trying to get through to her one more time.

I hung up and pulled my suitcase out of my closet. Most of my clothes were dirty, but I tossed them in anyway and then went to the bathroom to grab my toiletries. After adding the bag to my suitcase, I checked my phone, relieved to see that Belinda had sent me a text.

I need to talk to you in person, but not with Colt. After Delilah . . . I think it's best we talk alone.

Colt would never go for that, but it was ultimately my decision—and I wanted to see Belinda.

When? Where?

I still have clients back to back until six. After that? I can come to you or meet you somewhere.

She waited about ten seconds before sending:

If you're leaving town, you can meet me here at the office at six before you go. Leave Colt outside. I need to tell you my side.

I knew Colt would pitch a fit, but I was more than willing to take a chance on Belinda.

Okay.

As I'd suspected, Colt was not on board with my plan. "She can cancel an appointment to see you."

"She has clients, Colt."

He scowled; then his expression softened. "If this is what you want, Maggie. I don't want you leaving with any regrets."

His wording gave me pause. "You make it sound like we're never coming back."

He shook his head with a frown. "I only meant that I don't want you spending our beach time wishing you'd worked things out with Belinda. I want your undivided attention." He leaned over and gave me a kiss. "I'll book our flights for later tonight."

"Thanks for being so understanding, Colt."

He gave me a long leisurely kiss. "Belinda and I may not see eye to eye, but she's important to you."

"We still need to figure out how to get the memory card to the police."

"Why don't you call Brady and let him come get it?" Colt asked. "Maybe it'll help him out with the department."

"Even though he hid the whole thing about his cousin?"

He hesitated. "It's your call, Mags, but he always seemed to have your safety in mind."

"While trying to protect his cousin." But in the end, I called him, if for no other reason than I didn't want to see Martinez, and I had no desire to ever step foot in the police station again.

An hour later, Brady showed up at the front door. Colt let him in, then gave me a reassuring look before he headed upstairs to give me some privacy.

366

I was sitting on the sofa, and Brady stood behind the chair opposite me, looking less confident than I had ever seen him.

I gave him a hesitant smile. "I heard about your cousin."

"Yeah . . ."

"I'm sure this didn't work out the way you'd hoped."

His eyes pleaded with mine. "I was trying to make it right, Maggie. I had hoped it wasn't him."

I couldn't help but say, "He killed several more people while you were trying to make it right."

"I know. You have no idea how sorry I am."

"Is that why you were with me? Did you only like me because you worried he might be after me?"

"No," he said, his eyes turning warm. "I wanted you for *you*, Maggie. You're a beautiful, amazing, intriguing woman. I liked you before I knew who you were, and that hasn't changed."

I gave him a sad smile. "Believe it or not, that makes me feel better."

"Clint hasn't confessed yet, but the evidence is stacking up against him."

"Have they figured out that you're related to him?"

"Not yet. After I give them the memory card, I plan to confess my part in this . . . although they're putting some of it together already."

"Last week, you told me that you knew where I was because people in the police department knew I was living with you. But Martinez was surprised to hear there was any kind of personal connection between us. If your own partner didn't know, I can't believe that many people in the department knew to watch me." I looked him in the eye. "So how did you know where I was?"

He rubbed the back of his neck. "Remember when I told you that word had gotten around downtown that I liked you? I have a lot of friends downtown, and they all wanted to help set me up with you. You're not exactly the type to blend into the crowd."

"Then why didn't you tell me that?" I asked. "Why lie?"

Dropping his hand to his side, he lifted his shoulder into a small shrug. "Because I knew it would weird you out."

"Thinking the police were watching me freaked me out more."

"I can see that . . ."

"I'm leaving town with Colt for a few days, so I won't be able to take you out to the house until after I get back."

His gaze shifted out the back windows into the woods. "It can wait. There's no urgency now." He turned his attention back to me. "Where are you going?"

I shook my head. "We don't even know yet. I just know I need to get away."

"That's probably a good idea, but I suspect you'll need to give more statements when you get back next week."

"Okay." I paused, surprised my next question was so hard to get out. "Are the police looking for my dad?"

"Yeah," he said, perking up. "We are. Have you heard from him since last night?"

I shook my head. "No. And I'd like to keep it that way. He has some crazy idea that I'm going with him when he leaves."

"All the more reason to leave town until things die down," Brady said, and sadness filled his eyes. "I'm still here if you need me. That hasn't changed either."

"I plan on living a nice, quiet life from here on out."

He chuckled. "You seem incapable of that, Magnolia Steele."

I grinned. "Maybe so, but I'd like to give it a try."

Several hours later, Colt and I left the house and headed downtown. Our flight to Cancun was in the morning, so we'd decided to drive to Atlanta that night.

But first I had to try to make things right with my sister-in-law.

Colt parked on a side street, and we walked to Belinda's office together. She'd texted that she'd gotten held up in a late meeting and couldn't see me until after seven. To his credit, Colt hadn't said a word of protest. Since it was later than we'd planned, the sun had begun to set, and he was nervous.

"They caught the serial killer, Colt," I said, thankful that it was true.

"But they haven't caught your father. I've done his dirty work for three years. I know how devious he is. He'll do everything and anything he can to get what he wants, Mags, and he wants you to leave with him. I'll feel a helluva lot safer when we're far away from him."

Me too. "Then I'll make this as quick as possible so we can leave."

Colt opened the door to Belinda's office and gestured for me to walk in.

She was waiting for me in her front reception area, her hands clasped in front of her. She and Colt exchanged a long look; then Colt kissed my forehead. "I'll be sitting on the bench outside."

Then it was just me and Belinda, and I suddenly felt nervous. It didn't help that my nerves hadn't recovered from seeing the photos Roy had taken that night.

But Belinda looked nervous too.

"They caught the serial killer," I said. "It was Clint Duncan."

She pressed her fingertips to the base of her throat. "Thank goodness! You must feel so relieved."

"You have no idea. But that's not why I'm here."

She motioned toward two chairs. "Do you want to have a seat?"

"Sure." I sat while she pulled down the shades on the display windows.

"If I don't do this, we'll have people trying to come in," she said as she locked the front door and flipped the sign to say *Closed*.

But it also meant I couldn't see Colt, which made me anxious. Part of me wished I'd had him stay inside. Then I chided myself for acting like a helpless female. I had my gun in my purse and my pepper spray. And Colt was about thirty feet away.

After Belinda sat down, she watched me quietly, waiting.

I was the one who'd called this meeting, but I wasn't sure where to start. I decided to jump in with the thing that bothered me the most. "Why did you tell me you were an only child?"

Her face contorted with embarrassment. "Delilah disowned me. It's humiliating to tell people that I have a sister who refuses to speak to me." She pushed out a frustrated sigh. "It's all about appearances in the South. You know that."

Unfortunately, she was right. "But I'm not most people, Belinda. I'm your sister-in-law. I wasn't going to judge you. Look at the relationship I have with Roy, and I still claim him." I shook my head, overcome with profound sadness. "Hell, I forgave you after you held me at gunpoint. I would hope that you'd think better of me."

She glanced down at her lap and picked at the cuticle on her thumb. I noticed it was raw. I couldn't forget that Belinda was facing her own demons just like I was facing mine. I'd run away for ten years. Expecting her to jump ship from my brother at the snap of my fingers was unfair and unrealistic.

"Even though I'm disappointed, I forgive you. I love you, Belinda. I need you, and I only want what's best for you. I just don't want any more secrets between us."

She still kept her gaze on her hands in her lap. "Thank you, Magnolia. That's so much more than I deserve."

I leaned forward, and my stomach tightened. I wasn't sure how she'd react to this next part. "There's something you need to know about Roy," I said. "He had the camera I lost the night of my graduation party."

She shook her head, and her gaze lifted to meet mine. "No. How would Roy have that?"

I held her eyes for a moment to make sure I had her full attention. "He followed me out to the house that night. He found my camera and took photos of me and Melanie Seaborn in that basement. Then he bricked it up in Momma's basement fireplace."

She shook her head, her eyes wide with horror. "No. That would mean he was there. That he saw it."

I understood her reaction. I'd gone through the same emotions hours before. "He's sick, Belinda," I said softly. I got out of my chair and knelt in front of her, taking her hands in mine. "I'm scared for you, and the camera backs up my concerns. You need to leave him. Come live with me. We'll figure it out together."

Tears swam in her eyes, and her cheeks turned bright pink. "But you're leaving town."

Seeing her like this made me reconsider the trip to Cancun, but Colt was right. I needed to get away, if only to try to soothe my wounded soul. Besides, while I could be Belinda's support, she needed to make this decision on her own. "Only until the end of next week, and you can stay in the house until I get back. Or you can stay with Tilly. She's the one who encouraged us to go. She'd love to have you stay with her until we get back."

I didn't tell her that Tilly and I had discussed this very thing when I'd called to tell her we were leaving tonight. Though neither Tilly nor I had felt confident I'd get through to Belinda, Tilly was on standby, just in case.

She didn't say anything, so I said, "Please just think about it."

"Why are you still being so nice to me?" she asked, her voice breaking. "After all the lies and deceptions."

"Because I think you're a good person deep down and that you genuinely care about me and Momma. I'll never forget how loving and accepting you were when I came back home. And the way you stood up for me at that Bunco meeting . . ."

A grin tugged at the corners of her lips in spite of the tears now streaming down her cheeks. "I may have made a few enemies that night."

"I doubt it. You're too sweet. Everyone loves you. Including me." I squeezed her hands tighter. "I've done some terrible things too, Belinda, and *you* haven't turned away from *me*."

She leaned forward and pulled me into a hug. When she released me, she sat back and said nothing. Disappointment coursed through me. I was happy we'd made up, but nothing had really changed. She still hadn't said she was leaving Roy.

I stood and moved to the window in the front door, peering out so I could see Colt. He was sitting on the bench, tapping his foot anxiously. I waved and he gave me an expectant look, pointing his thumb toward where he'd parked his truck. I shook my head.

"So Colt, huh?" she asked, but there was no judgment in her voice. "Are you sure? I'm still worried you'll get hurt."

I shrugged and turned back to face her, understanding why she felt that way. "Colt and I get each other. He's different with me." I paused. "Is it hard for you since he was with your sister?"

"No," she said wistfully. "That seems like a lifetime ago."

My phone vibrated, and I wasn't surprised to see a text from Colt. Everything okay in there?

I smiled as I texted, I'm almost done.

"He's still worried about you?" she asked in surprise.

"We looked at the photos together, and they were pretty graphic. It shook him up pretty badly."

Her face paled.

"He'll hardly let me out of his sight," I said. "They may have caught the serial killer, but my father's still on the loose."

She nodded, but didn't say anything.

"Say," I said, "Colt and I are driving to Atlanta after I leave you. Do you mind if I use your restroom?"

"No. Of course not." She stood. "I'll walk back there with you. I need to see if my new assistant put the ring bearer pillows for the wedding I'm working on next weekend in the storage area. I can't find them anywhere, and the bride will throw a justifiable fit if we've lost them."

I left my purse by my chair, and we walked down the hall together. The restroom was past Belinda's office and a changing room. I opened the door and Belinda continued down the hall to the large storage room in the back of the store.

After I came out, I headed into the back room to find her and say goodbye, but she didn't answer when I called her name.

374

"Belinda?" I called out again, then saw the back door had been left ajar. I peered out the crack and saw her splayed on the ground outside. *"Belinda!"*

I hurried out and bent over her, relieved when I felt the pulse in her neck. She had a trickle of blood on her head. Someone had knocked her out. I reached for my phone in my jeans pocket to call Colt as I swung around to look for the perpetrator, but I found myself face to face with someone in a gray hoodie, the hood tugged down over his face. He lunged for me with a cloth in his hand.

Screaming, I scrambled to get away, but I was squatting next to Belinda. The man dove on top of me before I could rise to standing.

"Magnolia!" Colt shouted, but he sounded far away. He was on the other side of the building, and he'd never get to us in time. Belinda had locked the front door.

"Colt!" I screamed, elbowing the man behind me. He grabbed my chin, trying to put the cloth over my face, but I knew I was as good as dead if he did.

I rolled onto my back, reaching for his face with my hands, and sunk my nails into flesh. He shouted and used one arm to push my hands away, but the other clamped the cloth over my mouth and nose.

"Magnolia!" Colt shouted, sounding closer, but then his voice faded as my vision turned to darkness.

chapter
twenty-nine

The first thing I felt was the sting in my arms. Something cut into my wrists, and my shoulders were strained as my arms were pulled over my head. My toes pressed against something hard and cold.

Still deep in a dark sleep, I released a soft sound of protest and tried to reposition my arms, but I couldn't move.

It was then that I realized I was cold. Damp air clung to my bare skin.

Bare skin?

Where was I? But I knew before I got my eyes cracked open.

I was in the basement from hell, hanging from the same rafters where Melanie Seaborn had been tortured and killed all those years ago.

Terror flooded my head, and the darkness threatened to return. I wasn't sure whether to welcome it or fight it. If I was plunged into darkness, I wouldn't have to experience my last hours of hell on earth. But then I couldn't fight to survive either. I had no idea how I could escape with my life, but I knew I had to try.

"There she is," a deep voice said. "There's my sweet Magnolia."

A tall figure stood in the shadows, but my eyesight was still too blurry for me to make out his features.

"You know me?" I asked. My mouth was dry, and the words sounded funny. My head was still fuzzy, and my thoughts uncoordinated. Of course he knew me.

"Have you forgotten our reintroduction already?"

I recognized the voice, and I nearly gasped from shock.

He stepped out of the darker shadows and moved closer. He still wore a hooded sweatshirt, but he unzipped it, tugging back the hood as the sides parted to reveal a light gray T-shirt.

Tripp Tucker stood in front of me, wearing an eager smile.

"Why are you doing this, Tripp?"

"Magnolia, I know you'll probably find this hard to believe, but it's nothing personal against you."

I glanced down at my mostly naked body, bare except for my bra and panties, then back up at him, relieved that my head was clearing. "This feels pretty personal."

"It will probably get personal soon enough," he said, giving an almost careless shrug. "When Brian shows up."

"Daddy?" If he was my hope of salvation, my chances of survival were about 50-50. He'd already proven once that he was willing to choose money over me, and besides, I'd tattled about his crimes to anyone who'd listen. Maybe someone else would find me. Colt knew I'd been snatched, although he would have no way of knowing where we'd gone. And I'd been so busy trying to evade Brady and Owen, I hadn't brought either one of them to this house.

I was screwed.

Tripp moved closer, and it was then I noticed the shiny four-inch blade in his hand. "Aren't you curious about why you're here?"

The sight of the knife ratcheted my terror up multiple levels, and I couldn't stop the tears from filling my eyes. Only the balls of my feet touched the floor, which didn't give me much purchase as I scrambled to back away from him. "Please don't do this, Tripp," I begged.

A grin twisted his lips and glee filled his eyes.

I was close to breaking down and sobbing, but that was exactly what he wanted. He'd loved torturing Melanie. He'd loved torturing *me* ten years ago.

As if reading my thoughts, his eyes dropped to my thigh and his grin spread even wider. He reached for my scar with his left hand, his thumb tracing the indentation. "You've been a bad girl, Magnolia. This was to remind you to keep your mouth shut about what happened to Melanie."

He took a step closer and moved the knife toward my other leg. The tip dug into my skin, and I fought to keep from crying as he carved a new *C*. Fear exploded inside me, pushing me close to hysteria.

"You were so, so good when you went away, Magnolia. But then you came back, and you started spending time with that cop. And you forgot."

"No," I said. "He only figured out the connection because you killed Emily."

"And how did he figure it out, Magnolia?" Tripp asked. When I didn't answer, he leaned his face close to mine, his hot breath billowing in my face. "You slept with him. You were careless." He took a step back and his blade sliced a line into my skin to mirror the scar on my right leg. "When you're careless, I'm careless."

Despite my determination to stay silent, I cried out in pain and tears started to track down my cheeks. Warm blood slid down my leg.

Tripp backed up several feet, his gaze dropping to the fresh cuts in my leg, and a satisfied look filled his eyes. "I was sad when you left, but I knew that if I was patient you would come back. When it was time."

"You want my dad?" I asked, trying not to sound so desperate. "Cut me loose, and I'll help you find him."

"We don't need to find him. He'll be coming to us."

"Are you sure?" I asked. Was it wrong to hope that he would? "He's not very reliable."

"Let's hope he's more reliable than usual tonight, or I might get bored." He lifted his blade and ran his thumb along the edge. Blood beaded on his skin.

"You killed Tiffany," I said. "You convinced me that you didn't."

"I convinced the police too."

"But you said you loved her."

"And I did until she screwed me over by screwing your father. I trusted him with everything—my money, my girl . . . my love. He was like a father to me, and he threw every last bit of it away. I vowed that I would make him pay."

His words confirmed what I had already guessed. Tripp didn't plan for me to get out of here alive. He knew how much my father had doted on me. Killing me was only one part of making him pay. I needed to keep him talking until my father showed up so he didn't get *bored*.

"There was a murder before Tiffany," I said.

"That was an accident."

"An *accident*?"

He shrugged. "She pissed me off. I got bored."

"And the others? Besides Emily, every single one of them had a connection to one of the partners. You sent a magnolia to Steve Morrissey and a text to Walter Frey to make sure they didn't miss the message."

His eyebrows lifted. "Ava Milton's been loose with information." His voice lowered. "What have *you* been sharing with her?"

"Nothing about your murders."

"My murders? They aren't my murders. I didn't want to do them."

He was a liar. The gleam in his eyes told me he'd loved every minute of it, but I wasn't about to call him on it. He might decide to give me a demonstration.

"If you didn't want to murder those women, then why did you?"

His jaw set with determination, and his eyes darkened with anger. "A message needed to be sent to

380

Bill James and your father. I had to make sure I didn't get screwed out of my payoff. I'd agreed to drop the lawsuit for a portion of the twenty-million-dollar annuity, but I could see they were trying to cut me out. I wanted Brian Steele and his partner to live in fear that, if they didn't come through, I was coming for him and everything he holds dear."

His message might have worked with the partners, but it hadn't worked with my father. Unless my father had lied to me—which was possible—he hadn't even picked up on the murders. But I didn't plan on telling Tripp that.

Tripp frowned. "Brian Steele needs to start taking me more seriously." He pulled out his phone and swiped the screen. The phone rang on Tripp's speaker phone, and a man answered, his voice sounding strained. "I'm on my way."

"I thought you'd be more careful about the safety of your one true treasure, Brian," Tripp said, but he kept his focus on me.

There was a pause. "*Magnolia?*"

"Say hi to your daddy, Magnolia," Tripp said. His mouth turned up into a predatory smile, and he clenched and unclenched the knife in his hand, his bent fingers moving rhythmically. Oh yes, he was loving every minute of this.

Fear surged inside me as he stepped toward me like that, caressing his knife, but I told myself that he wouldn't actually stab me. None of the women had died from stab wounds. They had all suffered multiple slashes.

That didn't make me feel any better.

I gritted my teeth and tried my hardest not to cry, but my body shook with silent sobs. The cuts on my thigh throbbed, and I felt blood trickle down my leg to my foot.

Tripp's glee turned to irritation as he stopped in front of me, the phone in his left hand and the knife in his right. The name on the screen said *Dead Man Walking*.

My breath caught. Daddy wouldn't be able to save me from this. My only hope was Colt, and he had no idea where to find me.

The blade slashed across my abdomen, and only then did I realize he was retaliating because I hadn't followed his orders.

I screamed in pain, and the image of Melanie popped into my head. How many slashes had he made on her body? Countless.

"*Magnolia?*" my father shouted.

I closed my jaw, holding back my sobs. The pain was so intense my peripheral vision clouded.

"Tell your daddy that it's you, Magnolia," Tripp said in a cajoling voice.

Part of me wanted to refuse him. I didn't want to cooperate with him, but the punishment for defying him would be more slashes. No, I'd save my defiance for later.

"Daddy," I choked out, irritated with myself for calling him that. My stomach was on fire with pain.

"Oh God. *Magnolia?*"

"Remember Tiffany?" Tripp asked. "Magnolia will look five times worse."

"I'm coming," my father said, sounding frantic. "I'm on my way. It was hard to get the—"

"Save your excuses for someone who gives a shit, *Dad*." He spat the word out as if it were poison. Then his face morphed into a smile, and he said lightheartedly, "Let's play a game."

My hair stood on end. Any game Tripp created would be a horror show.

My father wasted no time before answering. "I have the money. I'm coming, Tripp. I swear."

"But not fast enough."

He growled out, "If you hurt her—"

My father's words were cut off by my scream as Tripp slashed my right thigh below my scar.

"Too late, *Dad*," Tripp shouted over my cries. "Your precious Magnolia is already hurt. Did you know I hurt her ten years ago? I gave her my mark, the one you created for me. I claimed her as mine, and tonight I'm going to make it come true."

"What mark?" My father sounded bewildered and scared.

"Are you fucking kidding me?" Tripp shouted, his face twisting into a mask of rage. "The logo for my ranch. The one I never got because you and your friends lost all of my money."

"What did you do?" my father bellowed in dismay.

"You can see it when you get here. It's on display. I'm giving you five minutes to get here. Magnolia will get another slash for every minute you're late."

"But I'm at least ten minutes away!" my father protested.

"Not my problem. And if you're not here in fifteen minutes, I'm carving the mark into her pretty cheek." Tripp ended the call, set the timer for five minutes, and then laid the phone down on the concrete floor. As he stood, he studied me, watching my body shake with sobs.

"You really are a pretty girl, but then you always were," he said, sounding like he was lost in thought. "You used to put on those shows after dinner."

Keep him talking. Keep him distracted, but the pain was so intense I struggled to form a coherent thought. "Daddy liked to hear me sing," I said in ragged breaths.

"In the hall at the dinner last night . . ." Tripp took a step toward me. "You said you didn't remember me coming to your house. Is that true? You don't remember how we used to sing together?"

I almost said no, that I didn't remember a thing about him, but then a memory wiggled free. Me sitting on the fireplace hearth next to Tripp as he strummed his guitar and we sang Johnny Cash and June Carter's song "Jackson." Momma was watching with guarded eyes, and the hate rolling off Roy was palpable. But Daddy . . . the memory of the love and adoration in his eyes made my breath catch in my chest. Of course, eight-year-old me had taken every drop of affection from that man for granted.

"Yes," I whispered, and more memories surfaced of Tripp at the dinner table—sometimes just him, sometimes Clint and a couple of other guys too. Memories of me and Tripp singing together, and of the boys, as dad had called them, singing on the back deck. Memories of Tripp hanging out with our family. He'd been there a lot . . . No . . . "You lived with us for a while."

How had I forgotten that?

"After your father lost all of my money. He was still pretending to love me then. Pretending to be my dad. And I believed it until Tiffany."

My mouth opened as I started to protest, but I knew it was true as more memories surfaced, memories I'd buried deep inside, locked away . . . to protect myself. "I'd forgotten . . ."

Oh. God.

My mind flashed back to that horrible night, and I realized I hadn't remembered everything. Right before Tripp had cut into my leg, the shadows hadn't entirely covered his face.

"Tripp," I'd whispered, and his grin had stretched wider as he made the first cut.

Why had my mind betrayed me? I wouldn't be here now if I had remembered that moment. And I could have saved so many women . . .

"Yes. How could you have forgotten?" he asked, sounding pissed. "You used to love me, Magnolia. More than your own brother, and he hated us both for it."

"We were kids . . . babies. You were older."

"Not that much older. I'm only fifteen years older than you. We were close, but I meant so little to you that you forgot me."

"I didn't forget on purpose," I said, struggling to catch my breath. Hanging by my arms made it difficult enough to breathe, but my sobbing hadn't helped. "After that night, I think I blocked all memories of you from my head." I still couldn't quite catch my breath, but focusing on talking seemed to calm me down. "When I woke up in the woods, I didn't remember anything about this house. I had a concussion, so I thought the memory loss was from that. But I was scared, and I knew Momma and Roy were in danger, so I ran away. I didn't remember anything until I came back to Franklin, and then only in bits and pieces. But I still didn't remember it was you. Not until now."

"The human mind is a funny thing," Tripp said. His grin was back—and it was *wrong*. "I thought you were ballsy when I saw you at the dinner. But then, you were always so fearless as a little girl. You'd take on a giant if he looked at you wrong, so I thought that serving me at that dinner was a way to get back at me. I followed you into the hall to confront you, but you asked me about Tiffany, and I realized that you really didn't remember." He looked amused. "I planned on exploiting that more, but unfortunately, things have progressed a little too quickly. It's time to wrap this up."

"Roy saw you," I said. "You threatened him to be quiet too."

"It doesn't take much to threaten Roy, and it helped that he didn't remember me. But I knew he was watching, and I wasn't surprised. He hated you, and I think he liked seeing you powerless and defenseless."

I closed my eyes, the thought too overwhelming. It was so similar to what Colt had said, and there was no denying the words carried a grain of truth.

"It hurts when the people who are supposed to love us don't. When they turn on us and betray us instead. I know exactly how you feel, Magnolia."

I didn't respond. He moved closer, close enough that he snaked his left arm around me and rested his hand on my lower back.

My breath caught in my throat as his gaze came to rest on my breasts. He slid his hand down and cupped my butt cheek.

This caught me by surprise. There was no record of him sexually assaulting the previous victims, not that groping would show up on an autopsy report. But my memories of Melanie's death didn't include anything sexual at all. Or maybe I'd blocked it out.

I held his gaze, trying to figure out what he was doing, and a grin lifted one side of his mouth higher than the other. He was amused.

"Do you know what I used to daydream?"

I was almost scared to ask, but I needed to keep him talking. "No. What?"

"I used to imagine us together . . . when you were older, of course. We would be married, and then I'd really be Brian Steele's son."

I gasped in shock, and it must have shown in my eyes, because his grin faded. "Is that so heinous, Magnolia?"

"No," I said, scrambling to come up with a plan. I could use this. It was time for the performance of my life. Literally. "When I saw you at the dinner . . . you caught my eye," I said, "even before I knew you were

Tripp Tucker. Something about you felt so right. Like something inside me had been missing."

He blinked in surprise. I'd caught his attention.

"When I found out who you were, I knew I'd never have a shot at being with you, but I thought of you . . ." I let my voice drop off, full of innuendo.

He watched me with interest.

"I hate my father. I hate him for what he did to me and my family. I hate him for what he did to you. We can both hurt him," I said. "Let's hurt him *together.*"

"What do you have in mind?" His hand tightened on my butt, and he pulled my body flush to his. The bulge in his pants told me he was interested. If I could get him to cut me down, I'd improvise. I just needed to be free.

"When he shows up, we ambush him together. How much do you think it will hurt him to find out that I've been working with you to bring him down? Especially after he rushes over here to save my life. You want him to pay, Tripp. This is how to do it."

He lowered his face to the side of my neck and breathed in deep before placing a tender kiss on my pulse point.

I fought hard not to cringe from his touch, but it was impossible. His hand with the knife rested on my waist.

His face lifted. "You smell like him."

My chest tightened. "Who?"

"Colt Austin. You slept with him and then tried to seduce me." He took several steps back, the blood from the wounds on my leg and my stomach smeared on his jeans and light gray T-shirt.

I shook my head, trying not to panic. "No! My father hired Colt to watch me. So I've been feeding him false information, trying to lay a trap of my own. But yours is so much better. We can work together."

His face softened, and his grip on the knife loosened. He seemed to be considering it when the alarm on his phone went off.

My heart skipped a beat.

Tripp's face fell and regret filled his eyes as he squatted next to the phone and turned off the alarm.

"I really wish you'd told me this before I called your daddy."

"It's not too late, Tripp," I pleaded shamelessly. I had no pride left. Only self-preservation. "We can still do this. *Please.*"

He shook his head, then swiped on his phone, setting the timer for one minute. I somehow resisted the urge to start sobbing. I couldn't fall apart. I needed to keep my wits and think this through.

"That's just it," Tripp said, advancing toward me. "I made your father a promise, and unlike Brian Steele, I keep my promises."

The knife blade glinted as it arced toward me, slashing my abdomen diagonally.

The cut was longer than the others, and I screamed in pain and fright, my feet unsteady beneath me. My body weight dropped, jerking on my arms and sending a fresh wave of pain through my shoulders.

Tripp took a step backward, wearing a grim look as he restarted the timer for one minute.

chapter
thirty

I felt the sting of a hand on my cheek, and my eyes opened, blinking in the light of the bare bulb overhead.

"Wake up, Magnolia," Tripp cooed into my ear. "I need you awake."

My peripheral vision was fading again, but the press of his mouth to my neck brought me back to awareness.

"You're a strong girl," he said as he kissed my cheek. "And such a pretty girl. Daddy must not love you as much as I thought he did. Let's hope he shows up soon. He's eight minutes late, and we both know what happens in another two minutes." He licked a *C* on my cheek with his tongue.

A fresh sob rose out of nowhere. After eight minutes of hell, I was sure I was out of tears.

I heard a creak on the floor overhead. Tripp must have heard it too, because he stopped and lifted his head.

"Daddy's home," he sang out, a smile lifting his mouth.

He moved away from me, heading toward the stairs as the creaking in the floorboards overhead moved closer.

I hadn't stood a chance ten years ago. Tripp had known I was there from the moment I'd walked in the door.

"*Magnolia?*" Colt called out, and my heart slammed into my ribs.

"*Colt!*" I screamed and started to sob.

Tripp shot me a look that screamed, *Shut up*. No words required.

"I have something you want," Colt called out. "Two somethings. Come up and get them."

"I don't think so," Tripp shouted. "But you're free to come down and see your girlfriend. She's sporting a new look since you last saw her." Then he laughed.

My entire body throbbed from the multiple cuts he'd slashed into me, and blood dripped to the floor.

I was sure I looked just like Melanie had when I first saw her. Had she been filled with the same hope of escape when she'd heard my footsteps overhead? She must have been devastated when Tripp had instead carried me down the stairs.

"I'm having a hard time wrestling one of them," Colt shouted. "Let our host know you're here, Steele."

"I'm here!" my father shouted. "And I have the money."

Tripp hesitated at the base of the stairs.

"Just come get the money and go," Colt hollered out. "It'll make your getaway a lot smoother."

The alarm went off and Tripp glanced at me, indecision in his eyes. "I'm in a dilemma, Magnolia. I told Daddy that I'd cut you for every minute he was late, and while he's technically here, he's not *here*. I need him to see you. I need him to see my handiwork."

He moved toward me, the knife at an angle that meant he was about to slash me again.

"No!" I screamed, letting the rope take all my weight as I lifted a foot and smashed it into his crotch. But my aim was slightly off, and although he doubled over from the pain, he wasn't totally incapacitated.

There was movement on the floor overhead and then on the stairs, but Tripp was upright and moving behind me. He had an arm around my stomach, and the pressure of his arm against my wounds was sending pulses of pain and fire through my body, but I was more worried about the knife tip pressed to my neck.

Colt appeared first, his expression a mixture of shock and outrage. Then anger. His body was tight with barely controlled rage as he reached the basement floor. He had a gun at his side, and he lifted it, pointing it to the side of my head—at Tripp's face, the only part of him not covered by my body.

My father was behind him, holding a black satchel. His eyes flew open when he saw me.

"Magnolia?" His gaze lifted to Tripp. "What have you done, Tripp? You've ruined everything, son."

"Son," Tripp spat out. "I'm not your son. You were full of lies. You told me you would never leave me and you did!"

"I didn't want to leave," my father said with a panicked look as his eyes scanned my body. "You know I never wanted to leave you or Magnolia, but they would have killed me if I'd stayed. Then you never would have gotten your money."

"You could have taken me with you!"

"You know that wouldn't have worked. It would have looked suspicious. I needed you to wait."

"I was tired of being patient. You told me you'd give me back my money tenfold, even after everyone else lost theirs. I've been living off residuals for fourteen years," Tripp said. "Every time you came back, you were full of excuses."

"I told you it would take twenty years before the annuity paid out."

"But *you* had plenty of money to come back and forth! You've had plenty of money to live off of, and you never shared a dime with me," Tripp shouted, his grip tightening around my stomach. I cried out as another wave of pain shot through my body.

Colt's hand tightened on his gun. How good of a shot was he? Could he miss me and kill Tripp? Because if he missed, I was confident Tripp would slit my throat.

"It wasn't just money, you stupid son of a bitch!" Tripp cursed, his body stiffening behind me. "I've been alone! You ruined my life! And now I'm going to do the same to yours!" The knife blade pressed harder into my neck, and I felt a prick of pain.

Panic rose up, choking me, and I struggled not to start sobbing again. I caught Colt's gaze, and the fear in his eyes gutted me. He'd never be able to handle seeing me murdered in front of him.

I mouthed, *I love you.*

His face hardened and he gave me the tiniest of nods. He was going to get me out of this.

"Tripp," my father said in a calm voice that hinted he thought he was regaining control of the situation. "I've missed you."

The pressure of the knife tip on my throat eased up.

"Come with me," my father said. "I planned to bring Magnolia, but why don't you come with us?"

"I can't come after this!" Tripp said in disgust, taking the knife away from my throat and waving it downward, then back up.

"You've made mistakes," my father said in a soothing tone I recognized from my childhood. He used to speak to me like that when I was scared. "I've made more than I can count. I've hurt the people I love the most. I've hurt Magnolia. I've hurt you. But we're family, and family forgives one another. It's the way it works."

Tripp turned his face to look at me. "Can you forgive me, Magnolia?"

I couldn't hold back my tears as I lied through my teeth. "Of course I forgive you. I understand doing drastic things because you feel unloved and alone." I struggled to get out the words. My breath was shallow and my face felt numb.

But what I said must have had an impact because Tripp's hold loosened.

395

My father took a step forward. "I have a plane waiting for me and Magnolia. We're flying out as soon as we leave here. Come with us."

Colt's gaze was still on me, and he looked alarmed. "You need to get Magnolia down. She's hurt, and hanging like that isn't going to help with her blood loss."

"Cut her down," my father said. "Let's put pressure on her wounds. Then we'll take her to the private plane I have waiting at the Murfreesboro airport."

"She needs help before that," Colt said, trying to look unaffected by the sight of my wounds. His voice shook slightly. "Some of her cuts are deep. She needs a doctor."

"We don't have one," my father said, then advanced toward me. "But we'll make do. Tripp, cut her down. We have to go. There's a storm blowing in, and we have to outrun it."

"I haven't said that I'm going," Tripp said. "I brought you here so you could watch me kill Magnolia. Then I was going to take the money and kill you too."

"There's a fine line between love and hate," my father said. "You love me, Tripp. Don't let your temper and impatience get the better of you. I can move past this. Can you?"

"You'll still bring me with you?" Tripp asked in disbelief.

"I've missed you, Tripp," my father said. "You were the son I always wished I had. There's nothing stopping you from coming now. But we have to hurry. With the storm blowing in, the plane won't be able to take off."

Tripp's hand shook as he pointed the knife toward Colt. "I want him to throw his gun over here. I don't trust your errand boy, Brian."

"He's not going to shoot you," my father said. "He's my employee, and he's loyal."

"I don't care," Tripp said. "He loses the gun before I cut her down."

Colt squatted and tossed the gun to the floor. It skidded across the concrete, stopping halfway between us.

Tripp hesitated for a moment, but then reached over my head with the blade. He leaned into my ear, whispering, "I hope you can get past this, Magnolia."

I didn't answer, my skin crawling with the anticipation of being cut down. I kept my gaze on Colt, telling myself he'd find a way to get me out of this. He slowly reached behind his back as he stood.

Tripp's hold on my abdomen tightened, sending a sharp wave of pain through my body as he cut the rope.

My body fell, slipping from Tripp's hold.

A gunshot rang out and then two more as I hit the floor in a heap. Tripp dropped behind me. I tried to roll to my stomach so I could crawl away, but someone grabbed me from behind.

I screamed and sobbed, trying to fling my arms at him, but they were useless and numb after hanging so long.

"Maggie!" Colt said, releasing his hold. "It's me."

I collapsed onto the floor, the throbbing of my wounds taking over all my senses.

"Tripp's dead. He can't hurt you anymore, but I have to get you out of here," he said, his voice tight. "I'm going to pick you up, okay?"

I nodded slightly, still crying uncontrollably.

He scooped me up and headed for the stairs, bounding up them faster than I would have expected since he was carrying me. He didn't stop in the house, carrying me out to his truck and putting me in the backseat. Reaching under the seat, he grabbed a cotton jacket and then wrapped it around my shoulders. He cupped my face with a shaking hand, and tears filled his eyes. "I'd call an ambulance, but I think it's faster if I take you to the hospital, okay?"

I couldn't answer through my sobs, but he must have taken my lack of protest as permission.

"I'm going to help you lie down." His voice quavered, and then his face hardened. "Killing the bastard wasn't enough. He should have suffered double what you did."

I shook my head. "Take me home, Colt. I just want to go home." My wracking sobs sent more waves of pain across my stomach, back, and legs, pushing me closer to the darkness.

He kissed my forehead and started to ease me down when I heard my father yell, "Magnolia!"

"I don't want to see him," I said in a panic.

"Don't worry," he said, his body humming with tethered rage. "That asshole will never get near you again."

He stepped back, his shirt and jeans covered in my blood.

The yard lit up as an engine started. My father stood in the headlights of his car, the key fob in one hand and the satchel in the other. He slipped the key fob into his pants pocket. "I need you to put Magnolia into my car," he said to Colt. "We have a plane to catch."

"This is done. You're done. Go catch your private plane and get the fuck out of our lives."

"Not without Magnolia. You know she's the main reason I came back."

"That's total bullshit, and we all know it, but it doesn't matter because she doesn't want to go with you."

"She's been traumatized. She wants to go—she just doesn't understand it yet."

"She's not a fucking child!" Colt shouted. "She's a grown woman who knows exactly what she wants. Try asking her."

Dammit. Colt was fighting my battle for me, and I loved him for it, but I had to finish this myself. I pushed to the edge of the seat to get out, and then I noticed the burner phone Colt had gotten me was lying on the front seat. I considered trying to lean over and get it, but I couldn't handle the anticipated pain. Instead, I slid out of the backseat and onto the grass, stifling a cry. I felt lightheaded and wobbled for a moment before regaining my equilibrium.

"So she can rely on *you*?" my father sneered. "Does she know the truth?"

"I know it all," I said, taking a tentative step toward Colt. Pain jolted through my body with every step.

Colt swung around to face me, his eyes wide. "Maggie, what are you doing? You should be lying down."

"You know about Delilah?" my father asked.

"Yes," I said, digging deep to find the energy to shout at him. "Now get in your car, go to your plane, and fly off to your island." Each footstep took more effort than the last, and my aching arms felt like deadweights.

"You're only saying that because of your attachment to Colt," my father said. "I knew I had to wait until your mother was gone. It was problematic that you were growing closer to Belinda, but the detective seemed willing enough to help sow some distrust. Enough that you wouldn't be encouraged to stay on her behalf."

"*Brady?*" Was there no end to my father's deceptions and orchestrations?

"Colt doesn't love you, Magnolia," my father said, taking a step forward and reaching a hand toward me. "He's using you to get to me. He hates me for forcing him to be my employee, and he wants to use you to hurt me."

I stood next to Colt. He reached for my hand and threaded our hands together. "He was the only one trying to save me just now," I said. "You think he's trying to get back at you. I think it's obvious who really loves me."

My father reached behind his back, and before I could register what was happening, he pointed a gun in my direction.

The gunshot sounded unnaturally loud as Colt crumpled to the ground, his hand pulling free of mine.

"What did you do?" I screamed hysterically. "*What did you do?*" I dropped to my knees and searched Colt's body for a bullet wound.

A blood stain began to spread on his upper left chest. I pressed my hand to the spot, my still partially numb hand clumsily putting pressure on the wound. "Colt!" I pleaded. "I love you, dammit. Please don't die."

He grabbed my upper arm, yanking me down. "Maggie," he whispered, grimacing with pain. "My gun is behind me. I'll roll to the side so you can get it, but first get my keys out of my jeans pocket. Then get in the truck and go."

"No! I am *not* leaving you here."

Colt shook his head. "He'll take you, I swear . . . he'll kidnap you. I think he's been planning it for years. You have to go *now*."

I heard a car headed toward us, and seconds later, I could see its headlights bouncing around in the woods.

"Time to go," my father said, marching toward me.

"Maggie," Colt whispered, sounding weaker. "Keys. Now."

I dug into his pocket as my father grabbed my other arm and tugged, and the jacket fell off my shoulders onto the ground. Colt held on to me until my fumbling fingers tugged the keys free. I flew upward, slamming into my father's chest. A new wave of pain shot through my body, making my vision start to black out, and I faltered.

"Magnolia, you're hurt. You need me to take care of you," my father said, wrapping an arm around my back. The pain in his voice caught me by surprise, but he continued to lead me toward his car.

I glanced back at Colt, who was motionless, and rage exploded inside of me. "You shot him!"

"It was for your own good."

"How can you say that?" I dug in my heels, but I was weak and exhausted, and I didn't have the strength to resist him. "Who made you God?"

"I did!" he countered. "I know best. Now stop fighting me, Magnolia!"

Where was the car in the woods? I heard no sign of it, and the headlights were gone.

It was up to me to save myself and Colt.

I let my father pull me closer, pretending to go along with him, and then I swung with the keys, aiming for his face. They hit his cheek, and I dug in and pulled down, stopping only when he released my arm. I ran for the truck, intending to get the burner phone to call for help, but I struggled to remain upright. I was almost there when I heard my father say, "If you get in that truck, I'll shoot him again and make sure he's dead."

"Maggie, *go*," Colt said with a cough. "I'm as good as dead anyway."

"Magnolia, if you willingly come, I'll call an ambulance right now," my father shouted. He held his phone out. "I'll even let you make the call. Colt doesn't have much time. You can still save him."

I hated my father. I hated him with every part of my being. How had I ever thought so highly of this man? Why had Momma and I worshiped him? I could see he was shiny and pretty, but deep down, he was hollow and selfish, only thinking about himself.

I had been like that in the past, but I didn't need to be that way anymore. If I went with my father, I could get help for Colt. I could save him.

I grabbed his phone and stumbled to Colt's side.

"Don't do it, Maggie," Colt said weakly.

I knelt next to him and landed on my butt as I fought a wave of dizziness. The darkness was back, eating at my peripheral vision. This was love. Sacrificing what you wanted to protect the person you care about. Colt had learned that lesson before me, but I caught on eventually. I pressed 911, and told him, "I'm sorry I was so stubborn."

The operator answered, and I told her Colt had been shot and needed help. Colt told me the address of the house, and I explained to her that it was in the woods, hidden from everything. I put every last bit of energy I had into telling her everything I could to make sure they'd arrive as quickly as possible.

"That's enough," my father said, taking the phone from me and pulling me to my feet.

I'd stood too quickly, and I wobbled with dizziness. The cool night air made me start to shiver.

"What trick is this?" my father demanded, and my legs turned to rubber and I fell.

I hit the ground, and the jolt sent pain rushing through me, strong enough to steal my breath away and make me black out for a moment.

"Magnolia, get up, or I'll shoot him again anyway!"

"Get away from her, Brian," I heard Belinda say.

A rush of warmth flooded through me. How had she gotten here?

My father walked toward her.

I could barely lift my head to see her, but she wasn't alone. A man stood with her. My brother.

"Maggie," Colt whispered in a raspy voice. "My gun. It's behind me. I can't reach . . ."

Roy stepped between our father and me, facing forward. Distantly, I registered that he had a gun in his hand. Belinda moved next to him, adding to the human shield.

I helped Colt roll to his side, remaining silent even though his face was contorted with pain. I nearly panicked when I saw the blood seeping through the back of his shirt.

"Roy," my father said in surprise. "What are you doing here?"

"I've come to get my sister." He cast a quick glance at me, seeing my exposed bloody body, before turning back. "What did you do to her?"

I reached behind Colt and tugged on the gun stuffed into his jeans, but I was weak and nearly fell over with the effort.

"You can do it, Mags," Colt whispered.

I tugged again, pulling it free. Colt rolled back down and grunted as his shoulder blade hit the jacket. I collapsed next to him, sure I didn't have any energy left.

"It wasn't me," our father said. "It was Tripp. I saved her, but now I'm taking her with me. Don't worry," he said. "You'll never have to see her again."

"What's in the bag?" my brother asked.

"Nothing you need to worry about," my father said in a smug voice. "But I left a present for you in the flower

404

pot in your backyard. One million in gold. Now, if you'll excuse us, Magnolia called an ambulance for Colt, and I need to get her out of here before they show up."

"You still want to take her?" Roy demanded. "After all these years?" When my father didn't answer, Roy said, "I heard you before you left years ago. I heard you talking to someone about going away, but you told him you'd be back for him and Magnolia. But you weren't coming back for me."

"You would never have wanted to go," my father said in protest. "Now let me get Magnolia. She's injured."

Roy turned to his side and glanced down at me, taking in my blood-covered body. "I think Magnolia needs an ambulance as much as Colt does. She'll stay." His words of concern and his dispassionate tone seemed at odds with each other.

"You don't get to decide that, Roy," my father said. "Either move out of my way, or I'll shoot."

I had a clear view of my father and the smug smirk on his face gave me one last jolt of energy. My hand tightened around the gun as I got to my knees, hiding the gun behind me.

"You'd shoot me?" Roy asked in an even tone.

"In a heartbeat."

I believed my father meant it. He had the gun trained on him, his finger on the trigger. It would only take a second for him to end Roy's life. My father had caused so many deaths, both directly and indirectly. I couldn't let that happen.

I lifted the gun, aimed it at my father's chest, and pulled the trigger, hoping my shaking hand didn't make me miss.

Belinda screamed and my brother dropped to the ground, and for a moment I thought I'd missed and accidently shot him instead.

My father toppled over.

I tried to stand, but my shivering became more violent. Instead, I dropped the gun and fell next to Colt. I was prepared for a shock of pain to shoot through me, but it was only a dull ache.

That was a bad sign.

I thought about trying to get up, but I was too weak. Too tired. I rolled to my side, facing Colt. "I'm sorry," I whispered. "I can't."

"Maggie," Colt cried out.

I was vaguely aware of Belinda dropping down next to me. She rolled me onto my back, crying out when she saw all my gashes. She started issuing orders to Roy, who actually followed them.

I heard the whine of sirens in the distance, and I told myself if I could just hang on, they would save me.

"Magnolia?" Belinda turned my face up to look at hers. "I need you to focus on my voice, okay?"

I felt my feet being tugged upward, and to my surprise, Roy was lifting my legs and putting a bag underneath them.

They covered me with a blanket, and Belinda made Roy press on the deep wounds on my leg and my stomach. Then she moved to Colt's other side, pressing down on his wound.

"I'm sorry," I whispered to Roy.

He nodded and then looked away, staring at our dead father.

"Hang on, Magnolia," Belinda said, but she sounded far away. "The ambulance is almost here."

I wanted to answer that I was trying, but I didn't have anything left in me. I turned my head to see Colt, and he was staring at me with tears in his eyes. I tried to focus on his face. If I had to die, at least I would be looking into the face of someone who loved me. Colt had made me believe I could have a happily ever after. Even if it never came true.

I fought to keep my eyelids open, but it was a losing battle. They were too heavy.

The darkness came back for me, and this time I let the nothingness swallow me whole.

chapter
thirty-one

The beeping woke me up and the pain kept me conscious.

I was vaguely aware that I'd felt this pain before, and that it was horrifically bad, so I fought against it, moaning as it tried to lift me up and then drag me under. It was a similar sensation to the undertow I'd fought when my parents took Roy and me to the beach one summer.

I'd been sure I was going to drown, but a hand had grabbed the back of my one-piece swimming suit and pulled me to the surface.

I'd expected it to be Daddy, but it had been Roy's face bobbing above the water as he clung to a noodle.

"I've got you," he'd said. Then he had ferried us to shore.

I knew the memory meant something, but my body was on fire. I cried out over and over, feeling myself on the verge of a sucking darkness. Just as I started to go under, I felt a hand on my forehead, smoothing back my hair.

"Rest, sweet girl," Tilly said, although her voice sounded very far away. "I've got you."

The next time I woke, I found Belinda next to me. She had knitting needles in both hands and the start of something hung between them, but the needles weren't moving. She was staring at them as though willing them to knit on their own.

"Belinda," I said, but it came out in a croak.

She startled and her eyes lifted to mine before she tossed the needles and yarn onto her seat and moved to my side. "Magnolia. You're awake."

"Yeah." My mouth felt like it had been stuffed with cotton. "I'm thirsty."

"I'll get you some water." She hurried out of the room, and I glanced around, trying to remember why I was in a hospital bed.

Then it all came rushing back—my father, Roy, Tripp torturing me, and Colt.

Colt!

I tried to sit up, but pain hit me from multiple wounds. Still, I couldn't rest a moment longer without knowing if he was okay. I fought against the pain, trying to sit upright.

Belinda came through the doorway with a plastic pitcher and a cup in her hand. She freaked out when she saw me trying to sit up, practically throwing the water pitcher on the tray table in her haste to push me back down. "What are you doing? You'll rip out your stitches."

"Colt. I have to see Colt."

"Colt is fine. He sailed through surgery, and he's healing just fine. I suspect he'll be in here soon trying to compare your stitches to his." She poured a glass of water and held a straw to my lips. I took several sips to wet my mouth, then pushed it away.

"How many do I have?" I asked.

She set the cup on the tray table. "More than you want to know."

I lay back down and stared up at the ceiling, trying to think about anything but the slashes of Tripp's knife. "No more bikinis for me, I guess."

"Tripp Tucker stole enough from you. Don't let him steal your bikinis too."

I turned to look at her as a tiny smile lifted my mouth. "You just want to share any bikinis I get in the future."

"Well . . ." she said, smoothing out some imaginary wrinkles in her pants. "I don't usually wear bikinis, but I suspect if I continue to hang around with you, you'll force me to do many things I'd never do on my own." She gave me her best interpretation of a mischievous look. "Which is a good thing. You push me out of my comfort zone. And wearing a bikini is one of those outside-my-comfort-zone things."

I narrowed my eyes and grinned. "So you're saying that you want me to continue to wear bikinis for your own selfish reasons."

She laughed. "Well, when you put it that way . . ."

"Maybe you fit into the Steele family better than I thought."

Her brow furrowed. "Magnolia, it makes me sick to hear you talk badly of yourself. I wish you could see yourself as I see you."

Tears filled my eyes. "And I wish the same for you."

Her mouth twitched and her eyes turned glassy. "Maybe I've started looking in that mirror. I left Roy."

I reached for her hand and squeezed. While my feelings for my brother were more complicated than ever, Roy had hurt Belinda. Maybe years of therapy would help him, but she didn't need to take any part in that after the way he'd treated her. "I'm proud of you."

"Are you?" she asked.

"Yeah. Very." I paused. "How did Roy . . . what made him . . ."

"Colt found me behind my shop and started to call the police, but I stopped him. We realized the killer had taken you, so he called your father and convinced him to let Colt meet him at the house to help save you. I called Roy and told him the killer had you, and he picked me up and took me out there. I called the police on the way."

"Roy came to save me?"

She frowned. "In all honesty, he may have partially been there to get revenge against your father."

I had no doubt about that, but I liked to think that in the end he'd wanted to save me too.

"Roy's . . ." Belinda trailed off and then started again, more conviction in her voice. "Roy realizes he needs help. He's checking into a center next week to help him work through his demons."

"I'm surprised he's self-aware enough to figure that out."

"Let's just say two Franklin police detectives helped him figure it out."

I suspected that meant Brady and Owen. I frowned. "It will only work if he wants it to."

"I think he does," she said. "He's known he hasn't been right for several years, but sometimes it's hard to admit that you need help."

I gave her a soft smile. "Yeah. I know. So what will you do?"

"I'm not going anywhere, if that's what you're asking. I love my job and my clients. I'll probably sell the house. Roy doesn't want it, and there are too many unhappy memories there. Owen, that friend of Brady's, says there are openings at his apartment complex. I'm thinking about looking there. What about you?" she asked. "Are you going to leave now that you have all of this wrapped up?"

I raked my teeth over my bottom lip. "No. Maybe eventually, but not any time soon." I pressed my lips together into a tight smile. "There would be a lot for me to leave behind."

"Including a certain guy named Colt?"

"I love him, Belinda. I know it's awkward because of Delilah."

"I want you to be happy, Magnolia. You're the one who's stuck with me, through better or worse. We might be sisters because of our last name and not blood, but in the end, it's love and loyalty that matter the most."

I nodded. "You're right. But he's only one of my reasons for wanting to stay. I couldn't bear to leave you or Tilly. We need each other more than ever." My eyelids felt heavy, and I had to put effort into keeping them open. "Why am I so tired?"

"Part of it is your pain medication, but part of it is your brain trying to heal," she said. "I was upset that you've slept for so long, but they said they weren't worried yet."

"How long did I sleep?"

"A day and a half."

The door opened and Brady poked his head inside the door. "The nurse said you'd woken up. Can I come in for a few minutes?"

"Yeah."

He moved to the side of the bed and rested his hand on the side rail. "Magnolia. I . . . Thank God you're okay."

"I'm sure my father told you to make sure I remained that way," I said in an icy tone.

His eyes widened, and Belinda looked shocked.

"Belinda?" I asked, turning to face her. "Can you give me a few minutes with Brady?"

"Yeah . . ." She gave him a hard stare before she left.

When the door closed, Brady asked, "So your father told you?"

"When did he contact you?" I asked.

"First, in my defense, I didn't know I was helping *him*."

I believed that. "Go on."

413

"It was after Walter Frey's murder. He contacted me with an anonymous tip. He told me that Lopez was involved, but you'd already figured that out. He contacted me again, after Lopez's death, and told me that you were still in danger. I already knew that too, but he seemed informed, so I listened. After your mother died, he told me that your brother and sister-in-law were out to hurt you. I wanted you to be safe, so I lied about Belinda. He also planted some evidence against Owen making it look like he'd been on the take, and I was hesitant to trust him. The captain called him in Friday afternoon to answer questions, but he's in the clear."

That must have been the call Owen received while he was with me at Momma's house. "Owen said Martinez was friends with Mahoney, the officer who arrested Colt on bogus charges. He thought Martinez might be dirty."

His eyes clouded. "There's nothing to prove that she is."

"But nothing to prove that she isn't."

"If she is, she's being watched very carefully," he said, his voice tight. I wondered if he would be one of the people watching her . . . if he still had a job.

"What about the annuity money?" I asked. "What will you do with it?"

Brady shook his head in confusion. "What money?"

"You didn't find any money?"

"No. The annuity money was there?" he asked, looking more alert.

"Maybe not. Maybe I imagined it. Or more likely my father lied." Or someone took it. But who?

Thinking about it made me tired. I closed my eyes and let myself sink into the pillows.

"I'm sorry," Brady said. "I really was trying to help you."

"While trying to cover your cousin's butt."

"Clint didn't do it. The reason he had info about the murders is because Tripp made sure to give him enough clues to get him searching."

"He did that to make Clint look suspicious?" I asked.

"And it worked."

"And they believe that Tripp killed all of those women?"

"He had plenty of evidence of his own in the safe in his house."

"What about his alibi for Tiffany's murder? The radio show interview?"

"It's usually live, but it turns out that Tripp's had been recorded. The detectives failed to ask."

I cringed. Would all of this have been avoided if they had? "Is Colt in any kind of trouble?"

Brady looked confused. "Why would he be?"

"For saving me in the basement."

"No," Brady said in a flat tone. "He did it to save you." He paused. "The gun your father used to shoot Colt is the same gun that killed Rowena Rogers and her hired hand. I hear you were the one to shoot your father."

"Roy was trying to stop him from taking me. He was about to shoot Roy too."

"You're not in any trouble," Brady said, but a bit of pride filled his eyes. "I guess that range practice paid off. You shot your father straight through the heart."

Talk about poetic justice. I closed my eyes. "Too many deaths."

Brady took my hand and squeezed. "It's all over now. You solved decades of crimes in only four weeks. If you ever want to be a detective . . ."

I laughed—then cringed from the wave of pain. It took several shallow breaths to ride through it.

"There's something else you should know," he said. "Bill James was murdered."

"Probably by my father."

"We're waiting on ballistics to see if the same gun was used, but it's a good guess. He was found in the basement of a burnt-out house in Leiper's Fork. Somebody killed him and dumped his body there a couple of days ago."

The bizarre part is the basement was partially dug up and there was a body of a woman buried underneath.

"Probably his first wife." So Momma had been right all along.

Bill James hadn't run off after Rowena was killed—Daddy probably kidnapped him and forced him to cash in the annuity. Even if Daddy's name had been on it, he needed Bill to sign his name, and the fact that Momma had declared Daddy dead meant his signature meant nothing.

"Did Owen get his job back?" I asked.

"He's decided to get some other job. Maybe security. He says if you're ever looking for a bodyguard . . ." He grinned.

I grinned too.

"Maggie," he said. "Maria needs to take your statement about what happened at some point. I can sit with you if you'd like."

I tried not to panic. "Why? Does she think I did something wrong?"

"Oh, no. The opposite. But she'll ask some difficult questions—details about what happened, and I suspect you won't want someone close to you to hear that."

"Then I'm not sure you should hear it either," I said.

He stared at me in surprise.

"I'm with Colt," I said, not wanting to give him the wrong idea. "I'm in love with him. But you and I were friends before we got romantically involved. I'd like to stay friends."

"And how will Colt feel about that?"

"It's my decision, and he trusts me."

He nodded. "Okay." His eyes shuttered and his cop face was back. "I can't help but feel that if I had handled things differently, Tripp wouldn't have . . ."

"Kidnapped me? Tortured me? The only way to have stopped him would have been to kill him or arrest him. He was going to do it or die trying."

"He cut you sixteen times, Maggie. Some of them were long and deep. You're going to scar."

"At least I'm alive."

"You're going to need therapy. You can't go through something like that and be just fine. Promise me you'll see someone. I know a few therapists who work with some of the domestic abuse cases I've handled. I can get you some names."

I almost told him I didn't need therapy, but then I thought about the countless nightmares I'd suffered *before* this happened. "I will."

"Good. I'll text you the contact info." He was quiet for a moment. "I'm here if you need me, Maggie. For anything." With that, he turned around and walked away.

The nurse came in to check on me and then upped my pain medication when my pain became more intense. Blissful sleep took over.

I was dreaming. Colt and I lay on a blanket in Pinkerton Park, staring up at the clouds, playing a game of naming the shapes of passing clouds. He slipped his hand into mine and whispered into my ear, "I love you, Mags."

My eyes fluttered open, and I realized I was only partially dreaming.

Colt stood next to my bed, holding my hand. He grinned. "Sleeping Beauty awakens."

"Should you be out of bed?"

"I'm supposed to walk. And once they told me I could walk, there was only one place I wanted to go. This is actually the third time I've been here. I was starting to get worried."

"*You* got worried? You scared me to death," I said. "You got shot. Because of *me*."

"At least it's a better reason than some people get shot for. Like arguing over a piece of fried chicken, or because you cut someone off in traffic."

He was trying to play off what he'd done. Not that I was surprised. "Thank you for saving me from Tripp."

His eyes darkened. "You should have never gotten taken by him in the first place. I should have been in there with you. I should never have let you go into Belinda's office alone."

"He would have found a way to snatch me and maybe hurt you in the process," I said. "No matter how careful we were. Besides, we thought Clint Duncan was the murderer. No one suspected Tripp Tucker."

"Brady didn't know anything about the annuity money. Do you know what happened to it?"

"Don't the police have it?"

"Please tell me you didn't hide it and plan to give it to me later."

His jaw tightened. "I want nothing to do with that money, and even if I did, I wasn't in any position to get up and get it. I couldn't even get the gun behind me and shoot the damn bastard. I couldn't save you." The bitterness in his eyes hinted that this would haunt him for some time.

"Then what happened to it? Did he really have it?"

"It was there in the bag when I showed up. And I have no idea who could have taken it. Roy? He's been after it all along."

"Maybe." Did it matter? Like Colt, I wanted nothing to do with it.

We were silent for a moment, and Colt's face paled. "What he did to you, Mags. Jesus . . . I nearly lost my shit when I saw you."

Images of the new scenes from that basement flooded my head. "I don't want to talk about it. I don't want to think about it." I took a breath. "I'm going to get therapy. Brady suggested it, and I think he's right. I'm sure I needed help before this attack. I can't sleep through the night without having nightmares, and it was starting to get worse. I can't keep doing that to me *or* you, and I want to make me better."

He squeezed my hand. "I'd do anything for you, Maggie."

"I think you proved that when you took a bullet trying to protect me."

"I love you, Magnolia Mae Steele. I'd do anything to protect you," he said. Then his eyes lit up. "I'm pretty sure *you* told me you loved me when you thought you were dying."

"Do deathbed professions of love count?" I teased.

"I'll take a regular hospital bed confession too."

I stared up into his eyes, wondering how I'd gotten so lucky. "I love you, Colt. I want to sell Momma's house and get another one. With you."

"Are you sure?" he asked. "Maybe you should take some time to think about it."

"Do *you* need to think about it?"

"No! It's just—"

"Life is short. I don't want to waste any of it." A mischievous grin lit up his face, and I tried not to laugh.

"If you say YOLO, I swear to God I'm gonna kick you out that door."

Happiness filled his eyes. "I love you too."

"You were totally going to say it, weren't you?"

"I plead the Fifth." His smile softened. "Are you sure, Mags?" he asked again. "And not about kicking me out if I said YOLO. I know you would have." He turned serious. "You just had this near-death experience, so maybe you need to take some time to think it through. And yeah, I had one too, but I'd already figured out that I loved you and didn't want to live without you before I almost died. Maybe you need time to catch up."

"I'd figured it out before then too," I said. "I was just too stubborn to admit it."

His thumb brushed the back of my hand. "So we've figured out what we're going to do about living together. What about your job? Don't you want to go back to acting?"

"Maybe someday. For now, I want to work with Tilly in the catering kitchen. And if you're willing, I'd like to sing with you. I think that will satisfy my need to perform. Maybe Maggie and Colt can play some gigs in Nashville. The manager at the Kincaid said he'd invite us back."

He grinned. "I'd like that too."

"And *maybe* if we got offered a record deal down the road . . . *maybe* I'd be more open to considering it. After everything dies down."

"Are you serious?" he asked, his excitement palpable. Then he frowned. "I don't want you to feel pressured into it because of me, Mags. All I want is *you.*

Singing with you is icing on the cake. It doesn't matter where. It can be on our back porch for all I care."

A thought filled my head, making me hopeful for the future. "Someday we'll sing to our kids," I said softly. "And our grandkids."

His voice lowered. "Yeah. I want to spend forever with you."

Tears filled my eyes when I thought about how close I'd come to losing him. "Me too."

Then he sat on the edge of my bed and sang me a love song he'd written for me.

The song that would become our first hit single on the country charts. Which was appropriate, since it was the song that started our happily ever after.

To find out more about Denise Grover Swank's releases and to have access to bonus content, join her newsletter!
www.denisegroverswank.com/mailing-list/

About the Author

Denise Grover Swank was born in Kansas City, Missouri and lived in the area until she was nineteen. Then she became a nomadic gypsy, living in five cities, four states and ten houses over the course of ten years before she moved back to her roots. She speaks English and smattering of Spanish and Chinese which she learned through an intensive Nick Jr. immersion period. Her hobbies include witty Facebook comments (in own her mind) and dancing in her kitchen with her children. (Quite badly if you believe her offspring.) Hidden talents include the gift of justification and the ability to drink massive amounts of caffeine and still fall asleep within two minutes. Her lack of the sense of smell allows her to perform many unspeakable tasks. She has six children and hasn't lost her sanity. Or so she leads you to believe.

For more info go to: DeniseGroverSwank.com

Made in the USA
San Bernardino, CA
05 August 2019